What people are saying about

The Renovation

"*The Renovation* is a beautifully crafted story about the broken relationship between a man and his son, and the joyful restoration of a mended heart and an old mansion. Engaging characters move the story along at a wonderful pace."

—LORI COPELAND, AUTHOR OF *SIMPLE GIFTS* AND *MONDAY MORNING FAITH*

"Renovate your reading schedule to include this great new title by Terri Kraus! In *The Renovation*, Kraus crafts a tale that both tugs at the heart and tickles the funny bone."

—CYNDY SALZMANN, AUTHOR OF THE HIGHLY ACCLAIMED *FRIDAY AFTERNOON CLUB MYSTERY* SERIES

"Terri Kraus has woven an absorbing and deeply felt story of forgiveness that touches both the magnificence of heaven and the tenderly drawn detail of human relationship. Subtly and with compassion she explores the struggle of ordinary people finding their way through the complex emotional legacies of past pain, to the simplicity and peace of experiencing God's forgiveness and love. This is a compelling, memorable, honest story, offering hope and deepening faith."

—PENELOPE WILCOCK, AUTHOR OF *THE CLEAR LIGHT OF DAY*

"In a captivating and evocative story, Terri Kraus skillfully weaves distance, longing, forgiveness, and redemption into a cast of unforgettable characters. This is a book to savor and ponder."

—NANCY ORTBERG, FORMER TEACHING PASTOR AT WILLOW CREEK COMMUNITY CHURCH AND AUTHOR OF *LOOKING FOR GOD*

THE RENOVATION

A PROJECT RESTORATION NOVEL

THE RENOVATION

by
TERRI KRAUS

David C Cook
transforming lives together

THE RENOVATION
Published by David C. Cook
4050 Lee Vance View
Colorado Springs, CO 80918 U.S.A.

David C. Cook Distribution Canada
55 Woodslee Avenue, Paris, Ontario, Canada N3L 3E5

David C. Cook U.K., Kingsway Communications
Eastbourne, East Sussex BN23 6NT, England

David C. Cook and the graphic circle C logo
are registered trademarks of Cook Communications Ministries.

This story is a work of fiction. All characters and events are the product of the author's
imagination. Any resemblance to any person, living or dead, is coincidental.

Scripture quotations are taken from *THE MESSAGE.* Copyright © by Eugene H.
Peterson 1993, 1994, 1995, 1996, 2000, 2001, 2002. Used by permission of NavPress
Publishing Group. Isaiah 44:22 and 1 John 2:12 in chapter 15 are taken from the *Holy
Bible, New Living Translation,* copyright © 1996, 2004. Used by permission of Tyndale
House Publishers, Inc., Wheaton, Illinois 60189. All rights reserved.

LCCN 2007941694
ISBN 978-0-7814-4846-8

© 2008 Terri Kraus
Published in association with the literary agency of Alive Communications, Inc., 7680
Goddard St., Suite 200, Colorado Springs, CO 80920

The Team: Andrea Christian, Ramona Tucker, Jack Campbell,
Theresa With, and Karen Athen
Cover Design: The DesignWorks Group, Charles Brock
Cover Photo: ©Shutterstock

Printed in the United States of America
First Edition 2008

1 2 3 4 5 6 7 8 9 10

To you, Mom—

Someone once said,

"God pardons like a mother,
who kisses the offense
into everlasting forgetfulness."

Thanks for unfailingly showing me
the meaning of such forgiveness.
You may not have written a book,
but your life speaks volumes.

*To preserve and renew
is almost as noble as to create.*

—Voltaire

Unforgiveness is like a scratch on an old record.
The song never goes on to the end.
It keeps the beautiful music
yet to be released unheard
and all that resounds
are the same old three or four chords
again and again and again.

—KATHERINE WALDEN

———

Forgiveness is a rebirth of hope,
a reorganization of thought,
and a reconstruction of dreams.

—BEVERLY FLANIGAN

CHAPTER ONE

ETHAN WILLIS PICKED UP a battered pry bar and wedged it under a loose attic floorboard. The nails gave way with a chorus of rusty squeals. He leaned back, and a shaft of light from the gable's eyebrow window lit the exposed rafters of the space.

Joel Brenner dug at the wood with the point of a long-bladed screwdriver. "Will we need extra bracing?"

"No," Ethan replied, "it's good wood. Look—these look like three-by-tens. Everything was built better back then. They'll hold."

"Everything was built better—except for all the stuff that already fell apart."

Ethan smiled. His assistant did not always share his passion for old buildings. "Well ... of course."

He slipped the hammer from his worn leather tool belt and, with a few practiced strokes, banged the floorboard back into place. The carpentry work dated back more than a hundred years. Ethan admired the old-fashioned, traditional craftsmanship. *What was built right still stands*, he thought.

Joel walked over to the small window and peered down. "Uh-oh. She's here."

"Who?" Ethan asked.

"Mrs. Moretti."

The muscles in Ethan's neck pulsed. "You have to cover for me," he said in a whisper. "Run down and intercept her. Keep her busy. I'll sneak out the back."

"Why me? She'll talk until dark."

Ethan was already unbuckling his tool belt. "Don't worry. You're still on the clock, remember?"

"So?" Joel answered, a nervousness in his eyes. "You're the boss. I'm just your lowly assistant."

"I know, I know. But Chase has a game today. So you get Mrs. Moretti. Besides, she owns the place and is going to be signing the checks for a long time."

Joel was anything but happy.

"Smile, Joel," Ethan said. "She's a nice lady. She just has too many words and too little opportunity to use them. And she knows what she wants. It won't be all that painful."

With a scowl, Joel responded, "That's easy for you to say."

"Maybe she brought some Italian food. It's all yours this time."

And with that, Ethan hurried down the attic stairs and ran down the back staircase. As he hushed the kitchen door closed, he could hear Mrs. Moretti's high-pitched laugh rattle from the entrance hall and echo through the empty house.

Mrs. Moretti was promising to be a wonderful client, providing Willis Construction the dream job of restoring the Old Carter Mansion. But it was not a relationship for anyone in a hurry.

Ethan waited a moment, then jogged quietly back to his maroon truck, parked halfway up the block. Relieved that Mrs. Moretti did not see him, he wondered if he would have stopped if she had.

Ethan hurried through the area that made up downtown Franklin, Pennsylvania—past the stately Franklin Club, across Chestnut Street, down

Buffalo Street, and a right turn onto South Park Street. Then he turned onto Liberty, flanked on both sides by a long row of elegant old brick buildings—some a bit tired and worn, some newly restored and repainted.

The welcome signs at the edges of the town boasted FRANKLIN: THE VICTORIAN CITY. It was once a town of many who prospered in the area's oil boom of the mid-1800s and who built remarkable structures downtown and lived in stately homes in the bordering neighborhoods. Downtown Franklin had struggled for decades to stay alive and vital. The town's Venango Historical Society promoted the preservation of the over two hundred buildings of historical significance, many of which displayed plaques boasting their years of completion. These buildings, once home to scores of thriving businesses—from haberdasheries to drugstores with soda fountains to millinery shops—now housed a curious mix of antique shops, one- and two-member law firms, offices of start-up insurance agents, two secondhand clothing consignment operations, and, increasingly, more upscale specialty shops.

Ethan drove past the old theater on Liberty Street. After years of community fund-raising and bake sales, it had been restored almost to its previous vaudevillian grandeur. A colorful banner draped over the entrance announced next month's concert—a big-band orchestra from Erie. He glanced over at the park opposite the theater. The same cluster of old men rested on the same benches by the fountain, watching the traffic as always. Ethan waved. A few waved back.

He turned right at the Shell station, then again on Elk. It ran parallel to the river. Two blocks downriver from town was Sibley Park.

He pulled into the parking lot of the baseball field. The truck tires bit and crunched at the loose gravel. He found that compressed munching to be enormously comforting—as if the very ground welcomed a traveler home.

The baseball game had already begun. Three zeros hung on the scoreboard. Ethan had only missed the first inning and a half.

The Franklin Flyers took the field as Ethan found his usual seat on the next-to-the-top row of the section of bleachers on the first-base side. He smiled and waved. Chase looked toward him. His son gave little indication that he saw his father, save an almost imperceptible nod.

Ethan leaned back against the seat behind him, took a deep breath, and closed his eyes for a moment to the warm afternoon sun. He reached to the visor of his hat and pulled it off, wiping his forehead with his palm.

He heard the pop of the ball against the leather of the catcher's mitt. The umpire drawled out, "Ball!" To his right, he heard the shouts and conversations of other parents—mostly mothers—who sat, like he, in the same positions for every Flyers baseball game. Behind him a car horn sounded, then another—two friends marking their passing on the street.

His eyes stayed shut. The whisper of a breeze slipped off the river, carrying the scent of the deep, slow-moving water.

The town of Franklin—population seven thousand—lay at the confluence of the Allegheny River and the much smaller French Creek, and was key to several hundred years of American history. Sibley Park was the location of an old French fort, designed by the foreign settlers to stave off the bullying English and Americans. But the French left without ever firing a shot in anger. They simply burned their handiwork to the ground as they marched off toward Niagara and ceded this stretch of riverbank to the British.

On warm evenings, Ethan often came to this park to walk along the river, imagining he heard the faint whisperings of French accents, muted murmuring as the waters rippled past the shallows by the shore. To have spent a long year building, hewing huge logs with dull axes, only to watch all that work go up in flames—it must have been so agonizing, so incredibly frustrating....

His reverie was interrupted by a brief shout. "Heads up!"

Ethan snapped his eyes open to see a baseball spiraling down toward him. Instinctively, he leaned to the right, lifted his hand—more from fear than athletic ability—and with some surprise, snagged the errant foul ball in his open palm. It smacked hard, and he tried not to wince.

A weak cheer arose from the other parents. "Way to go, Willis!"

He stood, offered a very theatrical bow, and tossed the ball back toward the pitcher. As he did, he saw his son roll his eyes and turn away.

Ethan was well aware of what that gesture meant.

Charles Willis turned away from his father and focused on the pitcher and batter once again. The young teen had been called Chase since he began to crawl.

His grandfather had been watching the child one afternoon and had spent a breathless few hours, always a few steps behind the crawling infant. When his mother had asked how the afternoon went, his grandpa, exhausted and exasperated, had replied, "I spent the whole afternoon giving chase."

His mother had laughed, and from that moment on the speedy infant was named *Chase*.

Chase always dreaded the start of school when his teachers would inevitably call out "Charles Willis." He would redden as his classmates giggled. "It's Chase, not Charles," he would correct ever so politely. "My mom gave that name to me."

Chase squinted at the stands and dug his toe in the edge of the infield, a few steps off first base. *Couldn't he have just tossed the ball back? Did he have to bow?*

Chase tried to forget his father's presence. He smacked his hand into his glove, adjusted the bill of his cap, and waited for the next pitch.

The Franklin Flyers were the heavy favorites to win the Little League Junior Baseball Tournament at the end of summer. Due to a string of late birthdays of their fourteen-year-olds, virtually their entire team remained intact from the previous year. If the Flyers won this year, their triumph would be the first time in years that any team had won the summer series back-to-back in any age division.

The Flyers' pitcher wound up and threw. The batter, a tall boy from Oil City with bleached hair, swung fast and solid. The ball skittered off his bat—a line drive hard into the dirt on the first-base side.

Chase hated those hard hits into the dirt, when the ball took mean and unpredictable bounces. He had a scar just below his bottom lip— so faint now that even he struggled to find it—that was a reminder of a fast line drive last summer. He tried not to shut his eyes as he bent down. He took two steps toward the pitcher's mound, smothered the ball with a graceful, athletic swoop, pivoted backward to the base, and beat the runner by two full steps. The runner threw his helmet in the dust, glaring over at Chase.

He had been robbed of a base hit.

Chase heard the chorus of cheers from the Flyers' bleachers. He let himself smile—but only a bit. He heard a loud voice, the loud voice of a woman shouting excitedly. It was Mrs. Bonnie Hewitt, his best friend Elliot's mom.

"Way to go, Chase! Good job!"

He shut his eyes for a second, wiping at his cheek with the strap of his glove.

And he wished, as he had done a thousand times before, that *his* mother had been there to see it.

"Are these stairs canting down on one side, or is it just me?" Cecily Carter Moretti called out to no one in particular as she swept up the winding staircase.

Joel waited in the shadow of a doorframe as the Carter Mansion's owner, a dainty, dark-haired woman whom he guessed to be in her late forties, reached the top floor. She was wearing a sophisticated blue suit that he was sure cost more than his entire wardrobe. Joel knew he wasn't an expert at detecting sophisticated, expensive fashion, but he was pretty certain that what Mrs. Moretti had on was it. Though quick to speak her mind, the crew knew her to be warm, energetic, and generous. She would come armed with some sort of delicious Italian food, as though always needing to be a hospitable hostess in her home even though the place wasn't anywhere near ready to welcome guests. Now a tantalizing smell emanated from the large brown grease-stained bag she held.

"They are," Joel answered. "It's only a degree or two—but you do notice it. That's not unusual. The foundation has settled an inch or so over the years. But don't worry, Mrs. Moretti, we'll get to them. When we're done, they'll be perfect."

"I sure hope so. I'd hate to feel like I had vertigo every time I went up these stairs. And these old doorframes—they're all crooked. I'm not going to have to live with that, am I?"

Joel let out a short laugh. "I'm sure they'll all be straight as an arrow when we're done, but I'll mention that to Ethan when he gets back."

"Oh—he's not here? Then who's going to eat all this food? I stopped at a new place called Crescendo's on the way. Their Italian beef is better than my mother-in-law's. But I would never tell her that! And you can't tell her either. Do you like sweet peppers or hot peppers on your sandwich? I bought both, although in my opinion an Italian beef isn't authentic without the sweet peppers. The hot peppers just drown out all the flavor of the meat. And there's extra juice if you want some. I always like having extra juice on the bread, but I order it on the side. Crusty on the outside, soft on the inside is the best."

"Thanks, Mrs. Moretti. Sweet peppers and extra juice it is," Joel said as he opened the bag. "It smells wonderful. Ethan doesn't know what he's missing."

"And you should taste their lasagna! They whip the ricotta cheese filling and it gets real smooth and creamy—to die for, really. Next time I'll bring some for you to try. With extra gravy. Not sauce—we Italians call it 'gravy,' and Crescendo's is the best—except for my mother-in-law's, of course." She winked and added, "And please, call me CeCe."

On the first step of the bleachers, directly behind the dugout, Cameron Dane scribbled on her notepad as Mrs. Cathy Hollister, a petite blonde with a multitude of animated expressions, rattled on. Cameron had been distracted when an attractive man stood and bowed. She only had come back to her task at hand as Mrs. Hollister had tapped her on the shoulder and began talking again.

Cameron nodded and hoped she looked as if she had been paying attention.

"It's not that I mind the time all this takes," Cathy Hollister said with a sweep of her hand, encompassing the entire field and all the players. "I really don't. We moms know that being on the ball field is better for our sons than just hanging around the house playing video games."

Cameron smiled as she wrote, hoping to encourage Mrs. Hollister into producing a more colorful quote on the subject.

"The thing that gets my goat," she said, in a conspiratorial whisper, "is the mothers who crow about being a 'soccer mom'—and then never go to a single soccer game. They expect someone else to cart their precious kids around. They're as much a soccer mom as I am Miss America. Don't get me started. That's another story. My gut's already in a knot over this base-ball game."

Cameron bit her lip. *I have the quote,* she thought, secretly celebrating.

Cameron laughed and flipped another page, filled with her sprawling but legible writing. She looked up and waved to Bart Renshaw, the staff photographer for *The Franklin Derrick.* Cameron guessed he was on his fourth roll of film. She could tell by the bulge in his shirt pocket—the place he always stored all his exposed rolls as he worked. He was the only photographer Cameron knew who still worked with real film, despite everyone's efforts to get him to switch to digital.

Cameron watched the Flyers' first baseman dive for a whizzing foul ball, skimming along at shin level.

Mrs. Hollister shouted out, "Way to go, Chase! Good hustle!"

Cathy Hollister attempted to act natural as Bart snapped picture after picture while considering the afternoon sunlight, adjusting his vantage point to include the small crowd behind her.

"I hope you use one that doesn't have my mouth wide open––like it usually is." She grinned.

"No, we want you to look as good as possible," Cameron assured her. "We're not *The Enquirer.*"

Cameron tapped Bart on the shoulder, catching his attention. "I know you like action pictures, but take one posed shot, would you?"

Scowling, Bart went to his knee, mumbling "Smile," and when Mrs. Hollister offered a weak, posed expression, he snapped two quick shots, then returned his focus to the game.

The two teams changed sides, and in the short lull in the action, Cameron turned and looked over the crowd.

"Anyone else I could talk to on this story?" she asked Mrs. Hollister.

Mrs. Hollister turned around and scanned the crowd. "Did you talk to Meg Walters—the big redhead over by the water jug?"

"I did. She was the first on my list."

"Then that's all of us, I guess."

The right fielder for the Flyers swung and the ball ricocheted off the backstop, making a metallic, wrinkled sound.

"Hey, wait a second," Mrs. Hollister said with a nudge. "You should talk to Chase's dad."

"Who?"

"The tall fellow who caught the foul ball. Ethan Willis. The Flyers' first baseman—Chase Willis—Charles—that's his son."

"Willis? Willis? Don't I know that name from somewhere?" Cameron said as she scribbled it in her notebook.

"Willis Construction. He does all the renovations on the old rat-trap Victorians in town. You may have seen his signs. He's working on the old Carter place over by the river."

Cameron pushed a strand of her long dark hair behind her right ear. She turned, shielding her eyes from the sun with her notepad, trying to get a better look. "Ethan Willis?"

"Uh-huh. You should talk to him."

Cameron turned back to Mrs. Hollister. "Is he always at the games?"

"Most of the time."

Cameron laughed. "Does he call himself a 'soccer dad'?"

Something dark crossed Mrs. Hollister's eyes—but only for an instant. "I don't know. He's always around, though." Then she added, in a confidential, nervous whisper, "He's a widower, that's why. He comes to just about every game. His wife, Chase's mom, is dead."

There was the briefest of pauses, as if Mrs. Hollister was struggling to add a list of large numbers in her head. "He's never remarried. Lord knows why. He doesn't have a beer gut and he has a steady job. That, and being as drop-dead good-looking as he is—well, I imagine that he could have his pick. But I guess that's another story for another day, right?"

Cameron stood and dusted off the seat of her tan slacks. Deliberately, she turned and looked in the direction of Ethan Willis. He lay stretched over two rows of seats. His cap had some sort of insignia on it—*a tool company, maybe,* she thought—but she was too far away to see clearly. His dark blond hair, covered by his cap, appeared to be cut close. She wondered if it were thinning. She wasn't close enough to see the color of his eyes. He wore a plain white T-shirt with jeans. A cell phone and tape measure were clipped on his belt.

As she began to make her way to him, her cell phone rang. For a split second, she was startled, forgetting she had the phone with her. She answered quickly.

After listening a moment, she sighed loudly. "But it's a grass fire, Paige. It'll be out by the time I get there. Can't I just send Bart?"

She scowled and nodded. "Okay, okay. I'll go. We'll take pictures of the smoking grass. Should I interview any survivors?"

A vacant lot across town was on fire and threatening an empty warehouse. The fire department had arrived, and Cameron knew there wouldn't be any decent pictures or an interesting story. But her editor wanted coverage, and coverage is what she would get.

She stopped at the end of the bleachers. "Mr. Willis?"

Ethan sat up straight. "Yep. That's me."

She brushed the same errant strand of hair from her face. "I'm Cameron Dane—from *The Derrick*. I'm doing a story on the Flyers baseball team ... well, actually the moms of the baseball team. I hear that the team is the favorite to win the Junior Tournament championship again."

Ethan waited a heartbeat, then nodded.

"Unfortunately, the story on the Flyers is due tomorrow, and I just got a call that a vacant lot on 7th and Egbert is on fire. I'm overdue for a Pulitzer, and my editor thinks that this fire story may push me over the top."

Ethan smiled easily but seemed most uncertain as to what to say in response.

Cameron gathered her notepad and backpack to her chest and squinted up at him. She didn't know why, but she made sure that he could see both her hands, outstretched over her backpack—especially the one without the wedding ring.

He was almost lost in the glare of the afternoon sun. She still couldn't make out the color of his eyes because of the warm light.

"So you're too late to be included in this story," she said, grinning. "And I bet you're disappointed to hear that."

He took off his cap and smoothed his hair.

She was right—his hair was thinning, but in a slow, gentle manner.

"Well, after you leave, you'll hear my cries of anguish," he said. "That's what the media is used to hearing, isn't it?"

"It is. Broken lives and trampled emotions. Scars. Lots of emotional scars," Cameron replied, hoping that his response meant he understood her sarcasm. She found that few people in Franklin really did. "I just heard that you're renovating the old Carter place. I'd love to do a story on what you're doing to it. You know, explain the progress to our readers."

His lips went tight.

She offered a bigger smile. "Please …"

———

Ethan squinted, trying to see this attractive woman more clearly in the blinding sun. He shaded his eyes with his hand to catch a better glimpse of her. But no matter how good-looking she was, Ethan, in his wildest dream, would not have considered himself fodder for any newspaper story—regardless of how small the market.

"Please. I know it would be fascinating," she begged. "You could be like Franklin's Bob Vila."

He tried not to wince when he heard the name. Almost every contractor disliked being compared to that man. Ethan considered the former *This Old House* host to be a showman who had the good fortune to find great carpenters, subcontractors, and craftsmen—though he wasn't one himself.

"Listen, the fire awaits," she said. "Let me call you tomorrow. We'll talk about this."

"Well …"

"Please?" she said, her expression neither coy nor apologetic. "Cameron Dane. From *The Derrick*. I'll call tomorrow."

Then she left without waiting for his response, either positive or negative.

Ethan shifted his position and watched the reporter jog toward the parking lot and her car.

Long dark hair, blue eyes, tall. Great smile. She's well dressed for Franklin, to be sure.

He turned back before she got to her car, not wanting her to see him looking. And as he turned, he saw Chase, standing by first base, frowning at him.

Ethan and his son sat in the cool, dim back room at McCort's. The front of the place was an old-style tavern, pure and simple, and the inside had a thickness of smoke hovering just above the faux wooden bowls filled with Beer Nuts. But through a separate entrance around the side, warm textures of old paneling and the scents of juicy hamburgers filled McCort's small dining room. A kaleidoscope of neon signs provided most of the light in the room.

Chase had declared the hamburgers at McCort's to be the best in all of Venango County. After every victory, Ethan allowed Chase to pick the dining establishment of his choice.

Midway into last summer's baseball season, Ethan had stopped asking and simply drove to McCort's, a block off the river in Oil City.

Chase slumped in the booth that was covered in bloodred vinyl lined with tarnished brass tacks along the seat and backrest. He tossed his cap to one side. His hair, lighter than his father's, more like his mother's, was damp from sweat. Ringlets coiled against his forehead.

Hazel took a healthy sip from her Seven and Seven and called out from her post by the kitchen door, "The usual, fellows?"

Ethan nodded and grabbed a handful of pretzel sticks from the bowl on the table. The other booths had similar bowls.

"Close game," he said as he chewed.

"Those guys were good," Chase said as he arranged the pretzel sticks on the table, making a series of squares and triangles. "We were lucky. That foul ball Elliot caught saved us."

"No, you played pretty well too. I think you had 'em the whole game."

Chase scowled as only a teenager who loves and hates the same moment can scowl. Ethan knew Chase loved the praise but had to deny it in public.

A papery wisp of music filtered into the room from the jukebox in the tavern. Depending on the time of day, the music could vary greatly. In the afternoon, it might be a polka or an old standard from the fifties. At dusk, the crowd usually chose country and western. And toward midnight, the music was straight rock 'n' roll, with the emphasis on metal.

Ethan often wondered if they changed bartenders for each crowd, or if the same fellow had to endure such radical shifts in styles.

The hamburgers appeared, coupled with a larger platter of cheese fries—French fries drenched in some sort of yellowy cheese topping. Ethan abandoned any health concerns when they dined at McCort's. He knew the food must be bad for him because it tasted so good.

Chase poured a fist-sized dollop of ketchup on his plate, for dunking both the cheese fries and his hamburger, usually before every bite. The two ate in silence, pausing only briefly to sip at their drinks or to grab another napkin from the chrome dispenser on the table.

Finally, Chase breathed a great sigh and pushed his empty plate to the side. "Good burger."

Ethan smiled in agreement. "Want dessert?"

Chase shook his head. "I'm pretty full. And kinda tired."

Ethan reached for the check and peered close, examining the figures and mentally doing the calculations. It was always the same amount. Chase would have rolled his eyes had he been with a friend.

As Ethan was reaching for his wallet, Chase cleared his throat. "Who was that lady?"

"What lady?"

"At the game. Who was that lady you were talking to?"

Ethan knew whom he meant. He heard a note of controlled anxiety in Chase's question.

"She's from the newspaper—*The Derrick*."

Chase stared at his father. "What did she want?"

Ethan shrugged, wanting to dismiss the subject. "She was doing an article on the moms of the baseball team."

Chase bobbed his head. "Oh yeah, Elliot told me. She talked to his mom, too."

Ethan pulled out a twenty-dollar bill.

"What did she want with you? You're not a mom."

Ethan shrugged again. "I know. But she said she heard we were working on the old Carter place. Wants to do a story on it. Like I'm the Bob Vila of Venango County."

Chase winced at the comparison. "You gonna do it? You gonna talk to her?"

Ethan, surprised at his son's questions and agitated tone, replied, "I don't know."

*If you stand up like a nail
you will get hammered down.*

—JAPANESE PROVERB

CHAPTER TWO

THE TREES CLUTCHED AT the darkness. A scant sliver of a moon peeked among the still leaves. Ethan carefully inched his way up his front walk. After supper he had dropped Chase off at the Hewitts' house for a weekend sleepover.

Ethan disliked entering a house that was too quiet, so instead of rattling around the rooms without the presence of his son, he had walked downtown as dusk fell. Then he had spent the evening at the Cumming's Stop and Chat Restaurant, reading the newspaper and drinking a succession of half-filled cups of coffee. It cost him $1.25 plus a dollar tip to spend two hours in the company of strangers. Now, in the warm dark, he had made his way back from town. The night grew thicker.

He came to his front steps. He had not switched the porch coach lights on when he'd left earlier in the evening. He remembered that inside the front door, in the alcove by the answering machine, lay an automatic timer for lights. It had been there for months, still in the box. He stared hard in the darkness and shuffled his feet forward. His right foot touched at the familiar loose sidewalk brick. Behind that were several bricks, wobbling and loose, just a few inches from the front porch steps. He promised himself again and again that he would fix them but knew he probably wouldn't get to the job anytime soon. He found his key and unlocked the door.

The hall was dark, quiet, and empty. The red eye of his answering machine blinked, indicating four messages.

He fumbled for the light switch. The wall sconces on the upstairs landing glowed softly. He made his way to the small alcove in the hall, tossed his keys onto the ledge, and nicked at the button just to the right of the red light. A beep and a busy signal. Someone had hung up without leaving a message. He smiled, feeling better that there were only three messages left.

The second message was from his assistant, Joel, detailing the list of concerns Mrs. Moretti had expressed during her visit. The job of restoring the Carter Mansion would keep his crew busy for at least six months—probably more. But Ethan was afraid she would become one of "those" clients—clients who stopped at the jobsite often and made a series of conflicting and confusing requests. With Mrs. Moretti, he was certain that her suggestions would be more like demands than requests. No, Mrs. Moretti's presence might just disrupt any sense of an orderly progression to the job.

The homeowner had to know—and Ethan realized that he would be the one who would tell her—that builders have certain requirements.

You have to respect the bones of an old house, he thought, rehearsing what he might say to Mrs. Moretti. *You have to honor what the original builders wanted to accomplish. Order and comfort come from keeping the past alive. You'll never go wrong staying true to the past.*

Ethan believed that no one, even with lots of money, should come in all willy-nilly and rearrange the original plans and style of any historic place. No—the original essence of the house needed careful preservation, loving restoration.

Otherwise you're just using the facade as some sort of elaborate stage set—like Disneyland.

He sighed, though he didn't want to.

I'll have to sit down with her.

He loved the careful work of restoration, returning to perfection a piece of history that had been damaged from use or worn down by time. That's what got his adrenaline pumping and brought him great pleasure.

His hands took easily to the work. They always had. And he knew a lot about historic architecture. But the real challenge was dealing with the human problems, not the construction problems. He knew that, in Mrs. Moretti's mind, the Carter Mansion project was a renovation, not a restoration, and she liked the "revise as you go" approach. He also knew that money was not a consideration with her. The situation felt far too fluid, far too slippery, for Ethan. He was a man who liked to know his limits from the beginning; he wanted to know and respect those boundaries. And he mourned the fact that, for the first time, he had a client with the resources to restore the home to its original glory, but she was one who didn't share his fervor to respect its history. Instead, she desired to remake the past so it fit into today, which Ethan considered an impossibility— even a travesty.

I'll talk to her. I'm sure she'll understand.

He tried to imagine how that conversation would go, and as he did, another thought barged into his reverie.

And … well, we really need this job. I need this job … if I want to keep the crew busy. It has been a bit of a dry spell.

The tape whirred again, shuffling to the next message. "Hi … Ethan …"

There was a pause and the shuffling of papers. There might have been the clack of a typewriter in the background.

Who still uses a typewriter?

He stopped and stared. He did not recognize the low feminine voice.

Then came a muffled curse—or what sounded like a muffled curse— and the crash of a glass or a dish before the phone was abruptly hung up.

The tape whirred forward to the fourth and last message. It began with a loud sigh. "Hi. That was me that just called. I dropped my coffee cup over my notebook and ruined my second-best chance at a Pulitzer."

Then the voice bubbled into a low, knowing laugh. "This is Cameron Dane. From *The Derrick*. I talked to you at the ball game today. I want to do a story on your work at the old Carter place."

Her voice sounds different over the phone … deeper … softer.

There was a loud sigh and a pause. "I hate answering machines. I always sound like I'm ready for a fight … or something."

I would never have said that about the voice, Ethan thought.

Then another pause followed.

"Listen. I would start over again, but then you would really think I'm a lunatic. I mentioned this idea to Paige Drake. She said she knows you, and she thought it would be a wonderful story. And she's the boss and you don't want to get me fired by saying no, do you?"

There was a sound like her open palm had smacked her own forehead.

"Don't I sound like some insane, freelance reporter for the *Senaca Heights Shopper*? Doesn't this message make you want to say yes to this story? Good grief, how pathetic can I get?"

Another long pause.

"Okay. This is it. My last and final attempt at sounding normal. I'm Cameron Dane. From *The Derrick*. We met today. I would really and truly appreciate it if I could do a story on your work at the Carter place. I love historic architecture and I adore old houses. I grew up in a Victorian house in Philadelphia. I could show you pictures."

She sighed again, loudly, and Ethan thought for effect.

"So … will you do it? And I'm sorry for calling you a Bob Vila. I bet you hated that. I dislike him too. Pretentious and unskilled, am I right? Right? Okay … I'll call you. Please say yes."

There was a long pause and then a resigned sigh, followed by the click of the phone being hung up. Ethan thought it was a most gentle sound.

Without really thinking about it, he hit the replay button and listened to both of her messages a second time. He would have listened to them a third time but felt a sudden wave of self-consciousness.

So should I talk to her?

Eleven o'clock had come and gone, and still Ethan couldn't fall asleep. He stared at the dark sky out his bedroom window for a long time. It was the quiet emptiness of the night that he found hardest to bear. With Chase gone, the silence felt louder than the roar of an angry river.

So should I talk to her? Might be good for business. I could really use the publicity.

He rolled over and plumped his pillow.

Probably get me the wrong kind of business.

The clock ticked over to 11:30.

And she is ... I don't know ... very attractive, I guess. My dad would have said she had gumption.

He sighed deeply.

Whatever gumption is.

11:45.

So ... should I talk to her or not?

By the time he fell asleep, he still had not decided.

———

Ethan heard the squeals of wood being torn from its moorings. The harsh squawk of nails, having spent decades in one place, and now disrupted and displaced, was unmistakable. His crew worked on the third floor, ripping down walls that had been erected in the 1940s, when sleeping rooms were added in the spacious attic.

He traced his fingers down a copy of the original blueprints for the house. The plans for large, expensive old houses were often kept in the official records of small towns such as Franklin. Not every blueprint was saved, and not every substantial home was represented, but the Old Carter Mansion was one of the fortunate ones. The dark, almost vibrant blue paper with white lines showed its age, but the drawings were still intact.

That made life easy for Ethan's crew.

We'll tear it down to the original walls, he thought.

Ethan unrolled the old floor plans and then the newly drafted version for Mrs. Moretti's project. Work on the third floor would be simple. When first built, the upper floor was one large room—a typically enormous Victorian attic with a large turret that was served by a winding, enclosed wooden staircase. The majority of the space had been used as a ballroom, with a full-height ceiling and inlaid-wood dance floor; the rest served as a large storage area. Basements of the era, usually constructed of stone blocks, were low-ceilinged, cramped, and often damp and moldy.

For storage, attics, even though hot in the summer and cold in the winter, would be more ideal to hold whatever was seasonal or unwanted.

The second floor—well, that would be a different matter. Ethan liked the old Victorian manner of dividing large spaces into many rooms—smaller spaces that were intimate, personal. The new owner did not share the Victorians'—nor Ethan's—sensibilities. Mrs. Moretti's architect had erased original walls, deleting so many that Ethan grew uncomfortable just considering the dashed lines on the new plan indicating the places where walls had once existed.

We'll need to talk about this. If we take down all those walls, we'll be forced to add a lot of spanning supports with headers. I don't like doing that. Mrs. Moretti needs to be sensitive to what this house was and still should be. There is no reason why anyone should throw out all the past. Those rooms are what make this house unique. She needs to understand that.

He flipped the page. The first floor had been completely reconfigured. Most Victorian homes had large front rooms with side parlors, small family spaces in the rear, and most often, tiny kitchens. The Carter Mansion was no exception. The new owner wanted it all renovated, with an office/library to one side of the entry, and a formal dining room on the other side. New walls, French doors, and transoms between the rooms were to be added. A large, open kitchen, all state-of-the-art, and a large adjoining space called the "great room" were to be at the back. She wanted another fireplace there as well, to add to the ten already existing in the house, which included an elaborate marble fireplace in the entry.

Ethan ran his finger over some of the newly designed areas on the first floor.

At least we won't get there for a couple of months.

He rolled up both prints.

It'll give me plenty of time to change her mind.

———— ✦ ————

Bonnie Hewitt, Elliot's mom, honked the horn as she pulled into the driveway and leaned out her window.

"He's probably hungry." She laughed. "Hasn't eaten for at least twenty minutes."

Ethan laughed and waved back. "Hollow leg, right?"

"Thank goodness for that new warehouse club. We'd be broke without it."

Chase bounded up the brick steps and slid under his father's arm, which was holding the front door open.

"Thanks again," Ethan shouted.

Elliot's mom, and all of the six Hewitt children, waved and drove off, the tailpipe of her scruffy blue minivan sparking on high spots of the asphalt.

"So, champ—how was the sleepover?"

Chase leaned into the refrigerator, as if looking for some manner of loose, chilled food source that might be lurking behind the milk container. "Fine."

Ethan poured himself a third cup of coffee. "What did you do?"

Chase pulled back, holding a yogurt. "Stuff," he said with a shrug.

Ethan glanced at the clock over the sink. He didn't really have time or energy to pry information from his son this morning. Elliot's mom had been smiling when she pulled up. The weekend must have gone well enough.

"Stuff?"

Chase slumped into a kitchen chair.

"Stuff. You know. Stuff. Me and Elliot sort of stuff."

"Did you remember to thank Mrs. Hewitt for letting you stay the weekend?"

Chase rolled his eyes. "Yes, Dad, I thanked her. And once more from the porch, remember?"

Ethan drank half the cup in one swallow. "Just checking." He poured the rest of the coffee down the sink. He would have several more cups before the morning was half over, and he didn't need the extra caffeine.

"You okay here this morning by yourself? Mrs. Whiting doesn't come today."

Summers were hard. Chase had been out of school for just a week.

The school district had a short one-day spring mini-break, opting instead to end the school year before Memorial Day. But now Ethan had to work, and Chase would be home alone. Mildred Whiting, an elderly woman from down the street, came in three afternoons a week to do cleaning.

With just the two of them, Ethan knew there wasn't that much to clean in the house, but Mildred was the classic version of what a grandmother should be. She'd been close to the family before Ethan's wife, Lynne, died and had been the godly "mother" in the young woman's life. Lynne's death hit her hard. Mrs. Whiting had taken Ethan and Chase under her wing and often came over more days than Ethan actually paid for, often checking in on the boy. She was there to fill in some of the gaps in a home without a woman—gently encouraging, softly guiding, and providing a loving touch when needed. She made sure Chase remembered some of the things his mother had taught him—to say his prayers, count his blessings, be a "good boy."

Chase didn't need a babysitter at his age, but Ethan did not relish the idea of him being on his own and alone so much. He was grateful for Mrs. Whiting.

"That's okay, Dad. I'll wash my dirty clothes this morning. Maybe I'll go to the park to see who's there. Or go fishing."

Ethan nodded. Franklin was still a small town. He knew it was not absolutely safe, but safer than most anyplace else that he could imagine.

"Okay. I'll be home early—by four. I have a couple of estimates to work on. We'll have dinner, okay?"

"Sure, Dad."

And with that Chase turned to the sports page of the local paper and bent to the box scores, no longer paying attention to his father, who slipped from the room and headed for his truck parked in the driveway.

Ethan loved the sounds of carpentry—the gnashing whir of a power saw; the tight, clicking hiss of a nail gun; the bang of a real hammer against a nail; the thick clatter of stacks of lumber. He stood on the first floor, in the foyer of the Old Carter Mansion, and listened with a smile. Most of their work for the next few months would be confined to the upper floors, so it was like listening to a symphony through closed doors.

The Old Carter Mansion had been called the Old Carter Mansion as long as Ethan could remember. He wondered if it had been called the Old Carter Mansion immediately after its completion.

The year was 1868. At eighteen years of age, Henry Carter—the illegitimate son of a Philadelphia barber—showed up in Franklin. Within a dozen years, he had declared himself the town's wealthiest lumber baron. He diversified into oil and cement and, at the age of forty, began work on his palatial abode.

He bought a piece of riverfront property up on a lovely ridge of land overlooking the water and the town—the most scenic view around.

Construction had taken two years.

The town's library housed a handful of pictures of the actual construction within its yellowed-newsprint archives. Before bidding on the current project, Ethan had spent a day in the archives, poring over the old photos and plans, attempting to discern what was now hidden behind plaster and wainscoting.

Carter's fortunes had not survived the dawn of the new millennium though. Overextended, he had not anticipated a glut of wood from Canada inundating the local lumber market, and at the end of his life, Carter's assets had been reduced to a mere few thousand dollars and his mansion—substantial for the times, but he was no longer a rich man.

His heirs had tried to maintain the house for a few years. Servants became expensive. None of his sons had inherited his business acumen or panache. By the end of World War I, his sons had sold the house to the owner of the Venango Coal Mine, who had added walls and bathrooms, turning it into a rooming house for his workers.

Now, well over a century after it was built, a great-granddaughter of Henry Carter, Mrs. Cecily Moretti, after making a substantial fortune in software design, had returned home to her ancestral roots, most recently residing in San Francisco, and had purchased the house with a desire to make this her summer home.

Her return to the area seemed odd. Franklin did have a smattering of summer homes, but the town was far from the cultured merriment of San Francisco. Local gossips worked overtime trying to decipher Mrs. Moretti's motives.

The original shingled house was a classic example of the Queen Anne Victorian style of architecture, with a round turret, a steeply pitched roof of irregular shape, and an imposing front-facing gable. A one-story wrap-around porch ran along the full width of the front of the house and along the sides. Its weather-worn, delicately turned porch posts still stood, but most of the ornamental gingerbread spindles and lacy brackets were rotted and broken. Most of the original clear glass of the home's many bay windows was either cracked or missing, but many of the beautiful stained-glass decorative panes remained intact.

A rabbit's warren of small rooms made up the second and third floors. Closets, if they existed at all, were the size of coffins. Added bathrooms were of World War II vintage. Due to inept remodeling attempts over the years, a number of shaky staircases led to nowhere. Layer upon layer of lead-based paint covered the woodwork. Major rooms had fireplaces; however, many were no longer in working order. Their mantels and hearths were badly in need of refinishing and repair. But, overall, the house was in remarkably good shape after all the life that had lived in it.

"The bones are solid," is how Ethan assessed the house.

The new Mrs. Carter—Cecily Carter Moretti—wanted her mansion taken down to the bare studs—and then some—and brought up to thoroughly modern standards.

The first time Ethan had walked through the house, he'd marveled at the grace and craftsmanship still showing through after all the degradations of the past. Even poorly built walls and partitions that had been added over the years could not spoil the perfect and pleasing lines of the architect's intent.

Ethan found it easy to tell the difference between what was original and what was not. When the mansion was built, Mr. Carter must have had his best quality lumber cut and milled to his specifications—the two-by-four lumber in the house measured a full two inches by four inches.

That was normal, given the age of the house, since standardization of sizes didn't start until the 1920s. Every stud smaller than an actual two inches by four inches could safely be removed.

Once the needed demolition was done and the house was brought back to its original spaces, Ethan was sure Mrs. Moretti would see the value in keeping most things as they were. Then she would stop her foolish dickering about what should be saved and what should be, in her words, "augmented."

———————

"Mrs. Moretti," Ethan said in his defense of maintaining the home's original layout, "you have to realize that the architect had a vision, and the builder knew what he was doing. This is all the work of skilled craftsmen." Ethan tapped on a bare stud wall as if emphasizing his point. "You can't just come in and dismantle what has stood for 125-plus years. It would be wrong."

"First of all, you have to stop this Mrs. Moretti business," Mrs. Moretti said, smiling. "It's CeCe. Remember? I answer to CeCe."

"Okay then … CeCe," Ethan replied.

"And secondly, I don't want a Victorian museum. Other than the exterior of this old place, I don't particularly like the Victorian style. Everything is too ornate, too awkward, too much like a funeral parlor. The outsides of these Queen Annes are wonderful. But not the insides, the spaces. They need updating to work for me."

"But the inside has to match the outside," Ethan countered. He had had this sort of discussion with other clients in the past, often to the detriment of his business. "You have to respect the past. You can't just use the building as a shell."

They were both standing in the turreted room above the third floor. From the expansive bay window that followed its round shape, one could see both French Creek and the Allegheny River—almost an aerial perspective of all of Franklin.

"But you can," CeCe countered. "I can, at least."

Ethan knew who was the client and who paid the bills but felt that he had to defend the original intent of the architect.

"Take that staircase there," CeCe said, pointing at the wooden spiral staircase, a continuation of the house's back staircase, which led from the third floor up to the turret room. "That's original, right?"

Ethan nodded. "Best use of space. A traditional staircase would use up almost an entire room on the third floor. It's what is needed here."

"But isn't there space for … like a hundred rooms on the third floor? It doesn't matter if one gets used for a staircase. All I know is that I don't like spiral staircases. They make me dizzy. What if I were wearing high heels? I would kill myself on those ridiculously thin steps. I don't wear high heels anymore, but if I did …"

"But Mrs. … CeCe … it's going to be really expensive to tear that well-built stairway out. And the way it is—well, that's the best use of space. The design works just fine."

She walked to the edge of the stairway and peered down. "I understand what you're saying … I think. But I don't care about what it's supposed to look like. I don't want the spiral staircase. Not at all. It has to go. It gives me the creeps. And you have to recognize that I don't want this house restored. I'm not a purist like you."

Ethan tried not to look shocked … or offended. He knew what was coming.

"I am *renovating* this house," CeCe continued. "I don't want what was here in the past. I want modern and nice and convenient and usable and safe. I want open. I want what I want."

Ethan could only shake his head in reply. He wanted to tell her that the history of things should be respected. *You should work around the quirks of a house. You could live with some odd corners. It's what gives the house its charm, its character. You could manage your life around some of the "defects" of the past.* It was important to have things as they should be, as they were, leaving the past to tell its story.

But instead of saying anything, he simply nodded.

She did, after all, sign the checks.

And, after all, Willis Construction really needed this job.

Ethan strapped on his tool belt.

He loved the feel of the hammer resting against his leg, the rattle of nails in the leather pouch, the clatter of tape measures and metal framing squares. Nail guns were faster and more efficient, but there was something alien about their popping hisses as compressed air drove nails into wood without benefit of hammer.

By noon, the crew had built new framing walls on the north side of a second-floor bedroom. Two small, original knee walls had been taken down, and two doorways were covered over in newer framing and plywood sheets.

"Lunchtime," Joel called. His watch kept the official time for the crew. A short, stocky man, Joel was about as unflappable an assistant as Ethan could have hoped for. Ethan knew Joel would keep things running smoothly on the jobsite in his absence. Joel had an ability to manage the workers on the crew with a strong yet kind manner. And he was a gifted craftsman as well.

The crew all made their way down to the first floor, grabbing their coolers and lunch carriers. It looked as if there was an official cooler for the team; nearly every one carried the exact same model, in different colors and stages of being nicked and scarred.

They assembled on the front porch. Of all the details on the house, the porch was one that had scarcely been altered since the mid-1880s. Although the gingerbread details needed work, the wide, sweeping curves of the porch—as it graciously wrapped around the house—remained the same as drawn by the nineteenth-century architect.

They ate in silence. From the third floor came the booming bass of the radio that constantly played as they worked.

Ethan sat, reclining against the shingled wall, just under a massive bay window. He looked up as a small, sporty white car in need of a washing pulled close to the curb and stopped at an awkward angle, its front a little too close to the brick entrance pillars and its trunk sticking out a little too far into the street.

The entire crew looked up.

The door opened, and a young woman stepped out into the bright sunshine.

Ethan immediately recognized her—Cameron Dane from *The Derrick*.

The rest of the crew fell into a deeper silence as she walked up the uneven brick sidewalk.

"Hi!" she called out. "I knew you were probably too busy to call, so I thought I might as well stop by and ask you again."

Ethan tried to swallow the bite of the salami sandwich in his mouth but found it wadded up at the top of his throat. He gulped again, then reached for his thermos.

Cameron stopped at the bottom of the steps. Her dark hair fell in relaxed curls around her shoulders. She was wearing black linen slacks that hung loose around her long legs, and a white blouse that might have been silk. Ethan imagined that even the stores at the new mall out toward Cranberry didn't sell expensive blouses like that. The first three buttons were undone. She put one foot on the bottom step and rested her hands on her hips. She smiled again.

He did not remember her being quite so striking.

"So?" she asked again. "Did you decide?"

Ethan could feel the eyes of his crew darting from this woman to him and back to the woman again. He hoped he wouldn't blush.

He swallowed again. "I didn't have a lot of time to think about it … I mean …"

Instead of a scowl, which is what Ethan expected, she tilted her head back and laughed. He watched her expose her white, smooth throat, circled with a simple string of pearls.

"That might have sounded plausible in a phone message. But in person … it just doesn't work."

Ethan felt his crew staring at either the back of his head or at this woman.

"Well … I would need to talk to the owner of the house. She's in California this week. It will have to wait until she gets back."

Cameron offered her best happy, not-smug expression in reply. "I already spoke with her. 'Call me CeCe,' she said, 'with two capital Cs.' The editor of the paper knows her father ... or uncle ... or someone. I called her, and she was excited about the idea."

He found himself smiling back, despite being scolded in a most pleasant manner. "Well," he said, finally, "I suppose it would be fine. When?"

She shrugged. "You're going to be here awhile—I know that much about construction. You're not going to have any 'after' photo opportunities for a while, are you?"

"No. Not for several months at least."

She looked happy that he had understood her verbal shorthand.

"Well, maybe we can do a two-part series with a long break between parts. Let's schedule the first interview for next Monday. I'd do it this week, but I have to head back home to Philadelphia this afternoon for a few days. I hope next Monday works for you."

"It does," Ethan said, nodding.

She brightened.

"Then I'll see you next Monday—about ten, okay?"

"Ten would be fine."

She nodded, turned, and walked back to her car. Before she got in, she looked directly at Ethan and waved.

He almost waved back but nodded discreetly instead.

As she drove off, he could feel the hard stares of his entire crew—none of whom had said a single word during the entire exchange.

———⊙⊙⊙⊙———

"She's just a reporter. Wants to do a story on this old place."

Joel shook his head in disbelief.

"About us? I don't think I'd like that."

"Not us. This house," Ethan answered.

Some of the crew laughed.

"It ain't the house she's interested in, Willis. A monkey with a pipe wrench could tell you that it ain't that at all."

Ethan stood up abruptly. "It's just a story. That's all. She just wants a story on the restoration." His words were not angry, but neither were they gentle.

He waited only a heartbeat until he turned and walked back inside, a full twenty minutes before their lunch break was over.

———◦◦◦———

"So, you still up for camping this weekend?"

Ethan carried the dinner plates back to the sink. Most often the sink would collect dishes for a day or two, but Ethan, as of late, had made a concerted effort to keep the clutter down. Now he washed the dishes as soon as they were finished eating. Chase most often pitched in but today sat in his chair and slumped farther.

He shrugged.

"Not much of an answer," Ethan replied harshly. "Do you want to go or not? No sense going if you're going to mope around all weekend."

Ethan tried to hold his anger in check. He was pretty certain that Chase was trying his best to hold his sullen mood in check as well.

"I dunno," Chase said softly, looking away. "I guess we could go. Only weekend for a while with no ball games."

Ethan and Chase had sat down weeks ago with the baseball schedule and calendar. During the entire summer, only four weekends did not have a game or practice or some other entanglement. Ethan did not like the excessive time demands but realized that the team gave his son a great outlet—an outlet that Ethan alone could not offer.

"You guess?"

Chase glared back this time.

"Okay. Sorry."

Chase's face softened. Ethan saw something in his eyes. It was not anger exactly, nor simply a sullen mood. It was something of loss, of emptiness, that flickered there, just out of his reach and understanding. It was the color of a gray afternoon in March, just before dark, under a cold, wet sky. He wondered if that veil had come upon his son that one unspeakable day so long ago.

Chase looked back at his father. "Yeah, we should go. To Lake Tionesta like you said, right?"

Ethan thought the words sounded hollow. But he also realized that Chase had made a move, no matter how slight. He blinked hard and tried his best to smile in return.

"Yeah, I think that's a great spot. We can take the canoe."

Chase nodded.

They had camped there several times last year, on the lake at the edge of the Allegheny National Forest. They had been nearly alone on the campground, and from the open tent flap they could have tossed a fishing line into the water, they were so close.

"Should I bring the big tent?" Ethan asked.

They had two tents—one an elaborate four-man affair with a porch and a few dozen poles and pegs. Ethan had bought the tent before he and Lynne were married. He'd anticipated children even before she had agreed to marry him. A year ago, he had purchased a smaller, two-man tent that could almost set itself up.

Ethan could not decide on which tent made him less uncomfortable. He still heard echoes of Lynne's laughter in the large tent, and the small tent was a constant, silent statement that she would never be with them again.

He thought he would let his son decide.

"The small one is fine. It's a lot easier to set up."

Both paused.

"But the big one is more comfortable."

Ethan nodded. He would decide later. "Firewood or Coleman stove?" he asked.

Chase bit his lower lip. "Firewood," he said, but added quickly, "but take the stove if it looks like rain."

Ethan recalled that their last trip had been marked with a steady, unrelenting drizzle. The nearest restaurant had been located over an hour away, so after two days of eating crackers and canned tuna, they had given up and headed home.

"Freeze-dried or fresh-caught?"

Chase let out an unexpected giggle. "Both. Please."

Ethan played at being insulted. "You doubt my ability to catch fish? Have I ever failed us before?"

Ethan caught his son's eye. When he saw Chase's expression, he knew they were both remembering a trip last year when they had planned to live off the land. The fish must have heard them coming because it had taken them all day to catch two small perch, which, combined, were hardly enough for an appetizer.

"Good. I'll get the tent and canoe ready. You gather up the food and your gear. I want to leave right after work on Friday."

Chase nodded.

"But we need to get back on Sunday evening."

Chase looked perplexed. Often they would stay through Monday morning. After all, Ethan was the owner of Willis Construction, and the position provided a few perks.

"There's a reporter coming to interview me at the Old Carter Mansion Monday morning."

"About what?"

Ethan shrugged. "About the restoration, I guess."

Chase leaned forward out of his slouch. "That reporter from the ball game?"

Ethan was surprised Chase remembered. "Yes. The same one."

There was a long pause, as if Chase was carefully measuring his words. "Sure. Okay. We can come home Sunday night."

His words were as blank as an empty chalkboard in a shuttered classroom.

Chase said nothing more about the proposed story. The evening passed quickly. The Pittsburgh Pirates were playing a night game in Atlanta, and Chase watched several innings. He and his father didn't exchange more than a dozen sentences.

Chase quietly left the room as his father began to snore from the depths of his leather recliner. He crept up the stairs to his room. For a long

moment, he hesitated in his doorway. He listened to the gentle hum of
the television and his father's occasional soft snoring.

He didn't turn the light on in his room. His antique pine bed, set at
an angle in the corner, had been unmade now for several days running.
His student-sized desk was nestled under the eaves. Since it was summer,
the surface stayed clean, save for the latest *Sports Illustrated.*

Two low three-drawer chests sat on the wall opposite. His mother had
found them along with a matching nightstand in a thrift store years earlier and had stripped them bare. She had planned to paint them. Now,
seven years later, they all remained unpainted. Chase kept them in reasonable order, but several drawers were filled with a jumble of socks and
underwear and batting gloves. One poster hung on the wall—this year's
Pittsburgh Pirates team photo. All the players and coaches were smiling at
some point off to the left of the camera lens. Next to it was an eight-by-
ten framed photo of the Franklin Flyers, sponsored by The Pizza Den.
Chase, unsmiling and squinting into the sun, was in the last row in a
number 14 baseball jersey.

He made his way in the dark and switched on the light in his closet.
He pushed aside a neat row of clothes, all hung carefully on matching
hangers, all notched in the same direction.

Behind the clothes was a rectangle of plywood, painted to match the
wall, and trimmed with door molding. The frame was about half the size
of a regular door. A handle jutted out on one side.

Chase slipped his fingers under the handle and pulled it toward him.
A patch of darkness lay in front of him. He carefully laid the plywood rectangle to one side and reached into the dark, his fingers spread. He found
the pull cord to the light switch and gently tugged at it. A small bulb filled
the space with cool light. Chase ducked his head and entered.

The Willis house was 120 years old. His dad always said it was his best
advertisement. Done in the Carpenter Gothic style, the large cottage had
stood longer than most of the houses in Franklin. Chase knew well the
story of how his family had acquired the house. His dad had always
admired its cross gables, its ornate bargeboards adorning the gable ends of
the roof, its windows with pointed arches, and its board and batten trim.

When Dad and Mom were newlyweds, the old place had gone up for sale. It needed so much work that it was affordable for the young couple—a real "fixer-upper." His dad had spent his nights and weekends lovingly restoring all the historic wooden exterior details. His mom had stripped the walls of over a century of wallpaper layers, and they had painted them in a palette of rich colors.

Dad had never fully finished the remodeling tasks Mom had planned—adding an island and moving a wall in the kitchen, putting up a chair rail and beadboard in the dining room—and now he didn't seem to want to do it.

Chase shrugged. Guess with only Dad and him now, the remodeling was no longer important. The house had its share of quirks and odd spaces. Under the steep cross-gabled roof, a narrow cleft of unused storage space lay behind Chase's second-floor bedroom—a tight, windowless hallway—or secret passageway—about fifteen feet long and four feet wide, with a low ceiling no more than five feet high. In it a small boy could stand and walk, but Chase now was too tall to walk without crouching.

Chase had pulled electrical wire from an outlet in his room and installed the pull light. A boy did not grow up in the home of a builder without learning some of the skills. He nailed in drywall along the exposed joists—in a jigsaw pattern—from scraps that he pulled from his father's work sites. They were carefully snugged tight together but never taped and plastered. The pattern looked like a mosaic of sorts. The floor was covered with a plush thickness of dozens and dozens of carpet squares—free samples from past projects that his father had discarded. At the far end of this hidden hallway was an eyebrow vent, its louvers facing the west, at the back side of the house. Two summers ago he had painted the drywall using some paint also left over from another old house his dad had worked on in town—a deep blue-green color, the color of the sea, the color of his mother's eyes.

He was sure his father had forgotten that this room existed. Or maybe he hadn't. Chase knew that even if his father remembered it, he would never invade this space without permission. They had that sort of a relationship.

Chase knelt and took a deep breath. He closed his eyes.

The walls were devoid of posters. The hall was decorated with a couple of old lawn chairs on one side, some beanbag chairs, and a dozen old pillows scattered about. A stack of old comic books and a few old *Sports Illustrated* magazines lay near the chairs. He walked to the far end and looked out the half-round louvers to the house next door. He turned and watched a car slowly cruise up their block.

Only he and Elliot ever entered this room. They had once talked about stringing wire between Elliot's house and this room so they could carry on secret conversations. As of yet, that plan had not gone beyond the daydreaming stage.

The night had grown dark, and a low scud of clouds obscured the moon. It was as dark as the neighborhood got, Chase figured.

He bent to his knee and from an alcove extracted a wooden box the size of a small footlocker. He had built it out of bits and pieces of one-by-sixes that he found in his father's truck. It had a hinged lid and a little clasping lock. He had once considered locking it but realized no one would ever tamper with his secret place.

He stared at the chest for a long moment. Then he opened the lid and paused for a long while. He didn't know how much time had passed. He then reached in and gently felt along the edge of a white fabric. His expression didn't change. He laid it back down and smoothed at the surface.

He pushed one corner to the side. He pulled out a folded paper and spread it open. It was the hockey schedule for the Franklin Oilers. It was seven years old. He refolded it and placed it back inside the box. Then he reached in and removed a Bible. The dark blue leather cover was creased and worn and had his mother's maiden name embossed in gold on the bottom-right-hand corner. He opened the front cover and traced at the writing with his forefinger.

From somewhere he heard his name being called out, ever so faint and ever so softly.

Then he blinked.

The voice was real. His father was calling up from the first floor. He hurried and replaced the Bible, closed the lid, slipped out of his secret room, snapped off the light, and replaced the plywood door.

"Chase? Do you hear me?" his father said in an agitated tone.

"Yeah, Dad?" he called back. Chase flumped into the overstuffed chair under his window, switched on the light, and grabbed one of the books in the pile by the chair. He flipped it right-side up and opened it halfway.

He heard the weary moans of the wooden stairs as his father climbed them. Fourth step squeal, seventh step creak.

"I was calling you. You didn't answer." His father now stood in his bedroom doorway. "Are you okay?"

"Sure. I was just looking at the moon," he replied. "I might have dozed off. Who won the game?"

"The Pirates—6 to 5."

Chase smiled. "Good. Well, I think I'm going to bed."

"Okay."

The steps squealed and groaned in the same manner once again but this time in reverse. That meant his dad had forgotten to check the locks on the front door.

Ethan stepped onto the front porch and looked up into the sky. There was no moon. Only the gray darkness of the clouds.

Forgiveness is the answer
to the child's dream of a miracle
by which what is broken is made whole again,
what is soiled is made clean again.

—DAG HAMMARSKJÖLD

CHAPTER THREE

Lake Tionesta wasn't the biggest lake in the area, or the closest. But if Ethan had been asked, he would have said it was his favorite. The campground at the lake lay at the foot of a steep bluff, layered with pines and oaks. The lake was quiet. Three years earlier, the state had banned all powerboats, citing environmental damage. There would be no sawing and whining of big Evinrudes at the tail of a Bassmaster boat. There would be no chopping complaint of Jet Skis clamoring about in the waves. Just the soft lapping of the water on the rocky shore. Just the gentle hiss of the wind in the surrounding pines.

After a week amid power tools, Ethan loved the chance to hear nothing.

It must have been a busy week for Chase as well, since he fell asleep as soon as they left Franklin and slept for over an hour—virtually the entire trip. Ethan walked quietly as he unloaded the tent and canoe. He had brought the big tent. Gray clouds filled the sky, and Ethan wanted a dry spot to sit if the rains did come. In only a few minutes, the tent was erect. He tossed the sleeping bags inside and set up the two collapsible chairs. He hung the lantern on one of the tent supports.

He slid the canoe from the truck and hoisted it to his shoulders, wobbling down to the lakeshore. He wedged it firmly on the shore. The calm wind produced no waves, and the leaves remained motionless in the graying afternoon. He turned back to the campsite and saw Chase sitting up in the truck, stretching, his right arm extending through the open window.

Chase had grown tall in the first year of his teens, losing all vestiges of his earlier, rounded, youthful look. He now stood two inches taller than his mother had been. His hair was the color of her hair, blond as a field of wheat in September. The afternoon light, fading gold from the west, lit his face in full profile. In the diffused illumination, Ethan saw the profile of his wife imbued in his son. He looked away, then pulled the canoe farther from the water.

"Dad," Chase called, "you should have woke me up. I would have helped." He stepped out of the truck and stretched again.

"No problem. You looked tired."

His son leaned into the bed of the truck and retrieved his tackle box and rod. "Fishing?" he asked. "Live off the land for dinner tonight?"

Ethan took a deep breath. "Why don't you try it alone, Chase? I'll finish setting up and start a fire."

"You sure?" Chase replied as he set his rod and tackle box in the canoe.

"Yeah, I'm sure."

Ethan helped maneuver the canoe into the water. He stepped on a flat stone just above the surface of the lake and gave the boat a shove. It slipped into the water with a silent rippling. "Put your vest on. I'm too old for a lake rescue."

Chase scowled, waited a moment, then grabbed the life vest from the prow of the canoe and put it on. Ethan heard the loud snaps of the plastic buckles as Chase fastened them together.

As he turned back to the campsite, he heard the ripple of a paddle in the still water.

Finishing the campsite took only another few minutes. A storm had passed through the area earlier in the week and the ground was littered with branches, some the size of a man's arm. In five minutes, Ethan had enough wood for cooking for the night, and probably for breakfast as well. Most branches he simply broke in half or fourths by stepping on them in the middle and pulling one end with his hands. He later cut the larger ones with a small folding camp saw.

He unrolled the sleeping bags in the tent. This was the job his wife had always done. He and Chase would have been in the canoe, and she would have done the final unpacking.

He placed the grate on the fire circle and set a blackened coffeepot to one side. He no longer tried to make real coffee but used instant instead. Lynne had the knack of knowing just how long to let the flames dance at the bottom of the pot. His always came out either weak as rainwater or thick as native petroleum.

He set a large pot to the fire and threw in his premixed bag of potatoes and carrots and cold water. Replacing the lid, he nudged the pot toward the center of the flames. Then he took his coffee cup, poured a cup of hot water, then added instant coffee and dry creamer. He pushed his chair closer to the edge of the tarp under the tent and sat down.

By this time, Chase had rowed nearly a hundred yards out into the lake as the sky cleared. Below the canoe, twenty feet down, lay a jumble of rocks and old trees—a perfect hiding place for bass and perch—in the cold, dark waters of the lake. The two of them had fished that same location often. He knew Chase had triangulated his position, sighting it in relationship to a jetty of rocks to the east and the ranger's tower to the south.

Ethan sipped at the coffee and watched his son cast his line into the water, slowly reeling it back in, jerking the line every few seconds, just as Ethan had instructed him so many summers ago. Four casts came back empty. On Chase's fifth cast, Ethan watched as the end of the rod tipped toward the water. Chase reacted smoothly and yanked the rod to set the hook. He began winding the reel, slowly at first, then more quickly. He reached into the water and pulled the line into the air. At the end was a perch, Ethan thought, though he was too far away to be sure. He thought he saw a lemon yellow flash in the sun reflected off the scales. Chase quickly removed the small fish from the hook and carefully set it back into the water, rinsing his hand off with a splash.

He looked toward his father and made some gesture, the intent lost on Ethan. He waved and Chase waved back, then cast his line again.

The sun was now twenty minutes above the western pines, scattering shadows across the far western shore of the lake.

Ethan stared out across the water, out toward his son. He sat the same way his mother had sat, Ethan realized, with his knees spread in a relaxed slouch. His hat, a Flyers baseball cap, was pulled far to the back, so the bill was nearly vertical. His mother had worn hers much the same, except she would pull her blonde hair through the back of the hat in a long, sweet ponytail.

He and Lynne had bought the canoe the first year of their marriage. Images of Lynne resting, leaning back against the gunwale, her right hand barely trailing in the water, tracing their progress with her index finger, came rushing to his thoughts.

He looked back at his son and felt that familiar, unwelcome snicking in his chest—a faint, insistent sputter below his heart.

Chase snagged his rod back with a snap. Whatever took the bait this time felt big. He didn't like using lures, preferring worms and leeches. He had a tackle box full of bait and spinners and jigs of all descriptions. None were as effective as the real thing.

But lures were cleaner and easier to use than live bait.

He wound his reel, feeling the great unseen tug at the line. After a long moment, he saw the golden, liquid flash just below the surface of the water. A bass, perhaps the biggest one he had ever snagged, circled once, then dove under the canoe. He sat up straight and leaned toward the fish, extending his arm to the side.

"Stay there, stay there," he said in an urgent whisper.

He pulled, tugging the fish toward the open waters to his side.

"Come on, now, come on."

The fish darted first toward the surface. Chase could see that one hook of his lure was snagged firmly in the mouth of the fish.

"I have him," Chase said firmly and yanked at the rod.

The fish broke the plane of the water, flipped its tail, and pulled once again away from the canoe. Chase let him have a dozen yards of line, wanting to tire him out. The line was thin and light, to add to the sport of fishing. Anyone could land a fish with a rope, his father said, but it took a sportsman with skill to use a thread.

Chase kept the line taut. Then all of a sudden it went limp. Instinctively, Chase stood in the canoe, bracing himself as best he could. He had to stand to see the shadowy ripples of the huge fish. He wound the reel fast.

Then he saw a glimpse of the fish—sleek, gold, green, and white, flashing toward him. He tried to wind as fast as the fish swam, but it would be impossible. A streak in the water, and then the fish dove beneath the canoe. The line went limp, then snapped tight. Chase pulled back hard. As he did, he realized with a thud that the rough, nicked bottom of the canoe would cut the line. As he pulled, the line broke free, and Chase knew in that second that the fish was gone.

He reeled his line in. The line was empty, and the lure was gone.

He looked toward the direction the fish had taken. It was free, but it had a lure snagged firmly in its flesh. It would not live long, perhaps a few days—and for that, Chase felt a sudden sadness.

He stood, watching the placid water.

At the shore of the lake, he saw his father striding toward the water, his hand raised. Even from this distance, Chase knew he was upset over something.

Chase leaned toward the land. He heard a shout but couldn't make out the words. He cupped his hand to his ear.

"I said sit down!" came his father's louder shout. "For heaven's sake, sit down! And come back closer to shore."

Chase stared at him for a moment. He knew he was guilty of a breach of canoe safety but did not enjoy being instructed from a distance. He glared back at his father, then sat down, threw his rod to the floor of the canoe, grabbed the paddle, and dug into the still water.

"Good grief, Chase, what were you thinking? To stand up like that in a canoe. You could have fallen and hit your head and drowned. What if I hadn't been watching? You would have been gone. Aren't you thinking anymore?"

Chase said nothing as he pulled the canoe up onto the rocks. He grabbed his tackle box and rod, yanked them out, and stomped off toward the truck, where he tossed them in the back with an indiscriminant clatter.

"Don't walk away from me while I'm talking to you," Ethan said, a little bit quieter than a shout.

Chase turned back and glared. "Okay. I stood up. So shoot me!"

Ethan took a step toward his son, his lips tight with anger. "Don't talk to me in that tone, young man."

Chase did not shrink back an inch. "Then you don't talk to me in that tone either!" he shouted back. "I just stood up in the stupid canoe. I forgot, okay? Nobody got killed, okay?"

Ethan lowered his voice just a bit. "Listen, I don't want you doing stupid things like that anymore. I may not be around all the time to save you."

"Save me?" Chase shouted. "I don't need saving! And I don't need you waiting around, waiting for me to screw up."

With that, Chase turned on his heels and walked away toward the tent. He slapped the flap open and ducked inside. If it had been a door, it would have been slammed.

Ethan unclenched his fists and took a deep breath.

It's not like it used to be, he thought. *Not at all.*

———

Ethan had the truck packed up by Sunday at noon.

The two of them had not spoken much since Friday night. Chase's anger had turned to a sullen quiet.

They awoke in silence.

Ethan quietly prepared the meals, they ate in silence, and Ethan cleaned up in silence.

Chase wandered along the lakeshore most of Saturday afternoon and spent all of Sunday morning casting his line into the shallow waters along the shore. He hadn't touched the canoe again.

Ethan had spent the time reading and staring out over the calm waters. It was as if there would be a winner and loser in the "who speaks first" competition. Neither of them wanted to lose.

Ethan looked at his watch for the fifth time in as many minutes. He poured another jug of lake water over the fire pit. Chase was a hundred yards away, sitting on the rock jetty, his arms draped about his knees.

"Chase!" he shouted.

The boy did not move.

Ethan shouted again. The pitch of his voice gave away the tension in his heart.

He knew Chase had heard him the first time. The boy rose, dusted off his jeans, and slowly picked his way among the tumbled rocks, extending one arm and then the other, for balance. He jumped to the shore and walked with great deliberateness toward the truck. He kept his eyes focused on the spot just in front of his father's feet.

"You ready to go?" Ethan asked, holding his voice even.

"Yep," Chase replied and reached for the door.

Ethan hesitated, then walked to the driver's side and slid in. When he started the engine, it sounded so very loud. He reached over and turned on the radio.

As the truck bounced and rutted its way to the main road, Ethan stepped on the brake and looked both ways. He switched on the blinker, even though he didn't see any cars around them for miles.

Ethan caught his son's odd glare.

The boy turned away and stared out the open window.

"Chase?" Ethan's voice was soft, almost conciliatory, as if asking for a favor following an argument that was lost.

Chase didn't turn completely around. His face was set to the road in front of them.

Ethan thought he saw his son's chin tremble—but only for the briefest moment.

"It wasn't my fault," he said in the barest whisper.

Ethan was certain he knew what his son meant. It wasn't the canoe or this day he was talking about. It was a long time ago. He had said the same words before—often at the end of arguments just like this one. Ethan could never answer quickly. Instead, he took a deep breath and let a minute sweep by them.

"I never said it was."

He knew his words were as unconvincing as his son's.

Then Ethan looked both ways again and pulled out onto the empty road and drove into the afternoon sun, toward home, in silence.

"You go in," Ethan said. "I'll unload the truck."

Ethan knew Chase hated packing and unpacking. *It must be a teenager thing*, he thought. *All his friends are the same way—just pick up and leave and never worry about putting things right again.*

"You sure? I don't mind," Chase replied, his angry tone softer now, almost even.

"Yep. I don't mind. You know how fussy I am about putting things in the right places. Everything in order and all that." Ethan attempted to grin at his son.

Although Chase didn't smile in return, his scowl slipped away for a second. "Okay. If you're sure."

And with that, he walked slowly toward the back porch and the kitchen door. He let the screen door slam behind him. In another moment, Ethan heard the mumbled sounds of the television. The Pirates were playing on the West Coast. The game must have just started. He sighed and reached into the truck bed for the tent.

Ethan would never store the tent folded; instead he hung it up on pegs he had installed in the garage. Sleeping bags, likewise, were stored hung, not rolled. He carefully emptied the gas from the camp stove. He hung the rods and reels by the handles so the fiberglass would not affect a permanent bend or flex. He manhandled the canoe upside down onto a pair of sawhorses so it would dry completely. Satisfied, he took a last look around the garage. It was filled with tools and equipment, but everything looked to be in its proper place. Almost out the door, he turned back, took a bottle of clear oil and an old rag, and wiped the bottom of the canoe clean. Regardless of warranties, he wanted to ensure that no metal part, no rivet or seam, would rust.

He closed the door, hearing the lock snick into place, and took a deep breath.

Home again. It's good to be home again.

He padded up the back porch steps and entered the darkened kitchen. He listened but no longer heard the buzz of any television … or radio either, for that matter. His watch read 6:00. The baseball game was still on, he imagined, unless it was rained out—but how often does it rain in California?

He opened the door of the refrigerator and peered inside. One of Mrs. Whiting's covered dishes caught his eye. Ethan lifted the cover. Homemade vegetable soup. At the back of the bottom shelf stood two Rolling Rock beers. He hadn't bought them. Doug, his lead carpenter, had brought a six-pack two months ago to an impromptu barbecue. Doug drank the four other bottles himself and forgot to take the remaining two home with him. Ethan debated a moment, then reached for a can of diet soda. It was a familiar debate, and the outcome had been the same for the past two months.

He took a long drink, then wondered if he should order a pizza. But, he eventually opted for Mrs. Whiting's healthy soup with some cheese and crackers for dinner.

Not a feast, but enough.

Instead of calling upstairs for Chase, Ethan sat down in the living room. The elegant Victorian homes in Franklin often had huge formal front parlors but terribly small living rooms at the rear of the house—just the opposite of what modern families wanted. When he and Lynne had bought this place so many years ago, Lynne had wanted to remove a few walls to create a better traffic flow and more usable space, but Ethan had never found the uninterrupted time to accomplish her dream. But, after living here for a few years, they had come to love the intimate, cozier feeling of each smaller space, so it had remained. He had upgraded the kitchen and the bathrooms, but the spaces were mostly original—the way Ethan had preferred them all along, but he had never insisted that his vision take precedence over Lynne's.

Looking back—the way he did whenever he found a quiet moment to just
sit within those walls—he was very glad it had turned out that way.

It's just right the way it is … the way it was … the way it was all sup-
posed to be.

The Sunday paper still lay on the front sidewalk. Ethan retrieved it,
sat in his chair in the back family room, switched on the light, and began
to make his way through the fat paper.

The streetlamps were glowing when he startled back awake. His
watch read 8:30.

He shuffled the papers into a neat pile, set them on the table by the
chair, and extracted the television listings. After tossing his empty soda
can into the recycling bin and the television listings onto the kitchen
counter, he snapped off the lights and made his way upstairs.

He was not hungry, but ever so tired.

Chase's room was dark.

He must have fallen asleep as well.

Ethan placed his hand on the knob and turned it slightly. Then he
stopped and let the handle creak back into place. He listened for a moment
and didn't hear a sound. He bowed his head, as if in defeat, and stepped
away, trying to avoid the loose, squeaky board in the middle of the hall.

Only when back in the darkness of his room did he exhale loudly.

———————

Chase sat in the window seat of his room and looked out onto Otter Street.
He had watched the darkness edge up on the neighborhood. He heard
the calls of children laughing and playing down the street. He watched the
sweep of car headlights.

He thought of the cemetery, more than a dozen miles from where he
sat. He sighed and closed his eyes.

The boards in the hall gave creaking evidence to his father's presence.
Chase knew he was standing outside his door. He heard the knob turn.
He waited. Chase knew his father would not come in this evening. He had
brought up the wrong subject at the wrong time again.

"I know you haven't forgiven me," Chase whispered.

He wasn't sure if he was talking to his father ... or the dark heavens above him.

On most workdays it took Ethan only a few minutes to get ready. In his closet hung a dozen identical work shirts—all blue denim. The only difference was the amount of wear each showed. A dozen folded white T-shirts were on a shelf. Half a dozen jeans slumped on hangers. Two pair of identical work boots sat on the floor. He could have dressed in the dark—and often did.

But this morning he shoved aside the jeans and reached farther into the back of the closet. He found a pair of khakis and slipped them off the hanger. He unfolded them and looked down. The hanger crease was hardly noticeable.

Ethan hated to iron. To do so today—a workday, after all—would have felt ... obvious, somehow ... and disconcerting.

He flapped the trousers, hoping the snap would serve as a quick pressing. It didn't, but he decided he would live with the few wrinkles at the knees. He placed his stocking feet on the cuffs and pulled up at the waistband. The wrinkles appeared to loosen some. He found his least worn work shirt and hurried downstairs as he buttoned it.

Normally, he spent twenty minutes reading the morning paper and sipping at coffee. Today he had spent too long in the shower and shaving. He heated a cup of water in the microwave, added instant coffee to an insulated travel mug, and sat down at the desk to write a note to Chase.

He did not like leaving his son alone and asleep. But he had little choice. Hiring nannies and sitters was expensive. He had done so for the first few years—he had to—because Chase was too young to be on his own. Now, during the school year, it was easy. They both rose at the same time, and Ethan would often drive his son to school. At thirteen, Chase would have been humiliated to suffer the stigma of having a teenaged sitter who was only a few years older than him.

For the most part, Chase had proven himself responsible. It was an agreement they'd reached at the end of the previous summer. One bad decision on Chase's part, one foolish choice, and a sitter would be there permanently. Mrs. Whiting came by on Monday, Wednesday, and Friday afternoons.

Every morning Ethan took a clean three-by-five index card from the stack by the phone and jotted Chase a note.

> *Chase—*
>   *At the Carter place all day. Call cell if you need me. Mrs. Whiting here p.m.*
>   *Gather up laundry. Be good—*
>   *Dad*

He hesitated to add the word *Love*. He did on some days. But he did not feel like it this morning. The silence of their weekend was deafening and still painful.

He was at the door, but then turned back, reached in his pocket, and pulled out a five-dollar bill. He picked up the pencil and added:

> *Buy breakfast at McDonald's.*

He stood, then bent over again.

He scribbled the word *Love* just above his name.

Ethan had looked at his watch a dozen times in the last ten minutes. He hoped it wasn't too obvious. The crew was dismantling old walls and framing new ones. Despite Ethan's original reservations about Mrs. Moretti's reconfiguration of the third-floor space, much to his surprise this newly defined area felt good—almost right—as if the original architect had been consulted. By lunchtime they would start their work on the staircase to the turret room.

He glanced at the crew. It might have been his imagination, but most of them looked as if they had dressed with more care this morning than usual. Even Sid, who favored rock-concert black T-shirts and tattered jeans, looked positively dapper in new jeans and a clean polo shirt.

No one made mention of the newspaper story, but Ethan was certain they were all well aware of it.

From below came a call: "Hello! Anybody here?"

It was not Mrs. Moretti, but a younger, more buoyant voice.

"That's the reporter," Ethan said aloud to no one in particular and bounded down the steps to meet her.

The news of her arrival brought the crew to a standstill for a moment. Then came a flurry of action. They all, almost in unison, readjusted their caps, brushed off some sawdust, hitched up their tool belts, and peered down the third-floor stairwell.

"Thank you so much," Cameron said as she extended her hand to Ethan.

Bart Renshaw, the staff photographer, hovered behind her, taking his last "before" photos of the house. Bart, a kind and cooperative man with salt-and-pepper hair, was always dressed in clothes that Cameron was sure were made of 100 percent unnatural fibers and purchased in the sixties. His stomach was smeared with sawdust from lying on the floor to get some more interesting camera angles. His pocket bulged with a dozen rolls of exposed film. He looked happy, clearly certain he had a full page of great photos. The crew worked awkwardly as he snapped his shots, not certain if they should stop and pose or pretend to be unaware of the camera's presence.

"It wasn't as bad as I thought," Ethan said as he shook her hand. He liked her firm grip. "You know a lot about construction and architecture."

Cameron smiled. "My father had the family home remodeled twice while I was growing up. It was a Victorian too—a farmhouse. I was the annoying little kid who hung around and asked too many questions."

Ethan found her expression warming. He reluctantly dropped her hand. She turned away and took a few steps toward her car.

She spun back around, perhaps surprised that he had not yet moved. "Listen …"

He listened.

"It's almost lunchtime," she said as she took a step closer to him.

His crew had begun to gather on the front porch.

She lowered her voice. "I mean, you did me a favor here by agreeing to this story. I know we slowed your work down this morning."

Ethan shook his head. "No, they actually got a fair amount done. It was okay."

She looked pleased. He hoped his crew was not paying attention to her, though he was sure they were.

"So … since you did me a favor, maybe you would let me do you a favor." She ran her hand through her hair that fell in long, loopy curls and smoothed it behind her ears. "Will you let me buy you lunch?"

Ethan swallowed. "Today? You mean now?"

"Sure. Today. I'm here. You're here. I'm hungry. I assume you're hungry."

Ethan could almost hear her smile.

"Well …" He felt his cheeks redden. It had been a very long time since he'd blushed.

"Please. I feel I owe you a lunch at least."

He wanted to turn around and see the expressions of his crew. He knew they had heard her invitation. He was sure they'd never seen him in such a situation. In fact, he couldn't remember ever having been in this type of a situation. He swallowed again. "Well, I guess so."

Her smile grew in breadth and intensity. "Good. I'll drive. I have to drop Bart off at the paper. And you get to pick the place for lunch. Okay?"

Ethan nodded mutely.

When he reached the car, he turned back to his crew. Joel stood at the staircase handrail, leaning against it, staring after him. The whole crew was staring, though some tried to be less obvious.

"I'll … I'll be back after lunch," he said a little louder than necessary. Then he opened the car door and slid in.

It smelled of flowers.

———◦◦◦———

"Cumming's?"

"Sure," Ethan said. "Don't you like it?"

Cameron shrugged as she turned the wheel from the curb in front of the newspaper office, where they'd dropped off Bart, and darted out into traffic. "I don't know. I've never been there. I always thought it was a Mafia front."

Ethan held onto the door handle and chuckled. "The Mafia? In Franklin? Around here, Pizza Den is as Italian as we get."

She leaned back and laughed, and he tried not to look at the graceful lines of her neck. Then she switched lanes quickly and turned onto Elk Street without using her signal.

"The way I see it," she said, "is that the shades are always closed all the way down. It looks like they haven't changed their sign in decades, and I never see anyone leave the place. And they have posters in their window from last year's county fair."

She spun the wheel again and headed onto 12th Street. The tires squealed for a moment.

Ethan grinned as she flew into a parking place just down the block from Cumming's.

"They have a loyal clientele," Ethan explained. "We overlook those shortcomings here, I guess. At any rate, the food's pretty good and it's not expensive. And they know me there."

She turned and smiled back at him as she pulled the keys from the ignition. "Well, I'm always up for new things. Cumming's it is."

———◦◦◦———

Ethan didn't have to glance at his watch. Over Cameron's shoulder, on the rear wall of the restaurant, was a large clock with an advertisement for a dairy, now long closed. The hands swept past one o'clock. If it had been a normal day and a normal lunch, Ethan would have stood up a half hour earlier, whether his host stood or not, and stated that he had to return to work. But now, ten minutes past one, he sat, sipping his fourth cup of coffee, and listening to Cameron talk.

"After I graduated, I moved to downtown Philadelphia and worked at a couple of temporary jobs, enjoying city life and all that, but still wasn't sure which direction to go," she said as she stirred a second packet of sweetener into her iced tea. She ate with gusto and finished her lunch with a piece of Cumming's homemade custard pie. Ethan liked that. Lynne, a slip of a woman, always had eaten with great enthusiasm too.

"I mean I had some offers, even at *The Enquirer.*"

"The one in the grocery store checkout lane?" Ethan asked.

She spurted out a laugh. "No, not that one—though they pay more than any paper anywhere."

"They do?"

"Yup. But I sort of had my heart set on a legitimate career. No, *The Enquirer* is the big daily in Philadelphia. But the job was on the bottom of the bottom rung. I would have worked for years before I had my first page-one byline."

She sipped at her tea. "My parents wanted me to stay near home, of course. You know, do the traditional thing—find a bright young man, get married. I told them there is plenty of time for that. My mother keeps sending me updates on all the eligible men in town—who's getting married, who's divorced, who's still living at home. The roster keeps changing day to day."

Ethan turned his coffee cup in his hand. He watched the afternoon light cascade over Cameron's dark hair. It made it seem as if she had a halo about her. As she talked, she coiled and uncoiled a single long loop of her hair, as if she were nervous. But Ethan could not detect any nervousness in her speech or demeanor other than that one gesture.

"So you came here instead? To escape? To Franklin?"

She nodded.

"Not escape, exactly, but the move made sense to me. *The Derrick* has a decent circulation. Apparently, it's profitable. The editorial section won some recent awards."

"It has?"

"Awards that only editors pay attention to, I guess," Cameron said. "I knew if I came here, I could get to do everything right away. Cover meetings and trials and investigative stories and crime—a bit of everything. Then, with experience, I could get a real reporter's job on a big metropolitan paper."

Ethan finished his coffee. "Then you'd leave here?"

She shrugged. "I don't know. I miss some aspects of living in a big city—the shopping, the restaurants, the museums, the excitement of parties or something always going on, like plays and concerts. But here it's simpler, quieter, more … wholesome, I guess—more like real America, you know? I like it … at least so far. Maybe."

She looked at him. He stared back into her eyes until he became uncomfortable, then looked away.

"What about you?" she said, leaning forward, almost touching his wrist with her fingers. "Why are you here?"

He watched her hand come closer, then his eyes quickly moved to his watch. "Good grief! It's nearly 1:30. I have never taken this long of a lunch. I'd better get back."

Her frown appeared genuine. "So soon? I'm enjoying this. I meet a lot of people on this job, but I seldom seem to have anything in common with them. You sure you have to go now?"

He stood. "Yes, I'm sure. I need to be on the job. Anyhow, thanks so much for the lunch. I appreciate it. You sure I can't pay half?"

She tossed a few bills on the table, leaving a bigger tip than Ethan would have. "I'm sure. Let me get you back to work. I'm sure your crew thinks I kidnapped you—or worse."

———

As Cameron drove off, Ethan's eyes followed her car as it sped down the street. He turned back to the house and looked up.

At least five faces in the third-floor window stared down at him. All of them ducked back into the shadows as he started walking toward the front door.

The sin was mine;
I did not understand....

—OSCAR WILDE, *THE NEW REMORSE*

———

From the body of one guilty deed
a thousand ghostly fears
and haunting thoughts proceed.

—WILLIAM WORDSWORTH

CHAPTER FOUR

THE OFFICES OF *The Franklin Derrick* were housed on the west half of the second floor of the Standard Bank and Trust Building in downtown Franklin. The bank name carved into the cornerstone no longer existed—the first-floor space being taken over a dozen years ago by a credit union, a title company, and an insurance company claims center.

After Cameron had graduated from college, she had interviewed at a dozen smaller daily newspapers. Most of the offices, she had discovered, were tucked into some nondescript office complex at the edge of some light industrial park somewhere near the edge of town.

Not how she pictured a newspaper office.

But when she opened the door to *The Derrick,* she realized it was exactly how a newspaper office should look, sound, and feel.

A dozen desks were set in a haphazard pattern around the large open room. In the two far corners were private offices—for the publisher and editor, no doubt. Half the desks still had typewriters on them, even though computer screens sat at the corner of each desk as well. One side of the room was the editorial area. The other side, advertising. And copies of newspapers lay scattered everywhere—on top of the bank of file cabinets, in corners, on tables and credenzas. Some were piled only three or four thick; other stacks were up to an adult's kneecap. A long black counter blocked direct access to the room at the entrance. Customers could buy extra copies of the paper, place want ads—some even came in to pay for their subscriptions. A tired, imitation ficus sat at one end of the entry, and a cash register, circa 1960, hulked in the middle of the counter. Next to it sat a brown hand-operated adding machine.

Franklin was that sort of town, and *The Derrick* was that sort of paper.

Cameron took over the desk that had been vacated by Sam Marshall. He had covered city, county, and township government for a dozen years. He'd surprised everyone by taking the editor's job on a small daily in Bemidji, Minnesota. His duties had been divided among the half dozen staffers. Cameron was assigned all township meetings—a task she found so stultifyingly boring that she wondered how the departed Mr. Marshall had maintained his sanity for so long.

Cameron walked in and nodded to Clara, the gray-haired, very permanent receptionist and customer representative. Her neck seemed to be frozen in a crick—most likely from cradling the phone between her shoulder and cheek for so long. She had turned down innumerable offers of a headset, though, claiming such a contraption would make her look foolish.

She pointed to the phone, arched her eyebrows, and made a jabbering gesture with her right hand. She was obviously talking to one of her friends—something she did often. Cameron smiled and mouthed the words, "Is Paige here?"

Clara turned and pointed to the publisher's office. The door was closed. Clara mimed someone drinking, then wobbled on her chair and laughed silently. Cameron dismissed her with a happy wave of her hand.

At her desk, Cameron tore out all the sheets from her stenographer's notebook and cut off the frayed edges. It was one of her personal affectations. She used a lot of stenographer's pads in the process. She kept one drawer in her desk filled with fresh, blank pads.

When on a story, as she asked questions and took notes, she wrote the answers and quotes on different pages, categorizing them into broad subjects, flipping back and forth as she did. That way, when she began to write her story, she would simply arrange the pages in the proper order. She was quick and organized. Her system produced a well-thought-out story with a logical progression to it.

She adjusted her blouse, buttoning one of the open buttons, and rolled up the sleeves. She tapped her password on her keyboard and waited for the computer to allow her access. As it whirred softly, she stared out the wide windows that faced Fountain Park and the theater. She rolled her head slowly from side to side, her neck making little pops, as she thought about her lunch.

His eyes are gray.

With a crackle, the computer program opened, and Cameron refocused her thoughts. She blinked, then began to tap out the Carter Mansion story, stopping every few minutes to shuffle and reshuffle her notes.

It came together with ease. She had no real research to do to make the facts work. She already had a fair amount of history concerning the Carter Mansion, and she had lots of pictures. The crew had provided some funny quotes and Ethan had given her some insightful remarks. While the story wasn't pure human interest, she found it easy to compose—and she was very interested in the subject matter.

Ethan hurried up to the third floor and was barraged by a chorus of silent stares—inquisitive and, he thought, reproaching. No one spoke, however.

"It was just a lunch, okay?"

The entire crew seemed to shrug in unison, and, after a moment, the shrill shriek of a circular saw slicing into a two-by-four broke the silence.

Mrs. Moretti had faxed a two-page, handwritten missive to Ethan that he had tacked to a bare stud in the hallway. She wrote much like she talked. Ethan could almost see her hands waving in the air as he read her latest directive.

Dear Mr. Willis,

My, that sounds formal, doesn't it? Ethan. I can call you Ethan, right?

Ethan … I want you to start on the staircase to the ballroom this week. The architect said that the drawings had been sent via overnight FedEx to you about this. I know you think it takes up too much space, but when I have a formal ball there, how do you think all the elegant ladies are going to make the climb in their hoop skirts if the staircase is too narrow?

Ethan, I'm just kidding. But we need that staircase as drawn. I know it's bigger than you said we need, but that's the way I want it.

You should be glad I'm not putting in an elevator! My family tried to convince me of that. I said no. See, you're already rubbing off on me.

I need to think about the simpler door trim for the third floor that we talked about when I was there last. It may not be the most Victorian of selections, but I think it's what I like the best. You said that means the trim around every door in the house will have to be replaced. Well, is there a rule written down somewhere that says it all has to match? I don't know if that's necessary, but I need to think it over.

I'll be in town at the end of next week. As long as you're still doing demolition or building the walls we agreed on, we'll be fine.

But no more than that. You know how fussy I can be.

When I come the next time, I'll bring calzone and cannoli for everyone.

Thanks—
CeCe

The crew had more than enough work in demolition alone to keep them busy for days. The trim decision, Ethan knew, was a bit premature. He still had some time to try to make CeCe see the error of her ways.

She'll have to decide on trim well before all the drywall is installed if it's going to be custom. But Mrs. Moretti doesn't seem to be in the mood for custom. That would be a big mistake, Ethan thought as he began measuring the risers for the oversized stairway to the ballroom that was no longer a ballroom. *This is going to be a long project.*

An hour into work on her story, Cameron saw the door of the publisher's office open and Paige Drake slip out, closing the door firmly behind her. She saw Cameron and rolled her eyes. Cameron stifled a laugh.

"The story on the Old Carter Mansion?" Paige asked.

Cameron nodded. "I'm nearly done. Bart said he had scads of great pictures. Maybe we can use it on Sunday."

"Maybe. I hate to waste such a good piece in the summer when nobody seems to read anything."

Cameron leaned back and locked her hands behind her head. "I can make this a two- or three-part story if you'd prefer. Do some on the history. Profile the current owner. Do a before-and-after sort of thing."

Paige gave a disappointed look. "It'll be Christmas before they're done. You can do an 'after' article once the first installment runs. Tell Bart to save a bunch of photos. Can you have the first one done for the Sunday edition?"

Cameron nodded, then pulled out a page of her notes. On the top she had written *Ethan Willis/Profile*. She had not written a single word on that page.

She looked over to the editor. "What do you know about Ethan Willis? He didn't give me much personal background."

The phone in Paige's office began to ring.

"Finish the story. Then come to my office. I may have an old file on him."

Cameron thought it odd for Paige to have kept a file on a contractor, but she didn't want to mention it … yet. She shrugged and turned back to her keyboard and screen and began to finish the last dozen paragraphs to the article.

"You have a file on Ethan Willis?" Cameron asked as she tapped at the doorframe of Paige's office.

"I do. I think I do. I should have. At least I had one," Paige replied and spun on her chair to face the bank of black file cabinets that lined the rear wall of her office. She opened one drawer and shuffled through the folders. Pages of newsprint peeked over the tops of the folders. Papers lay on top of the folders. Paige brushed them aside. A few clippings fluttered to the floor.

"This may take awhile. Have a seat," Paige growled toward the files without turning around.

Cameron sat in the creased leather chair in the corner and stretched. The Carter Mansion story had come quickly, and Cameron liked how it sounded—all except for any hint of a background on Ethan Willis.

She slouched in the chair and watched Paige edge along the cabinets, opening one, closing it, opening another. She appeared to have no true system for retrieving information. Every so often, Paige would snort and slam a drawer to open another.

The office was what an editor's office should look like, Cameron thought. Stacks of papers, letters overflowing an in-box, a real typewriter on the desk, clippings from twenty years ago in frames on the wall, pictures of Paige with an assortment of state officials and even two presidents.

It's perfect.

Even though Paige claimed to have quit smoking five years earlier, there was still a lingering scent of tobacco faintly smoldering just below the surface.

"The typewriter's lousy with it," Paige had snarled one day after Cameron had asked who was smoking in the offices.

On the front of Paige's gunmetal gray desk, a HONK IF YOU LOVE JESUS bumper sticker was placed at a slightly askew angle. Cameron wished she could straighten it. She had this same urge every time she entered the office. On the desk stood a small wood crucifix. On the wall behind her hung an ornate certificate from St. Mark's Church, naming Paige Drake as the Volunteer of the Year from three years ago.

Cameron heard Paige growl again. She held her giggle.

"I should fire somebody for screwing up my files like this."

Cameron would have replied that Paige was the only person authorized to open the files, but she held her tongue.

"Good heavens," Paige snarled. "Here it is. Filed under C—probably for Construction. Why would anyone put it there?"

She spun around and faced Cameron.

Paige, at nearly sixty, showed her age with enthusiasm. She was a big woman, full-figured, with a great crown of white hair that seldom saw the inside of a beauty shop. She combed it back in the morning and let nature take its course for the rest of the day. Her smile was energetic and expansive, but so was her acidic tongue.

It hadn't taken too long for Cameron to learn the details of her employer's life.

Clara, the receptionist and office gossip, had entertained Cameron over a long lunch her first week on the job. Clara had been a fixture at the paper for decades and knew amazing details about the personal lives of everyone on the paper—as well as just about everyone in town.

"Paige outlived her first two husbands," Clara whispered to Cameron that day. "Hard living takes its toll. She just had more stamina than the both of them."

Paige's grandfather had founded the newspaper, and her eighty-year-old uncle was now the top name on the paper's masthead as publisher. Paige was the only child in any of the Drake family with an interest in journalism.

Cameron had asked Clara during their first lunch for hints as to the best way to get along with the paper's editor. "I have to admit that she scared me a little during my interview. She was kind of cantankerous," she had told the older woman.

"You don't have to worry none," Clara had explained. "She used to be a real pill. But five … maybe six years ago now, after her second husband passed on … well, she went and found religion. She came to the office with that cross and a Bible and a fish decal on her car and, land sakes, she was just a different person. She could be as gruff as a nanny goat in spring, but you could tell that it was all bluster and that wasn't who she really was anymore. The whole newsroom saw it. *The Derrick* became a much better place to work."

Cameron nodded. She almost understood. Cameron's aunt—her mother's "difficult" sister—had made a similar transformation when Cameron was in high school. Her uncle had suffered a heart attack, and her aunt had started going to church five times a week until his health

improved. She declared it a miracle and started carrying and quoting the
Bible. It had not made sense to Cameron. Her mother would simply nod
and say, "Everyone needs some religion in their life." But her aunt was a
lot easier to live with after that.

Cameron's recollection ended as Paige flipped the folder closed.

"Not much here. I thought there was more," Paige said.

"What is it? I could use a little more background."

Paige glanced at the clippings. "Nothing about him personally. Most
of it is about his wife."

Cameron nodded. "I'd heard that his wife had passed away. How long
ago was it?"

A nearly perturbed look crossed Paige's face. "Passed away? I don't call
it 'passed away,'" she snapped.

Taken aback by Paige's harsh reply, Cameron stuttered, "But …
well … I mean … I don't know. Should I say 'died' instead?"

Paige snorted. "No, you shouldn't. She didn't just die. She was
murdered."

To have said Cameron was shocked would have been an understatement.
As a reporter and a self-confessed news nerd, she was well aware that people died in all manner of untimely fashions and in all manner of accidental
ways. But she had never known anyone who had been touched by the act
of murder. It just didn't seem real, that's all, to know someone who had
lost a loved one through an act of such violence.

And as she thought of the implications of that act, the act of murder,
there was the memory of another incident, an accident, when she was
much, much younger. Its terrifying images made yet another attempt to
breach her steady defenses and force their way into her consciousness.
Once again she did her best to push them—all of them, and that day …
all of those days—out of her consciousness and far, far away, where she
kept them locked, dark and secret. She could not have them intrude on
her here, not in Franklin. The distance between here and there, between

Franklin and home, was perhaps the most important unacknowledged reason she had left Philadelphia—and friends and family—to find a place where the memories would not bother her anymore.

She shook her head to clear her thoughts and stammered a reply to Paige. The editor's phone rang as she did.

"It's okay," Paige said with her hand on the receiver. "You didn't know."

She handed the file to Cameron, who backed out of the office feeling shame, though she had no real reason to be ashamed. After all, what Paige said was true. She hadn't known the particulars. If she had, she wondered, would she have treated Ethan any differently during the interview?

She felt fairly certain she would have—but did not know how, exactly.

———— ⤚⤙ ————

The file was thin. It consisted of only three clippings.

The first one was a very brief report—probably added just as the paper was going to press that day—stating in two paragraphs that a local woman, Lynne Elizabeth Willis, had been killed in Erie, Pennsylvania. It listed her address and age. It did not indicate how she had died.

The second was nearly as brief, but it contained most of the pertinent information.

Lynne Willis, age twenty-nine, wife of Ethan Willis, of the Willis Construction Company. She had been shot in her car. Local authorities, the report said, were still trying to determine if the incident had been a random shooting, an attempted carjacking, or a robbery attempt.

The third clipping was her obituary.

Cameron paused as she read it. She knew Ethan had a son, of course, but did not realize until she read it that Chase was only five ... or maybe six ... when his mother had ... passed on. She carefully placed the clippings back into the folder and laid it on her desk.

She looked at her watch. It was 7:30. She peered over at Paige's office. Paige was chatting away with great animation, her feet up on her desk, gesturing at the ceiling.

Cameron glanced at her story again. She knew it didn't require any
additional background information on Mr. Willis. If Paige was inclined to
want more, she could always ask Clara in the morning. Or she could talk
to Ralph at the chamber of commerce. Ralph, a short, oily man with the
worst toupee she had ever seen, had asked her out when she'd first arrived
in Franklin. So kind was her refusal that he still asked her out on occasion.
She had yet to say yes.

Cameron waved good-bye. Paige waved back.

The air was warm with the hint of a breeze from the river as Cameron
walked out of the office. Her car was parked just out front, but she
decided not to drive it home. Her apartment over the Franklin Club was
only a few blocks away. She began walking and hoped that it would not
rain tomorrow morning.

On a sunny morning three days later, Cameron rolled down the windows
in her car, opened the sunroof, turned up the radio, and headed north
along Route 322, heading toward Erie. By a curious serendipity, Penny
McElroy, a classmate of hers from the University of Pennsylvania, had
married the managing editor of the *Erie Times Standard*. To be honest,
Cameron had never much liked Penny but called her anyway and asked if
she might ask her husband a favor.

All it would cost her was taking Penny to lunch. Afterward she would
have access to the archives of the *Erie Times* and a promise from Penny's
husband to introduce her to anyone who might have any additional information on the murder of Lynne Willis.

Penny did not ask why Cameron needed the information, and neither
did Cameron volunteer any reason.

Lunch was pleasant enough, Cameron realized, and it was amusing to
keep up with the news of her old friends. She had never been much of a
letter writer, but Penny had been. For two hours, Penny told tales of other
classmates' marriages and hires and fires ("Wow!") and divorces ("So
soon?") and even a death due to a skiing accident in Switzerland.

Marriage had suited Penny, and she had become less shrill than she had been back at Delta Delta Delta.

Armed with directions to the newspaper office—in an office complex on the eastern outskirts of town—Cameron zipped into a visitor's space and asked for Mr. McElroy at the reception desk.

In less than fifteen minutes, she was alone in a large, windowless room with dozens and dozens of huge shelving system units, each section holding decades of newsprint, bound in full-sized journals. A few years ago the paper had started archiving material in electronic form, but before then, they simply saved the actual newspaper itself.

She knew the date of Lynne's murder. Retrieving the correct journals was a simple matter.

Unfortunately, and to her great disappointment, the news reports in the Erie papers were not much more complete than what appeared in *The Franklin Derrick*. The paper had a photograph of the car, canted at an odd angle to the curb with the door flung open. In the background were lines of police tape marking off the accident scene, and a few uniformed policemen, conferring together. One policeman pointed off into the distance. In the foreground of the picture lay a shopping bag with the sleeve of a light blouse or shirt peeking out. There was a dark patch on the asphalt, just by the door. The photo was black and white, so Cameron could not be sure if the stain was blood or not.

She felt a chill.

She paged through the papers for a few days following, just to be sure. No additional word on the murder. Random violence involving an out-of-town visitor must not have warranted a lot of news copy.

She sat back in her chair. The wood squealed softly.

She wondered what she would write if the same thing would happen in Franklin. After a moment, she came to the conclusion that it might not be all that different.

Replacing the volume in the rack, Cameron snapped off the light switch and made her way to Mr. McElroy's office. He did not look busy, she thought, so she tapped on the door.

He looked up. "Find what you needed?"

"I did, thank you. Your paper didn't have much more than ours did, unfortunately."

"Well, that's too bad. I wish I could offer more help. Penny said to extend all courtesy to you. You must have been close friends back in college. Wild Tri Delt girls."

"We were," Cameron said, hoping that she sounded sincere. "There is one other thing ..."

"And that is?" he answered, his palms flat against the blotter of his desk.

"Was there anyone on staff then who might know more about this? Anyone working here today that was working back then?"

Mr. McElroy pursed his lips as if tasting a lemon to indicate deep thought. "Well. Turnover has been high ..."

Cameron sighed. She knew that was most likely the case. At *The Derrick* the long-term positions were receptionist and editor. Even the newspaper's lifestyle editor, often a local maven of long standing, was only five years into the job.

"But ... I think Hank was here back then. It's before my time. He's been here a long time. Maybe he remembers. It was a quite a ways back, you know."

She nodded.

"Was this murdered person a friend of yours ... somehow?"

She shrugged. "Sort of. A friend of a friend, really. Where is Hank?"

Mr. McElroy sat high in his chair, as if trying to perch on the armrests, and craned his neck about. "Over there. The desk by the window. The fellow who's smoking."

Cameron looked. There was a skinny older man, hunched over a newspaper, holding a cigarette in his left hand, above his head.

"I thought this was a nonsmoking place," Cameron said. "I mean, isn't everywhere nonsmoking?"

Mr. McElroy shrugged. "It is. If I enforce it, he just stays outside longer and gets less done. I polled the office staff. No one seems to mind. I sort of don't see it anymore."

Cameron extended her hand. "Thank you. Thanks for your help."

He shook her hand longer than necessary. His palm was wet, and Cameron hoped he didn't see her wipe it on her coat as she left his office.

———=∞=———

"Yeah, I remember it," Hank said, then coughed. "Didn't write it. But I remember the story."

"You do?"

"Yeah. Pretty girl. I felt bad. Being out of town and having some punk do that. Didn't seem right."

He coughed again and reached for another Pall Mall. "This bother you?" he asked, just as he struck the match. The cigarette was already dangling in his lips.

"No. It's okay." She hoped it didn't sound too much like a lie.

He took a deep drag, coughed, then blew out a long cloud of blue smoke. He leaned closer to her. She wanted to lean back but did not.

"Tell you a secret," he whispered in a gravelly voice. "I could quit anytime, but then I'd have nothing to bug that goofy McElroy kid with. My smoking drives him crazy and I enjoy that."

He leaned back and took another drag. "No one likes him. That's why the rest of the office doesn't complain about me." He cackled and began to cough again.

Cameron waited until his fit passed. "Do you remember anything else about the story? Did they ever catch anyone?"

"Naw. I heard the cops wanted to pin it on one kid—a minor dealer they said—but he wound up on the wrong side of some drug deal. They found him floating in the lake a few months later. It was an 'accidental' suicide murder. No great loss, I guess."

"Nothing else?"

Cameron wondered if this whole trip had been a waste of time. She didn't know what she'd expected to find. But she kept seeing Ethan Willis's face and seeing the hint of something behind his eyes—some graying to his smile. Now she knew what the something was and wanted to know more. She was certain that any enlightenment would not be coming from Ethan.

He had a silent something in his bearing and attitude. And even if she found out additional information, she wondered what import it might have.

That thought had consumed her attention during the ride north to Erie.

As she drove, she had pondered the reasons—and she kept seeing Ethan's face as he sat across the table from her that day for lunch. In truth, she'd finally realized she really wanted to see him again. She wanted to talk to him again, to sit across from him at a table having coffee. She liked his smile. She liked his sense of reality.

And she wanted to know more about his past. A murder, the loss of a spouse, was not a subject an acquaintance simply brought up out of the blue. But what he must have gone through …

Hank squirmed in his chair. "Don't think so. Carjacking, robbery—whatever it was, it was just a stupid thing to have happened. That woman was just in the wrong place at the wrong time."

"Was that part of town really so horrible? I wouldn't think Erie would have such a bad area."

"Naw. Isn't the best part of town, for sure. But it isn't like people are getting shot there all the time. You know, that was one of the few murders that year. Might have been the only one up till then."

Cameron didn't know what else to ask. It was obvious that he had little additional information on the incident.

"Well, thank you so much. I appreciate your help."

Hank took a last drag, stubbed the cigarette out, and half stood. He offered his hand. "You know, the person I feel worst for is that little boy. To see something like that. The poor kid's gonna be living that nightmare forever. Is he doing okay?"

Cameron stopped. "Little boy? What little boy?"

Hank appeared confused. "Her little boy. He was in the car with her. When she got shot. He was there. In the car. In the backseat."

The radio blared the entire trip back to Franklin, as if Cameron wanted to drown out her thoughts. Cameron had stumbled back to her car after learning the news. She had asked a few more questions, then had felt a compulsion to leave, to run away, to turn off the images that ran through her thoughts.

Hank had explained why no report mentioned the fact that the small boy, the woman's son, was in the car.

"I remember now. They found the kid crouched in the backseat. I bet the jerk who pulled the trigger that day didn't even know he was there. Tinted windows, I bet. A small town like Erie—well—if the cops ask a reporter to ignore something and you can see the logic in it—well, you ignore it. I bet the cops thought the killer might try and come back for the little boy if the bad guy had known the kid was in the car. So whoever wrote the story left that part out of the newspapers. If the floater in the lake really was the killer, the little boy has nothing to worry about. It has been a long time. I'm betting that whoever it was wasn't the brightest bulb on the tree, anyway. To shoot somebody in broad daylight like that." Hank had shaken his head. "That little boy—seeing his mama shot like that. Had to be hard on him."

Cameron had listened, nodded, then had stood, saying she had to go. "Is he okay? That little boy? What was his name again?"

For a moment she could not remember. "Chase. His name is Chase."

Hank had nodded. "Is he okay?"

Cameron had tried to smile but couldn't. "I think he's doing fine."

<hr/>

To her credit, Cameron made it the whole way to Meadville and kept her car in control, her speed under the posted limit, her breathing regular, her eyes clear.

Then, in a wave of piercing thoughts and emotions, she could do none of those things. She pulled off the freeway and around to the back of a Cracker Barrel, where there were no other cars beside the fence that hid the restaurant's dumpster. She was gripping the steering wheel so tight that her hands and forearms were white, her muscles only a moment away from spasm.

The poor kid's gonna be living that nightmare forever.

She closed her eyes and willed the tears not to come....

She was ten years old. A storm had come up on Rehoboth Beach along the Delaware coast. Just north of Rehoboth, the gray clapboard oceanside cottage with white shutters that her parents rented for a month every summer sat in the storm's path. The cottage was right on the beach, where Cameron and her brother could haul their rubber rafts, tubes, and floats to the porch each night, only to wait for the sun the next morning, when they would charge off into the surf again.

A storm was at the eastern horizon, not a large storm by storm standards, but with higher winds and bigger waves. Her parents had left Cameron, her little brother, and her older brother, William, alone as they went to the store for groceries.

"No child would go out in that sort of weather," they had told themselves as they drove away.

Ignoring his babysitting chores, William had busied himself with a book.

Cameron and her younger brother had not.

Always in bathing suits, they had bolted for the deserted beach: to shout at the waves and to wade in, waist high, and let the surf buffet them back to shore. They laughed and taunted the ocean's power.

Cameron had run to the porch and dragged the rubber raft to the waves. It was an old but large raft—big enough to hold six people, with two canvas seats stretched across the inflatable chambers. Cameron pushed it into the surf and jumped in. As a wave crashed against it and pushed it vertical, Cameron screamed in mock terror.

"You shouldn't do that, Cam."

Cameron looked at her little brother, folded her arms under, and squawked like a chicken. "You scared?"

"No!" her little brother shouted back defiantly and jumped into the raft with his big sister. He was no sibling's chicken.

For twenty minutes they played and paddled and were pushed back, laughing, by the waves. They stood up to be tossed out in the sea and scrambled back on board like little white crabs.

Then a wave had come up that was different than the waves preceding it. It was larger … not by much, but it knocked over the raft with indifference, then hurried back to the sea. It pulled with a great force, so much stronger than any wave that had crashed earlier that same morning.

Cameron's little brother shouted … shouted something Cameron did not understand.

Cameron swam as hard as she could and grabbed him by the wrist. In a moment, the raft bobbed farther out to sea, heading into the darker ocean, farther from shore. The waves broke harder and higher and saltier and blacker.

"Cammie!" her younger brother screamed, his shriek a pitch higher, more terrified, more panicked.

"I've got you," Cameron yelled back. "I won't let you go."

Her screams had been all but drowned out by the next wave, crashing between them, tumbling and turning. Then a turbulent roll and Cameron no longer had the arm and wrist and fingers of her younger brother.

She screamed and screamed as a wave took her up. She couldn't see anything but water … the raft so very far away … and the shore. Another wave and her head went underwater. Arms flailed. Another wave came, then another …

When she woke, Cameron was in the surf, on her knees. Her older brother stood in the surf up to his waist; her father farther out, swimming hard. Her mother was standing at the shore, afraid of water, afraid of this salty sea, screaming, her hands over her mouth, her screams taken by the wind.…

Cameron could never remember past that scene. Her older brother, William, told her that her father had made it to the raft in hopeless hope of finding her younger brother clinging to it.

But of course he was not.

Her mother had collapsed to her knees in the sand and held her head in her hands, sobbing, screaming, then ran to Cameron and clutched her young daughter so very, very tightly.

Her brother had told Cameron later that her mother knew Cameron had gone in to save her impetuous little brother who, no doubt, had jumped into the waves against her command. When William had told her this, a week after the memorial service, he had waited a long, long moment, to see if Cameron would validate that statement. Cameron had said nothing. She remembered nothing.

   She never told anyone of the horrific feeling of her younger brother's tiny fingers, slipping, clutching, and grasping, as the sea took him away from her and carried him to heaven.

You can't forgive
what you refuse to remember,
any more than you can
seek treatment for a disease
whose symptoms you have yet to notice.

—CAROL LUEBERING

———⊰∘⊱———

When we forgive evil …
we look evil full in the face,
call it what it is,
let its horror shock and stun and enrage us.
And only then do we forgive it.

—LEWIS B. SMEDES

CHAPTER FIVE

SINCE HER TRIP TO Erie, Cameron had felt disconnected, as if her internal clock was blinking twelve and she had lost the instructions on how to reset it to the proper time. The recurring image of a small boy, hiding in the backseat of his mother's car, cowering from the sound of gunshots, continued to haunt her.

She kept wondering what Chase had gone through but refused to again revisit her own past. She was most expert in keeping that memory buried—the vivid memory of her wrongdoing, the one that no one else needed to know. It would do no one well to open that box, that hidden compartment, again. So she closed the door and locked it, letting the pain stay right where it was supposed to stay.

It's better this way, she thought.

She awoke early on Saturday morning. Other than the mellow clang of church bells, the town was quiet under a brightening blue-orange sky. Her apartment on the top floor of the old Franklin Club was small and not entirely tidy. The place consisted of one bedroom, one bath, a tiny galley kitchen, and a large living room with ten-foot ceilings. It also came with a turret that was filled with tall windows all around, overlooking the street.

The first thing Cameron had done when she moved in was to fill the benches of the window seat in the turret with big, colorful pillows. It became her favorite place to read. She had brought little of her own possessions, other than a TV, some basic furniture, a couple of large framed exhibition posters from the Philadelphia Museum of Art, her clothes, her computer and CD player, her books, and a small collection of photographs of her family and friends. When she first moved in, she told herself it would only be for a year or two, so she hadn't planned on doing much decorating. But somehow making the turret her most comfy and welcoming place had been important.

She had only enough coffee for a single cup, which was two less than her normal allotment for a Sunday morning. She flipped through the newspaper, but not a single headline held her attention. She remote-controlled through a dozen news programs on television, but the thought of spending an hour listening to the minutiae of politics today made her shudder.

A red leather-bound book lay nearly buried on the bottom shelf of her bookcase. She bent down and flipped the blank journal open. Only the first page, front and back, bore her writing. She had purchased the journal, discounted by 50 percent, during her last trip home. It was her intention to keep a journal of these days by herself in Franklin.

She had not done well with the task.

Am I this much of a perfectionist? she asked herself, as she grabbed a pair of scissors from her desk and carefully cut out the first page with the quick scrawls on it.

If I'm going to start this again, I'm going to start clean. And neat this time.

She grabbed a favorite pen, slipped on her sneakers, and made her way into the warm sunshine.

Ethan peered out the open second-floor window of the Carter Mansion. He had heard a car door slam, and he looked down as CeCe Moretti and another woman walked up to the house carrying several colorful shopping bags and a rolled-up blueprint.

I'll just stay up here for as long as possible, Ethan thought, turning back to his measurements as footsteps echoed up the staircase of the empty house.

"Honey, I'm home," CeCe called out.

Ethan could hear the women's laughter. He pushed at the button on the case of his tape measure. It rolled up with a snap.

"Anybody home?"

"I'm up here, Mrs. Moretti," he called as he made his way downstairs.

"I didn't think anyone would be here today. How's it going, Ethan?"

"Good. Good. I'm just here trying to get ahead on some things for next week's work schedule."

"That's what I like to hear!" CeCe answered.

They both turned to the other woman—short, highlighted brown hair, about fifty, Ethan guessed, elegantly but casually dressed, with a warm smile and an easygoing demeanor. She was wearing an elaborately engraved gold locket on a long, thick chain that Ethan was sure was an antique heirloom. CeCe introduced her as her interior designer—Tessa Winberry, of Winberry Design in San Francisco.

Tessa's multiple gold bangle bracelets jangled softly as Ethan shook her hand.

"I brought Tessa here with me from home for the weekend. She did my house there, and I can't imagine working with anyone else on this old place. She'll make it sing," CeCe declared. "Tessa knows my style and she's done a lot of Bay Area Queen Annes."

"Then it sounds like you're the right person for the job," Ethan answered.

"We've been having a great time putting some schemes together," Tessa said, "but I wanted to see how they'd work here in person, you know, in the Pennsylvania light."

And how is Pennsylvania light so different from California light? Ethan thought, but just replied, "Then I'll just get back to work and let you two do your thing."

"You mean you don't want to stay and give us your opinion?" CeCe asked with a bit of a sly smile.

"I think I'll leave all that to the expert," he answered.

For the next couple of hours, Ethan could hear CeCe and Tessa going from room to room, pulling out fabric and wallpaper samples from the shopping bags, taping them up on the walls next to the windows, lining up carpet samples on steps. Their voices were occasionally punctuated with higher notes of pleasure and agreement. When he came down for his lunch, CeCe asked him if he could brush some squares of paint on the walls in the foyer, the great room, and the master bedroom from the collection of small sample containers Tessa had brought. The colors ranged from dark, jewel tones to lighter, grayed-down shades of yellows, greens, and blues with accents in the red family.

At least they look like halfway historic colors, Ethan thought with a grin. *Here in the Pennsylvania light, anyway.*

———— ✦ ————

Too bad we don't have a Starbucks. It would be nice to have a coffeehouse or someplace I could walk to on days like this, like in Philly.

She knew that toward the mall there was a cluster of chain establishments, but Cameron didn't want to drive anywhere. Two blocks east, and one block toward the river, there was a twenty-four-hour convenience store.

"Coffee? We have lots of coffee. There's hazelnut and French vanilla, and then there's this Irish creamer that tastes like mint. I don't know if they grow mint in Ireland, but I sure like it. We have decaf as well, but I don't think I made that mint stuff with the decaf yet. I could. Do you want some? Will only take a minute."

Cameron leaned backward slightly in the midst of the verbal avalanche. The clerk's nametag read *Vera.* Vera, a very short, very energetic woman past middle-age, wore her glasses on a beaded cord around her neck. Her hair was graying and coiled tight like a poodle's. From a distance she looked like she was wearing a fuzzy helmet.

Cameron smiled. "No latte, though, right?"

"Latte? You mean like at one of those fancy coffee places?"

Cameron nodded. *I wouldn't be having this conversation in Philadelphia.*

Vera's lips pursed as tight as a Cheerio, then she bundled out from behind the counter and peered around the last set of shelves, toward the coffee bar.

"Well lookey here—we do. I wasn't sure what this machine made. Mike does all the servicing. I don't touch this one. So I wasn't sure what it squirted out. I charge by the cup size and I never really pay attention to what's in them. See there," she said, turning back to Cameron. "The middle button. It says *latte.* So we do have it. You press this button here, the one with the big cup on it, not the small one over here, if you want a large one. You want me to do it for you?"

Cameron shrugged. "I guess so. A grande, then."

"Grande?"

"The large button."

Vera appeared all at sea for a moment. "Grande means large, right?"

Cameron nodded.

Vera giggled. "I guess I knew that. I must have seen it in a movie or probably on television—I mean somebody saying 'grande' and all. I should have known that right away. A grande latte—that's what they serve at those fancy places, isn't it?"

A whirring, steaming noise came out of the stainless steel machine. The illuminated sign just above the buttons proudly claimed that the beverages here would be *Piping Hot* and *Gourmet Quality.* The machine gave a final whoosh, and the last few drops fell into the cup.

"Well, now, here you go. All set. You want sugar or that pink stuff? I usually use the pink stuff. Somebody said the blue stuff is bad for you. I never use the blue stuff anymore. And I sure don't use the real stuff. They say that's even worse for you. I heard the new yellow stuff is supposed to be good, but we don't have any yet."

Cameron took a packet of "pink stuff," shook it, tore it open, and poured it into the latte.

Vera grabbed a lid and carried the cup back to the cash register, humming. She tapped at the keys. Cameron took a five-dollar bill from her pocket and waited for change.

"Well, now, there you go. A nice hot grande latte. You going to the park this morning? I noticed that you didn't drive here. We don't get that many walkers. Or are you headed to the river? I like the park 'cause it's much quieter. You go to the river, and the Jet Skis and the fishing boats set up such a racket that you can hardly hear yourself think."

Vera stopped talking and grinned.

"The park, I guess," Cameron replied. "I was planning on writing. Quiet is good."

Vera brightened as if illuminated by an inner spotlight. "Write? Are you a writer? My goodness. I wanted to be a writer too, but I can't spell. Writers have to be able to spell, don't they? So what do you write?"

Now I know what it feels like to sail into a whirlpool.

"Well, this is just a journal. But I work for *The Derrick*. As a reporter."

Vera leaned back against the cigarette rack. "Really? *The Derrick*? You're a reporter? What's your name? I read that paper every day. I mean, we sell it and there's always a few copies left over. I don't have to pay for it if I wait till afternoon to read it. Is that illegal or anything?"

"I'm Cameron Dane. And I don't think anyone will arrest you," she said, taking a sip of her latte.

This isn't all that bad. Coming from a machine with a big button.

"Cameron Dane."

Vera brightened more, if that was possible. "You wrote the story on the baseball moms, didn't you?"

Cameron nodded.

"The story was great. You pegged that snooty Cathy Hollister just right. She could talk the bark off a stump. Jiminy Christmas. The woman can talk, for certain. She comes in here and I hide. I let Mike wait on her. That story was great."

Cameron's role as reporter, her slight tint of small-town celebrity, had never been noticed in public before and she was unsure how to deal with it.

"And you did the story on the Old Carter Mansion. The house Ethan

Willis is doing. He stops in here all the time. He gets regular coffee, though, cream only, and a couple of Butterfingers most days. Sometimes he gets beef jerky. That's something I don't eat either. How do you know what's really in it? That's what my husband always says. Like hot dogs. But that Carter-place story was good too. I liked the pictures. Woo-hoo—he's one good-lookin' fellow, don't you think?"

Taken somewhat aback, Cameron shrugged.

"I asked him how it felt to be famous—being in the paper and all—when he came in that next day and he just laughed. I think he was embarrassed. He said he thought you did a fine job. You got all the details just right. I think he was really pleased. He bought five copies of the paper that day. He was all smiles."

Cameron couldn't help grinning.

"Well, Vera," she said, "I should be going—if I want to get any writing done at all."

"Okay then, Miss Dane. It is Miss, isn't it?"

"It is."

"And if you ever want to do a story on a convenience-store clerk, I'm your gal. They made a movie about us clerks, but it had too many swear words. I wanted to walk out, but I already bought popcorn and a Coke and the movie cost seven dollars. Seven dollars for a movie! I think that's just outrageous. Best to go to a matinee when it's cheaper."

Cameron took a step to the door and grabbed the handle.

"Well, Miss Dane, you have a good day. And write good, okay?"

"Thanks, Vera. I'll try," she said as she stepped out and began the three-block stroll to the park.

The river would be too noisy for sure.

As she walked and sipped her coffee, she came to the quick and final realization that, despite her noble intentions, she would not write a word today. Instead, she'd spend the morning staring out at the rippling waters of the Allegheny River and trying her best not to think too much about Ethan Willis and the color of his eyes.

Ethan pulled his truck to the curb and beeped his horn as softly as he could, being Sunday morning and all. They were running late, and by the time Chase would get his seat belt undone and saunter up the walk to Elliot's house … well, a lot of time might pass.

Elliot ambled out of the house in his standard church uniform—nicer jeans, blue T-shirt, and, over everything, one of four Hawaiian shirts he owned. In the summer, the style worked fine. In the winter, Ethan wasn't so sure, but he would never mention his misgivings to Elliot.

"Morning, Mr. Willis," he said as he wedged himself in the small jump seat behind the front bench seat.

"You can sit up here with us," Ethan said.

"No, I'm fine back here. Honest, Mr. Willis."

Chase rolled his eyes. "You two say the exact same thing every Sunday. Don't you get tired of it?"

Both of them responded, almost in unison, "Nope."

Chase slunk farther in his seat, even farther than usual, especially after noticing the smiles on both his father's face and his friend's.

In five minutes, Ethan had steered the truck toward the curb in front of Creekside Bible Church at the edge of town. He held the brake down as Chase clambered out.

Elliot wedged his way out from the back. "Thanks, Mr. Willis."

"You're getting a ride home?"

Chase nodded. "Mr. Carwell said he doesn't mind. It's on his way."

"And you both promise to stay in the church and not wander off like you did last week?"

Chase's eyes narrowed. "It wasn't last week. It was, like, two months ago. And we only went across the street for a Coke. Come on, Dad, everybody was there. And it was only for three minutes before church."

Ethan had heard the story from Ken Carwell, the boys' Sunday school teacher, of how a gaggle of students had sneaked out of church before the service had started and had to be rounded up by the youth pastor. Ethan hated getting bad news from a third party.

"We promise, Mr. Willis," Elliot said, then leaned back toward the truck. "I brought two cans of Coke with me. We don't have to go to the store."

Ethan waved a quick good-bye and headed away from the church.

His wife had been the real churchgoer of the family. She had nudged and pushed and prodded to get Ethan to come with her to Sunday services and special events. He would always relent, sometimes begrudgingly, sometimes less so. Since her death—since the funeral—he had not stepped inside their church, or any church for that matter, more than a handful of times. Mrs. Whiting's gentle encouragements that Ethan go with Chase went unheeded. He would make sure he was there for a Christmas Eve service, and most likely Easter—anytime Chase participated with the youth group, or whenever Chase insisted.

Ethan often found himself driving aimlessly around Venango County on Sunday mornings. In the past he would try to read the paper at home, but without Chase around, the silence became too deafening. He tried to have a quiet breakfast out on his own, but felt as if other diners were staring at him in his solitude. He had tried going to church on occasion but could not sit through the service without imagining his wife beside him— or worse, the scene of the funeral. It had happened only a few times … the sweat, the heart palpitations. The sadness was too much for him to bear.

Ethan didn't blame God for his wife's death. He was fairly certain he didn't blame God.

But maybe he did … a little.

And if he did, who could blame him?

And why were Lynne and his son in Erie in the first place?

They didn't need to be in Erie.

She never once had mentioned she and Chase going to Erie that day.

It was not to buy important school clothes or supplies.

To go all that way for a hockey jersey, when she never liked to drive and Erie was over an hour away?

They had no business in Erie.

He remembered the funeral. And then he tried not to remember the funeral.

He hated it when people said her death was all part of God's timing or in His plan. That didn't make sense to Ethan. Was God surprised at what happened? If He was, then who was really in charge of life here on earth? Was her death some sort of angry coincidence, some tragic serendipity? And what good could come of taking the mother of a young child like that?

She was gone. Nothing any pastor could say or do would make her come back and heal this huge hole in his heart. He would not remember what that man said the day of her funeral. He would not. He would not remember the silent sobs Chase cried. He would not. He would …

Ethan found himself on a road he did not recognize.

He looked behind him. The road was empty. It was a country road, on a Sunday morning, with a pellucid sky and the scent of corn growing in the fields. He thought of his wife. This time Lynne's image was slow to form in his thoughts, and it wasn't as clear as it had been in the past. When he closed his eyes tight, he could see her—but as if he were looking through a hundred windows. Not like before. Her face used to appear in his thoughts with a burning intensity.

Now it did not. And for that—for that tiny failure—Ethan felt a tide of guilt wash over his heart. He breathed deeply, looked both ways along this unfamiliar, familiar road, and began to search for his way home.

———⊙⊙⊙———

That afternoon, Elliot called through the front screen door of the Willis house. "Is Chase here?"

Elliot was almost a head taller than Chase, and built like a coal miner—his grandfather's occupation.

A shout came from the kitchen at the back of the house. "Come on in. I'm back here."

Elliot opened the front door and closed it gingerly. His mother nagged at him constantly to be more refined and pay attention to his manners. He tried, but he often found himself galumphing into furniture or people or even trees and shrubs, so an apology and a smile was always at the ready.

Chase sat at the sturdy kitchen table with a loaf of bread, a stack of

yellow cheese slices, and a small boat-shaped container of shaved ham. A
knife was stuck in a mayonnaise jar that sat next to a plastic squeeze bottle of mustard.

"You hungry?" Chase asked as he chewed on a healthy bite of sandwich.

Elliot shrugged. "I just had lunch, but I could eat another sandwich,
I guess."

Neither spoke. The knife clacked against the glass jar. Elliot grabbed
the mustard bottle, and it snorted out a healthy dollop.

He looked around for a dish but elected to use a paper towel instead.
There was no chance he could break a paper towel, although he once
pulled the entire holder out of the wall. He and Chase had fixed it before
his dad got home, using big butterfly bolts.

Both boys finished at the same time.

Chase looked at his friend. "Want another?"

Elliot shrugged and reached for the bread.

After they had cleaned the kitchen, they sat on the front porch. Lynne
had bought and repainted some vintage wicker furniture that she'd carefully placed on the porch flanking the front door of the house. The glider
chairs, a rocker, and a sofa were now a pleasant blue color that matched
some of the house's trimwork and had thick, comfy, multistriped cush-
ions. The hanging baskets she had added across the front as the finishing
touch, once home to lush maidenhair ferns, now hung empty except for
a few remaining dried brown fronds that drooped over their edges.

Chase brought his radio out to the porch with them and tuned it to
the Pirates game. They were playing in Philadelphia. Chase didn't like the
Phillies. He wasn't sure why, except that his father didn't like them either.
He always wondered how his mother felt about them. She was from
Philadelphia, and Chase thought you couldn't be against the hometown
team.

"What do you want to do?" Elliot asked. He sprawled on the wicker
couch. No one could sprawl quite as well as Elliot.

Chase shrugged. "Finish listening to the game?"

Elliot pondered for a moment. "We could go fishing. We could take
the radio with us."

Chase shrugged. "Okay. I'll get my stuff."

"You got an extra pole? I don't want to go home and ask. I think my mom would say no."

Chase nodded. Elliot's mom was often moody and had seemed more explosive than usual over the last several weeks.

Their favorite site, on the rocks just by Sibley Park, shaded by a thick stand of evergreens, had been taken over by a half-dozen older teenagers. Their shouts were loud, and Chase heard a new variation on a familiar string of curse words.

They did not argue but simply made their way up the river, past the picnic grounds, past the public boat launch and by a small nudge in the shoreline. The riverbank was grass right up to the waterline, and was cut short and tidy by city workers. The water was deep and still, with a tangle of exposed tree roots just below the surface that offered great hiding places for smallmouth bass.

They spoke only a few words as they set their lines. Chase knew Elliot was a skilled fisherman. He wanted a fly-casting system, but even as a birthday present, his family couldn't afford it, Chase imagined.

Chase put a shiny spoon bait on his line, cast it into the river, and slowly began to crank the reel. He sat down on a large flat rock at the water's edge. Elliot was still carefully threading the line through a minnow lure. He always seemed to struggle with the small things in life.

"You want me to help?"

"Naw. I'll get it."

Chase looked to the far shore. "Your mom being hard again?" he asked.

He didn't expect an answer. A lot of their questions didn't have answers.

Elliot shrugged. "Sometimes she gets that way. My dad just says she's going through the change."

"What's that?"

Elliot shrugged again. It was a most familiar gesture. "I don't know. Means she gets a chance to act weird, I guess. Moms can be pretty much a pain sometimes."

Chase looked away.

"Sorry," Elliot said softly.

"'Sokay," Chase replied. And it was. He thought about his mother a lot—more in the last few weeks—but he never minded when anyone who still had their mother mentioned that his mother was gone. It just made her real again—even if only for those few minutes.

They made numerous casts and retrieves without garnering the slightest interest of the fish. Sounds of the ball game filtered and drifted between them. The Pirates were leading by one going into the fourth inning.

"I saw your dad in the paper the other day," Elliot said as he cast into the waters again. "My dad said he never had a reporter follow him on his job. I think he was jealous or something."

Chase smiled.

"Did that lady reporter write it?"

"What lady reporter?" Chase asked.

"The one at the ball game. The real pretty one."

Chase didn't change his tone, but a muscle in his jaw flexed. "I dunno. Maybe. I guess she did."

Elliot nodded. "My mom said she's a real looker. And she's looking for a man. She said she could tell."

A long breezy silence took over.

"Do you think your dad is looking?" Elliot asked as he pulled off a strand of river weed from his hook.

"For what?"

"You know. A woman. Like a new wife, you know?"

Chase shrugged again. He laid his pole down, leaned forward, his elbows on his knees and his chin in his hands. "I don't know. Do you think he is?"

"I dunno," Elliot replied. "I can't figure out grown-ups. They say one thing and do another."

"He's never said anything about that. Or her, I mean. He wouldn't," Chase said.

Elliot opened up the tackle box and began to very carefully rummage through the lures. Chase couldn't blame him. Last summer he'd managed to get a hook into his thumb so far that his dad had to pull it through and cut off the top to extract it.

"You ever ask?"

Chase rubbed his nose. "Naw. We don't talk about stuff like that."

Elliot stopped looking for a hook and simply waited.

"Since my mom ... you know ... we don't talk about a lot of stuff."

"But you're always doing stuff with him. Camping and stuff," Elliot answered.

"Doesn't mean we talk. I think ... I think he thinks that somehow it was all my fault ... you know ... back then."

"Was it?"

The muscles in Chase's throat tightened. This subject lay in a new territory for the two friends.

"Naw. I was just a little kid. How could it be my fault? I mean, I was just a kid."

Elliot offered a tentative, knowing smile. "Hey, all kinds of stuff is my fault at home. Stuff that I didn't even know about. It's easier to blame me than to figure out what really happened."

Chase turned to his friend. "Doesn't that drive you crazy?"

Elliot stared up at the sky, his eyes unfocused. "Naw. I mean, it does, but I don't let it bother me. If you fight it, that makes it worse. Like they taught us in Sunday school. Blessed be the peacemakers and all that sort of stuff."

"Yeah."

Elliot nodded back. He understood. He understood without saying. You could just tell he understood by looking at his face, his eyes, as if he understood everything that couldn't be put into words.

"Life is just so messed up," Chase said.

Elliot sighed. "Yeah. Sometimes it is, I guess."

All but Death, can be Adjusted—
Dynasties repaired—
Systems—settled in their Sockets—
Citadels—dissolved—
Wastes of Lives—resown with Colors
By Succeeding Springs—
Death—unto itself—Exception—
Is exempt for Change—

—EMILY DICKINSON

CHAPTER SIX

PAIGE WINCED AS SHE swallowed the last of her coffee. She looked at her watch. "Goodness! It's nearly ten. We haven't been this late in months."

Cameron yawned and stretched her arms over her head. "I know. What happened tonight? We only had thirty-six pages."

Paige shrugged. "I miss the days of hot lead and linotypes. Now those were deadlines."

Cameron held her grin. Even in her short tenure on *The Franklin Derrick,* she had heard this same refrain many times.

Paige rummaged about her desk. "Even wax and paste was better than this. You could hold a headline in your hands and lay it down. You had a physical connection to the paper. Now it's just us and these idiot computers."

The Derrick had gone computerized several years earlier, one of the last holdouts in an increasingly electronic world. All page layouts were done on computer screen. No one touched a real paper anymore—not until it came off the press. At the touch of a button, the pages would transmit to a printer located in the anonymous nondescript industrial park on the outskirts of town, between the airport and the American Legion Hall.

"I wish we could go back. When I handed the pages to the printer, I really felt something," Paige said. "There was a finality about the process. Now I press *Send* and—*poof!*—it all just goes away. Hardly seems right."

Roger Corkel, a fussy middle-aged man who lived with his mother, was responsible for the majority of the design and layout of *The Derrick*, but he worked only five days a week and the newspaper came out six times a week—Tuesday through Sunday. On Monday evenings, Paige and another staff member would handle all the design chores. Cameron imagined that the Tuesday edition always looked both tense and loose at the same time, as if the hands putting it together were tentative and unsure. Most readers would have been hard-pressed to see any difference, but Cameron noticed. She always noticed.

Paige hiked her large drawstring handbag—red canvas and bigger than most backpacks—to her shoulder. She shifted her weight to compensate.

"Are you coming?" she asked as she dug into the depths of the bag, shaking it every so often, listening for the jingle of a key ring, jammed with dozens of keys.

"In a minute or so. I think I'll send some e-mails. Lock up. I'll make sure the door is closed when I leave."

Paige pursed her lips. "It's late. Shouldn't you be getting home?"

Cameron giggled, then realized Paige was serious. "Well, I'm not due in tomorrow till afternoon. I'll sleep in."

Paige nodded in agreement, though Cameron knew Paige never slept in, no matter what hour she left the office. She always arrived at work at eight in the morning—no matter what. Paige hefted her bag again, and cocked her head and stared at Cameron, as if studying her. Then she sidled up to the desk opposite Cameron and sat against it.

"What's the question?" she asked.

"What question?" Cameron replied. "I didn't ask a question."

"No … but you want to. I haven't been in the newspaper business for all these decades without learning a few things about how to read people. You have a question. Ask me."

"No, really. There's nothing."

Paige turned her head and stared harder—just like Cameron's mother used to do.

"Well … I don't want to bother you. It's late, Paige."

Paige leaned on the empty desk and let her bag thump to the ground. "So? All I have waiting for me at home is an old, scruffy tomcat with a bad disposition. Now or ten minutes from now, he'll still be in a bad mood."

Cameron looked at her hands, then toward the windows. All she could see through the tinted glass was a row of streetlights leading to the theater and Fountain Park. The red lights of the marquee flashed and wobbled in the strong river breeze.

"So what's on your mind? Man troubles?"

Cameron looked up as if she had heard a shot echo in the empty building. "What?"

"Man problems." Paige exhaled a soft whistle. "Am I good or what?"

"It's not man problems … exactly." Cameron had not looked up from the desk. "It's nothing. I shouldn't bother you with this. I'm not even sure I should bother with it myself."

Paige slipped off the desk and into a chair. "Can't be analytical standing up. And it's times like these that I truly regret giving up smoking. Late-night philosophy and cigarettes seem to go together. Even if they do kill you early. So who's the new fellow?"

Cameron didn't answer. She did not look up until she heard Paige's very throaty laugh, soft at first, then full-bodied, resonant and hearty.

"Sorry," she said, holding up her palm, "but I just stepped back and looked at us. Here I am, an almost sixty-something, twice-widowed old lady assuming to know something about men. All my experience happened in the last century, remember?" Paige took a deep breath. "Doesn't all this seem a little like a French absurdist play to you?"

Cameron didn't answer.

"So you're really serious about this?" Paige finally said. "I'm sorry for making fun of it. It just seems …"

Cameron could only muster a sidelong smile. "I know. Women today are supposed to have everything figured out. To know what we want and how to get it. Men are supposed to be the easy part of the question. They're supposed to be there and ready—when you're ready."

Paige laughed again, a friendly, pat-on-the-back sort of laugh. "Cameron, there are men out there that are very, very ready. But I just bet they're not the kind you want. And I should know that. I married two of the worst choices God ever put in western Pennsylvania."

"I don't think this one fits into that sort of 'beware' category."

"So tell me, who is he? Do I know him?"

Cameron took a deep breath. She brushed back a loopy strand of dark hair that fell across her cheek. She looked up at Paige, who was the closest thing to a grandmother she had ever known.

"Ever since I did that piece on the old Carter place ..."

Paige's face showed her surprise. "No. Not one of Willis's crew? The blond one—the mysterious one with the ponytail ... and very nice frame?"

Cameron grinned. She had no idea that Paige knew any of the carpenters on Ethan's crew. "No ... not Doug."

"The one with the motorcycle? He's pretty easy on the eyes too."

"No ... not Jack either."

Paige winced as she appeared to be mentally reviewing Ethan's crew. "But other than Doug and Jack, the others are all married, aren't they? Please don't tell me it's with a married man."

Cameron looked up. "No. He's not married. Well ... he was. He's a widower."

A few seconds later realization dawned in Paige's eyes.

"Ethan? Ethan Willis?"

Cameron nodded.

"Really?"

She nodded again.

"But he's a good bit ... older than you, isn't he?"

Cameron shrugged. "I didn't ask his age. Maybe a few years older."

"More than a few."

Cameron hesitated. "Maybe under ten."

"More than likely over ten. He's got to be close to forty."

A car horn sounded from the street below. Cameron watched the sweep of headlights as the car turned into the alley, apparently on its way to the rear parking lot behind Ernie's, a tavern four doors down from the newspaper.

Cameron looked up. "So I should forget about it—just because he's a little older?"

Paige's eyes narrowed. "I didn't say that. I was just surprised, that's all."

Cameron was silent. Her mind swirled with a mixture of confusion and pain.

"I'm sorry," Paige said as she leaned closer. "I had no idea. I mean … I just would have never thought … the two of you. You know?"

Cameron waved her hand in an odd sweep, as if trying to communicate all her uncertainty in a gesture.

"Have you two gone out?" Paige asked. "I mean, this is a small town and all, and sooner or later, I hear about everything."

"Not really. Not yet. But we did go for lunch after the interview. We spent two hours at Cumming's. I think … well, I think there was … something there."

"Has he called you?" Paige asked, as if she were a mother with a teenage romantic crisis on her hands.

"No. But I want to call him. Ever since I found out about his wife and all that. And his son … being there when it happened and all."

Paige's face grew visibly surprised. "What do you mean—he was there?"

"Chase was there when his mother was killed."

"What?"

"In the backseat of the car."

It was obvious this was news to Paige—who knew everything about everyone.

Cameron related the story of her trip to Erie and her conversation with the reporter at the Erie newspaper.

"Well, no one in town has a clue," Paige said with finality. "Whoever knew about this did a very good job at keeping the secret."

A pool of silence settled around them. Cameron heard the ticking of the clock on her desk, the wheezy hiss of the air-conditioning. She considered Paige, realizing the woman was in the midst of processing too much information.

Cameron looked out at the darkened street, then glanced at her watch. *I've done a very good job at keeping my secret too.*

"I should be getting home. Would you give me a lift?" she asked Paige.

"Sure," the older woman replied. "Give me a minute to find my keys again."

Cameron opened the door and started to get out of Paige's silver Volvo station wagon. The engine rattled and ticked softly. She sat back down and pulled the door closed, then turned back to Paige.

She had to ask. She was surprised at how much the older woman's opinion mattered.

"So, I shouldn't call him, then? He's too old for me?"

It was apparent that Paige had been thinking of an answer to Cameron's question during the short ride to her apartment.

"Cameron," she began, her words maternal and cautionary, "I can't tell you what to do. He is older. But then my first husband was ten years older than me. I can conveniently forget all sorts of things like that. But here's what I have to say about this: If it's meant to be, then it will be. But I also know that if anything is going to happen, you'll have to be the one to make the first move."

"You think so?"

"I do. He'll never ask you. The age thing, I would guess. A fellow like Ethan, he just won't call first—no matter how many hints you may have dropped. Remember: The worst that can happen is that he says no."

Cameron deflated. "But he's a really nice guy. I know that much about him. He seems like a decent man. He would have to be a good person to raise his son on his own like he is."

"But you do have to be aware … that he may be …"

"What?" Cameron asked.

Paige was silent, then said, "I'm not one to talk, obviously, but he may be … well, damaged. He may be damaged in a way that you can't fix. My second husband was like that. There was something major in him that needed fixing and I thought I was the person to do the fixing. But in the end, we almost wound up breaking each other."

"So, a man with a past … I mean, should I avoid any man with some sort of past? That includes just about everyone, doesn't it?" Cameron asked.

And poor Chase … isn't he just as damaged? she thought.

"No. It's true that we're all broken in some ways. And maybe I'm wrong here. I probably am wrong. But you need to be aware of how a person's past colors their present. Maybe this is different. Maybe Ethan does need your help. Maybe. He's had his share of problems. After his wife … he had some business troubles. I don't know if that's the case now. Contractors always seem to be living on the edge of disaster. But maybe he's ready now … for some positive steps in his life. And you never know unless you try."

Cameron looked at Paige, then reached over and gave a gentle hug to a surprised Paige. "Thanks," she said softly. "Thanks for everything."

"So, you're going to call him?" Paige asked. "I mean … this is purely journalistic interest on my part."

Cameron laughed. It felt good. Then she stared at Paige and shrugged. "Maybe. I don't know." She slipped out of the car. "Probably," she said. "Someone needs to take care of them both. You know … his son, too. Chase."

"True. So, you're going to call?" Paige asked.

Cameron shrugged again. "I don't know. Maybe. Probably. That's if I can figure out what to say."

Then she turned and bounded up her steps and into the entrance of her apartment.

Cameron had been nervous before. She knew what a fast, fluttering heart-beat felt like. After all, she had given the valedictorian speech at her high school commencement. She'd almost gotten sick before stepping to the podium. She had interviewed visiting dignitaries and politicians as they'd traveled through Franklin. She'd almost had the opportunity to ask the president of the United States a question during a stop at her college several years ago.

But nothing compared to the near panic she felt as she at last picked up the phone and tapped out Ethan's number.

"Hello?"

"Uhh … hi, Ethan. This is Cameron. Cameron Dane."

Silence.

He doesn't remember me!

"From the newspaper. Of course. How are you? Have you won the Pulitzer yet?"

She grinned wide.

He does remember me!

Then her palms went moist. She had forgotten what she was planning on saying. She forgot at what restaurant she had decided to ask him to join her. She forgot what day she had intended for this get-together. And he had flummoxed her more soundly by asking a question.

Answer him! Answer him!

The conversation had lasted only a handful of minutes. As she hung the phone up, she felt a bead of sweat roll down between her shoulder blades.

Do guys feel this way when they ask a woman out?

He had been charming and kind, and he'd even thanked her for her story on his work at the Carter Mansion. He said he was pleased with her writing. She might have just imagined it, but he had sounded more than a bit nonplussed when she finally blurted out the reason for her call.

"Dinner?"

Her eyes were shut tight. "Yes. That meal after lunch but before the piece of chocolate cake that you eat standing up in front of the open refrigerator."

He laughed. She felt a huge weight lift from her stomach.

"Dinner, you say?" he repeated.

She nodded, then smacked her head with her palm. *He can't see you!* "Yes, I say dinner. Though some people call it supper." She gritted her teeth.

Please laugh, she pleaded and hoped he could not hear her fast-beating heart.

"Well … sure," he said, and she thought his words sounded as if he was actually pleased at the prospect.

Please be pleased!

He then repeated the time and place. She imagined it was as much for her benefit as his. She said, in a hurry, that it would be easiest if they met at the restaurant. Cameron knew it wouldn't really be easier, but felt that picking him up in her car was problematic—she wasn't sure how, exactly, except that she knew it was. And she couldn't ask him to pick her up, since she was the one doing the inviting.

"Great," he had said. "I'll see you then."

Afterward, she collapsed on the sofa, staring blankly into space for a long time.

He said yes.

And then she got up and spent the next five hours, until she heard the bell from St. Mark's toll midnight, obsessing on what she might wear.

"With who?"

Ethan felt the prickliness of Chase's voice. They had just sat down to a less-than-elegant dinner of macaroni and cheese. Ethan had come home late that night and had rushed to put together a quick meal. And Chase had always loved macaroni and cheese.

"Cameron. That reporter from the newspaper. The one who did the article on your team … and the story about the Carter place."

"The story was on the *moms,*" Chase added with a touch of venom. "Not the team. She didn't talk to me or anyone else on the team."

Ethan shrugged.

"When did you talk to her?"

After a minute of hesitation, Ethan replied, "Yesterday evening. She called. You weren't home, remember? You spent the night at Elliot's."

"She called you?"

Both were aware that their tone was drifting from polite civility to something harder, something more caustic.

"Well, are you going?"

Ethan closed his eyes for a long moment. He had not been on an official date for years. After his wife's death, and for several years after, a few well-meaning friends and relatives had arranged dinner parties or barbecues with a single woman in attendance. Chairs had been shuffled discreetly, and people had contrived to bring Ethan into close proximity with a single friend or cousin or someone's acquaintance. The evenings had always gone pleasantly enough. Ethan was more often than not a personable, polite man. But he'd always felt awkward both during, and especially after, the event.

The relative or friend would sidle up and ask, in a conspiratorial whisper, "So ... did you like her? Isn't she nice?"

Ethan had found himself forced to agree that whoever she was, was indeed nice, that he was sure she was a wonderful person. Smiles all around. He was sure there would be a flurry of phone calls back and forth, his friends and relatives dissecting the details of the evening.

The phone calls would never originate with him.

Then he would feel guilty for never pursuing any of these available options. A week or two would pass and he would be forced to defend his inactivity.

Eventually, his friends and relatives stopped their unofficial sponsorship of any matchmaking events. Ethan had felt a great sense of relief as he realized the invitations tapered off. He still was invited to parties, and there was often a single woman or two, but no longer did anyone expect any relationships to ensue.

Ethan had a son to raise—alone. He didn't have time for dating. And after his wife died, his construction business struggled. He lost jobs, he was late paying for materials, checks bounced on occasion. Lynne would have never let that happen. Now it was just him. It was a struggle, but Ethan felt he had made it through that dark patch without needing anyone else.

Now ... well, maybe now was different.

He looked at his son and tried to read his eyes. It could have been anger; it could have been confusion. And then it could have been that innate roll-of-the-eyes children seem to have.

He had never promised his son that he would never date. He had simply never dated.

"I am. I told her I would go. I am going."

He said the last few words with more firmness than he intended.

Chase glared at him before lowering his eyes. He dug his fork into his macaroni and cheese. After three forkfuls, he looked up. "I can stay with Elliot that night."

Ethan couldn't find the words to respond. What did he think he would do—bring her home with him? After a single date?

Ethan felt a sigh in his heart but would not give it voice.

What these young people grow up thinking, he thought.

"No," he said. "You don't have to do that. We're meeting for dinner. At Wilson's. At seven. I'll be home by nine, nine thirty at the latest. You're good by yourself till then, right?"

He hoped his words had the right bounce to them.

Chase shrugged. "I guess."

And those were the last words the boy spoke all evening.

Ethan waved to his crew, pushing the air in front of him, then pointing at the cell phone at his ear. He tried to make his face say that he couldn't hear Mrs. Moretti. After a moment, the saws stopped, then the hammering stopped.

"Yes, I know you said the staircase should be wider, Mrs. Moretti ... CeCe ... but we had it laid out and seven feet was just too much. That's too wide for the space. We'll lose a huge chunk of the room off the hall if it's that wide."

The crew stood almost motionless as Ethan argued long distance over the staircase. Ethan had decided seven feet wide was too wide for an upstairs stairway, and instructed them to cut the treads at five feet.

"Once we've cut them, she can't expect us to change them back," he had told them. "You can't add inches to a cut board, now, can you?"

But now Mrs. Moretti, on the phone and upset, was doing exactly that.

"But we've cut the treads already. You'll be much happier with the smaller staircase. You have to trust me on that … CeCe. You don't build this big of a staircase without a bigger staircase as its base. It needs a reference point to connect it to the ground level. You just don't do it that way."

Ethan averted his eyes as he listened.

The smell of cut pine board thickened the air. Doug, very silently, put down his circular saw. Joel flipped the safety switch on the nail gun. Both men acted as if they assumed the conversation would go long and CeCe would prove victorious. Joel moved slowly to the pile of lumber still in the middle of the room.

"But that means we'll have to go back and order more tread board. That's really expensive."

Ethan turned away, his back to everyone. "I know you wanted seven feet, but that means a lot of extra expense …"

He could feel the slump in his shoulders grow more protracted and pronounced. "All right. Okay, Mrs. Moretti. I'll order the extra tread board. My fault. Okay. My fault. Okay. Seven feet. Regardless of whether it's right for the space or not. Seven feet. Fine. Okay. This weekend. Sure. Fine."

When Ethan turned back, Joel was maneuvering the three uncut tread boards out from the pile. "I think we can get by with ordering another thirty-six feet. That should be enough."

And no one spoke directly to Ethan for the rest of the afternoon.

"So you've been here before?" Cameron asked as they walked up to the front door of Wilson's.

He nodded. "I grew up in this town, remember? There aren't that many restaurants. Eventually, you wind up eating in all of them—at least occasionally. Except the truly bad ones."

Wilson's had been housed in a rambling stone building, overlooking a bend in the river, for the last fifty years, he told her as they waited to be seated. Ownership had changed infrequently, and the dark, clubby atmosphere had remained constant. White tablecloths and tall goblets marked it as one of the better establishments in the area.

Paige had grinned when Cameron told her of their destination. "You've picked the most romantic spot in Venango County," she had said with a little cough.

Cameron had been horrified but knew it was too late to change her plans.

After a couple of minutes, they followed the maître d' to their table.

"I've only eaten here once," Cameron explained to Ethan as she slid into the seat opposite him. "When I was interviewing for my job, we came out here for lunch. I remember the food being very good."

Ethan smiled at her.

What was that for? she wondered.

"It is good food. I don't come here often. My son doesn't exactly require anything gourmet. The way he views food is that if you can't put ketchup or cheese on it, then you may as well not eat it."

Cameron laughed nervously. She started talking about her day at the newspaper. She found herself reaching for the one strand of hair she always twirled and twisted at times like this.

His eyes followed her hands and then found her eyes. She stopped talking in midsentence. "Uhh ... what was I saying?" she asked, flustered.

"Something about the mayor and zoning," Ethan replied. "I think so, anyhow."

Her eyes fluttered. "Uhh ... well ... then ..."

She folded her hands on the table and lowered her eyes. When she looked up, she tried to smile. "I have no idea what I was saying," she admitted. "I guess I was simply … prattling on. Silence makes me nervous sometimes."

Ethan looked around the restaurant. It was midweek and perhaps only half-filled with patrons. He leaned forward a few inches. "Can I tell you a secret?"

"Okay." Surprised and curious, Cameron leaned in to hear it.

"When you called and suggested this place, I was worried about the same thing. What was going to happen when neither of us could think of anything to say? At least at Cumming's there's the low rumble of that relic of a dishwasher that would drown out any uncomfortable pauses."

Cameron smiled. "Is that what that noise was? It sounded sort of like a subway train, and I didn't think Franklin had a subway. But I didn't want to ask and sound stupid."

Ethan laughed. "This isn't so bad. I was worried about nothing."

"You were worried? Really?"

Ethan nodded. "I guess. I mean … it has been a long, long time since … you know … I've been on a date. Like tonight."

A look of mild alarm came across Ethan's face.

"I mean … this is a date, isn't it?" he quickly added. "It isn't another interview, right? You're not going to try and sell me something, are you? Please tell me this is … sort of a date so I don't evaporate from embarrassment."

"Yes … it is sort of a date. I … I haven't much practice at this sort of thing. I mean, asking a man out."

Ethan tilted his head. "A modern woman like yourself? I would have thought this is standard operating procedure." Ethan reached for a thick slice of bread from the breadbasket.

She watched as he gently tore a smaller piece from the slice and actually used the butter knife to place a pat of butter in his own bread-and-butter plate. She watched as he laid his knife across the plate— just like the rules of etiquette suggested. It had been a long time since she had dated a man who seemed to know that there is a difference between dining and eating.

She watched his hands. They were powerful and callused. She could tell he had spent extra time cleaning them this evening. She looked at him as he studied the menu. He wore a simple blue cotton shirt—starched, button-down—with sharply creased gray slacks. If she had not known, he could have passed for a stockbroker or a schoolteacher.

She listened to him order his meal—steak, medium, house salad with Thousand Island dressing, au gratin potatoes, and an iced tea. He seemed assured. He treated the waitress with courtesy and humor. He smiled as she laughed.

To Cameron, the evening passed by as quickly as a summer sunset. She had done most of the talking that night, and when the second cup of coffee was finished, he reached for his wallet and began to extract a credit card.

She leaned over and placed her hand on his. She had been right—it felt strong and competent.

"No," she said firmly. "I called you. I invited you out. This is my treat."

Ethan looked both pleased and a little unsettled. "Are you sure? I would be more than happy to split this."

Cameron shook her head. "Not this time," she said, as if she knew right then that there would be other times. "My treat."

"All right," he said, slipping his wallet back into his pocket. "Next time, I get to pay."

She nodded.

He said there would be a next time!

"But you can be assured that I'm not going to pick such an elegant place."

She laughed. "You mean expensive, don't you?"

He grinned. "Well … that too."

In the parking lot, she stood by her car door and unlocked it. He had escorted her there. She saw his truck parked on the other side of the lot.

"I had a very nice time," she said. "Thank you."

"No, thank you," he replied. "It was a nice treat. And I enjoyed myself too. There weren't too many awkward silences, were there?"

She shook her head. "Only a few. But they gave me a chance to think of something witty and charming."

He stepped back. She saw his eyes dart from her to his car, then to his hands, as if he was now so very uncertain of what to do next.

She thought his indecision was utterly adorable and wished she could tell him so.

She saw his hand move slightly, as if to offer a handshake to end the evening.

That is not an appropriate way to end the evening, she thought.

She leaned toward him as she opened her arms. He obviously saw her and responded in kind. They exchanged a short, chaste hug in the parking lot of Wilson's.

He dropped his arms first and backed away a step, nearly stumbling into a Buick parked next to her.

"I'll … I'll call you," he said, then turned and walked into the Buick's side rearview mirror.

She held her laugh. "Thanks. I'd like that."

And as she sat down and closed her car door, she realized her heart was pounding as if she had just run up a flight of steps.

Ethan waited in his truck until she had pulled out and headed back into town. He had to take the same route and did not want to appear as if he were deliberately following her. Then he wondered if his waiting would make it look like he was intentionally not following her.

He shrugged and breathed in deeply.

That didn't go so bad, he thought. *Actually, I sort of enjoyed it. She seems nice.*

He rolled down the window as he drove, turned up the radio, and let the wind whistle about the truck. He began to sing along with the song on the radio, even though he only knew a few of the words, plus the chorus.

It had been a long time since he had sung out loud like this.

As he turned the corner just before Sugar Creek, he felt his heart lurch. Dinner was quickly forgotten.

A half-mile ahead, on the right, overlooking the river, was the River Bend Cemetery. It was where his wife had lain these past seven years. He had, for most of the evening, forgotten she was there.

And in that moment of realization, he stopped singing. His heart seemed to thump with a familiar, slower cadence.

He drove by, trying not to look south, to the gentle rise, to the small headstone—LYNNE ELIZABETH WILLIS—set among a trio of red maple trees.

He told himself again that it wasn't too soon, that it was time not to look. Yet the truck slowed, he turned his head, and …

He sighed.

Then he switched the radio off and drove home in silence to his son.

———

Cameron danced up the steps to her apartment and twirled about the living room as she tossed her keys and purse onto the couch. She would have turned up her stereo to a painful level, but this was a meeting night of the Franklin Club and the cadre of stodgy members would be banging on the ceiling in a heartbeat.

She kicked off her shoes, pranced about into the bedroom, and threw herself onto the bed, reviewing once again the entire evening. She wished she had someone to call. She thought of calling Paige but decided against it.

Too soon.

She lay there, grinning, and recalled the brief hug in the parking lot.…

———

Chase sat on the couch with his arms folded.

The Pirates, in contention to take first place in the division, had taken the Braves into extra innings.

"You said nine o'clock."

Ethan looked at his watch. It was 9:15.

"I said about nine or nine thirty."

"How come I have to be on time and you don't?" Chase snapped.

Ethan tried his best to be even-tempered at all times. But sometimes he just couldn't.

"Because I'm the dad. Because I make the money. Because I go to work every day. Because I pay all the bills. Because I have all the headaches. That's why—and don't be smart with me again."

Chase kept his arms folded and whipped his head back to the television.

Ethan waited a moment, huffed out a breath, and sorted through the stack of mail lying on the entry table.

The Pirates were batting in the bottom of the eleventh inning. Chase stood up, walked to the television, and clicked it off with an obvious and deliberate move. He turned and slowly walked out of the room and up the steps. As he reached the top of the steps, he mumbled, "Good night."

Ethan muttered a "good night" in response.

Chase clicked off the light at the top of the stairs. Ethan stood at the bottom, in darkness. He listened to the sounds of running water, then the closing of a door, then silence.

He took a deep breath and let it slip from his lungs.

He could still smell the scent of her perfume on his shirt.

Since nothing we intend is ever faultless,
and nothing we attempt ever without error,
and nothing we achieve
without some measure of finitude
and fallibility we call humanness,
we are saved by forgiveness.

—DAVID AUGSBURGER

CHAPTER SEVEN

FLYERS LOOK STRONG!

Ethan folded the newspaper back and smoothed the crease. He folded it in half again. He would have called to Chase, but his son had spent the night at Elliot's. Local sports were light in the summer, and *The Derrick* highlighted the Little League championships. Ethan read through the article—a couple of standard quotes from the coach about "playing their game" and "giving it 110 percent."

Chase would get a kick out of seeing this, Ethan thought. *I wish he were here.*

Ethan knew his son enjoyed being a part of the pleasant chaos of a family with six children at the Hewitts', but Chase seemed to be spending more time than usual over at Elliot's.

Ethan sighed and refolded the paper carefully. He would save this issue, along with all the other bits and pieces of memorabilia he had collected over the years. A large blue plastic bin under the basement steps held a stack of clippings, drawings, report cards, awards, and pictures—all evidence of the life he and Chase had shared since his wife had died.

Up until seven years ago, everything was glued into scrapbooks or placed in photo albums. Ethan could never summon up the energy or desire to do the same. Saving the material was all he could do. Organizing it artistically, or even chronologically, was beyond him.

The Flyers were scheduled to play in the semifinal game on Saturday afternoon. The winner of the Franklin tournament would play the winner of the Oil City tournament. The playoffs, a double-elimination series, would last through the end of summer. Ethan saw the Flyers as having a good chance of heading into the championships. This weekend they were slated to face the Senaca Royals, a team they had already beaten once this year.

He carefully laid the folded paper on the hutch. He grabbed his keys, thermos, and lunch, and headed out the door.

———◦∞◦———

"Here's our latest revision of the first-floor rear area," the architect said as she unrolled her blueprints on a makeshift plywood table in the entry of the Old Carter Mansion.

Ethan peered at the neat lines and marks. Neither he nor Joel had much good to say about most architects, claiming that they never understood the realities of actual construction work and materials. But so far, Mrs. Moretti's architect, Michelle King from 3R Design, was different. She actually visited the jobsite and asked Ethan for his input.

She didn't listen to it, though, Ethan politely fumed to himself.

The first time Ms. King had arrived on the site, both Ethan and Joel had stared in wide-eyed surprise. Architects were usually rare at project sites, and women architects were just rare—period. Michelle was an attractive, tall, sturdy-looking woman, well-dressed, with a no-nonsense bearing.

At their first meeting on-site, Ethan had traced a thin blue line on the third-floor drawings with his finger and then muttered, shaking his head, "Well—I can see that you don't know lumber. Look here. You need a bigger header. There's too much of a span."

"I don't think so. Look at the note. I mean ... you do read the blueprints, don't you?" Ms. King replied confidently.

Ethan had looked closer at the plans. "Oh. Okay. I see the note. Four two-by-twelves. But ... wouldn't a composite wood beam be more cost effective?"

He had hoped his words did not sound too contrite.

"You could use either—depending on the best pricing you get from your lumber yard," Michelle answered.

Ethan appreciated that the architect visited, but it made it harder for him to defend his keep-everything-the-way-it-was approach. He was pretty sure that Mrs. Moretti ... CeCe ... insisted her architect show up from time to time, not only to check out the progress and lend her moral support, but to provide ammunition on technical and style conflicts as well.

Today Ethan felt overwhelmed. CeCe was joined by her architect and now her kitchen planner, Scott Anderson of Anderson and Harrington Kitchens. CeCe had touted them as Pittsburgh's premier kitchen specialists. CeCe first noticed their work in a design magazine, and she'd insisted on using them for the Carter Mansion project.

"I want this area as open as possible," CeCe declared with a sweep of her hand. "People love to be in my kitchen, so I need lots of space." She smiled. "If Ethan wouldn't give me a headache about it, I would make the entire first floor one big kitchen."

Scott walked over to the west wall. "I think the Wolf range and ovens should go over here—their stainless steel hood will catch the sun perfectly. And the double Sub-Zero refrigerator-freezers go on that wall. They'll balance out the heights," he said as he walked and pointed.

"Italian Carrera marble tile, right? And a pot-filler faucet over the stove?" CeCe said. "I love my pasta." She smiled and added, "And don't forget my warming drawers."

"When guests come in here," Scott said, sweeping the air with his outstretched arm, "CeCe wants them to think they're in Tuscany ... in some wonderful villa on top of a hill in an Italian vineyard."

Ethan did his best not to roll his eyes. *It's just a kitchen, for Pete's sake. Every house has a kitchen.*

"I want my kitchen to knock people's socks off. It's the most important room in my house, where people love to gather. I want people stunned when they come in."

"No problem," Scott answered. "We can do that."

"And, Scott, I want to be in on all the finish selections—the marble slabs, the hardware, the flooring—everything," CeCe reiterated. "I know what I want ... right, Ethan?"

Ethan felt that if he offered more than a silent nod, he might say something he would regret.

"I'll have some elevations drawn up within a few weeks, including the layout for the cabinetry for the entertainment wall in the great room, and then we can start with selecting the cabinet style," answered Scott.

Mrs. Moretti left in the early afternoon after a long discussion with both the architect and the kitchen planner. Scott stayed on for another hour, taking measurements and making notes on the back area of the first floor. By the end of the afternoon, Joel and Ethan were alone and closing up shop for the week. The rest of the crew had taken off. Everyone wanted out on time on Fridays.

Joel rolled the blueprint into a tight tube and snapped a rubber band around it, twice. "So, you think you're going to make any money on this job?"

"I'd better. I don't want to have to make another trip to the loan officer with my hat in my hand," Ethan answered.

"What time's the game tomorrow?" Joel slipped the blueprints under his arm. "Be fun to see Chase play."

"Two o'clock," Ethan replied. "But you don't have to go. I mean, you must have better things to do on a Saturday afternoon."

"You don't know my life. The Little League Junior Championship Series is a big deal in comparison to the rest of my mundane existence."

They both laughed.

"So you taking Chase out for a spaghetti dinner tonight? Stacking some carbs for the first round of the playoffs?"

Ethan didn't answer right away. "No ... he's spending the night with a friend."

"Oh."

"I ... have a date tonight."

Ethan was not certain why he'd said that, why he felt a near compulsion to admit this fact to someone. He was surprised, and the words felt odd as he formed each one.

If Joel was surprised, he tried his best not to show it. "Oh?" he answered calmly. "With who? Do I know her?"

"Cameron Dane. The reporter from the newspaper. The one who did that story on the house. We're having dinner at Moore's."

Joel nodded.

"You look surprised."

"No," Joel replied. "I'm not ..."

But it was clear that he was trying to find the words to describe his response—somewhere between surprised and more surprised. He ran his hand through his hair. It looked as if he were about to speak, then changed his mind. He tightened his lips into a fine line. "Oh, what the ... yes, I am surprised."

He took a deep breath and continued. "I thought you would never go out on a date. No one did, I bet. I lost count of the number of times people tried to set you up. Your sister, Carol—does she know?"

Ethan shook his head. He felt sheepish.

Joel continued. "You've never taken anyone out. Never. I bet all your friends and relatives have given up trying by now. What's it been ... six years?"

"Seven."

"Long enough. Long enough for sure."

"You think so? I mean ... I look at Chase and he doesn't say a word, but it's like I'm doing something horrible. I know that's what he thinks."

Joel settled against the doorframe and the wood creaked comfortably. "It has been long enough. And Chase ... well, he's only a kid. He doesn't understand. You need to consider yourself. You're still a young man ...

sort of," Joel said with a smile. "You should have been doing this a long time ago."

Ethan stared at his hands. "I never felt like it, really. Until now. And even now ... well, I'm still not sure how I feel. I guess it feels okay. But it also feels plain weird. And then ... well, I sort of feel guilty ... like I'm cheating on my wife or something. And then there's Chase. It's just all so complicated."

A moment of silence passed. Ethan realized with a start that he had shared more personal information with his assistant than he had with any other living person—except Lynne.

Joel looked almost uncomfortable having heard the confession. He coughed and cleared his throat, happy to make some sound, other than talking. "She's younger than you, isn't she?"

"Some. A few years. Think it's a problem?"

"I don't know. Maybe. I stopped worrying about all those complications when I got married. I don't envy your position."

"Tell me about it," Ethan replied. "I feel so awkward. But she's nice. She's easy to talk to."

"And easy to look at. Has Chase met her?"

"He knows who she is. He saw her at the ball field. But he hasn't met her."

Joel nodded. "He probably should, don't you think?"

Ethan shrugged. "I don't know. It's only a date. And I can't talk to him anymore without us fighting about something. Doesn't matter what we talk about."

"He's a teenager. We were all like that. Obnoxious most of the time. He's a good kid. He'll come around."

They walked to the front door. Ethan closed it behind them and fastened the lock.

"So is she going to be at the game as well?"

"Don't know. Haven't asked her. Might be too soon."

"Well, if you're going to ask her, do it now. I think women like to be asked earlier rather than at the last minute. Especially to a semifinal game."

"They do?"

"All I know is my wife gets testy if I spring a dinner invitation without at least a few days' notice."

"Well … I don't know. Maybe she'll have to go to do a story on the game. Maybe she's been planning to come all along. You think?"

Joel smiled. "I wouldn't worry about it. Have a good time at dinner tonight. And maybe I'll see you tomorrow."

Elliot and Chase stood on the porch, recounting their escape before heading to the Willis house. Elliot's mother had launched into a cleaning frenzy, and the two of them had slipped out the front door before she tried to involve them in her whirlwind of activity. She was on her hands and knees in the living room of their large old house, spraying and wiping baseboards and muttering. Her hair was tied with a ribbon knotted at the top of her head.

"She's getting weirder," Elliot said softly as they crept off the porch and onto the sidewalk.

"Don't be so hard on her," Chase answered. "She's not that bad. Just once in a while."

Elliot snorted. "You're only at my house once in a while. She's like that most of the time. I think that's why my dad works so much overtime."

The two walked in silence for a block.

"You ready for the game tomorrow?" Elliot asked. "First game of the playoffs and all that."

"I dunno. I mean, what should we be doing? We just play baseball."

"Well, like before the Super Bowl, the teams always do something different to get ready. Like special exercises or something."

"Nah. If you're good at baseball—well, you're just good at it," Chase explained. "There's not a lot more you can do. If you got it, you got it."

Elliot sighed. "So I'll never make the big leagues?"

Chase punched him on the shoulder in a friendly way. "You're okay. You're better at other stuff. Baseball just isn't your best game."

"Yeah. I guess. I'm pretty good at football."

"Better than me."

"'Cuz I'm bigger."

"And not quite as bright."

Elliot snorted a laugh and returned the punch to Chase's shoulder, but a little harder than Chase thought appropriate.

They walked through the neighborhood in the direction of the river.

"My mom said your dad had dinner with that lady reporter."

"How did your mom know that?"

"Hey, she knows everything. Or she has friends that do, I guess. Nothing much ever happens in this town—and what does, she knows about. That's what my dad always says."

Chase looked at his shoes. "Well, he didn't bring her home or anything. It's not like they're hanging out all the time."

"My mom says she's a looker, all right. She saw her at the Piggly Wiggly. Says she was buying a cart full of frozen dinners. Says she probably doesn't know how to cook or anything. She says the pretty ones never do. She says they get to coast through life. Do you think she's pretty?"

Chase shrugged. He wished Elliot would stop talking about this woman and his father so he could forget all the mind-numbing complexities those thoughts brought with them. He wished all of this other-woman stuff would simply disappear. Right now, Chase felt that his father was both happy and sad at the same time.

It was weird, he thought, for a grown-up not to have life all figured out.

That uncertainty troubled Chase more than any other new reality— a reality that included women and dates and his father, although Chase would have had trouble placing those nervous feelings into words.

Elliot kicked an acorn with the toe of his worn sneaker. The acorn bounced off the windshield of a Toyota minivan across the street.

"I mean, is it weird or what to have your dad go out on a date? You gonna set a curfew for him or something?"

Chase's grin had an edge to it. He then went blank. "I dunno. I ... you know, I don't think I want to talk about this anymore."

Elliot stopped. "Why? It's not like your mom is still alive or anything. It's been a long time since she died."

"Hey, Elliot—just leave my mom out of this, okay?" Chase snapped back and continued to walk toward the river, faster, not seeing if Elliot was following or not.

"Wait up, Chase! I didn't mean anything by it. Honest!"

Elliot caught up to Chase as he stood by the riverbank, pitching pebbles into the placid water. He picked up a tree limb, pitched it upriver, and began to toss rocks at it. It was a familiar pastime for them. Three more sticks followed.

"My arm hurts," Elliot said.

"That's why you stink at baseball," Chase said with some cheer. "You don't practice."

"I just don't like baseball all that much," Elliot answered. "The games take too long. A lot of standing around in the hot sun."

He sat on a rock and began to skip small stones in the water.

Chase stood staring out across the river. The far side was a blanket of trees—dark, green, and mysterious. A strip of land lay beneath a jagged bluff, protected from development by a sheer wall of rock. Occasionally at night there would be the ghost of fires dancing among the dense foliage. Most people assumed them to be teenagers with an illegal six-pack or two. Chase imagined the fires set by runaways drifting down the river, escaping from their tormentors.

Chase turned to Elliot. "What would you say if your dad was going out with some other lady?"

Elliot laughed. "Before or after my mother killed him?"

Chase threw his last rock at Elliot's feet. It splashed water on his calf. "I'm serious. You know what I mean. If your mom wasn't around anymore."

Elliot flicked another pebble into the water, making a *splunking* sound. "I don't know. It would be weird. Real weird. But not having a mom is weird. If the person was nice, it might be different. I don't know."

Chase sat back in the grass. "He seems sad sometimes. Or worried. Then he gets mad. He gets mad a lot."

"Your dad? I've never seen him mad," Elliot replied.

"You don't live with him. He does. And I think he's lonely ... and it's all my fault."

"It ain't your fault. Isn't your fault. You were just a kid. It just happened. Just like you told me. It wasn't your fault."

Chase's lower lip trembled, and he turned away from his friend. Then he drew his forearm under his nose, sniffed loudly, stood up, and put his hands on his hips. He took a deep breath. "You want to go to Cumming's for ice cream? I can treat."

Elliot almost fell into the water scrambling up the bank.

On Friday afternoons, the newsroom of *The Derrick*, even during the languid days of summer, seemed to hum a little louder. Not that a dozen employees could truly be bustling, but it was payday, the county fair started on Sunday, and Cameron always noticed a certain higher pitch at the end of the week.

She had finished up her two stories of the day—one on the 125th anniversary of the town's cornet band scheduled for the following day and the other on the rising and falling fortunes of the county's farm-implement dealers. Neither of them were prize winners, but Cameron took some pride in the solid writing both required.

Some reporters go weeks without a byline, she told herself.

She straightened up her desk, then looked up at the corner office. Paige was alone. Cameron tapped at the doorframe and took a half-step inside the editor's office.

"Hey, come on in," Paige called out. "You must have been busy. I haven't seen much of you all week."

Cameron gave her a thumbnail of the farm-implement story, then she and Paige had fun handicapping the Miss Venango County Fair contestants. The odds-on favorite to win was Brittany Gardner, a blonde cheerleader from Franklin High School whose talent was belting out show tunes from Broadway musicals. At sixteen years of age, she looked to be around twenty-four—in all judging categories.

"Big plans for the weekend?" Paige asked as she leaned back in her chair. It groaned as if unaccustomed to the angle.

Cameron stepped farther inside the office, hesitated a minute, then sat down. "He called."

"Who? Who called?"

"Ethan. Ethan Willis. On Wednesday night."

"He did?"

"He asked me to dinner tonight."

Paige arched her eyebrows. "Oh. This is a new development, isn't it?"

"I guess. I … I sort of thought he would call. No, I knew he would. You can just tell that, right? After our dinner I took it for granted that he would call me. I knew he would take a week or two to decide, but I knew he would call. I can't explain why exactly."

Paige waited. "You don't seem too excited."

"I don't know. I was. I am. I still am. He's a nice guy."

Paige coughed. "Just a nice guy?"

"No. He's a really nice guy. I mean … I don't know what I mean."

Cameron knotted her hands together as Paige shuffled a stack of papers from one corner of the desk to another.

"Is it the age thing?" Paige asked quietly. "Or the damaged thing? Or something else all together?"

Cameron glared, but only a little. "No. It's not the age thing. He's a very interesting person and we seem to get along well. He's easy to talk to. He laughs easily. I like that. He treats me like I'm a lady. You know how rare that is? If I'd asked any other man in town out, they would have thought I was asking for something—and most likely been all too eager to give it to me."

Paige appeared surprised.

"Pardon my bluntness, Paige. But you know what I mean."

Paige held a laugh. "It has been a long time, but I know what you mean."

Cameron sighed. Her shoulders hunched down.

"So why aren't you excited?"

"I don't know. I guess I keep thinking about what you said."

"*Moi?*" Paige held her hand to her chest.

"The damaged part. I keep thinking about it. I'm waiting to find something bad, I guess. Something nobody can fix."

And my damage. The thought came to Cameron's mind, and she quickly shushed it away.

Paige stood up, came around to the front of her desk, and rested against it. "Cameron, you only went out once officially. Don't put the cart before the horse—or whatever old cliché fits here. It may come to nothing."

Both women sighed, almost simultaneously.

"But what do I know about waiting?" Paige continued. "I married my first husband two weeks after we met. We both knew what we wanted."

"He's not going to ask me to marry him," Cameron said in a tone that indicated she hoped he might just do that, eventually. "But I like him. I really do."

Paige sat down next to Cameron on the other battered leather chair in the office. "I remember what I said about the differences between the two of you. But … this is only your second date."

"Paige, he was married when he was in college. She was his girlfriend since grade school, I bet," Cameron said, her hands in the air, trying to explain.

"But that was a long time ago, Cam."

"His wife was the only woman he ever seriously dated. He told me that. He said he was never one to sow wild oats."

Paige waited. "So …?"

"Paige, I have dated lots of guys. Life in the big city. This is, like, the twenty-first century and all. Dating is a little bit different now."

Paige wrinkled her forehead. "Oh," she said, finally realizing what Cameron meant.

"His wife dies tragically. He stops seeing women. All women, I guess. Like he's still married. Like he's still being faithful to her … to the past. I mean … does he have any space for someone else in his life? Especially for someone who is not that sort of faithful, if you know what I mean? I know … I know. I'm getting all worked up before I have to be worked

up. You said that nothing might happen between the two of us. I know.
But what if it does? What if I want something to happen? Can it? Is he
too damaged, like you said? Or what's harder—am I too damaged or …
tarnished … for him?"

Paige took Cameron's hand in her own.

"Listen," she said almost at a whisper, "I'm not sure if you believe in
this or not—but you need to have faith. With God … well, with God,
anything damaged can be fixed. Second chances, clean slates … it's all possible. You just have to have faith."

"I have faith," Cameron said, as much to convince herself as Paige.
"I've been to church and Sunday school. I know that God has powers."

Paige obviously wanted to say more, but she remained silent.
Finally, she said, "Then just trust Him and have faith. Faith that if
Ethan is ready, you'll know. And faith that God will guide you. And
when you're ready, you'll know that, too."

But maybe there are some things that even God can't fix, Cameron
thought.

Ethan was sitting in his truck outside the Carter place when his cell phone
warbled. "Willis here."

"It's CeCe, Ethan." He held the phone away from his ear. CeCe's conversations could be on the loud side—and this perspective from a man
who made his living hammering nails and sawing wood.

"I meant to ask you about the bay window on the second floor, on the
north side of the house—the one that will be in the largest guest bedroom.
The window I don't like."

Ethan had planned on bringing the subject up with Michelle King,
the architect, but he must have been preoccupied that day.

"Yes, that bay window … we opened it up yesterday. Took off all the
trim and dismantled some of the support. It's not good news."

"Not good?"

"Well, no. We might not be able to save it."

"What?" CeCe said with a laugh. "You mean there's something you don't want to save? That sounds like good news to me."

Ethan took the good-natured ribbing in stride. He and Mrs. Moretti battled over the same sort of issues every day—restoration versus renovation.

"The supporting wood is just about gone," he said. "Bay windows are really notorious for hiding wood rot. Their little roofs are nearly impossible to keep waterproof. Over the years the wall and the window separate, and water gets into the wood. This has been going on for years. Joel was surprised that the windows hadn't simply fallen out of the frames years ago."

"So we can get rid of that ugly thing?" CeCe asked.

"But we could rebuild the walls around the window so it's exactly as it was," Ethan replied.

"Can we put a flat window there instead? That bay looked out of place up there on the second floor."

Ethan wanted to sigh in resignation. She had fought for a change in that spot since the beginning of the project. It pained him to agree.

"I'm sure we could restore it. You want to think about it?"

"No. A flat window. That's what I really want," she answered.

"Do you want Michelle to draw up new plans?"

He could almost see her, shaking her head so hard that her hair covered her face.

"No. I trust you. Match it exactly to the other second-floor windows. Does that sound reasonable?"

Ethan really wanted to bring the window back—exactly as it had been designed over a century ago, but he realized that it might involve more expense and aggravation than anyone wanted.

"It sounds reasonable," Ethan said. "I guess sometimes things need to be replaced."

"Not restored, right?"

"Right," he replied, not entirely sure if he meant it or not.

Forgiving is one way
of becoming the person
you were created to be—
and fulfilling God's dream of you
is the only way to true wholeness and happiness.

—Carol Luebering

CHAPTER EIGHT

CAMERON SPENT MOST OF her time at home in her turret room, as she called it. She remembered how as a little girl she dreamed she was in the tower of some ancient castle—a room like this—with a handsome knight in the courtyard and a dragon in the distance.

This particular afternoon she sat in that space, with a pillow clutched to her chest, staring at the street below. Because of the maze of one-way avenues in town, the only practical route to her door was to head south along West Park Street and turn into the alley just south of the Franklin Club.

Cameron had arrived home around five, showered and dressed, and by five thirty, had begun her vigil. Ethan said he would be there at six thirty. She could not recall any time that she had been ready for a date a full hour before the appointed time.

She looked at her watch for the twentieth time in the last few minutes. With every sweep of the minute hand, she felt a new ripple of nervousness. It was not altogether unpleasant nervousness, she thought, but it was altogether unexpected. She was a strong, modern woman—too much a grown-up to be nervous over a silly little date, wasn't she?

Cameron had been out on scores of dates. She had been in several relationships, and had felt all the things lovers feel, she imagined. But there was something about how she felt now that was different from how she remembered feeling with the others …

She tried watching television, but it was filled with aimless electronic chatter that did not come close to holding her attention. She popped a CD into the player on low volume instead.

Looking back on those other relationships, she realized now that from them she'd come to believe love could never be more than an unstable, shifting, fluid thing. She didn't want to believe that now, and this was an unexpected hope she didn't think she was able to trust.

Could things be different with Ethan?

Pushing that thought away, she sighed loudly, drew her knees up to her chest, and resumed staring at the southbound cars on West Park Street.

He had told her it would be a casual dinner, that he would take her to a comfortable place. The night before she had torn through every garment she owned, attempting to find something casual and comfortable.

Immediately she dismissed the notion of wearing sweats—even her fancy, go-to-the-club-but-don't-sweat-in sweats—as being much too casual. She saw her favorite silk blouse and tailored slacks as too precise and sophisticated. She decided against wearing jeans, thinking that might be too casual as well, then reconsidered when she found out she disliked everything else in her closet.

She chose a pair of new jeans that fit just right and coupled them with a tailored white linen blouse with shell buttons, freshly starched, with dressier black shoes and a classic leather belt. She tried a silk print scarf around her neck, then tossed it back into her closet, thinking that it made her appear either affected or presumptuous, or possibly both, and chose a simple gold chain instead.

She hoped her current outfit appeared more comfortable than she felt inside.

She checked her watch for the hundredth time. Then she looked at the street once more and saw a familiar pickup. It slowed, and she saw the flash of the blinker. She waited until it made the turn into the alley, then jumped off the window seat and ran to the long mirror behind her bedroom door for one last look, front and back.

"If I'm not together now, I never will be," she said, tossing her hair a few times. She turned to the side and cocked her head—first to the right, then the left.

She heard the buzzer. Her heart tightened one last time.

"I wonder if he's as nervous as I am," she said to herself as she grabbed her purse and opened the door at the top of the stairs. "I bet he isn't."

Ethan took a huge gulp of air, shut his eyes tight, and tried to remember what it was like not to have what felt like a sock wedged below his throat, just above his heart.

Work happened today, but Ethan was only marginally aware of what had gone on. He recognized after his first cup of coffee that he should stay away from anything complex, anything requiring deep and thoughtful analysis. He thought he should stay away from power tools as well.

Instead, he spent the day hauling up lumber to each floor, carrying boxes of nails, erecting some scaffolding around the fireplace—anything that could be done in a mindless sort of daze.

He had been surprised that Joel had reacted with such calm to his revelation about asking Cameron out on a date. Ethan carried an image of Lynne with him almost all the time, and he imagined other people did the same.

But it was clear Joel did not.

Perhaps no one did ... save Ethan and his son.

Now that image, that closely held vision, was going to be compromised—or diluted in some way—with the flesh-and-blood image of another woman.

A *young* other woman, who was so unlike his wife that it made it hard to hold her image and the image of his wife in his thoughts at the same time. Would he be able to accommodate both? Would that precious image of Lynne be further diminished after tonight?

Can I do this? Should I do this? Is all of this too late … or too soon? Have too many, or not enough, years passed?

He was not sure which image he would discard and which he would need to keep. Even the thought of having to make that choice some time off in the future was disconcerting and disorienting, like being in a familiar forest at dusk with no map or compass—only the setting sun to light your path.

All of that rushed past his thoughts as he rang the bell. He had seen Cameron's silhouette in the turret windows as he'd turned in the drive. He was certain she had seen him in her street. It was too late to make any escape.

And he didn't want to, really. He simply wanted the confusion to be gone … for that leaden feeling to vanish.

He pressed the doorbell button and sucked in another deep breath of air. He held it a few seconds, then exhaled noisily, like the pitcher on the mound facing a 3-2 count with a home-run hitter in the batter's box.

He adjusted the collar of his shirt.

Silence.

Do I press it again? Is she nervous? That can't be. Not her.

From two stories up he heard the unlatching of a door, then the creak of footfalls on a ninety-year-old staircase. He saw her shoes before he saw her.

Jeans. That's a good sign, he thought.

And then he exhaled again.

Cameron remembered little about the short drive to Oil City. Ethan said something about a nice place overlooking the river, and then her mind had gone blank. She was pretty sure she'd spoken some, because she recalled Ethan laughing a few times.

Unless he was laughing at me not talking?

No, she remembered speaking a few words at least. She remembered that she really liked the sound of his laugh … deep and silvery.

"I hope you like this place," Ethan said as he exited the car. Cameron forced herself to wait. He was that sort of man. Normally, she would have simply bounded out her side, ready to investigate. She waited, and he opened the door, his smile knowing—at least that's how she interpreted the gentle wrinkling around his lips. The phrase *wry grin* came to mind, and even though it didn't fit exactly, it was as close as she could come to describing him.

Wry grin ... and *gorgeous*—but she quickly pushed that thought away. It was much too early to be deciding on gorgeous. *Maybe fine-looking.* She chided herself. *And soon you'll be practicing writing your name with his last name on the front of your social studies notebook to see how it looks, I bet.*

"Moore's. It's been here forever. Almost forever."

Cameron nodded.

Moore's was housed in an imposing old stick-style Victorian, painted the lightest gray with dark brown trim—*the color of rich velvet,* Cameron thought. It stood at the southern edge of Oil City, with the river at its back. Its rather austere style, unusual for the Victorian era, imitated the architecture of the medieval past, with decorative half-timbering, brackets, rafters, and braces. Trim boards called *stickwork* marched around the entire facade, and three thick brick fireplace stacks towered above the dormers protruding from the roof.

"They repainted it last year, back to the original shades, they said. It used to be sort of a purple. I never liked the color. Maybe it would have been fine for a private home—one of the Painted Ladies perhaps," Ethan said, "but that color just didn't work as a restaurant color."

Cameron nodded again. She had never once thought of any color as a "restaurant" color. Well, maybe McDonald's red and yellow, but that was it.

The interior couldn't have had a more different mood than the exterior. Warm and inviting, done in pleasantly understated tones, sleek furnishings, soft lights, and subtly patterned Wilton carpeting did not add up to any restaurant Cameron had visited in the area. Quiet live music came from somewhere. She glanced around and saw a male pianist at a gleaming ebony baby grand tucked into a far corner.

"You said this was casual," Cameron protested as Ethan pulled the cushy upholstered chair out for her at the table. "This is not casual. This is … well, this is fancy—white tablecloths and all."

Ethan gave her that smile again—a genuine smile coupled with something else altogether. "I know. I lied. Sort of."

She tried her best to glare at him, hoping the glare would be received with good humor—the way she intended it.

He opened his palms to her. "If I said it was fancy, we would have had to dress up. I don't like dressing up. And you would have worried about what to wear. Then you may even have asked me what sort of 'dressy' it was. How could I have answered that?"

An elegant waiter appeared at the table and handed them each a very fat leather-covered menu.

"Wine? A before-dinner drink, perhaps?" he asked.

Cameron would have felt at ease ordering something "adult," but had decided well before tonight to follow Ethan's lead. She wasn't sure why, but she felt it might be important to him.

The waiter, of course, turned to her first.

She was flustered but tried not to show it. "I don't know … Ethan, what are you having?"

If he was unsettled about ordering before her, he didn't show it. "Just a club soda. With lime. That's elegant enough."

Cameron felt off balance, still unsure of his humor. "Me, too," she added, and the waiter glided off.

Ethan returned to their original conversation. "You see, to me, there's work clothes—that's jeans and T-shirts. Then there's business attire—like asking for a loan at the bank. That's a sport coat, hopefully without a tie. Then there are weddings and funerals. That's my one dark suit, tie, white shirt, and uncomfortable shoes."

He looked right in her eyes. "So what sort of fancy is this place, Cameron from the big city? Business fancy or weddings and funerals fancy?"

Cameron immediately forgave him for not telling her. As she glanced around the room, she noticed a substantial number of older patrons. Many of them looked just like her parents—tanned, leathery, and wealthier than they let on. There were more than a few pastel-colored cotton sweaters draped over shoulders.

"This place is country-club casual," she concluded. "My parents cruise a lot, and they often require 'country-club casual.' Sometimes it's called 'business casual,' but this is a little more comfortable and stylish than that."

Ethan took a sip from his club soda, which had just arrived. "If this is country-club anything, then I would have been lost in trying to explain that. But I think you look perfect here. I mean ... what you're wearing is ... you know—perfect for this place."

How sweet, she thought. A compliment, no matter how awkward, was still a compliment.

She moved her hand toward his, without thinking. Then she stopped. She saw him watching. And then, deftly, he picked up the breadbasket and handed it to her.

"Would you like some bread?" he asked. "I hear it's baked here on the premises."

She had to take one, even though she had promised herself she wouldn't overdo the carbs—no matter how tempting.

She had two more slices of the delicious homemade bread before the waiter descended again with their salads.

Chase ran down the steps. No one knocked quite like Elliot. If the doorjamb could be broken or dislodged by knocking, Elliot would be the one to do it. The house rumbled, more or less, when he announced himself.

"Hey."

Elliot thought for a moment, then replied, "Hey."

He lumbered in, careful not to catch his sleeves on the door or the banister.

"Hungry?" Chase asked.

"I just ate. But I could eat. If you're going to have something. To keep you company."

"I got a frozen pizza."

"Sure."

Chase opened the door to the freezer. "I have sausage or pepperoni."

Elliot's forehead tightened. "I like 'em both. They're not that big. They're the kind my mom gets three for ten dollars at the warehouse club. Two of 'em fit on one rack in the oven."

Chase switched the oven on. "Just as long as you promise to share, okay?"

"Sure," Elliot replied, switching on the television. Without the drone of some electronic device, the room grew too quiet for either of the boys.

"So where's Mrs. Whiting? Isn't she supposed to be here?" he asked.

"She called and said her husband wasn't feeling good. She said he's been having a bad couple of days. My dad said I would be fine alone."

"Where's your dad?" Elliot asked, looking around, as if he expected Chase's father to suddenly materialize.

Chase hesitated. "He's ... well, he's on that date."

Elliot tilted his head, not unlike a dog that hears a high-pitched whistle. "Oh, yeah, that date. With that girl?"

Chase didn't smile. "I guess. That reporter lady."

Elliot looked at his fingernails. "You think they're, like, dating now?"

"No. This is only their second time."

Elliot leaned over to grab the remote control, which was farther away from him than the actual TV. He thumbed through the channels until he hit ESPN. "That's weird. Your dad out on a date."

"I know," Chase replied, then opened the refrigerator and removed three bottles of Orange Crush. One would be more than enough for him. The other two were just as necessary—especially if Elliot and a pizza were involved. Or two pizzas.

"I can't believe I've never heard of this place," Cameron said as she scooped the last of her mango-tangerine crème brûlée into her mouth. "Everything was just delicious."

Ethan looked pleased. "I'm glad you liked it. I don't come here all that much these days. Chase doesn't quite get the charm of the place. He says that looking at the river is no fun unless you can skip stones on it. I don't think they would encourage that here."

The setting sun lit the waters of Oil Creek to crimson, the ripples sparkling. At this point, the creek was as much a river as the Allegheny River it emptied into a few hundred yards to the south.

Ethan spoke again. "Did you feel at all out of place here during dinner? Neither of us is wearing true 'country-club casual.'"

Cameron's voice echoed her contentment—a wonderful meal and pleasant, comfortable conversation. "I have seldom felt more at home, if you want to know the truth. I have always ... I don't know ... felt a half-step out of pace with everyone else. Even in school. I got good grades and had a lot of friends, but I never felt I understood any of them—or any of them really understood me. Like we were all on different wavelengths or something."

Ethan's expression did not change, not really. But Cameron still wondered if she had shared too much.

"It's the food," she continued. "All this food has made me light-headed."

Ethan's wry grin reassured her without him having to resort to clumsy words.

Somehow Cameron found herself outside, with Ethan gently shepherding her toward his truck.

"It's still pretty early. Would you like to go for a drive or something?" he asked.

Cameron willed herself to wait a moment until she answered and willed herself not to sound too enthusiastic, even though she felt as close to giddy as she had ever felt since moving to Franklin.

"Uhh ... sure," she said, hoping her words didn't reveal more than she wanted to convey.

"Only if it's okay … maybe you have to get up early tomorrow or something."

She jumped in too fast—she knew it was too fast—but she jumped anyway. "No. It's okay. Really. I just have to run over to the newsroom in the afternoon. I could stay out all night. I mean … I could. But it's okay to go for a drive. Digest the food and all that."

She mentally kicked herself. *Who talks about being able to stay out all night and—worse—digesting food on a date … except old people who have a problem with it? Now he probably thinks I have stomach problems or gas or something. Good grief.*

Ethan drove more carefully than Cameron did. He aimed the truck north. The sign read TITUSVILLE—15 MILES.

He rolled down his window, and she did the same. The air was warm, almost humid. They passed a few farms, houses nestled up close to the two-lane blacktop, and gradually, the trees crept closer to the roadway. The late sunlight flicked through the canopy of leaves.

"Ever been to Titusville?" Ethan asked, breaking a long, comfortable silence.

She shook her head. "No. Isn't that terrible? I've never been there."

Ethan nodded. "Do you know why the town is famous?"

Cameron was caught. "Well … no. Except that everybody says I should go there. Oh, wait! It's the oil well, right? Something about an oil well."

"The first oil well. 1859. Edwin L. Drake. The birthplace of the American petroleum industry."

"Yes," Cameron chimed in, "that's it. That place." She tried to read his smile. "Are we going there?"

"No. Every school kid within a hundred miles seems to go there at least once a year on a field trip. I've seen it often enough, thank you. If you're interested, though …"

Turning in her seat to face him—to at least see his profile—Cameron tried to read his face. She could see the tiny wrinkles at the edges of his eyes. They looked deeper now, as if he were enjoying this.

"No," she said. "Unless you really want to experience the history of petroleum again." She paused, then asked, "Do you?"

Now he smiled. "No. But let's take a drive. We'll take the scenic route. I want to show you one of my favorite places. It's pretty close, and it's not that late. But it's not exactly a tourist stop."

She settled back against the seat, happy to be riding with him, happy to feel the vibration of his truck, happy to be driven. He drove north for a while, cut west on a side road, then headed back south. The truck slowed. Cameron looked and saw nothing but greenery on both sides of the road.

"It's a little hidden," he said as he steered his truck into a thin mesh of greenery.

"A little hidden? Is this where I should start getting scared?"

"No," he said quickly. "It's not like that. It's just ... well, you'll see."

In another moment they came to the crest of a small hill and the road opened up onto a pocket version of a picture-postcard sunset.

"That's Oil Creek down there. We're only a mile or so from the river," Ethan explained as he slowed the truck, pulling off onto a grassy patch. "It used to run with oil—at least that's what the guides at the Drake Well say. It's better now."

He shut off the engine and opened his door. She waited again until he came around and opened hers.

"It's just over there," he said. She followed him as he walked a few yards to the right. They stood on a little hillock, whose one side was draped with a weeping willow. Before them was the meandering Oil Creek, snaking back and forth in the perfect but petite valley. Grass, calf-high, grew lush and full, pocked with stands of extravagant day lilies in orange and red and yellow, all catching the last glints of the setting sun, looking as if they were illuminated from within by some magical light source.

"I hoped the sun would still be up," Ethan said softly. He held out his hand.

She wondered, in that split second, what to do next.

She took his hand, and he helped her down a steep ledge.

"I didn't want you to fall."

She was sure he held her hand for at least a few seconds longer than necessary, but she liked that comforting feeling.

"Over there. That's what makes this place so ... different. Beautiful and unsettling at the same time."

On the other side of the creek, perhaps seventy-five yards away, nearly hidden by lush foliage, stood an old house. Maybe it was a mansion.

"Wow!" she exclaimed. "I'd never have seen it, or expected to see it. It's like it was hidden and then it wasn't."

"I know," Ethan said. "You can look right at it and not completely distinguish it. Like one of those trick drawings ... an optical illusion sort of thing."

The structure loomed in the growing darkness of the woods. Three stories hulked in the shadows, and an enormous turret rose at the far end. It must have been painted white at some recent time, but the boards had weathered to a milky yellow. A deep porch leaned against the front of the structure. The tall windows appeared opaque, like shiny obsidian.

"Does ... does anyone live there?" Cameron asked, surprised that her voice had suddenly grown small.

"No. They haven't for nearly a decade. The last person—the grand-daughter of the original owner—moved to a nursing home. She may still be alive, but I haven't checked recently."

"Have you ever been inside? It looks huge."

Ethan nodded slightly. "Once. The interior is amazing. I tried to buy it ... several years ago ... when my wife ... but the woman's grandson thought my offer was ridiculously low. He took it off the market after that, and it's been empty since then. And slowly crumbling, I'm afraid."

"You really wanted to live there?" Cameron asked. "It looks kind of ... spooky."

"It does now. But imagine the grounds cleared out around it and the house restored and repainted. See how it sits there, looking out over this wonderful scene ... like a painting." He lowered his voice. "And look over there, at the far edge of the meadow."

A deer stepped into the lowering sunlight, tentative step followed by tentative step, ears switching, almost swiveling to catch hints of danger. A few yards behind followed a smaller deer, most likely her fawn from the spring.

"This would be at your doorstep," Ethan whispered. "And the sound of the creek and the scent of grass and the lilies. It would be so perfect."

Cameron would have asked why he didn't try to buy it again, then realized why he hadn't. She wanted to tell him it was magical, but an image fluttered into her thoughts ... an image of a woman, now dead, and her hold over this man. At least Cameron imagined she had some sort of hold on him. Was this the sort of damage Paige meant? The impossibility of Cameron breaking into a perfect memory—a ghost from the past?

"It's beautiful," she said without much conviction.

Whatever acting she had done, apparently it was enough for Ethan.

"I'm so glad you can appreciate this. I don't know many people that would. It's such an old house, so quiet and isolated. You know ... most people want something modern and right next to a mall or something."

Cameron smiled back at him. She did love vintage houses, and a peaceful setting, but she also liked knowing that she could run to a mall in a few minutes, rather than having to plan out a daylong excursion.

She turned her head ever so slightly, just enough to watch Ethan stare at the scene. She saw the earnestness in his eyes, the appreciation for nature and craftsmanship, the desire to see the past live again—and his realization that the past is gone.

What was ... is not now ... and never will be.

She began to retreat from being angry at the intrusion of the ghost of his wife into their evening, and then grew upset with herself that she had resented the disruption. She leaned a few inches closer to him. It seemed like a natural move to Cameron, but she thought she saw a twitch of tension in his jaw muscle. She decided she would let the proximity stay as it was—close enough to be noticed, but not close enough to make either of them uncomfortable.

They stood in silence for a long time, until the sun was completely hidden and the sky was almost completely red.

"We should go back. It gets dark fast in the woods."

Cameron thought that an odd statement. How much quicker could darkness come here than in a city? But when she turned around, the truck had all but disappeared. She blinked, thinking it must have been moved, or covered with brush somehow.

Ethan stepped forward and climbed the steep slope, then stopped and extended his hand down. She grasped it hurriedly, fearing being left behind in the growing darkness. He pulled gently but firmly and she scrambled up the slope, colliding with him at the very top, her feet sliding on the damp grass. He grabbed her around the waist, steadying her. His arm felt very secure and very powerful. She could feel the muscles in his upper arm tight against her shoulder.

"Are you okay?"

She nodded. After a long moment, he took her hand and led her through the darkness to his truck. She would have been lost had he not been there leading the way. He opened the door and kept hold of her hand as she boosted herself to the seat.

Neither of them spoke as he started the truck, turned around, and bounced back to the road. The truck rocked as it climbed onto the asphalt roadway, and she slid a few inches closer to him on the bench seat of the truck. She had read, in a dating-advice column when she was a teenager, that a girl should not sit against the door, nor against her date, but somewhere in the middle. She stole glances left and right and realized she was more like two-thirds of the way from the door and one-third closer to Ethan.

It was advice from a long time ago, she told herself and did not move as Ethan accelerated down the road back to Franklin.

Despite his earlier dinner, Elliot downed one full pepperoni pizza himself and another two slices from Chase's selection.

"Don't they feed you at home?" Chase said with a laugh.

"These hardly weigh anything," Elliot said, defending himself. Chase was pretty sure that Elliot considered weight to be the deciding factor in consumption choices. A full bag of potato chips was pretty much equal to two microwavable burritos—you could heft both of them in your hand and the weights would be close.

Chase leaned back in his chair—something his father continued to instruct him firmly never to do.

"See all those scrapes and gouges in the floor?" his father would rant. "It's all because you lean back in the chair like that when you watch TV."

It was a long-running battle. Chase figured the floor was already nicked and scarred, so why be so concerned about it?

"The house is already like a bazillion years old," he'd once said, thinking that his logic would defuse the situation.

"And that gives you the right to destroy it?" his father had replied sharply.

But his father was not here tonight, and Chase liked leaning back, balancing himself with a foot on the cabinet.

The ball game droned on, the sound turned down, barely audible. Chase professed to dislike the television announcers, preferring the radio team on KDKA instead. He bounced forward in his chair, then snapped off the TV.

"Hey!" Elliot said. "I was watching that."

"I know. That's why I did it. Just to aggravate you."

For a moment, Elliot appeared to believe him … then recognition of Chase's sarcasm dawned on his face.

"Let's go upstairs to the cave and listen to it on the radio."

"Sure," Elliot said, as he grabbed another Orange Crush out of the refrigerator.

Once inside the hidden room, Chase settled into a rescued and rickety folding chaise lounge. Elliot threw himself into a pair of mismatched beanbag chairs. The air hissed as it escaped from their vinyl coverings. Chase switched on the radio. It was twenty years old, with a lighted dial like a speedometer, and a real turning knob—no fancy digital tuning. The game came on, gently protesting with a ghost of static—a perfect sound for a still summer evening, hidden in a secret room.

———— ∞ ————

Ethan knew Cameron was sitting closer to him on the ride home than she had been when he picked her up. He knew that must mean something, but it had been so very long since he had attempted to interpret exactly what those subtle signals might imply.

Maybe she's just comfortable. I never sit on that side. Maybe the seat sort of sags that way, he thought.

He took pride in his safe driving but managed to steal a long glance or two in Cameron's direction as he drove. Night enveloped the truck, and the glow from the dashboard instruments offered a soft illumination. She sat with her hands folded in her lap, one on top of the other, and her legs crossed at the ankle. She almost caught him looking at her.

"You want a final coffee?"

His words seemed to startle her.

"Coffee? I—"

"There's a new Starbucks just over the bridge in Oil City. I know we had coffee at the restaurant, but if you want …"

He caught her eyes as they waited for a traffic light to change. He thought she might be hiding a hint of disappointment … about what, he had no idea.

Then she brightened. "Starbucks? Really? A small decaf latte would be great," she chirped.

For a moment, I thought he might be inviting me back to his place, Cameron thought. *But his son would be there. And this is sort of only a second date. Or a third date, sort of. But another coffee would be nice.*

She wanted to sidle up closer to him and put her head on his shoulder.

But she stayed where she was.

Elliot slowly slipped down to a nearly prone position in the formless chairs. He turned and smushed one beanbag behind him and put his legs on the small wooden chest under the eave.

"Hey," Chase called out. "Not on that. Get your feet off of that."

Elliot reacted quickly. "Okay. It's only my feet. I didn't, like, walk in from a swamp, you know."

Chase knelt by the chest and pulled it toward him. "It's just my private stuff in here. I don't want it getting dirty, that's all."

Elliot looked as if he was about to bark out a reply, but he didn't. His face softened, his lips moving away from their smile to something less than that. "I'm sorry. I know it's your private stuff."

Chase leaned back in the chaise. "It's okay."

Elliot sat up. Both boys knew that Elliot didn't consider himself as smart as Chase, or as adept at things. It didn't matter what things they were—Elliot was a quarter step behind. But his heart was different. Chase knew it. And so did Elliot. It was as if Elliot could see what hurt looked like and sounded like.

"I know it's got your mom's stuff in it," he said slowly, not looking at his friend but at the radio instead.

"What does?"

"That chest. It's got stuff in it from … you know … from before."

Chase had never showed it to anyone.

"How do you know that? I never showed it to you. And it's always closed."

Elliot looked at his feet. "I know. But nobody hides stuff like that, unless … unless it's real important … or if you have to keep it hidden. Some stuff you have to hide or it gets wrecked. I hide stuff sometimes. Sometimes you have to hide the past from the present. I don't know why. You just do."

Chase didn't reply.

Elliot looked up. He let a long, long moment pass before he spoke. "Man, Chase, it's not your fault. I keep telling you that. It's not your fault. You were just a little kid. Nobody thinks it's your fault."

Chase stared at Elliot, hearing how his friend had shared his heart, yet holding his lips almost tight, and with a tense jaw, hoping to hide his own feelings. "Yeah … well, maybe you're right."

But I know you're not.

"I love their lattes," Cameron cooed as she poured a packet of sweetener into the cup.

"I do too ... now, anyways," Ethan said as he sipped his. "If they could offer coffee like this at church, they would have no trouble filling up the pews."

Cameron nodded with a smile. "It's all in the marketing, right?"

"Let's walk over by the river," Ethan said.

Cameron followed him down the block to the park near the bridge. They sat on one of the benches. A few other families and couples ambled about. The warm night filled with stars and moonlight.

"You go to church, don't you, Ethan?"

Ethan turned to her, almost staring, carefully considering his answer. "No, I don't. Not much anyway. A few times a year. If Chase is in something. And holidays. That sort of thing. I make sure Chase goes. That's important. And he likes it."

Cameron didn't respond right away. He expected more questions, so he waited. Finally, he asked, "Do you? Do you go to church all the time?"

"Not all the time. I go—sometimes. My parents went fairly often. They brought me to church and Sunday school, and I went to youth group in high school. I have a very religious aunt who keeps asking me about it."

"Why do you ask?" Ethan said as evenly as he could.

She shrugged, then added, "Just curious. Getting to know you. That sort of thing."

Ethan wanted to say he hated being in church ever since ... the funeral. *Ever since they said those meaningless words over my wife.*

"Is it important to you now? I mean ... going to church and all that?"

Cameron tightened her lips. "I don't know. Maybe."

Just then a young boy shouted from the riverbank, his figure outlined in a circle of illumination from a streetlight. He was fishing with his father, his reel bent toward the water. Squealing, he reeled his catch in, laughing proudly. His father hovered just behind, ready to take the rod if his son faltered. The fish caught the streetlight like a jewel. The boy's father gently removed it, held it close for his son to examine, then carefully lowered it back into the water.

"Bye-bye, fishy," the young boy shouted, waving to the water.

Cameron and Ethan were quiet. As quiet as the darkness that settled about them.

Ethan moved slowly, transferred his latte to his right hand, and reached, with great deliberateness, taking her free hand in his. He held it like it was a fragile baby bird. He did not entwine his fingers, but cupped her fingers inside of his, nestling them together.

"This has been very nice, Cameron. I have really enjoyed myself tonight. You're nice to be with."

Is he going to try and kiss me? Would he do that so early on? No. He wouldn't. But would I let him if he did? I might. What do I do to be neutral? Move closer? Move away? Squeeze his hand?

He solved her dilemma by turning back to the river. She waited a few seconds, then offered a long, silent exhale, almost a sigh, a mixture of regret and relief—but mostly regret.

Cameron forced herself to wait again when they reached the parking lot of her apartment. Ethan hurried to her side of the truck and opened the door with a smile. She moved slowly as she slid down from the seat.

"Let me walk you to your door," Ethan said.

Cameron was going to say something about him being so chivalrous and gentlemanly—unlike most every other man she had ever dated—but realized in a hurry that her talking about her dates might be just like him talking about his wife. Then in another heartbeat she scolded herself for even thinking like that.

He's just a gentlemanly guy, she thought, *and I am not going to embarrass him for being a gentleman.*

She unlocked the door, pulled it open, stepped inside, and immediately turned to face him. She was one step higher than him, so their eyes were now on an almost even plane.

"I had a really good time," she said, having decided that there would be no invitations upstairs. She knew he would not accept and did not want that lingering discomfort of the possibility of misinterpreting intentions.

"So did I," Ethan quickly replied. "You're really easy to talk with. I like that. I like a woman who likes good food ... and good conversation."

"You, too," she answered, her hand still on the doorknob. She brushed at the hair on her forehead. "Well ..." she said, trying not to smile.

"Well ..." he replied.

A silent moment jutted between the words, and Cameron knew what he would do next. She just knew it, even as he hesitated, even as she knew he was dismissing logic and the past and any experience he might have had a few decades ago.

She knew it.

He leaned forward, just a little. He put his hand on her hip, just so gently. He leaned forward a bit more, tilted his head, perhaps more than he needed, and kissed her.

She tilted her head in apposition to his.

It was not just a peck, nor was it long. The duration was right in between those two.

A perfect finish to a perfect evening, she thought.

"Well ..." he said again as he leaned away. "Thanks."

He turned and stepped away, almost smiling, but recovering smoothly enough to most likely imagine that she hadn't noticed.

He turned back to her. Her hand was still on the doorknob.

"I'll call you."

She waited there, without moving, until he got into his truck, started the engine, and drove away. As she turned, she almost tripped. Then, almost stumbling up the steps, she caught herself on the handrail at the last minute ... and giggled more than she ever had since moving to Franklin.

———

"Are you guys still up?"

Elliot and Chase had heard the truck pull into the driveway and had scrambled out of the hidden room and tossed themselves into Chase's bedroom.

"West Coast game," Chase replied.

"Okay. Elliot—does your mom know you're here?"

Elliot nodded. "I'm sure she does. I mean ... sure. I told her. I think I did."

Ethan looked at his wristwatch. "You want me to give her a call for you? Let her know you're here and all that? It's not too late, is it?"

"No," he replied. "She never goes to bed until midnight. Thanks, Mr. Willis."

Chase stared hard at his father. He could see something different in him—something new, something unsettling.

But he wouldn't be the first to say anything.

Ethan looked back at his son, as if surprised by his intense stare. "What?"

Chase opened his mouth to say something, then didn't.

"Well, I'll call your mother, Elliot."

"Sure. That would be swell."

Chase kept staring.

"What?" Ethan asked again.

Chase didn't answer.

Yet he somehow knew that his father knew what the question was.

The church bell at St. Mark's rang twice. Ethan sat up in bed and folded his hands across his knees. He didn't bother with the light. The moon provided enough illumination. He wondered if the neighbors of the church would ever be successful in silencing the clock, which sounded at every hour. Despite a campaign a few years back, the congregation had stood firm and the city fathers had issued a stern no.

It was so unlike Ethan to be awake after midnight. Well, if he was being honest, it was unlike him to be awake after ten in the evening. And here it was, hours past midnight, and he remained wide awake and far, far from sleep.

He ran the images of the evening over and over in his head, wondering how Cameron viewed the same event. He wondered if he had erred in his restaurant selection, if he had erred in taking the ride up to Titusville, if he had erred in answering her questions about church the way he did. He was pretty sure he hadn't. She had never talked about church before that moment. Ethan knew there were women who were very committed to religion, and he was pretty certain the idea would have come up sooner—and that she would have reacted more strongly to his honest answer had she been one.

He wondered if she was just being polite.

He'd had a good time this evening. It was the first good adult-only time he had had in … well, in years. Not that time spent with Chase wasn't good, or that time spent with his extended family wasn't good. And he wasn't one to hang out with friends regularly.

He replayed the end of the evening again, when he had placed his hand on her hip and when he'd kissed her. He was pretty certain that she had kissed him back—not only politely, but as if she meant it—even if it was just a brief kiss.

He liked the feeling. It had been a long, long time since he'd felt this way.

As he tried to recall the touch of her skin against his own, that image from his past wavered into view. A thud of guilt grazed his chest. He imagined his wife. Then he saw Cameron's face, her closed eyes and lips, outlined in soft crimson.

He swung his feet out of the bed, as if the movement would change the view. It was not entirely successful. He stood up and peered out the window, up and down the street. All was quiet. He heard the gentle creaks and hum of the house.

As he recalled the scent of Cameron's perfume again, the guilt returned. He closed his eyes and his head dropped.

This is never going to work. This will never, ever work.

He sat down on the bed heavily, his shoulders slumped.

I can't do this to her. I just can't.

Cameron heard the church bell toll twice. She loved the sound—the deep rolling chime as it blanketed the downtown. The first time she'd heard it, she had smiled, certain that Franklin was going to be a wonderful town to live in.

She sat up in bed and watched the reflection of headlights from the street below on the wall. She folded her arms across her knees. She replayed the evening in her head again, wondering if she had done everything right. She remembered him laughing and smiling, and remembered the touch of his hand on her hip and how thrilled she was that he'd initiated the kiss. She wished, now, that it had lasted a little bit longer, but tried to resolve that she should not be greedy.

She wondered why she had asked him about church. Was it because of Paige's comment about God being able to restore a damaged person? Cameron wasn't a devout churchgoer. In fact, she had only been to church a couple of times since moving to Franklin, and usually after a conversation with her aunt—the religious one.

It was not a question she normally would have asked.

Other than that one blip—or sort of a blip—she considered the evening a success. He was funny and considerate and charming, the sort of person she would want to be with—always.

It was just so right. I'm sure he's going to call again. He will.

She felt again the hopefulness she had felt earlier. And then a fleeting image of the sea came to her mind.

The poor kid's gonna be living that nightmare forever.

She had moved to Franklin to be farther from the sea and farther from those memories.

It wasn't my fault.

And then she closed that door once again.

*Without forgiveness
life is governed by
an endless cycle
of resentment and retaliation.*

—ROBERTO ASSAGIOLI

*Forgivers ... reject the possibility
that the rest of their lives
will be determined by
the unjust and injurious acts
of another person.*

—GORDON DALBEY

CHAPTER NINE

ETHAN TOSSED THE BAG at Joel. "Think fast!"

Joel almost dropped his thermos but switched hands and caught the bag before it hit the floor. He didn't spill a drop of coffee in the process.

"I got you a couple of donuts. A reward for the first man on the job."

Joel dug into the bag with obvious pleasure. "Marcy won't let me stop at Donut Heaven anymore. She said that if she finds another greasy crumpled bag in the truck, she's going to make me join Weight Watchers with her."

"You're not fat," Ethan said, defending Joel against this outlandish accusation.

"It all depends on your definition, boss. Marcy's dictionary is much different than mine," he said as he munched into the chocolate-covered, custard-filled donut. "Do you think Donut Heaven will sell me donuts in plain paper bags?"

"You know, you could just throw the bags away before you get home. Try being neat for a change."

Joel responded, his mouth half full, "That's not the way of the contractor, Ethan. You should know that by now."

Ethan smiled, but painfully. It was a common complaint—carpenters and construction crews were pigs, people said—never cleaning up after themselves. Ethan defended the process to a point. "'Why clean a site when it will get dirty the next day?' my crew says. At the end of the project we'll get a high school kid cheap to pick up all the debris."

He did take exception to the pop cans and drink containers left littering the space, insisting that the crew keep the site relatively neat.

CeCe hated the clutter and debris left over at the end of the week. "Can't your crew sweep up once in a while?" she'd chide.

Ethan tried to explain that she would be paying a carpenter's wage for manual labor—not the best use of their time ... or her money.

CeCe said it didn't matter. She liked the site clean—regardless of the cost. "This will be my home, after all," she'd said.

Joel leaned against a stack of drywall and bit into his second forbidden treat. "Seeing your girlfriend again this weekend?"

Ethan could feel his eyes narrowing. Was Joel trying to get a rise out of him? Date a woman once, and the local observers would classify that event as a get-acquainted date. Dates two and three started to change that identification. And now that Ethan and Cameron had had six official dates, they were a "couple," at least in the eyes of most casual observers.

Ethan didn't consider his relationship with Cameron that way, but it was too early in the morning to argue.

"Yes, Cameron and I are going out again. She's a pleasant person. We laugh a lot."

Joel obviously wasn't compelled to investigate the situation any further since he simply nodded while he ate. Then he asked, "How's Mrs. Moretti?"

Ethan looked pained. This was a wonderful project, a project that would keep Ethan and his crew employed for months, a project that had the potential to put Willis Construction solidly in the black ... but that was not all of it.

"She's fine. She's happy so far. Or she was happy yesterday. Or at least happy at the end of yesterday."

Joel wiped his sleeve across his face. "Ethan, I know it's your job and your company and all that … but you should lighten up. If she wants a seven-foot-wide staircase, you shouldn't even say anything. You should just start cutting treads in seven-foot lengths. You're going to have a heart attack here if you and her argue about every detail in the place. There are a lot of details. And a lot of arguments to come, probably."

Ethan was shocked. Joel had always supported him in his preservation-not-degradation arguments. Or at least he had never contradicted him.

"But what she wants to do isn't the right thing," Ethan replied with early morning passion. "What she wants doesn't work. It doesn't look authentic. I can't keep my mouth shut when she ignores history. She should honor the past. I do. Deeply."

Joel drained the last of his coffee and screwed the lid back on his thermos. "The rest of the crew will be here in a minute. And it would serve no useful purpose if they hear us arguing about this. But they already are getting confused as to who to listen to—you or Mrs. Moretti. She's here a lot and she talks a lot, Ethan. She tells everyone what she wants. She brings food with her. You got to realize that she is the boss here—even if what she wants don't exactly line up with history. Sometimes the past just ain't worth holding on to, Ethan. You should know that. You battled too many times with too many people over the same sort of thing. And where has this purist thing gotten you?"

Ethan was perturbed now, almost angry. *What right does he have telling me how to run my business? He's an assistant, that's all. He doesn't have any money in this. If what she's doing is wrong, then I have a right to call her on it.*

"You know that I like working for you, Ethan. We all do. But we all know that … that you need this job. Willis Construction needs this job. We don't like bounced checks and dirty looks at the lumberyard. Why don't we just do like the nice lady asks and everyone will get their bills paid and everyone will be happy … okay?"

Ethan was thinking of the right answer when the front door opened with a slam and the familiar sounds of Z102.3—ErieZ Classic Rock—came blasting as Doug hauled up his boom box to the third floor.

Ethan remained silent. And remained silent all through the morning.

"You want to get a what?"

"A latte. You know—coffee and steamed milk, I think."

"And where do you know about lattes from?" Ethan asked, wondering when and where Chase had tasted a latte.

"I was with Elliot and his mom. She stopped at that new Starbucks in Oil City. She said she was treating, and I saw on the menu board that a small latte was the cheapest thing, so I got one. It was real good. I thought we could go for a ride … get some coffee?"

His son had not been what Ethan would call communicative for weeks, perhaps ever since he had started dating Cameron. Sometimes doors opened ever so slightly.

"Okay. We have nothing important to do today. Hop in."

Chase switched the radio on, rolled down his window, and turned the volume up.

At least he's smiling, Ethan thought. *That's a good thing these days.*

Minutes later at Starbucks, they both stood, staring at the menu board, which proudly presented several thousand options. Ethan had seldom stopped at these places for this exact reason. He was confused over what to order.

"A small latte," Ethan eventually said, without much confidence. He loved coffee, but loved it as plain coffee, not encoded with odd ingredients and confusing sizes.

"A tall latte," the clerk called out.

"No … a *small* latte … the little one," Ethan said, explaining his choice.

"A tall is small," the clerk said evenly, as if he had explained this very thing a hundred times already this morning, mostly to children and ignorant customers.

"Oh. Okay then. A tall latte."

Chase stepped up. "The same thing. But with a shot of caramel."

Ethan shuffled off to one side of the counter, looking up to see where the PICK UP ORDER sign was.

After receiving their drinks, they scouted for an open table. And there, right in the middle of the not-so-crowded coffee shop, at a large table in the center, sat Cameron, with her laptop. Three sets of eyes met and triangulated in an instant.

Cameron raised her right hand, almost timidly, as if she wasn't sure she should be saying anything. "Hi. I saw you come in. I was reading the news. I didn't expect to see you here."

Ethan looked at Cameron, then at his son, trying to gauge the mood and tenor of this all-so-awkward moment.

"We don't normally come here. Chase wanted a latte—and I don't think there's any place in town … so … we came out here … and …"

Chase, in a most epiphanic moment, took a step forward. He extended his hand and announced, in a relatively clear voice, "Hi, I'm Chase. You must be Miss Dane."

Where in the world did this person come from? Ethan thought, amazed … no, astounded. *Has a polite alien taken over my son's body?*

"Chase, it is so nice to officially meet you. I saw you that day when I was doing the stories on baseball moms.…"

It was obvious that Cameron almost stumbled on the word *moms.* Anyone could see the confusion in her eyes—as if her saying the *M* word might cause Chase pain.

"Yeah, I remember seeing you there. It was a pretty cool story. Mrs. Hollister didn't like it much, but then she doesn't like *anything* all that much."

Cameron laughed, in spite of her nervousness. "You have time to sit down? I'm alone here … so …"

Chase pulled out a chair and sat before the two adults had moved a muscle.

"I guess we could sit for a minute or two," Ethan said.

"We have no place to go, Dad. You said that yourself," Chase corrected him kindly.

"But Miss Dane might be busy."

Chase looked over to Cameron and screwed his face up tight. Cameron laughed again, in spite of the fact that Chase was making fun of his father.

"You live on the third floor of the Franklin Club, don't you?" Chase asked.

Again Ethan wondered just where Chase got all his information. He
had never once mentioned Cameron's address.

"I do. It has a turret."

"I know. We all thought it would be a cool place to have a club. But
somebody said it was haunted. You see any ghosts there?"

Cameron leaned in close. "No. But when it's real dark and foggy, I can
hear things."

"Really?"

"I do. But I think it's just one of the club's ancient members who fell
asleep in the clubroom—snoring."

This time Chase laughed.

Where did this person come from? Ethan wondered again. *When he's
with me, he never says anything.*

Cameron asked Chase about the upcoming school year, about baseball, and she told him that her older brother worked for the front office
of the Philadelphia Phillies baseball team and that she would see if he
could get an autographed picture of the team. Chase said that would be
really, really cool. He asked her if the newspaper was going to send a
reporter to the championship game and Cameron said she thought so. She
added that she knew a little bit about sports, but not a lot. Chase said that
was okay because girls hardly ever did.

Ethan watched them talk, watched this son of his talk with a woman,
a woman he was … well, dating. He knew his was an odd, odd situation,
but he watched them laugh and smile and talk like they had been old
friends for a long time.

Several minutes later, Cameron sat up, startled by the ringing of her
cell phone. She placed it to her ear, listened, and said, "Okay. I can be
there. Give me ten minutes."

She stood. "That was the paper. There's been a mix-up. Our photographer isn't where he's supposed to be and no one can find him. I need to
run back to town to take a picture … of somebody."

She gathered up her purse. "It was so nice to meet you, Chase. Your
father has told me a lot about you. I hope to see you again."

"Sure. Thanks. And it was nice to meet you, too, Miss Dane."

Ethan wanted to shake his head in amazement but held his head steady. *Maybe they're teaching him manners in school ... or church.*

They both watched her walk quickly to her car.

"She seems real nice," Chase said.

"She is."

And then, as if a veil of silence fell around him, Chase returned to his latte, quietly drinking it through the plastic lid. He grabbed the sports section of the *Erie Times* from a table nearby, flipped to the baseball page, and began to read.

Ethan sat for a moment, not knowing what to do or say. He finally joined his son, picked up the front page of the paper, and began to read as well.

———◇———

The relaxed, easy days of summer seemed to quicken as the season raced to its final ending. School was only a handful of days away, and there was a different feeling in the air.

The Flyers continued their winning ways and found themselves scheduled for the Junior League Championship Series. The team photo ran in the newspaper. Ethan dutifully saved the entire page, placing it carefully on the pile of clippings in the blue bin under the basement stairs.

If Chase had been nervous about playing in the final championship game of the season, he didn't show it. Ethan was much more anxious than his son, even though he wasn't the sort of father, or so he claimed, who lived life through the on-field accomplishments of his son.

No, he was more rational than that. He was much more evolved.

But Ethan woke early that championship Saturday morning, the Saturday of the final game for the Flyers, instantly fidgety and anxious, even before his morning coffee. Chase, on the other hand, slept late.

———◇———

Chase, fully dressed in his baseball uniform, had calmly made his own breakfast of toast and cereal and a large tumbler filled with orange juice.

He was putting his few dishes in the sink when his father walked hurriedly into the kitchen.

"Hey, sport," he said, forcing his tone to be cheery and optimistic, "you ready for the game?"

Chase wasn't sure how to respond. His father never called him "sport." In fact, it was sometimes a joke in the house—fathers who call their sons "sport" because they can't remember their names. His dad had only one name to remember, and Chase was pretty sure he hadn't forgotten it.

"Yeah, I'm ready. But it's just another game, you know."

Chase watched his father's face. He couldn't tell if his father was in pain or just confused.

"Well, that's a good attitude. But you are going to try your best, right?"

The teenager part of Chase wanted to reply, "No … I might only try half my best. That would be okay, right?" He wondered if dads ever realized how goofy some of their questions were, and how they forced their kids into saying the right thing—even if they didn't mean it.

"Absolutely," Chase said with some degree of assurance.

"Then that's all I can ask for," his father said, as if wrapping up the conversation and the question into a neat little ball. After a short silence, he added, "Cameron's going to be there. Is that okay with you?"

So that's why he's so goofy.

"Sure," Chase said.

"You sure?"

"Sure. She's nice."

Chase knew his father wanted to ask something else, some other question, but he didn't know how to ask. Did he want to know how his son felt about his father seeing another woman—a woman who wasn't his mother? But there was nothing. It was as if he was perfectly fine with his father seeing another woman—not his mother—but another woman.

"You're okay with her being there?" Ethan asked again, with a note of uncertainty in his voice that Chase wasn't used to hearing from his dad. "She doesn't have to come. I just thought it might be a nice day and she might like to watch the game."

"It's fine with me," Chase said. "I'm going to go to Elliot's house. His

dad will take us to the park. We want to get there a little early. Elliot said
he had to practice his throwing."

"I'll see you there."

Chase was sure his father almost said, "*We'll* see you there," and was
glad he didn't. Cameron seemed like a good person, Chase thought, but
it was still very weird to imagine his father on a date, holding hands ... or
trying to kiss her.

———

Ethan watched his son leave, carrying his bat and glove and satchel filled
with baseball things. He wondered why Chase hadn't been upset—at least
a little—with Cameron coming to the game. Ethan would have been, if
the situation had been reversed. He was sure of it. This was a woman who
threatened to take his mother's place and Chase said nothing—no rise, no
concern, no problem. Ethan figured there would be more. But Chase had
seemed so cavalier about it. Something tightened in Ethan's gut ... or was
it his heart? Either way, he felt out of kilter—and maybe a little hurt.

He turned away from the door and walked upstairs, wondering what
he was going to wear to the game.

And that was a totally new and disturbing experience for Ethan.

———

"I'll go get two hot dogs and sodas," Ethan volunteered as they found their
seats at the ballpark.

"Sounds good," Cameron said cheerfully. "I'll be here. I'll save your seat."

He grinned at her as he left, heading down the bleachers, around the
dugouts, and toward the concession stand on the far side of the field. As
he passed by the Flyers' bench, he called out, "Go get 'em, Chase."

Chase looked up, but only for an instant. He nodded, but only
imperceptibly.

Ethan had not felt this jumbled for ... well ... for as long as he could
remember. Courting his first wife—and wasn't that a terribly curious way

to think about her?—he'd had no considerations other than her and himself. He had no son to think about, no concerns over what the neighbors might say, and no guilt in how he felt.

But now, with Cameron, all those elements came into play.

He worried about how Chase was reacting. It appeared to Ethan that his son was simply acting too nonchalant and too unaffected to be believed.

They had not talked about Ethan dating—really talked, since ... well, since never.

Since the evening Ethan had invited Cameron to what she called "the purple restaurant," he had kissed her a few more times, and she had kissed him twice—taking him completely by surprise both times.

If he had said that compatibility was based on conversation and its ease of taking place, then he would have to say they got along well together. He enjoyed spending time with her. She laughed easily and often and had a wicked, biting sense of humor that he found stimulating and refreshing. And he liked the way she looked—a lot. But more than just physical, he saw in her a strong, mature woman, smart and passionate and willing to take risks.

He wasn't so sure what she might see in him.

Joel did repeat his observation that Ethan was "way older than she is ... right? I mean *way* older."

Ethan only nodded in reply. He had not asked her how old she was, but he could figure things out within a year or two. Working in Franklin for a year. Maybe working at odd jobs out of college for a year or two. Maybe she took five years to graduate. If he rounded up for each situation, he was ten years older.

That's not so bad, he told himself ... often.

Cameron watched him walk down the bleachers, paying attention, without being obvious, to the way he moved.

He's so graceful, she thought. *He moves like a dancer. Must be all the construction work that keeps him limber.*

She rested her back against the seat behind her and let the sun warm her face and arms. She had dressed modestly today. Not that she dressed immodestly on other days, but this was their first "official" time together in the presence of Ethan's son. Everyone had been aware of everyone else, almost from the beginning, but like asteroids, their trajectories did not collide—except for the time in Starbucks—until today. Today she was not completely certain they would all get together after the game, but she thought the odds were good. If the Flyers won, a celebration of sorts would surely follow. She would have to be invited along to that.

If the Flyers lost, then something smaller, a more sedate and quiet gathering, no doubt, but she took heart even at that. Ethan had remarked, several times, that Chase didn't seem to be all that concerned, winning or losing. The three of them would commiserate in a loss, or celebrate for a victory. Cameron was pretty sure of that.

Either way, Cameron and Ethan would be together—and she would get a chance to be with Chase. After all, Chase was a big part of Ethan's life … and maybe a part of hers in the future.

And just maybe, because of something dreadful in both their pasts, she already felt close to the young boy.

The two teams—the Oil City Tigers and the Franklin Flyers—appeared to be evenly matched. Through five and a half innings, the score stood at 2-2. Chase had gotten one hit but didn't score a run and was thrown out after a weak infield grounder. Defensively, there had been no close plays at first base yet.

Both teams played in the Junior League, and according to league rules, teams were required to play every player at least three innings during the game, and no player, except the catcher, could play all nine innings. The rule guaranteed equitable participation, and all but the most driven coaches endorsed the rule and substituted freely.

Chase and his team took the field. It would be his last time in the field for this game. The first Tigers' batter connected with a low curve and drove it out into the gap between center and right field. By the time the outfielder returned the ball to the infield, the batter had slid safely into third base. This was a serious scoring threat. The Flyers' best power hitters would be out of the game after this inning, and Ethan felt a collective groan emanate from the Flyers' side of the bleachers.

"Hold 'em, Flyers!" came a shout.

"Heads up!"

"Stay focused!"

"Keep your head in the game!"

Cameron looked over at Ethan. He was sitting at the very edge of the bleacher, his hands in tight fists on his knees, staring hard at the action on the field. She wanted to say something, even encouraging, but could think of nothing that didn't sound clichéd. So, she remained silent alongside Ethan and stared out to the field.

Ethan took off his ball cap and twisted the brim in his hands, back and forth, folding and creasing, folding and creasing. Cameron tried her best not to look.

A short, burly player from Oil City came to the plate. He did not appear to be a particularly intimidating or dangerous batter.

"Pitch 'em hard, Justin!" Ethan shouted.

The first two pitches were balls, wide to the outside.

"Make 'em work for it! Don't give it to him!"

Another pitch went into the dirt, followed by a series of soft groans. The catcher blocked it and the runner held at third.

The next pitch came fast and dead center.

The batter swung and caught nothing but air.

The crowd on the Flyers' side applauded.

"Two more just like that!"

The Flyers' pitcher nodded to his catcher, reached back, and threw another fastball. The batter swung nervously, as much trying to protect himself from the ball as he was trying to hit it. It was more a case of the ball hitting the bat than the other way around. The ball plinked off at a curious angle and headed, looping and spinning, toward first base.

Had Chase a few more years of experience, he would have stepped

back, toward the outfield, and let the ball corkscrew its way to foul territory. But Chase did not have that experience, and the throaty yells
from the crowd helped propel him to dive toward the ball. He nicked it
with the top edge of his mitt, almost catching it … coming within two
inches of making a wondrous play. Instead, his glove touched the ball
and made it a fair hit. Then the ball hit the dirt, took another strange
hop, and rolled away from him. He scrambled to get to his knees, lung-
ing at the ball, tripping himself in his haste, booting the ball farther
from his reach.

The runner made first with ease, well before Chase found his foot-
ing and the ball. The runner at third walked home, scoring the go-ahead
run, amid cheers from the Tigers' bench and fans, and groans from the
Flyers' loyalists.

Cameron knew some of the intricacies of the game, having played
girls' softball all through high school. She knew Chase's effort would be
ruled an error—as honest as it may've been.

Ethan stood, his arms raised first in hope, then sinking in defeat.
"Chase! What are you thinking! Get your head in the game!"

Cameron could see the red flash in Chase's face—anger, embarrassment, shock. She felt an urge to run to the field, to put her arm around
the young boy and tell him everything was going to be fine.

"Come on, Chase—think! That was totally your fault!"

Although Cameron was surprised by the harsh tone Ethan had taken,
she didn't say anything. A few minutes later the second and third outs
were made, and the Tigers finally retired to the field.

"Tough break for them," Cameron said, keeping her words calm and
even and without judgment.

Ethan only grunted in reply and slapped his cap against his thigh.

———◦∞◦———

The Flyers failed to score in the seventh, eighth, and ninth innings, losing
the final game of the year by one single run.

The teams gathered in midfield, each player offering each opponent a handshake. Cameron scanned the boys—winners happy and ecstatic, losers glum and tight-lipped. But there were no tears, at least not yet. If they had been girls, there would have been tears—lots of tears—hugs and tears and promises that they would return victorious someday.

But the Flyers didn't cry. They returned to their dugout for their equipment. She could hear the words of their coach, praising them for a good season and a good effort. He said they should all be proud of what they did.

That will make them cry, she thought.

She stood at the bottom of the bleachers while Ethan walked toward the dugout.

He did not have a smile on his face. It was not what she had ever expected to see from him.

She didn't want to eavesdrop on a private moment between father and son, but she couldn't turn off her hearing.

"That was your fault—you stopped thinking. You let the run score," Ethan accused, his voice louder than it needed to be.

Chase, head lowered, his eyes averted, mumbled something in reply.

"It *was* your fault!" Ethan said back.

Chase raised his head, squared his shoulders, and, with a look of anger and grit, shouted back, "It's *always* my fault, isn't it? That's what you think, isn't it?"

Then, without waiting for a response, Chase turned on his heels and walked away, heading to the far exit of the park, the exit by the river.

"Hey!"

Chase kept on walking.

"Hey!"

He had no hint of hesitation in his steps.

"You stop—now!"

Chase didn't stop, or slow, or even flinch.

Ethan stared after him for a moment, then turned away.

Cameron looked down at her hands, as if she had not been listening. To be honest, there was a lot of commotion on the field and in the bleachers as the winning side continued to celebrate. Perhaps no one else had really heard what father and son had said to each other. Perhaps it was not an unusual occurrence.

But Cameron couldn't believe that was true. She didn't want to be there, not just now, not having heard what she'd heard and not having seen what had just happened.

Ethan came around the backstop, slowing his steps with obvious deliberate effort. He moved to stand by her. Most of the Flyers' families had dispersed. No one stopped as they left.

"Sorry," he mumbled.

She wondered what was in his eyes but was hesitant to look up.

"I didn't ..." Her words were almost inaudible.

Finally, she raised her head. She swallowed, her throat dry, her chest tight. "Ethan, that wasn't fair. He's just a boy. It wasn't really his fault. He tried his best. And it's just a game."

She felt herself recoil, physically, from the withering stare that took over Ethan's face. His eyes had narrowed until they were tight, flashing.

"Hey," he said, snapping the word in cold precision. "You don't know what this is all about, okay?"

She thought, for just a split second, that he would offer his sort of silly, wry grin, and make the moment better, as if he were just playing some sort of joke that went badly, badly amiss. And she thought she saw, in his eyes, a glistening of something—something like fear or panic or an overwhelming desire to stop and take all of it back. But like the flash of a bolt of lightning on a summer night heralding the start of a thunderstorm, there was no taking back, no silly grin. There was nothing—except that cold, angry, almost malevolent stare.

"Just stay out of it, Cameron. He's my son, remember?"

He turned back to look for Chase, but his son was now lost in the crowds arriving for the second game.

Ethan spun back around. "It *was* his fault and he knows it. I don't need you saying it wasn't. This is none of your business. He's *my* son."

The words were harsh and brittle. And they were aimed directly at Cameron.

"You have no business interfering! Okay?"

She willed her eyes, harder than she had ever willed anything before
in her life, not to well up with salty tears. She bit on her lip to focus her
energy and concentration.

And then he turned away again.

——————

Chase didn't turn around, nor look back, nor listen, nor care. If someone
followed him, fine. But he was not going to turn around and find out if
they had.

He walked out the southern entrance to the ball fields, crossed the
street, walked past the boat launch, past the picnic tables and portable toi-
lets the city set up in the summer. He didn't stop walking until he reached
the far end of the city park, where the riverbank gave way to rocks and
cement and brambles. It was his and Elliot's favorite place to fish, throw
stones into the water—and talk.

*It's always my fault. He said it. He thinks that way. It was my fault. I
should never have done that.*

His vision became watery.

I am not going to cry.

He still held his baseball glove close to his chest, the baseball glove his
father had driven to Butler to find, a Wilson A2K model, with the single
post web and deep pocket.

He held it in his hands and stared at the stitches and the Wilson logo
in black and yellow. He lightly traced the leather webbing, brushed his
hand over the logo once more. Then, without thinking any more about it,
he leaned back, coiled his arm, and threw the baseball glove, as far as he
could throw it, into the dark water of French Creek, a quarter mile from
where it joined the Allegheny River heading south, south through
Pennsylvania and the Ohio River and the Mississippi and on to New
Orleans.

He watched the ball glove bob in the murky water, holding its head
above the ribs of the river until the darker, stronger current grabbed hold
and drew it under.

Then, almost as if he had planned it this way, Chase put his elbows on his knees, formed a V, buried his face in his hands, and began to sob.

———⧫———

When Ethan had turned away, Cameron felt something snap in her heart. And she knew, in that instant, that if he looked up, she would not know what to do, or what to say. She would wind up blubbering like a foolish, lovesick teenager who had just been jilted by an equally foolish young swain who was testing his muscles by inflicting pain on the unsuspecting— just because he could.

Cameron, in a most pellucid moment, knew she could not let that happen, regardless of what Ethan needed. She had to turn away before he turned around. So she spun on her heels and began to walk, as swiftly as she could without resorting to running, and headed away from him, heading north, getting away from the tears she knew were only a few steps away.

———⧫———

Ethan didn't turn around right away.

I am not this sort of father.

He stared to the south, looking for his son.

I am not that sort of father.

He could see nothing.

He's not at fault.

He twisted his hands into fists.

It's not his fault.

He turned back around.

And Cameron was gone as well.

If we wait too long to forgive,
our rage settles in
and claims squatter's rights to our souls.

—Lewis B. Smedes

———

Forgiveness is a funny thing.
It warms the heart
and cools the sting.

—William A. Ward

CHAPTER TEN

SUMMER HAD ENDED IN Venango County.

Each year, the Stoneskipping Championship Festival on the River, when professionals and amateurs alike vied for the *gerplunking* state championship on the third weekend of August, marked the end of the summer season. Books, backpacks, and supplies had been bought, and school had begun.

The days remained warm, but in the evenings an unmistakable intimation, a waft of the scent of fall, tinged the air. An early edging of leaves at Two Mile Run Park had already turned to gold, hinting at the season's fallow colors soon to come. Flocks of geese and birds assembled in great, squawking crowds at the river's edge, jostling and strutting, making noisy preparations for their journey south.

For Cameron, something about the end of summer caused a restlessness in her, an unnamed longing. Each year the feeling brought with it a certain sadness that she found difficult to describe. And this year that sadness was intensified.

Activities at *The Derrick* also intensified in the weeks before the start of the school year. Cameron had been assigned both publishing and editing duties of the back-to-school style and special fashion supplement to the newspaper. This job entailed making sure that the sales department actually sold advertising for the section, that models from the local high school were recruited, that the clothing stores in Franklin and out at the Cranberry Mall were solicited for special back-to-school outfits for the models, that stories and editorial assignments were given out so the pages would be filled. The job was complex, time-consuming—and just the thing Cameron needed.

Since the Flyers' loss at the championship game, since those explosive minutes just after the game, since Cameron's carefully constructed daydream had collapsed in her hidden, bitter tears, she and Ethan had not spoken. He had not called or stopped by. During the first few days following the game, she had hoped for some word, even as slight as an e-mail, but nothing was spoken, or written.

To her, Ethan's silence was more damaging and potent than any cruel word could ever have been.

It was obvious to Cameron that what she had thought was there between them … was not. It was not the first time a woman had fooled herself into thinking that a man was committed to a relationship when he really wasn't.

But how can he just walk away? Cameron wondered. *He didn't even feel the need for closure. Nothing. I can't believe it.*

She found herself thinking as much about Chase as she thought about Ethan.

The silence grew so loud that Cameron felt grateful for her hectic schedule. By the end of this day, she had to complete several five-hundred-word articles on the current "hot" styles for today's teens, and she had no idea what kids considered "hot." Early into the process, she had visited the local stores that specialized in teen fashions. Her time wandering amid the racks of jarring styles confused her. It seemed there was not a single article of apparel in those stores that she would wear, could wear, or would ever have considered wearing.

But she gamely interviewed owners and clerks and the kids themselves. She thumbed through scores of magazines, looking for trends and

ideas that she might extrapolate to the local scene in Franklin. She began
to show pictures to Paige, who showed an interest at first. Paige's interest
quickly grew to shocked silence—especially at the more skimpy and
revealing fashions that seemed to be *de rigueur* for today's teens. And then,
instead of interest, Paige simply waved Cameron away when she appeared
holding a magazine in hand.

"I'm already offended, Cameron. Old and offended." She coughed
from her office. "Don't make me feel even older than I am. Or more
offended … if that's possible."

If Paige had wondered why Cameron had stopped talking about
Ethan, she had the sensitivity not to ask. Cameron knew her boss must
have been wondering. Cameron also knew that Paige already may have
heard about what had happened.

Franklin was that small of a town, and this story of anger and public
humiliation would have been so wonderfully delicious.

———

Chase approached the start of eighth grade with neither happy anticipation nor glum acceptance. School was, as he had once told Elliot, not a
bad way to spend a few hours a day. This would be his last year at the
Franklin Area Middle School.

Since his final baseball game, he and his father had barely spoken.
What they were sharing between them, in their tight silence, was not
anger. It was something else altogether—a mutual emotion that twisted
them, made words unnecessary, even hurtful, and made the silence an
angry addiction.

It wasn't that all words had stopped—just words that spoke to things
other than what was necessary and right in front of them.

His father could talk about food and what they might eat for supper.

Chase might answer in a word or two, most often noncommittal.

His father might suggest listening to a ball game.

Chase might accept, but often would demur, claiming fatigue or
disinterest.

Less than a few hundred words between father and son had been scattered over the three weeks since that last game, that last grievous error, their last silent parting.

Chase turned it all inside and let his feelings wind and coil. It was a familiar process to both father and son.

And if Ethan had noticed that Chase's favorite baseball glove was missing, he didn't say anything about it.

———

That morning Ethan sat in his kitchen, staring at *The Derrick* without reading a word, nursing a fourth cup of coffee. He could have simply slipped out and headed to the jobsite. Perhaps he should have. He knew Chase was awake; had heard the hiss of water from the bathroom, and the shower spray echo hard against the tub. Chase was dressing, rattling about upstairs. Ethan no longer had to worry about a lunch. This year the middle school offered a hot lunch for a few dollars a week. To Ethan, it was a small price to pay for not having to worry about finding food that would please Chase—most often at six in the morning.

There were other issues Ethan faced, troubling issues as well. He and his crew were weeks behind schedule on the Carter Mansion project. They had run into plumbing problems on the second floor and spent an angry week slowly working around and behind a plumbing outfit from French Creek.

The stairs groaned as Chase made his way down. Ethan could clearly see that Chase was surprised to see his father still at home. Ethan had decided that their uneasy cease-fire, their unstated armistice, had gone on long enough.

"Chase," Ethan said calmly, "we need to talk."

"Okay."

Ethan put his coffee cup on the counter. He wasn't going to drink it anyhow. The coffee was tepid at best, tasting more like cough syrup.

"I'm sorry for what I said to you at the game."

"It's okay."

"No. I was wrong. I always told you it was only a game, but I didn't act like it."

"It's okay, really."

"No, it isn't. I shouldn't have yelled like that."

Chase only glanced up for a moment. "It was a bad play."

Ethan had a speech prepared, and he was following that speech. But Chase's part was not going quite according to the lines he had written in his head.

"No. It was just a game," Ethan said again. "I'm really sorry for yelling at you like that."

Chase simply shrugged.

Ethan wanted to shout at him all over again. In spite of his best intentions, his shoulders tightened. *What is that shrug for?* Ethan wanted to say. *I'm apologizing here, and you just shrug at me?*

But he kept his words as even and as calm as he could. "Am I forgiven?"

Chase looked up at him, stared into his eyes, and almost shrugged again. Ethan saw his shoulders move just ever so much.

"Sure, Dad. Forgiven. No big deal."

Ethan waited and fumed silently. *It was a big deal, and Chase dismisses it like it was nothing—like it's not even worth his time to discuss it.*

Chase didn't speak.

After a long time, Ethan added, "So, we're okay then?"

"Sure. We're okay," Chase replied, not giving his answer any time for reflection.

"Good. You're sure we're okay?"

"Yep."

Neither Ethan nor Chase spoke for a minute.

"Well, I'll see you tonight."

"Sure. I'll be here."

Silence.

"Maybe McCort's?"

"Sure."

But as Ethan picked up his lunch box and thermos, he wondered why his carefully planned apology felt so absolutely and horribly wrong, like none of his feelings that lay behind and under the words mattered.

———

Forgiven. Easy for him to ask. He doesn't understand any of this. He doesn't understand anything, Chase thought as he cinched up his backpack and headed out the door. He saw Elliot coming down the street. He grinned at his friend, offered a wide wave, and waited as Elliot started to jog toward him, taking loping, circular strides.

Forgiven.

I wonder what that feels like.

———

Ethan was not having a good day. In fact, he had not had a good day in several days. Immediately after his clenched-teeth apology resulting in a clenched-teeth forgiveness from Chase, he entered another situation filled with tension—but including none of the clenched-teeth drama. It was just out-and-out yelling.

It had all begun two days earlier, when Todd Thomas and Sons, a plumbing outfit from French Creek, began to complain about the location of the third-floor powder room.

"Too far from the soil stack. Never be able to make the grade. You gotta move the room—or move the pipe," declared the senior Thomas loudly, arms folded across his chest, his son several steps behind, holding a tape measure in one hand and a blueprint in the other.

Ethan had years of experience dealing with subcontractors. *You yell back—it's the only way.*

Ethan did exactly that. Not mean, aggressive, angry yelling, but passionate yelling.

"We can't do either!" Ethan explained—loudly. "She wants the toilet here. That's what the plan says, and at this point I can't move that soil stack short of tearing up the entire house. I'm not doing that."

"Easy for you to say. I gotta rip all the floor between here and there—and none of that work is in my quote."

Ethan shrugged. "You had the plans and drawings. It had better be in the quote. You looked at the job. If you misquoted, too bad. You'll just have to eat the difference. You've been in business too long to pull this."

The senior Thomas muttered, turned away, and snatched the blueprints from the hands of the still-silent Thomas junior.

Ethan stayed out of the plumbers' way for the rest of the day. Plumbers worked on different schedules than carpenters, and neither felt at ease working with each other. It would do no one any good to get into another shouting match. Arguments on the jobsite always meant an afternoon of jumbled and sometimes substandard work.

As a gesture of conciliation, Ethan said he would call the architect that afternoon—"to see if there was anything that could be done to help." He was sure there wasn't, but he needed the Thomas boys to stay on the job. They had been the least expensive bid on the plumbing. Every added and unforeseen cost escalation was money out of Ethan's pocket—money he could not afford to spend.

Ethan held the cell phone tight to his ear. He was standing in a quiet corner on the third floor, looking out to the street below.

"Well, Ethan, what a surprise. I was just thinking about you," said Michelle, who always seemed as if she was genuinely happy to hear from him. "So, tell me what problems we have today."

"What makes you think we have a problem?" Ethan asked.

"A contractor calling the architect? Please. I've been around long enough. It's for a problem. Is it something I caused?"

Ethan laid out the concerns of the Thomas boys. Michelle kept repeating "uh-huh" as Ethan suggested some possible alternatives.

"Don't we have two feet between the floor and the ceiling below? That's more than enough for their angle. It's what—a one inch of drop per horizontal foot? They have to lay less than twenty feet of pipe. It should work fine."

"That's what I thought too. They may be worried about cutting through too many joists."

"They're covered there too. I'm sure that they only cut through two—but make sure they rebrace the area, and then they have a straight run to the soil stack. Should be an easy fix."

Ethan conveyed the architect's diagnosis and suggestions to his plumbing subcontractors.

"Sounds easy, but she ain't here to see the mess," the senior Thomas growled. "She wants us to run the pipe under two walls. That's too much work. I didn't figure on that. I ain't doin' it that way."

Ethan stood up straighter. "You have to make it work. You quoted the job. You saw the plans. Now do what your bid said you're going to do."

The following day, the Thomas crew did not show up until after lunch, and then cut massive holes in the two walls and into the ceiling below before Ethan or anyone else saw them do it.

"You want pipes? You got pipes," Thomas senior barked out at Ethan.

It was just at that moment that Mrs. Moretti breezed in with her interior designer, Tessa Winberry, in on another visit from San Francisco, both carrying shopping bags of carpet samples, fabric swatches, and biscotti.

CeCe stopped in her steps and stared hard at the hole in the ceiling by the second-floor landing. The soil pipe angled awkwardly through the plasterboard, protruding at least a foot into the space.

"We can't have that there," she said with dismay, pointing at the pipe, the pipe still dripping purple with plumber's glue. "That's all wrong."

The Thomas and Sons plumbing team picked that moment to swagger down the stairs, banging their dolly filled with equipment on the steps, chipping a nice divot of wood from the stair tread, the piece landing on Tessa's foot.

"You need a pipe? You got a pipe," Thomas senior said as he turned the corner and bounced down the remaining steps, banging the front door open and closed.

CeCe looked over imploringly at a silent Tessa, then stared hard at Ethan before speaking again. "That … pipe … has to be removed."

"We'll fix it. We can lower the ceiling a bit in that area. You'll never notice it."

CeCe dropped the shopping bag and walked closer to the wall. "No.

Not lowered. Removed. Do you hear? Removed. There is not going to be a lower ceiling in the hall. There is not."

Ethan could tell his crew was trying hard to *not* hear what was going on between their boss and his client. But that was impossible. So they all tried to find something to occupy themselves as far from the field of battle as they could.

"Removed."

Ethan could only nod in reply, as CeCe and Tessa picked up their designer shopping bags and went downstairs.

———

The Franklin Area Middle School had been built on former farmland, three miles south of town, across the highway from the Venango County Municipal Airport. Aircraft noises were seldom interruptions; the airport was rarely used.

Virtually every student had to take a bus to school. Chase and Elliot were no exceptions. The thirty-minute, meandering trip gave them a last-minute opportunity to finish any homework they had forgotten, either deliberately or accidentally, from the day prior. Since school had just begun, Chase did not felt overwhelmed with schoolwork. He did most of his work in study period or during class. Elliot, however, always seemed to have a sheaf of papers needing correction or revision.

"I'm not stupid," Elliot would insist. "I'm just not as organized as you."

Chase would help as he could.

Today, as always, the bus turned along the river, stopping every block, allowing students to jostle aboard, the noise increasing at each stop.

"So your dad finally said he was sorry?"

Chase just nodded. Ethan and Chase may have thought no one heard their brief argument that day, but virtually the whole team—or at least the parents of the entire team—had heard. The parking lot was only steps from the field, and voices in anger carried well on the breeze. Chase had invited himself to Elliot's house for dinner the evening of the game, and no one made mention of anything relating to baseball. They talked about fishing, and school, and church, and movies—but not a word about Chase's dad or what he had said that afternoon. It was obvious from their silence that everyone had overheard, and everyone was acting polite.

"Yeah. He apologized."

"So?"

"So, what?"

"I mean … like, did you guys hug and make up? Did he say he was going to take you to dinner? Is he going to buy you something cool, like an iPod, to make up for it?"

Chase shook his head. "No. But he did say we might go to McCort's."

"McCort's? That's not much of an apology, if you ask me."

Everyone inside the bus swayed in time with the bus as it turned the corner on Buffalo Street.

"No. But he wasn't really apologizing."

"He wasn't?" Elliot asked. "How do you figure that? He said he was sorry, right?"

"He said he was sorry for yelling at me. That doesn't mean he thought it was okay—I mean, what I did and all. He was just sorry for yelling—especially in front of people like that. That's all. He still blames me for losing the game."

"But the coach said it was nobody's fault. Somebody wins, somebody loses. None of the guys think you screwed up. I mean, we all screwed up. I didn't get any hits that game. And I don't feel bad."

Chase shrugged. Elliot unzipped his backpack, stuck his hand into it, rustled about, and extracted a wrinkled and creased bag of Fritos.

"Want some?"

"That your lunch?"

"Nope. Saved 'em from last week. I traded for them."

Chase took a few and tossed the handful into his mouth. "Who trades away Fritos?"

Elliot shrugged. "Dunno. Some dumb sixth-grader."

As the two friends finished dividing the bag, the bus bounced against the curb in front of the school, and they joined the stream of students charging toward the main entrance.

Paige may have been waving her hand in greeting as Cameron dropped her bag and purse onto her desk in a heap. She couldn't be sure. Paige also could have been swatting at a fly.

"You waved?" Cameron said as she stuck her head in the doorway.

"I did. Come on in. Take a break. Sit down. Have some coffee."

"All at once?"

"Sure. You're good at doing more than one thing at a time."

"After this week, it feels like I've had more than my fair share of practice at multitasking."

"The fashion section looks great. I saw the galleys. Everything looks terrific. I'm impressed. Really, really impressed. Our best ever."

Cameron felt as if she were beaming. Paige gave compliments, but seldom were they this effusive.

"Thanks. I had fun doing it, though my days of knowing what's 'hot' fashion must be over. None of what they wear nowadays seems to be feminine in the least."

Paige waved the air again, as if swatting at invisible flying bugs. "Don't get me started. Young girls looking like streetwalkers. Terrible. I feel bad for parents."

Cameron took a deep breath and exhaled, feeling a sudden wave of age and fatigue sweep over her.

"You should take a break for a few days after you're finished with this. Take a long weekend. Get off by yourself somewhere. Recharge."

Cameron's face gave away what she had been hiding for the past few weeks. "You heard?" she asked, her voice a whisper.

Paige pursed her lips, then said, "I did. This is Franklin. After all my years in this business, I still get surprised."

"Surprised?"

"People love telling secrets. They love telling *me* secrets—I think just to see if I'll put them in the paper."

Cameron offered a very brittle laugh. "I hope this isn't that sort of secret."

"No. It isn't. Twenty years ago, this would have made it to near the top of the society page. Today, not so much. To be honest, the few people who mentioned it to me did so because they were actually concerned about you. They said it was such a shock to hear Ethan talk that way—to both you and his son. 'That's just not him,' they said."

Cameron tried to say something in reply, but no words came.

"Cameron, don't let this get to you. He'll get over it. His son will get over it."

The young woman shook her head in reply. "I know it was only a few words, but you didn't hear him. It was like he was a different person. He was so mad. I don't know what happened. I hardly said anything."

Paige opened a desk drawer and rummaged about the contents. She sat straight up. "Goodness. You know what I was doing? Looking for a smoke. It's been decades, and all of a sudden, I wanted one. Must be the subject matter."

"I'm sorry, Paige," Cameron said. "I didn't …"

"Not your fault. Old habits die really, really hard, I guess."

Paige appeared as if she were considering standing and giving her young editor a hug. But she didn't. "You think I'm crazy, don't you? You think it's hopeless."

Cameron squeaked out a yes.

"It isn't. This is just a little bump in the road. If it's meant to be, it can get fixed."

"No. I think this situation is screwed up completely. I was going too fast. He's not looking for someone to share his life with. He's not ready. I can see that. I blew it."

Paige did stand this time and began to pace behind her desk. "Hey, stop feeling sorry for yourself. It's not that bad."

"It is too," Cameron replied, her words edging toward a wail.

Paige sat on the front of her desk. "Listen, girl, you have no idea of what bad is."

The older woman waited, then resumed speaking, her voice darker, softer, deeper. "I have done more screwing up than you could even dream of doing. My second husband … he was a good man, but he was lost, had a bad past ... overwhelmed by life ... and everything. I was lost too. I was drinking all the time. He was drinking all the time. He was as bad as I was.

"One Sunday night we came back from a party and kept drinking. I passed out. I guess I did, anyway. When I woke up, my husband was on the floor, blue and cold. They told me later that his heart had stopped. I was ten feet away from him when he died and didn't know it.

"After the police left, I staggered over to the church down the block, sick from a hangover, and just started to cry. For him. For myself. For what a mess I was making of my life. The pastor was kind. The people were accepting. God is good."

"I'm sorry, Paige," came Cameron's almost silent reply. "I had no idea."

"Well, I'm not telling you this for sympathy or pity or anything like that. I haven't told this story to many people, Cameron. But you need to listen to one thing: Don't be like I was, blind and deaf. Don't waste time. Make it right, Cameron. And most important, get forgiven. God can do that for you. Then tell Ethan what a jerk he was—and maybe admit you were too—and start over. You owe it to yourself. And to him. You will never know if tomorrow is one day too late."

Cameron stared up at Paige, her eyes wanting to brim with tears, yet she did not cry. "I don't know if I can do that. Any of that. I don't know."

But Chase needs me. And Ethan. So maybe ...

CeCe and Tessa busied themselves with their samples, feeding her crew Italian pastries and asking them about wives and girlfriends and children and plans for the weekend. After the homeowner's unequivocal demand that the pipe on the landing be moved, she left Ethan alone.

Perhaps they were both surprised by her anger.

The crew cleared out early, and CeCe claimed that she and Tessa were meeting someone for drinks somewhere. Joel and Ethan were left in the silent house to stare at the pipe, still protruding.

"Well, I'm not paying him now, for sure," Ethan said.

"He'll just put a lien on the house. He's done it before. You don't want that to happen. CeCe would get those papers, you know. She'd hit the ceiling. Literally."

Ethan lowered himself to the second step of the landing and stared upward.

"You mean I have to pay him—and then pay more to correct his mistakes?"

Joel pulled a biscotti from his shirt pocket and chewed off one end. "Yep. I told you—don't go with the cheapest bid on this. Those French Creek guys are pirates."

Ethan ran his hand over his face. "We can fix the upstairs, right?"

"Yeah. That's easy. But this pipe is the problem."

"We could move it," Ethan said, his words not all that certain.

"No," Joel answered quickly. "We're carpenters, not plumbers. Remember that time at the Travers' place? I think their toilet still leaks."

"So, I'm supposed to pay for another plumber? I don't want to."

Joel chewed softly. "You have to. I heard her talking. CeCe. On her cell phone. I don't think she knew I was there. She said something about maybe having to go in a different direction. You know as well as I that when a customer says anything about 'a different direction,' it means they want to fire who they got now and get somebody new."

Ethan was startled. "She really said 'a different direction'?"

Joel nodded.

After a long exhale, Ethan spoke. "We can't lose this. I'm already buried under a second mortgage. We can't."

Joel's eyes showed an uneasy glint. "I can call my cousin. Maybe I can get him in tomorrow. It's Saturday. Maybe it won't slow us down."

The only sound was the creaking of the house in the cooling afternoon breeze.

"Yeah. Call him. Ask if he'll cut us a break on his labor. Tell him I can help."

Joel nodded again.

Ethan despised acting as anyone's assistant—especially a plumber's assistant—but he was desperate.

Somehow Joel knew. He understood. And he didn't say another word.

Cameron sat on the window seat, looking out at the dark street. Only the occasional car passed by on West Park. The wind rustled through the trees outside her window. The leaves had gone from the silken hush of green to a scratching, brown, ominous rattle.

She opened her journal on her lap. She wiped at her eyes, clicked the pen, and began to write:

> *What do I do now? I am pretty sure Paige was talking about a lot more than calling Ethan when she said, "Make it right."*
> *I don't think I did anything wrong.*
> *And maybe he didn't do anything that bad.*
> *A few harsh words is all that happened. That's not so terrible.*
> *But why do I hurt so much? I can't let it go.*
> *We're both so screwed up.*
> *Why doesn't he call me?*

She clicked the pen again, slowly closed the notebook, and blinked, trying to get the trees back in focus. She kept seeing Chase's face crumble under his father's words. And every time she remembered that painful look, she felt a resonance of an earlier time in her own life.

Forgiveness frees the forgiver.
It extracts the forgiver
from someone else's nightmare.

—LANCE MORROW

———⋙⋘———

Once forgiving begins,
dreams can be rebuilt.

—BEVERLY FLANIGAN

CHAPTER ELEVEN

ETHAN AND CHASE DID not go to McCort's that evening. When Chase returned home he found a scrawled note on a three-by-five note card propped up between the salt- and peppershakers on the kitchen table. It was the one spot where all notes between father and son were left. The kitchen was the first stop for anyone entering the house.

Chase,
   Have to work late tonight to catch up. Called Mrs. Hewitt. She said to go there for dinner. I'll be home by 9.
   Dad

Elliot was the oldest of six children, so mealtimes at the Hewitt house were often hectic affairs with multiple choices to satisfy multiple palates. After a dinner of macaroni and cheese, hot dogs, Fritos, meatloaf with real mashed potatoes and gravy, green beans, and Jell-O, Chase and Elliot slipped out of the house.

They walked toward town, not having a specific destination, but walking. If you lived in the older sections of Franklin, you could walk just about everywhere. If your house was in one of the newer subdivisions south of town, you had to drive. Sidewalks didn't go that far, and both 13th Street and Route 322 out of town were narrow roads.

"You want to go to Fountain Park?" Elliot asked.

"I guess."

"Maybe we can stop at the Minute Mart. You have any money?"

"Yeah, but we just ate."

"Oh, yeah, we did," Elliot replied. He thought for a minute, then added, "So, can I borrow some?"

Chase reached into his pocket and pulled out three wadded and wrinkled singles. "Will this be enough to get you to the park and back without fainting?"

Elliot screwed up his face. "Maybe. I don't know. I guess we'll have to try it and see."

They each bought a small Slushee—one grape and one wild berry—and Elliot promised to divide the bag of Sweet Tarts equally between them. They slurped as they walked down Liberty Street, pausing several times to stare into windows. They passed the Senaca Outpost, the local sporting goods store, filled with athletic jerseys and hunting gear.

"How come you didn't try out for football this year?" Chase asked. "You're big. You're a natural. You're good at knocking things down."

Elliot poked his friend with an elbow, careful not to spill the remains of his Slushee in the process.

"Hey, careful," Chase answered and poked back.

They kept walking, and Elliot tossed his empty cup into a trash container.

"My dad wanted me to. He thinks I could be good. My mom didn't. She thinks you have to be sort of mean to play football. She tells everyone that I have a gentle temperament."

Chase laughed out loud.

Elliot took a mock swing at his friend's shoulder and connected by accident, almost knocking him down.

"See! You *are* mean. You hit people for no good reason." Chase made a show of nursing his injured arm.

"I think she might be right," Elliot explained. "I don't particularly like football. Last year when I played on the seventh-grade team, there was a whole lot of practice for not a whole lot of time to play."

Elliot looked over at Chase. "So why didn't you go out for the eighth-grade team? You have a good arm. You could have played quarterback or something like that. You wouldn't get stuck as a lineman like I was."

Chase shrugged. "My dad wants me to play hockey. I think he was some big sort of star hockey player when he was a kid like me."

They sat on the ledge around the fountain, in the center of the park, listening to the splashing water. Elliot made a game of pretending to reach in for the coins that lay at the bottom of the fountain. He had actually tried it once, but a police car had stopped in midblock and had used the bullhorn to tell him to cease and desist.

"Yeah, well, my dad wasn't that good at anything in school. He doesn't push me that way."

Chase lay back on the ledge. The stone was still warm from the sun.

"He's not pressuring me, I guess. But I know that's what he really, really wants."

"So, you going to try out for the Oilers hockey team?"

Chase shrugged again. "I don't know. Maybe. If we're talking by then."

"He apologized, Chase."

"He didn't mean it."

Elliot took three pieces of candy and pushed them into his mouth. "The pastor talks a lot about forgiveness. He says we need to forgive people. Otherwise we get stuck."

"Stuck?"

"That's what he said. You might have missed that Sunday when you were camping. I'm not sure what that means, exactly, but it sounds bad, doesn't it? Stuck. Like you have chewing gum all over your backside."

"That doesn't sound churchlike." Chase laughed.

"Well, that's what it sounds like."

Chase sat up then and began to walk around the fountain on the ledge, pretending as if he were walking a tightrope, his arms extended for balance.

"But isn't everyone supposed to forgive everyone … for things that went wrong? That's what Mrs. Whiting says."

Elliot chewed thoughtfully. "Sure. I think. I mean, if something's not your fault and you ask—then yeah, they should forgive you. Like God forgives us."

Chase was on the opposite side of the fountain. He called over to Elliot, who remained seated. "Maybe I should ask the pastor to talk to my dad."

Elliot looked mystified. "Well, maybe. He does stuff like that. I bet he wouldn't mind. He's nice. Even though my mom says he never visits people in the hospital anymore."

"Are they supposed to do that?"

"I guess. That's what my mom says. My dad just waves his hand when she says that."

Elliot attempted to imitate his father's silent, dismissive wave, and in so doing dropped one of his last pieces of candy into the fountain. He toppled over trying to rescue it, barely holding himself out of the water with one arm, while flailing for the errant candy with his other.

From somewhere on the east side of the park came a loud voice. "Hey, kid, get out of the water!"

Chase jumped from the ledge, ran to Elliot, and grabbed his free arm, pulling him upright. "Hey, I could have bought another bag. No sense drowning—or being arrested for one lousy Sweet Tart."

"But … it was the last one. I was waiting for the last one. If you don't know it's the last piece, then you don't get to appreciate it as much. You know?"

And with that, Elliot carefully blew on the last piece of candy, trying to dry the fountain waters. When it was sufficiently dry, he popped it into his mouth with a lopsided smile.

———◦∞◦———

Cameron let her car slowly come to a stop. She had driven past Ethan's house three times, trying to get up her nerve. She hoped no one was taking note of her circling around the block. She switched off the ignition. The car engine pinged loudly as it began to cool. She glanced at herself in the rearview mirror.

I have to do this. I have to.

She opened the door, stood up, brushed imaginary lint off of her slacks, turned, with some purpose, and walked toward the front door.

If he's never going to call me, I need to know that. And he needs to tell me in person.

She stopped, or almost stopped, halfway up the walk. It was more a slow step, a stutter step, but she would not allow herself to back down now.

Cameron had scarcely slept the night before. Paige's story of lost opportunities and last chances for restoration echoed in her thoughts.

It's not like we had announced anything. It's not like we made anything official, or even talked about it. But it was going there. I knew it. He knew it. There was a spark. More than a spark.

Cameron had talked at a whisper to herself as she paced back and forth in her dark apartment. She had staged elaborate confrontations between herself and an imaginary Ethan. Most of the time, their reunion would go well, and he would profess profound regrets over his stupidity and callousness. Occasionally, Cameron would allow the scene to end in his denial of any attraction between the two of them. That would not happen often because it made her cry. Instead, she would start another scenario, this one with a happier ending.

And I keep thinking about Chase. He needs …

She realized she was driving herself slightly crazy. Why on earth must she think about Ethan so much? Summoning her strength, she reminded her heart that there is a certain grace in just letting go, in forgetting. She resolved that, either way, all of this pent-up, bottled-up emotion had to be released. They both lived in a small town. Eventually, they would cross paths. Sometimes she longed for the anonymity of the big city again, where you could just disappear.

But Cameron was not the sort of person who left loose ends lie—not professionally, and not socially. Things should be tied up. Uncertainty was unhealthy.

The stairs creaked as she stepped up to the porch. Her heart, beating fast as she drove up, now began to sprint. Her thoughts began to race— *What am I doing here? What am I going to say?*

She let her legs move her forward without giving the act of walking any conscious thought. She raised her hand, pointed her finger, and pressed the doorbell. Like jumping into a swimming pool of chilly water, it was best to get it over with in one sudden, irrevocable move. She heard the bell chime inside the house, behind the door. She waited and willed herself not to hyperventilate. She waited and heard nothing—no steps, no muffled calls from inside.

Now what?

She pressed the bell again.

It's a big house. It could take awhile to get here.

She inhaled deeply.

Silence.

Her shoulders began to drop—not that she was aware of the slump, but the adrenaline was seeping out of her, blood pressure was lowering, heart rate was calming. She pursed her lips once more and pressed again.

Nothing.

She looked over her shoulder. Her car was the only vehicle in the street.

Now what?

She had to force herself to move, to walk slowly off the porch. Once she reached the sidewalk, she hurried, not wanting to be caught here in the middle of everything and have to explain whether she was coming or going, and the purpose of her aborted visit.

Her car lurched forward, and she reached an illegal speed much quicker than normal for her.

Upstairs, in the Willis house, a young boy slipped out from the shadows and moved closer to the window.

Chase had watched as Cameron pulled up to the curb. He had watched as her car stopped, watched her as she made her way toward the house, watched the way she held her arms close to her body, watched as she stared at the walk. When the doorbell rang, he jumped, even though he knew it was coming.

He stayed in his secret room, counting the seconds between the chimes. He was, after all, only obeying his father's instructions. He had been commanded, in no uncertain terms, to never answer the door when alone—especially if it was a stranger. Chase figured that she wasn't a complete stranger, but she still was sort of one.

He sat in the darker shadows of his secret room, waiting, hiding. He heard her steps on the porch as she walked away. He watched her walk around her car, knowing that she could not see that deep into the shadows of a small window on the top floor of the house. She wouldn't be looking for his face anyway.

He waited until her car moved away from the curb. Then he put his face against the window and followed her car as it sped to the corner, then turned left and out of sight.

I wonder what she wanted?

Chase may not have been the most mature observer, but he knew that his father and that woman had not seen each other since … since that last baseball game.

I wonder what happened to them that day?

Seeing Cameron at his house did not feel as shocking as he thought it might. When he first learned that she and his father had been out on a date together, he'd anticipated feeling horrible and abandoned and pushed aside. But none of those emotions had welled up inside of him this day. He could see Cameron's face—no smile, but no frown either. It was just like Miss Patterson in fifth grade. When she was mad or really, really serious, her face would sort of go blank—like no one could tell what she was thinking. As soon as you couldn't tell what she was thinking, everyone in her class knew to be very, very careful, and very, very quiet. She could easily be pushed into assigning four or five extra pages of homework.

That's what Miss Dane had looked like—like something was inside that she was trying her best not to let outside. He knew that for a fact, because that's the way he felt so often. He knew what it felt like, for sure, and he could tell Miss Dane was right there too.

I wonder what she's holding inside?

He crawled back into the shadows. He opened his secret box.

He carefully laid the old hockey jersey on the floor and smoothed out any wrinkles. He wished it would still fit him, but he hadn't been that size for years. He carefully turned the jersey over, folded each arm to the middle, then folded it again, so the jersey formed a small, tidy rectangle. With a gentle hand, he picked it up and placed it back inside the box. Before he closed the box, he stared at the jersey for a long moment.

I wonder.

The days grew shorter as autumn began to give way to a gray, dreary winter. Ethan promised everyone concerned that the Carter Mansion project would be done by Christmas.

Even though it was steady work, he felt his crew grow restless over long projects. A few years back, just after his wife … he found a yearlong project building new homes between Senaca Heights and Franklin. Midway through, he knew it had been the wrong decision. He became bored with the repetitions. His crew also grew bored and tired. Two of them quit and started taking on small remodeling jobs. None of them enjoyed the routine, the sameness, of a long project, no matter the quality.

Now they were falling behind on Ethan's ambitious, original estimation of time required to finish the Carter place. Large jobs and a lot of small tasks remained undone, and the punch list began to snowball. It would grow longer, Ethan imagined, with each passing day. No one liked to play catch-up, and Ethan took it upon himself to work longer and harder than anyone else on the crew. Some days, Joel would stay with him. The two of them, dedicated to one task, could accomplish much in the span of three or four hours.

Tonight Ethan had made a lot of noise, cutting framing lengths of two-by-fours for a new wall on the second floor. Mrs. Moretti had changed the plans once again, shrinking the master suite and adding more room to the walk-in closet.

No one likes having to tear things out—especially tearing out things that take days to put back up.

Ethan had volunteered for this one. He liked working alone. He liked the solitude. It gave him time to think.

He stacked the cut lumber on one side of the room. He snugged the pieces tight against the wall, taking some pride that each cut board was identical to the one below—no angled cuts, no short pieces, no long pieces.

He stopped and wiped his forehead with his sleeve.

He wondered what Cameron was doing.

He had tried not to think about her, not at all, since that day, that bright and sunny day of the championship game. Ethan told himself over and over that he hadn't been that upset, that bothered by the loss of the game, nor his son's mistake. That's what his head said to his heart. But once his angry words had started coming, he couldn't stop them. He had been angry—angrier than he had ever been—and unsure what he was really angry about. But there it was, vile and venom, spewing out—even in that short burst. Its power had surprised him.

Yelling at Chase was bad, yet he knew that most fathers and sons sometimes tangled. What he'd said was no worse than some of their disagreements in the past. He didn't see what had his son so upset that kept him silent, or sullen, for so many weeks now.

He was a teenager, of course, and teenagers can behave in some terribly odd ways, but this was so unlike Chase.

And Cameron—what he'd said to Cameron—was it all *that* bad? He told himself it wasn't. He and Joel had exchanged worse words—several times—and the next day, they would be best friends and shaking hands and working together like nothing had happened.

He was pretty sure Cameron did not intend to shake his hand—not just yet.

I hardly even got mad.

And when he'd turned around, she was gone.

I don't know how she could have just disappeared like that. And why didn't she call me? She was the one who left.

Ethan unsnapped his tool belt and laid it to the side, out of the way, so no one would trip over it. He switched off the overhead light, a big-watt bare bulb in a pull-chain socket. The room went dark and the light from the streetlamp outside filled up the void, shining through the stud wall in the bedroom. It cast long, narrow, linear shadows over Ethan, the shadows like prison bars—tight and running from ceiling to floor, offering no exit, no exit at all.

Franklin had few taverns that respectable, single women might feel comfortable entering alone. Reed's on the river was not one of them. But CeCe did not want to drive any farther, and she spotted a parking spot right next to the entrance.

"We're meeting Michelle here at six. It's early," CeCe called out to Tessa as she switched off the car. "The biker and hoodlum crowd won't show up till later."

Tessa hoped she was kidding and hoped she didn't have personal knowledge of when the harder clientele actually did show up.

"I don't want a piece of pie or coffee or some stupid mocha-flavored iced decaf latte," CeCe said, explaining her choice. "I want a real drink. And I don't want to drive to the mall. This place is fine. We just need to sit down and talk with Michelle for a few minutes."

Michelle pulled into the parking lot just minutes later, and after introductions, the architect and interior designer followed CeCe inside….

As the ladies' eyes adjusted to the darkness of the tavern, CeCe pointed to a booth by the window. "See? Hardly anyone here. And the smoke isn't all that bad yet. You want a diet something, right?"

She returned with drinks and a bowl of pretzels. "Free dinner, too. This place is great," CeCe said, laughing.

Michelle grabbed a pretzel. "Well … do we have a problem?"

CeCe took a large swallow, then another, then sat back in the booth. "Direct question—means we're all tired and want to get home. Okay.

Direct answer: Should we consider changing construction crews? We are weeks behind schedule here. He told us Christmas. I'm not an expert, but it'll be more like Easter."

Michelle liked her client. She liked her honesty and enthusiasm. She liked that she paid her bills on time. But she knew that her unbridled urgency to complete tasks would be a problem.

"No. We're fine. Really. Willis is doing a good job for you. Schedules always slip a little."

"But, Michelle, he doesn't get it. He's always fighting me about everything. He doesn't want a wide staircase. He doesn't want to move the wall in my bedroom—even though I told him a dozen times. He wants to put a lower ceiling over that blasted pipe that sticks out in the hallway. He wants to use the old 'authentic' windows. Every day it's something else to fight about. I'm writing the checks. Why doesn't he ever say, 'Yes, CeCe, I'll do that for you right now, Mrs. Moretti, ma'am'?"

Michelle felt weary. It was the same argument she had with virtually every client. Construction realities and client expectations rarely matched—even on the perfect jobs. When things got complicated and involved—like with the Carter place—the expectations of both client and craftsman could be, and often were, at polar opposites.

"I don't know, CeCe," she said, hoping to soothe her. "But you want a contractor who's passionate about your project. Ethan really cares about his work—and the quality of the job."

"A true craftsman like that—that's rare. It really is," Tessa added.

"But I want him to say yes—just once. I don't like arguing over everything," CeCe claimed.

"I can talk to him again. I'll try. But he's one of those guys who thinks that all good carpentry practices stopped around 1910."

"He likes things to look the way they used to look. He has great respect for the past," added Tessa.

"But I'm not a Victorian. As Tessa and you both know, Michelle, I don't like Victorian—other than the shell. I love the outside, but the inside has to work for twenty-first-century life—my life. I said that from the beginning of this project—didn't I, Tessa? He refers to that as 'Disneyland.'

I want a big bathtub and a big shower and big closets and windows that actually go up and down. And if I want to have an electrical outlet every two feet, he should do that without giving me a hard time."

That was their most recent battle. In the first-floor office, CeCe had insisted on twice the number of outlets as the building code—and the architect's drawings—required. And she wanted them higher than the standard distance from the floor.

"I have lamps and an electric pencil sharpener and a computer and a printer and fax machine and a copier—and I do not want cords snaking all over the floor! And I don't want one of those annoying—and ugly— power strips! I want real outlets. Higher. And lots of them," she had said.

"But that many outlets up high will be like little dots around the room," Ethan had answered. "It won't work in here."

CeCe had stormed off, calling over her shoulder that there had better be twelve outlets in that room or "I'll take a sledgehammer to it myself and make some really big dots."

"I think your contractor is just a purist," Tessa said. "He's not intentionally trying to be obstinate. He just really believes what he believes. And he does wonderful work."

"CeCe … I understand," Michelle said. "I'll try and talk to him. But I agree with Tessa. I wouldn't try and talk you out of making a change if he didn't do the best work I have ever seen. And you can't change now. Instead of Easter, it will be the Fourth of July before you're in. I know how much you want to spend this summer here with your family."

"But I hate that I feel like I have to be on-site almost every day," CeCe complained. "That if I'm not there, they'll do what Ethan thinks is right—and I'll have to come in and yell at them to change it. I don't like this part of the process at all. On Wednesday … I stopped in and they were framing out the guest bathroom. And I noticed that they had capped off the plumbing for the second sink. I said, 'I want two sinks here. There were two sinks before. Why would I want to eliminate one?' And they just sort of stared at me like I was an alien, and answered, 'Ethan said that they only had one sink in each bathroom when this house was built … so we thought …' I was ready to scream."

Tessa held her laughter. "Men don't think too far in advance, do they?"

"They don't. Men—especially contractors—act like small children. You have to follow them around and make sure they don't get themselves into trouble," CeCe answered as she downed the last of her drink. "And for that, I have to pay them too."

Cameron disliked autumn. Not the good autumn with red and golden leaves falling in a gentle breeze against crystal blue skies, or football games, or crisp air and brilliant sunshine. No, she disliked the mean, gray, dismal autumn days, when rain would fall steadily, the sky would turn the color of wet slate, the temperature headed close to freezing, and the wind whipped along the banks of the river—all in a grand summation to make her miserable and depressed.

Sunday was just such a day—a perfect example of a perfectly miserable autumn day. She awoke to rain pelting against her window. It had started on Friday and had not really let up.

Cameron was not good with nothing to do.

It was the weekend of Applefest, western Pennsylvania's big autumn event. Each year an entertainment stage for band concerts was erected, and hundreds of local food and craft vendors set up booths on the grounds of the old courthouse. Families wandered through the farmer's market and the antique-car show, sharing apple strudel, caramel apples and candy apples, apple cider, apple cider donuts, and apple pie. Cameron imagined that the event, including the morning's 5K run, would be a complete washout. So, she couldn't take a walk there as she had planned— too wet. She was too out of sorts to read. Even the Sunday paper, usually a grand treat, irked her by sitting fat and thick and almost insulting, on the kitchen counter.

She toyed with the idea of taking a car ride but didn't like driving in the rain. Besides, her car really needed new wiper blades. She could barely make out the road through the streaks of water left on the glass. A bike ride on the cycling path was out of the question. She thought of going out for breakfast, but then she'd just end up eating alone, or with a book, or with a newspaper.

None of the options appealed to her.

If I still lived in Philadelphia, I wouldn't have this problem. I could have gone to the art museum.

But she knew she could never live in Philadelphia again.

Instead, after hearing the morning church bells, she decided to do something completely atypical.

She decided to go to church.

Maybe it will be entertaining … or at least distracting, she thought.

She thought of the church around the corner at the end of her block. It was a beautiful stone Gothic-style building, with magnificent Tiffany stained-glass windows of biblical scenes and religious figures. Cameron had been astonished when she had walked by it for the first time. It had a huge rose window with iridescent glass that flamed in the sunlight, but would now be pale in the cold morning light. She had gone to two services there—both within a month of her arrival in Franklin. She recalled loving the church's interior, with its marble floor worn to a soft patina, and its simple stone altar, and wondered, now, why she had never returned to such a beautiful place.

Maybe I was just busy. And the church was … well … it seemed full of mostly old people.

As she dressed, Cameron gave little thought to the oddness of her choice that morning. Had she been pressed, she might have said that the idea of church just fit the inclement weather—providing shelter from the storm, perhaps. She might have said that Paige's urgings from weeks prior had gotten her thinking about … she would hesitate to say "spiritual" things, but she had felt herself toying with that.

Paige had said something about getting things right in her life. Cameron didn't feel she had much to get right—not huge things, at any rate. But she wondered if there were some things in her past that needed … something.

Forgiveness. Maybe it was important. But nothing about that stormy morning so long ago was really her fault—was it? She was too young then. Right?

It's funny that, after all these years, my parents have never once discussed what happened that morning. They never asked. I never told them.

Paige said something about God and "getting right" and all that, didn't she?

Yes, I have a past, but … doesn't everyone? Especially these days …

But she still felt unsettled as she stepped out her door.

The rain had softened to an invasive mist. She pulled her coat close and hurried down the block.

The sign outside said FRANKLIN COMMUNITY CHURCH. Cameron had not paid attention to exactly what that meant or what denomination the church was. The name didn't commit one way or another, she figured.

Her aunt's church—the religious aunt—spelled it all out: EVAN-GELICAL FULL GOSPEL ASSEMBLY. You knew where you stood when you entered those doors. The service there would be intense, with a capital *I*.

But a "Community Church"? It almost sounded like you would walk in and see ping-pong tables and soda machines along the walls—like in every community center she had ever visited. Recently, a new banner that read SKEPTICS WELCOME in big magenta letters had been draped over the archway at the top of the church's main entrance.

On this Sunday, as she hurried up the steps, music came pulsing through the closed doors.

A well-dressed older man, balding, with a fringe of white hair like a halo around his head, hurried up to her.

I was right … they are all old here, she thought.

He was very tan and fit but still looked every bit like everyone's favorite grandfather. His right hand was extended, left index finger point-ing at her, almost as if ready to scold her. But he was smiling, not angry. "It's … it's … Cameron, right?"

Cameron nodded.

"I met you when you visited our church the first time. Charlie Ochs."

She put out her hand, more or less amazed.

He took it in both of his. "I'm good with names. I've been a greeter here for … well, for longer than you've been alive, I bet. And it's Cameron … something Norwegian … or something Scandinavian … Dane. That's it! Cameron Dane."

"You're right. I'm amazed. I only came here once or twice."

He kept hold of her hand longer than normal, in his very firm and steady grip, in a comforting, avuncular way.

"And you work at the newspaper. I see your name all the time. You write well."

"Thanks."

"You don't know that Brad Hitchcock columnist, do you? You print his column, right? He should be arrested for impersonating a writer."

Cameron retrieved her hand. "No. We just reprint his pieces. I've never met him."

"Well, if you do meet him, tell him Charlie says to knock it off, okay?"

Cameron nodded then looked to the closed doors of the sanctuary, expecting Mr. Ochs to lead her to a vacant seat.

"You have to wait until the music is over. We have a new worship director. Says no one is supposed to come in while they're doing music. Says it interrupts the 'worshipful mood,'" he said, making quotation mark signs with his fingers.

Charlie's smile was warm. "He's a nice young man, and I guess you have to learn to adapt. This has been my church for fifty years—and, Lord willing, it will be my church for a few more."

Cameron smiled back, and Charlie leaned close again.

"How about a cup of coffee? Those folks are good for another fifteen minutes of straight singing. Once they get started, they really get into it. And all that standing! Sometimes we old folks just sit down. Even if he never lets people sit down. Being old has its privileges." He laughed.

He led her through a set of double doors into a large multipurpose room—a combination of a gym, a meeting hall, and classrooms.

"They don't want us sneaking in early to get coffee, either, but what they don't know won't hurt them—right, Miss Dane?"

She took the cup Charlie offered. "They think they can keep us from snitching coffee by hiding the cream and sugar until it's refreshment time—so you're going to have to have it black."

"That's good," Cameron said, fibbing as sweetly as she could. "I drink it like this all the time."

He ushered her back through the doors. The music, she noticed, was much more contemporary and upbeat than Cameron recalled from her previous visit.

"I myself prefer more traditional music," Charlie said. "But if the upbeat type attracts younger people like you—then it's a good thing. You are the future of the church! Do you like our new music, Miss Dane?"

"I do. What I can hear of it, anyway," Cameron answered, as she peered in on the service.

Charlie looked at her face closely, and Cameron could see genuine concern in his eyes. "You're troubled by something, right? I haven't been around all this time without getting a little smarter."

Cameron didn't answer. She didn't know if Mr. Ochs was expecting an answer.

"Well, if so, you have come to the right place. We're not perfect, of course. But if you're at all unsettled and worried—then you're at the right place. You'll find us to be friendly people, and maybe you'll even get an answer to a question or two. Once the music stops, I'll get you a good seat. Our new pastor—he's another young one—is very smart. He's talking about living a Christian life. Book of James. He's good. You'll like him."

The music stopped. There was applause and Charlie took that as his cue.

"Let's get you inside, Miss Dane. Glad to have you back with us. Pay attention today. You'll feel better for it."

I would build a bridge a hundred meters long,
To see the other side of what I did wrong.
Well, you say you don't hate me
But I guess that I'm scared,
That with a river between us
You'll no longer care.

—MARC GUNN, *THE BRIDGE*

CHAPTER TWELVE

AUTUMN WAS BEING EDGED out by winter. Venango County had yet to receive any measurable snowfall. The sky had been the color of lead for several weeks, and the cold gray of the days matched exactly the way Cameron felt.

Her work at *The Derrick* proved to be an answer to a prayer—a prayer she would not have prayed, even if she had been a praying woman.

What kind of prayer would it be? she wondered. *Lord, keep me busy because if I'm not busy I'll start obsessing over Ethan again? And Chase?*

She worked longer hours than required, spending a few nights a week at her desk, typing, researching, making phone calls, learning more about page design and layout, telling herself that this extra time was an investment in her future career.

One afternoon, the week after Thanksgiving, Paige summoned Cameron into her office. "Nice work on the county board article. You made a boring subject almost interesting."

Cameron immediately replied, "I could redo it. I knew it needed more of a human angle to it. Let me rework it. I can make it better."

"No, Cameron. No more. This was a compliment. Really. You actually made an article about that bunch of old, cranky men readable. No one else on this staff has even come close. No need to fuss with it."

"But I had some great quotes I didn't use," Cameron protested.

"No more. And besides, you've only had the assignment for two days. I expected you to take a couple of weeks."

Cameron didn't shrug, but it appeared as though she wanted to. "I've had a bit more free time these past weeks," she admitted. "It's nice to keep busy."

Paige waited an uncomfortable minute before speaking again. "You haven't talked to him, I take it."

Cameron shook her head. "Nope. Not a word since … since that baseball game. Since the end of summer." Her words were tinged with defeat.

"Cameron, it's been a couple of months now. I know I'm no paragon of relationship wisdom—seeing as how none of my marriages worked out very well."

Cameron was sure a lecture was coming and was feeling an odd mix of fear, guilt, and anger, with a dash of sullenness thrown in.

"You know what I'm going to say, right? Wasn't there a book a few years ago … something about *He's Just Not That Into You?* I so dislike using 'into' as a substitute for the concept of love … or even attraction. Terrible thing, this new language. All sorts of connotations, if you ask me. We're becoming a nation of sloppy writers and lazy readers."

Paige sat up straighter. "That's off the subject. Sorry. But this thing with Ethan Willis— if it only took that one time—that one blowup … if that's all it took, then maybe it was …"

Cameron sat up straighter. "Please don't say it was for the best. Maybe it was. Maybe. But I don't want to hear that it was for the best."

Cameron's surge of passion made Paige lean backward in her chair.

"So you thought that you were falling in love? Is that it?"

Cameron shrugged, using her whole body to make the gesture. "I don't know. Maybe. I mean, I have been with other men … longer relationships, and more … more intimate. When those relationships ended, I may have been sad for a few days, a few weeks, and in some cases, extremely relieved, but I kept moving. I guess I figured that's how love is. I never felt this derailed."

"I know you just told me not to say it—but I have to. Have you ever thought that this *could* be for the best? Maybe this was the way it was supposed to happen. There is a plan for our lives, Cameron, whether we acknowledge it or not. Ethan seems like a very nice man, but maybe he isn't healthy deep down inside. Maybe he would have been totally wrong for you."

I don't believe that for a minute, Cameron thought.

"I don't know. It seems like I had the new beginning of my life here all figured out, and apparently I thought I had the next step figured out. I mean, it felt so right and so comfortable ... so unlike anything else I had experienced. And that's what threw me. It was just so good and then it blew up. That, I didn't see coming at all."

It was obvious to Cameron that Paige wanted to nod and commiserate with her but held herself back. "Still, you have to be aware of that one big possibility—that this is exactly the way things are supposed to be."

But I don't want to be aware of that. I don't.

Both women were silent for a long time, letting the discussion echo and reverberate within the office and themselves.

Cameron broke the silence by sighing with resignation. "I don't know. I don't know anything. Maybe you're right, Paige. I thought I would never say that. But maybe you're right."

Then a young boy's face came swimming up toward her—and she somehow knew that it wasn't right. Not right at all.

Ethan stood in what would eventually become the kitchen of the Old Carter Mansion. By late afternoon, the weary wintry sunlight had all but disappeared. He switched on the work lights that were attached to a tripod stand in the corner. Wallboard had yet to be installed, making it much too early for any lighting to have been wired.

He stood next to a sheet of plywood serving as a table held up by two sawhorses, and unrolled the blueprints for the kitchen area. He pinned the corners flat with a hammer, a box of finish nails, a twenty-five-foot tape measure, and his thermos. He smoothed out the paper, taking care not to create any ridges or folds in the paper. By the end of the job, the prints would be torn and tattered, but Ethan liked the document as pristine as possible for as long as possible.

He had come back to the house for a meeting with the kitchen planner. He whisked away a tumbling of sawdust from the plans and unfolded the preliminary outlines for the kitchen cabinets. The thin overlay paper held the first draft of a very complicated kitchen drawn by CeCe's kitchen designer, Scott Anderson, from Anderson and Harrington Kitchens in Pittsburgh.

Having a separate design firm for the kitchen was different, and having one from out of town was even more unusual. People in Franklin didn't usually hire kitchen planners. You put in the appliances and cabinets in an efficient sort of way—what more design did you need?

He wondered why a Pittsburgh outfit would have bothered. CeCe's extensive kitchen meant a decent commission, to be sure—but the distance between Pittsburgh and Franklin, Ethan surmised, would have created a large logistical headache.

It could be the possibility of a magazine shoot when the kitchen is completed, Ethan thought. *A project like this would look good in a portfolio.*

Ethan glanced at his watch—a few minutes after five. The house was empty, save for himself. His crew had decided that starting early—at six in the morning—was better, since it allowed them to leave early.

"At least we'll have a little daylight left to enjoy," Joel explained.

Joel had volunteered to come back for the meeting, but Ethan had declined the offer.

"I'm fine. Don't you think I can handle our fancy Pittsburgh designer?" Joel did not argue.

The house was quiet when he heard a tapping at the front door.

About time he got here.

Ethan swung the door open.

He stopped and stared.

On the other side was a woman.

It was close to quitting time—the official quitting time for the hourly staff at *The Derrick*. Cameron anticipated staying around for another hour or so, so she could surf the Internet, looking for Christmas gifts for everyone who was hard to buy for among her family and friends. In fact, Cameron had concluded, everyone she knew was hard to buy for—except herself.

If I had to buy myself something for Christmas, that would be so easy.

Cameron had finished her story on the finances of the Venango County School Board and printed out the pages. Even if she didn't need paper copies for her stories, she liked to have them. She found editing much easier on paper than on screen.

She stacked the pages neatly, making sure that all the corners were even, then laid the stack on the right corner of her desk, making sure that no pages slipped out of alignment.

I am becoming so obsessive-compulsive, she thought.

She heard Clara say, "That's her over there."

Cameron didn't look up until a shadow crossed the corner of her desk. "Miss Dane?"

"Yes … I'm Miss … I mean, I'm Cameron … Dane."

A young and very attractive man standing in front of her desk bent slightly at the waist and extended his hand to her. "You have to forgive me. I hadn't planned on stopping here tonight … tomorrow, yes, but not tonight. But I am a firm believer that when opportunity knocks, you should try to answer the door. Don't you agree?"

Cameron wondered what she had missed. She looked over and saw Clara shrugging mightily, raising her hands in submission.

"Obviously, I have lovely Miss Clara confused. I bet that doesn't happen all that often, does it?" he said as he nodded toward the older woman.

How did he know her name? Cameron wondered.

"Miss Dane, please allow me to do introductions. I am Paul Drake." He waited a moment, as if he had the timing rehearsed. "Sounds like a bad soap-opera name, doesn't it?"

"Drake. You mean … like the oil well?"

Paul Drake laughed. "No. No relation to the Drake who drilled the oil well. That question is only asked in Venango County by the way. History can be so provincial. And, Miss Dane, that branch of the Drakes died penniless, I am told."

Cameron tilted her head, baffled, then brightened. She turned and pointed to the empty office in the corner. "Like the Drakes who own the newspaper?"

"Well, yes, Miss Dane, at least in the general sense. The newspapers are on the other side of the family. Aunt Paige and all them. I'm from the black sheep side of the Drake line." He leaned closer and whispered, conspiratorially, "We left Venango County eons ago—before the Ice Age, I believe—and made our way to the balmy southern climes of Pittsburgh."

Cameron liked this young man already, although she had never once heard Paige mention having relatives in Pittsburgh.

"We are involved in—" he whispered, the last word the softest of all—"television."

Then Paul Drake stood tall and resumed his normal speaking voice, which was bold and clear. "Actually, Aunt Paige is a great-aunt, or is that called a second aunt?" Paul said, batting the air, as if dismissing the complexity of his genealogy. "But we are related in some convoluted, backwoods fashion, I'm sure."

Cameron found herself grinning.

"And I am surprised that Aunt Paige is not here. After all, she did invite me here—to talk to you, actually."

He waited for the words to have effect.

"Sort of, anyway."

Cameron had no response.

"So—are you free for dinner?"

At the corner of her vision, she could see Clara, so confused and desperate to figure out who this stranger was.

—⚬⚬⚬—

Emily Harrington thrust out her hand to a surprised Ethan Willis.

"Mr. Willis? Scott said to express his regrets. He had planned to come today but was tied up with a family ... situation. You're a dad, right? Then you must understand how these things sometimes happen. I'm Emily Harrington. Scott and I are partners. I am the Harrington of Anderson and Harrington."

Ethan recovered the ability to speak. "Oh, yes, sure, that's okay. I just had expected Scott. We had talked some, you know. And he said, well, he was going to be here."

Emily stepped into the large foyer. "You knew that Scott had a partner. But he never mentioned me, did he? He never mentioned that he had a partner who happened to be of the female persuasion, I'll bet."

Ethan smiled. "No. He did not. Not once." He ushered the designer back through the house toward the kitchen. "Not that I mind. This project has lots of women involved. It's just that I was just expecting ... someone named Scott."

Emily surveyed the large open area that would someday be a kitchen. "If it helps, Mr. Willis, you can call me Scott."

She smiled at him, broad and warm, and from what Ethan could tell, in great earnestness. She was very pretty, Ethan would admit later. Pretty, and actually a lot more than just pretty, but in a middle-aged sort of way. Her form was trim, not thin, and her medium-blonde hair was short, precise. Red-framed glasses matched her lipstick and fingernails.

"No. That's okay," Ethan replied, almost recovered from his surprise. "Just a little startled at the end of a longish day. I think I'll be able to handle it."

The designer set her ample Louis Vuitton bag on the makeshift plywood table, pulled out a case, unzipped it, flipped open a thin and chic laptop, switched it on, and retrieved a small, digital camera from her bag.

Paul Drake straightened his Italian silk tie. It did not need straightening.

Cameron would later guess he could not have been more than two years older than she. If she were writing his description for use in a book, she would have written, *And he was devilishly handsome … a fact that he knew of, approved of, and ignored.*

He pushed a hand through a shock of dark brown hair. His hair was unmoussed, she was sure, but it obeyed as if it were.

"So, Miss Dane, are you mentally considering which fine local dining establishment you shall recommend for the two of us? We do have some important business to discuss."

Cameron looked over her shoulder to see if she had missed a large section of conversation and it was lying behind her, unused.

She saw no such pile of words there.

"Yes, yes, I know my aunt is not one for telling the appropriate parties of important conversations between herself and her nephew … or great-nephew—whatever. But that does not answer my question. Dinner? Where?"

Clara almost fell from her chair at the desk. She offered a small shriek that got both Paul Drake's and Cameron's attention.

"I'm fine," she called out as she grabbed the edge of the counter and pulled herself upright. "Why not Gibson's? Best steaks in Venango County."

Cameron shot a harsh look at Clara, then softened when she turned back to Mr. Drake.

"Obviously, Aunt Paige was negligent in her duties. She did not let you know I was coming. She did not discuss this at all with you. I must talk to her about this. But now, we must attend to the matter at hand—dinner. I am famished. It has been a long day."

Cameron almost stood, as if being swept along by the force of Mr. Paul Drake's personality. "But … but why are you here? What do I have to do with—"

Paul smoothed the camel-colored cashmere overcoat he had draped over his right arm. "Well, I suspect I will be forced to disclose my plans before I can coerce you to leave your desk. Miss Dane, I know a good bit about you already. We get copies of *The Derrick* down in Pittsburgh. A few days late, but we get it. I have admired your work. I asked my aunt to tell me about you."

This time Cameron did stand. Somehow it felt more appropriate.

"And I have come all this way to …"

Cameron listened closer.

"… to offer you a job."

Cameron had to force her jaw to remain closed, but somehow she accomplished it. Clara was much less successful than Cameron.

Emily snapped dozens of pictures of the kitchen, making sure that every angle of the empty room was documented and every perspective explored. She tapped at her laptop and typed for a moment.

"This is much more grand than I imagined," she finally said. "Scott isn't the best at describing a room. A room always feels so different in person than it does on a blueprint, doesn't it? The light. The flow. The height."

She looked directly at Ethan, her eyes catching him full on. He felt observed, examined. "How long until you start on the finish work down here?"

Ethan had anticipated the question. "We have another three weeks on the top floors. We're waiting on some custom glass bathroom tiles Mrs. Moretti ordered from Italy. If they show up … three weeks. If not … then maybe we'll finish the basement first."

"Good," Emily said, nodding and typing. "Of course we have some preliminary planning done. We knew that wall would be cabinets," she said, pointing at the north wall. "They're close to being selected."

"What about the appliances?"

"Mrs. Carter was very, very certain about what she wanted—as long as it was the absolute best. That makes our job a little easier. I have a tentative layout here," she said as she pulled a rolled blueprint from her bag. "I wanted to walk it all out with tape so I could check on traffic patterns."

Ethan helped hold one edge of the blueprint down on the plywood table. As he bent close to her, he smelled a hint of citrus. It might have been a lemony fragrance, but sweeter. On the work site, that scent was not a regular occurrence. He told himself not to breathe deeply, thinking that the gesture might be considered rude.

"The Wolf range and ovens are here, and over here are the Sub-Zeros," Emily said, pointing. "And we have the island right in this area. That's the one dimension I need to check. We like architects. Especially the team from 3R. It's just that we don't trust them."

Ethan found himself laughing in agreement.

"Help me with this tape?" she asked as she extended a thick roll of bright orange masking tape to him. In her other hand, she pulled out a battered forty-foot tape measure—just like the one Ethan used.

———

"Gibson's it shall be, Miss Dane. Clara would not send us to a mediocre establishment, would you, Clara?"

"Certainly not," Clara responded with some pride. "I don't go very often. But Gibson's is real good."

Paul Drake slipped his coat on in a single smooth move. "I adore 'real good,'" he said as he extended his hand to Cameron. "I hope you like 'real good' too."

As Cameron took his hand, he turned back to Clara. "Miss Clara, would you be so kind as to call that fine establishment and make reservations for the two of us? At their nicest table—one with a view, if they have one."

Clara was already in the phone book. It was obvious to Cameron that Paul Drake was a man who was used to getting his own way—and to having people help him get it.

Paul drove. Cameron had forgotten how smooth and supple a luxury car could be. His black Lexus, though maybe a year old, looked immaculate and still smelled of new leather with the tiniest hint of some woodsy aftershave.

The maître d' at Gibson's escorted them to a table overlooking the river. Though it was early, the dining room was three-quarters filled.

"Winter brings out the early crowd," Paul said as he slid in Cameron's chair. "Pittsburgh in the winter is exactly the same."

A trio of waiters scurried over with water, bread, and menus. Paul did not take one.

"The lady will take her time, but have your chef pick out the best New York strip in the house for me. When he cooks it, make it medium rare to medium, no blood, please. Instead of the baked potato—grilled asparagus, plain, and a double order of a house salad—no radishes, bleu cheese dressing on the side. And a large glass of water. With a slice of lime, not lemon."

Paul folded his hands on the table. "But, Miss Dane, please, take all the time you need. I admit that I can be a distraction in restaurants. I have only a few favorite foods—and I order them over and over."

Cameron held up her hand, bidding the waiter to stay. She knew she wouldn't be able to function well with Mr. Paul Drake watching her decide on dinner.

"A large salad, the house vinaigrette, extra croutons. The petite filet, medium well. Baked potato with everything. And an iced tea if it's fresh brewed, lots of lemon slices. If not, a sparkling water. With a slice of lemon, not lime."

It was clear that Paul was nearly impressed. "Not many people, women especially, come to quick decisions in a restaurant. I like those that do. Not that it proves anything at all, but I like that quality in a woman—and in a man, for that matter."

Cameron folded her hands in front of her on the table. She forced herself to say the words evenly and calmly. "So, Mr. Drake, what sort of job are we talking about?"

———⋙⋘———

In fifteen minutes, Emily and Ethan had lined the kitchen floor with the fluorescent masking tape, outlining the shape of the cabinets, the appliances, the island, the built-in desk, and had taped the counter height on the raw stud walls. Emily tapped scores of measurements into her laptop. She walked through the room, stepping aside of the tape, entering and exiting at each door. She knelt where the dishwashers were to be located, she paced backward from the stove as if taking out a large turkey, she walked between the refrigerator/freezers and the sink, and the ovens and the sink—what she referred to as "the working triangle." She spent several minutes learning the distances between those points on foot.

"Paper can be so misleading. It's such a blessing to have the space unfinished so I can really see how things will fit together."

Ethan watched with admiration. Seldom did he find architects or designers who took this sort of care with a project, working hard to make the design fit for humans. Most often it was vice versa.

"Well, Mr. Willis, I think I am done for tonight. Our specifications expert is coming tomorrow morning."

"Right. That's what Scott said."

"I don't think he really needs to be here … but I think he just wants to get out of the showroom for a day and take a long drive."

"Should I roll up your blueprint?" Ethan asked.

Emily looked over her shoulder as she was packing up her computer.

"No. Unless it's in your way. We'll need it tomorrow."

"You'll be here tomorrow?" he asked, a little surprised.

"Yes. Jacob, our specs 'consultant' is—well, to be kind—a little high-strung. I don't want him getting too excited about any change in the plans or dimensions. It's easiest if I just spend the night in Franklin so I can hold his hand, if you know what I mean, in the morning. You know how temperamental some designers can be—and kitchen designers are simply the worst."

Ethan nodded, though he didn't really understand any of this. But he did know what *high-strung* meant, and he knew it was better if someone else dealt with it.

"I have a room at The Franklin House. That's the historic hotel on the main street of your downtown, right? I hope it's a decent place."

"It's not bad. I can't say I've ever been in the rooms. I imagine they're not spacious, but the dining room is … well … it's okay. And other people who have stayed there said that … that it was clean and friendly. It's an okay place."

"Okay is fine. There aren't that many lodging choices in Franklin. It was either this or the Holiday Inn in Oil City. And I didn't want to drive there after dark." Ethan helped Emily pack up her tools, then walked over to the light. "You're done, right?"

Emily shouldered her bag. "I am. But I do have one favor to ask. It's a long drive from Pittsburgh to Franklin. And I'm tired. But more than that, I'm really hungry. What's the best place to eat around here? I'm in the mood for meat—a good steakhouse would be great."

Without giving it a lot of thought, Ethan replied, "Gibson's. But it's out on the river highway—a few miles out of town. There's no steak place closer than that, I'm afraid."

Emily didn't try to hide her disappointment. "No. I'm no good driving strange roads after dark. I'm not that good even with places I know once it gets dark."

"I could draw a map. It's real easy to get to."

Emily hoisted her bag higher on her shoulder. "No. That's okay. The Franklin House will be fine."

Ethan saw something in her eyes, then, without thinking about the words, said, "I could take you there."

Emily brightened. "Would you? I mean … could you? Your family must be waiting for you. I would hate to impose on your time."

"No one is waiting. My son is at his friend's house tonight. There's nobody waiting." He was not sure if he should explain further, and he did not.

"That would be great. Is it a fancy place?" She didn't really look at his clothes, but she did glance.

He looked down at his clean denim shirt and pressed khaki pants. "No. I think I'm fine. This is Franklin, after all."

"Then you have a dinner date."

The word stopped him for a moment. "Well, then—okay."

———

Chase lay on his back on the floor, his legs elevated on Elliot's bed.

They both could hear Elliot's mom clattering in the kitchen. She was rearranging the cabinets, moving dishes from one cabinet to the other, cleaning the shelves and laying out new shelf liners. When she was in one of these moods, which were now known as "Mom's frenzies" in Elliot's house, everyone avoided that specific room, lest they be recruited into a cause for which they had not expected to volunteer.

"You going away over Christmas?" Elliot asked. He was lying on his bed, tossing a Nerf ball up and down, seeing how close he could come to the ceiling fan without hitting the blades.

"No. My dad's still working on the Carter place. I heard him and Joel talking and that it's taking longer than they thought it would. Maybe spring break, he said, we could go someplace not too expensive," Chase replied. "You guys going anywhere?"

Elliot snorted a laugh. "And when was the last time we went anywhere? You're the lucky one who went to Disney World last year."

From the kitchen Chase heard Elliot's mom bark out his younger sister's name. "Elaine! I see you there. Come here. Hold these plates. My word! Every time I start to clean, it seems like everyone disappears."

Elliot snorted another laugh.

"Yeah. Real lucky," Chase said with more than a little sarcasm.

Not to forgive is to be imprisoned by the past,
by old grievances that do not permit life
to proceed with new business.

—LANCE MORROW

———◦◦◦———

Forgiving what we cannot forget
creates a new way to remember.
We change the memory of our past
into a hope for our future.

—LEWIS B. SMEDES

CHAPTER THIRTEEN

"You seem to be a direct person," Paul said as he carefully took a single croissant from the basket of various types of dinner rolls. "Aunt Paige said you had moxie. I like moxie."

Cameron could not help smiling.

"I know. *Moxie* is such an out-of-date word, isn't it? Like *gumption*. No one has gumption anymore. I mean, sure, people have it. They simply call it something else."

He stopped talking long enough to take a rather large bite out of the flaky roll, foregoing the addition of butter.

Cameron remembered the croissants as being made with a substantial portion of butter, or maybe lard.

This is Venango County, after all, she thought.

He chewed, swallowed, took a drink, and brushed his lips with the napkin. "Cloth napkins. In Franklin. Imagine that."

Cameron liked him even more.

"Well, Miss Dane, enough of my pathetic cat-and-mouse game. I admit to taking some measure of perverse pleasure in such activity. Though my father is the master at this game. Such dialogue with him can extend for weeks."

Paul pointed to his water glass as a busboy scurried past.

"Well, I mentioned to you earlier, did I not, that we are in that horrid television business? A brother of Paige's father moved south to Pittsburgh way back when. Said the newspaper business dirtied his hands. Literally. He didn't like the way newsprint rubbed off on his hands. And he claimed that your daily work winds up in someone's trash bin the next day. He didn't like the imagery involved."

Cameron sat back in her chair and crossed her legs, anticipating a longish story. She was glad she was wearing slacks.

"He was one of the original investors in KDKA."

Cameron still didn't get it. Her face must have showed it, because he went on.

"Well, obviously you did not grow up in Pittsburgh. KDKA was the world's first public radio station. And even then, there was a Drake with his hand in the till."

"Did he own it?" Cam asked.

"Oh, no. Just a little part of it. And a few other stations. I suspect he bought a majority holding in some of them for a few hundred dollars. And presto … wait twenty years … sell at a huge profit."

"The American way," Cameron said.

"And they bought into television when it was very much in the infancy stage. Now the family is into cable and transmission services and advertising rights. None of our side of the Drake dynasty really seems to own anything outright, but the little pieces all add up."

He relaxed in his chair. "The one thing we do own outright, curiously enough, is an operation that does not make money. Some sort of wicked Drake curse, I suppose. We have an independent cable station—and that includes an odd franchising operation. If one franchises television, one needs shows to franchise. Our little operation produces programs. We own the rights to a few cooking shows, a few exercise shows, and we are beginning a new show—to compete, if you could call it that, with Home and Garden Television—a remodeling and decorating and renovation show. It will be grand—grand on a western Pennsylvanian scale."

Cameron uncrossed her legs, took a croissant from the basket, slathered two pats of butter in the middle with her knife and smushed it back together. Before she took a bite, she asked, "But what does any of this have to do with me?"

Paul smiled. "Well, Miss Dane, we want you to be the host."

She almost dropped the croissant in her lap but caught it before it hit, nearly crushing it in her fist.

———— >∘◦∘< ————

Ethan hurried around to first open the car door and then the restaurant door. He'd discovered that Emily was not a woman who walked slowly. She insisted that he drive her car. He had not driven a car as luxurious as hers since … well … since forever.

"I don't know much about cars," Emily said. "But Scott said this model of Jaguar is a good value for the money. And I like its rather feminine lines. They had a red one in stock. So I bought it."

Ethan was going to ask what her husband had to say about that, but then looked at her ring hand and saw it bare of jewelry. *If she asked her business partner what car to buy, then she's probably … single.*

Ethan had no idea what to do with that information or if it should make a difference in how he should act this evening. He hoped not, because he was not standing on ground that felt all that solid.

"Why, this is just lovely," Emily said as they sat down. "So charming. I was expecting something more like a roadhouse. This isn't like that at all."

Ethan was glad that she seemed pleased but wasn't sure what the difference between a roadhouse and this restaurant was. Subtle perhaps, he concluded.

Emily only glanced at the menu, and when the waiter came for their drink order, she said she was ready to order food as well.

"There is nothing on the road between here and Pittsburgh except that dreadful fast food," she said for the benefit of both the waiter and Ethan. "I am mostly to fully famished, so dinner needs to progress on the quicker fashion, rather than the slower."

After they ordered, Emily took a crusty roll, broke it into small pieces on her plate, and added a delicate dab of butter.

"So, tell me, Ethan, how did you come to land the Carter restoration project? Mrs. Moretti just goes on and on about how wonderful your work is. Do you specialize in historic projects like this? I wouldn't think Venango County would host that many careful restorations. And why aren't you working in Pittsburgh? I could use a good contractor to recommend. Clients are always asking for trustworthy craftsmen. You could do very well in a bigger market, I would bet."

Ethan took a sip of water and wondered which of her questions he might actually get to answer.

———<small>◦◦◦◦</small>———

"So, Chase, what's it going to be for the big science project?" Elliot's mother asked as she ladled out a large spoonful of macaroni and cheese onto his plate.

This was not the sort of mac 'n' cheese that came out of a box. Elliot's mom took real macaroni and melted a chunk of real cheese— Chase thought it was Velveeta, or the warehouse version of Velveeta, the size of a softball. When that was melted and gooey, she added milk and lots of butter, then poured it all into a full pot of macaroni—the kind that looked like seashells. It was Elliot's favorite dinner. Chase, as well as all of Elliot's younger siblings, liked it too.

Chase would have shrugged at the science-project question at home, getting a glare back from his father for sure. But he liked Elliot's mom a lot and, after all, they were feeding him once again.

Both he and Elliot had been seated at the far end of the table, closer to the adults and farther away from the mayhem at the kids' end of the long, long dining-room table.

"I'm building a house … I mean, it's a model house. Out of balsa wood. I'm showing how the walls are made and the trusses and joists and how all that stuff works together. I'm using a book that my dad has. It shows how to calculate the loads and stress and that sort of thing. Like if you need a ten-by-two or OSB or steel. The model shows all the hidden stuff in a house."

Mrs. Hewitt nodded and pointed at Elliot. "You should do something interesting like that. It sounds real brainy and just the thing that would impress those snooty judges."

Elliot looked pained, just a bit, and Chase gave him a second's worth of a shrug, as if to say, *I didn't mean to make you look bad.*

"I don't know, Mom. But I'll think of something to do."

His mom just looked at him.

Elliot quickly added, "Maybe I'll do a presentation that shows how to make the world's best macaroni and cheese. I think that's kinda brainy."

Mrs. Hewitt looked both peeved and pleased at the same time. She smiled at her oldest son. "I don't know if that would qualify as science, but thank you, Son, for the nice compliment."

After dinner, both boys helped clear the table, much to the surprise of Elliot's mom. Then they headed back over to Chase's house.

"It's easier to study there—it's real quiet," Elliot explained.

"Thanks for dinner. It was really good," Chase added.

They cut through backyards, shortening their walk.

"Is your dad home?"

"Dunno. He works late a lot these days."

"He never used to."

"This is a big project. And he said something about meeting a kitchen designer or something. From Pittsburgh."

"Really? From Pittsburgh? They come the whole way up here, like with refrigerators and stoves and that sort of stuff?"

"Dunno. Just said this guy was coming up. He said there was a pizza in the freezer if he didn't make it home for supper."

"A pizza? Really? A warehouse club pizza?"

"Probably. You want some?"

Elliot shrugged. "Maybe. Okay. A piece or two. If you're hungry. Sure."

"But I don't know a thing about television," Cameron said in protest. "Though I did take a television-production class in college, I hardly paid attention."

Paul leaned closer. "Then you know at least as much as I do about the business. I nod a lot and ask other people what they think, then agree with them—with enthusiasm. Works like a charm."

"But host? Me? You must be joking."

Their food arrived and Paul did not stop talking as he dug into his steak.

"No, Miss Dane, I am not. You are articulate. I could tell that from the way you write. You seem to know quite a bit about construction and renovation. We could all see that from the articles you did on the Carter Mansion. You have a fresh face—you're very attractive. Aunt Paige said that. And I can see why. That's all you need to be successful on TV."

Cameron was pleased about being judged attractive but would not let her thoughts linger on the delightful feeling that gave her. "But don't you need a screen test to tell? Or some sort of interview?"

Paul chewed more quickly. "Maybe some people might. I don't."

"But I don't see how ..."

"Let me ask you a question," Paul said, waving a thumb-sized piece of sirloin in the air. "When you read a story, or a book, or a newspaper article, even, how many pages or paragraphs do you need to read to know that it is something that's good, well-written, something that you would want to continue to read?"

Cameron thought. "Maybe a page?"

"I would think a single paragraph would be more likely," Paul said, popping the meat into his mouth. "One can tell early on. I think you would be a grand host. Somebody else will write the scripts. You can do some editing, if you like, if the words don't sound like you. We have a small crew that will do the filming. Someone else will edit, add music, graphics ... whatever. All you have to do is look at the camera and not trip very often. You could do that, right?"

Cameron felt pushed along, like a dandelion caught in the wind.

"Listen, Miss Dane. Being a TV host on a cable show will not make you rich. In reality, it is just a glamorous-sounding part-time job at the beginning. Unless it takes off. Then—who knows? You would not have to move to Pittsburgh. I envision your being our delightful host for merely a few days a month. I could work out a time-share deal with Aunt Paige. It would be great fun."

Cameron looked at her steak and realized that she had yet to take a bite.

"I said earlier that a man … or a woman … needs to seize the moment. I think I said that earlier. If I didn't, then I should have. And if you hesitate in your response and fail to eat your steak—then I will be forced to eat it for you. And you don't want that, do you, Miss Dane?"

She waited, then grinned, and picked up her knife and fork and began to eat.

"Thank you for the kind words," Ethan said, avoiding calling her Emily— or Miss Harrington—which she probably was, but he wasn't sure and had limited skills in navigating the turbulent waters of modern manners. "I don't think I could get any of my crew to move to Pittsburgh. I bet the deer hunting in Pittsburgh is terrible. And there's a lot more traffic than in Franklin. Everyone that works for me hates traffic. So, no, I have not considered advertising for work there."

"A pity," Emily replied. "You could stay very, very busy—just on my referrals alone."

"And as for specializing in restorations … I love old houses and the care that people took in building them. You don't see that today. People cut corners, use cheap material, shoddy workmanship. It's a shame, and I try my best to give the customer not just what they ask for, but what the building needs. It takes a lot of time with some of these jobs to uncover what's underneath, what was hidden by lots of layers of paint, cheap paneling, or bad drywall. A lot of the bones, the intentions of a house, get lost or buried, and it takes some care to uncover all that. I find the work fascinating and rewarding."

Emily nodded during his speech, and Ethan would say later that she was just about to take his hand in the middle of it.

She did not.

And when he was finished, he turned his head slightly away from her, somewhat embarrassed by his passion.

Had he not turned, he may very well not have seen Cameron and a well-dressed man sitting in the far corner of the dining room, both heads leaning in toward the center, as if discussing a matter of great importance or something of deep personal significance.

Whatever their discussion was about, Ethan felt his chest tighten, as if having some sort of major medical emergency, which he knew he wasn't. He wondered how long he could stare in her direction before making a fool of himself once again in front of a woman.

When one door closes, another opens;
but we often look so long
and so regretfully upon the closed door
that we do not see the one
which has opened for us.

—ALEXANDER GRAHAM BELL

———

Life is an adventure in forgiveness.

—NORMAN COUSINS

CHAPTER FOURTEEN

THE PIZZA WAS BIGGER than Chase or Elliot had anticipated. But, gamely, they finished it, although they both left a few crusts; something they seldom, if ever, did.

"So, what are you doing for the science fair? You only have a few weeks."

Elliot shrugged. "I dunno. None of the stuff Mr. Hardwick suggested seems very interesting—and most of it seems pretty hard."

The boys sat in Chase's small, hidden room.

"You wanna test concrete? I thought of doing that. Might be cool."

"Concrete? Where am I going to get that? From one of those giant cement trucks?"

"No, dummy. You buy one bag of the stuff at the Home Depot. It's called Sakrete. Then we have to build some small forms for the concrete. You could use paint stirrers—they're just the right size. We mix up the concrete with different amounts of water or sand or gravel. Then we put weights on them to see when they break in half."

"Sounds really hard," Elliot said as he scooted back against the wall, picking up a *Justice League of America* comic book.

"It would take, like, a couple of hours at the most. I was going to do
it myself—before I started building the house. It would be cool. See how
much stress it takes to break things."

Elliot appeared concerned. "But don't you need to prove something?
What's it called—a thesis or something?"

Chase readjusted his lawn chair. "It has that. All the concrete will look
the same from the outside, but it won't be the same on the inside. The
weak concrete will look just like the strong concrete, only the weak stuff
is brittle and breaks easy. You could have a title like 'Breaking Points,' or
something cool like that. Like how it can look normal and all on the outside and be ready to break on the inside."

"I dunno," Elliot said as he flipped the pages. He had read the comic
book several hundred times. "Would you help me?"

"Sure. I'm almost done with mine. Sure. And we can make things
break."

Elliot set the comic book down. "Okay. Thanks. I mean that," Elliot
said, his words tight with honesty.

"No problem."

⸻ ❧ ⸻

For the most part, except for in her hometown, Cameron never anticipated seeing anyone she knew anyplace she went—especially in Franklin,
where she knew a few people through her work on the paper but considered only a handful as friends.

Just as Mr. Paul Drake was in the midst of laying out his proposal for
Cameron to host the initial three episodes of *Three Rivers Restorations*, she
stretched her back and pivoted in her chair, hearing her vertebrae pop and
click. When she reached her fullest extension, she saw into the other section of the dining area, connected by wide French doors. She saw Ethan
and some other woman, a woman much closer to his own age than
Cameron was.

She supposed that in Franklin, given time, everyone would see everyone, regardless of potential or imagined discomfort. It was different in

Philadelphia. Circles may never intersect. But she had known that, sooner or later, she would run into Ethan.

And there he was, sitting there, plain as day, smiling ... then not smiling as their eyes met. While the look they shared was not happiness, it was not displeasure, not anger. It was something else altogether—a look of longing or pain or something akin to seeing an image of a lost past that was once attractive and perhaps now is gone, but perhaps not.

Cameron didn't know what to do or say or where to look.

Paul asked a question that she didn't hear. He repeated it. She had to turn away and look at her dinner partner. She had to look away from Ethan, though she didn't want to.

She didn't want to admit how her heart felt, how her throat tightened, and how much she wanted to run from the restaurant. She wanted to run into the snowy woods, where she could hear nothing except the creak and hiss of the pines as a cold wind threaded through the branches and needles and swept along the dark, bare forest floor.

<hr />

Ethan stared a moment longer at Cameron after she stopped looking at him. He turned back to Emily, who was happily dissecting her steak, dipping it in crimson steak sauce, turning the slice of meat in and out and through, and drawing it to her mouth with great gusto.

Grateful for the food, grateful for the silence it commanded, he picked up his fork, hoping he might still be able to swallow that evening, hoping the food would not lodge in the lump in his throat.

And as he chewed, he thought about Cameron.

I didn't call her ... because I could not dishonor Lynne. Calling her would be a dishonor. And hurt Chase. That's why. Really. That's why. It would hurt Chase. It would reopen memories.

Ethan held that lie up and turned it about, hoping that the lie, the lie he was telling himself, would hold tight, become real, and make whatever it was he now felt simply go away.

I will not dishonor Lynne. Or hurt Chase.

In reality, Ethan perceived only snatches of what Emily was saying. But he smiled and nodded in what he hoped were the appropriate places, and that seemed to be enough for her. The conversation continued, seemingly unimpeded.

At some point, she spoke of a challenge awaiting her back home—restoring an old Victorian house, her dream house, on top of Mount Washington in Pittsburgh, with a view of the entire city below. Emily said she planned on completely gutting the interior spaces, and the exterior needed complete restoration.

That snapped Ethan back to the present and back to their conversation.

"You have to respect the past," he declared. "The past should be your best guide."

Emily smiled and tilted her head at him. He would think, later that night, that she was flirting with him.

"Of course a builder would say that. But let me play the devil's advocate here. The past is no good if it gets in the way of today," she said. "Tell me, would you want to live in a true Victorian house? With no closets? With no family room? With a kitchen the size of a phone booth? I understand tradition. But should the past always dictate the way we live now?"

Ethan did what he hated when his son did it—he shrugged. He could come up with no cogent response. He could offer no new defense of his position. In fact, he was not even sure if he believed it anymore.

"Well, Mr. Willis?"

She paused, smiled when it was obvious that he was not going to answer her, put her fork down, and allowed him to wriggle free from her tenterhooks.

"Ethan, we should simply agree to disagree. And since you won't come with me to Pittsburgh to do my renovation, I guess you will never be troubled by what I do to the old place."

She waited. "Unless you might consider taking me up on my offer. A plum assignment in Pittsburgh. How does that sound? I would make it worth your while. As soon as you're done with CeCe, that is."

Ethan couldn't help but wonder if she was offering something more than just a building proposition. He wasn't sure, but he knew whatever the implications of her comments, they were making him a little uncomfortable. He hoped his face didn't betray his feelings. He wanted to change the subject and be done with eating.

"I know I wouldn't like it in Pittsburgh. Too many people. Too much traffic. And too many choices."

"And that's a bad thing? Choices?"

He shrugged again, but kept talking. "It can be. If you want fancy food around here, there are two … maybe three places. I know that seems like too few, but it makes the decision so much easier."

As Emily replied, he saw Cameron and the man she was with walk across the dining room toward the exit. He stared while trying his best not to. She seemed taller and leaner than when he had seen her last. He was not sure if she even looked his way.

He wished he could see the parking lot from where he sat, but couldn't and knew it would be rude to excuse himself to follow the pair outside.

Emily continued to talk for some time—amusing, interesting conversation, Ethan was sure, but conversation that barely registered in his consciousness.

————◦◦◦————

Ethan drove Emily back to The Franklin House and escorted her inside. It was what a gentleman is supposed to do. Emily seemed a little surprised but very pleased.

She extended her hand to him, saying good night. "I'll see you in the morning," she said, holding his hand tighter than a handshake required, and longer.

He was quite certain that if he had said something clever and appropriate, they might have adjourned to have a drink or two in the small bar off the hotel's restaurant.

But he didn't say those words. He was pretty sure he didn't even know what words he would have needed to say and didn't attempt to find them.

However, he was aware enough that some combination of words might have been sufficient.

He handed her the set of keys from her car. "Bright and early. Joel will be there from my crew as well. He's more skilled at kitchen work than I am."

"You're just being modest, Ethan," she said, her eyes sparkling. "I bet you're very good at everything you do."

Later, he would realize that she was flirting with him again.

And he knew that, again, he was being offered a slow pitch right over the plate—a pitch he let sail past his bat without moving it from his shoulder.

He stepped backward half a step. He could feel Emily's eyes on him as he exited the lobby and walked quickly through the cold to his truck. He thought about turning and waving, but that would mean he expected her to be watching him. He didn't want to presume that she was.

———⊙⊷⊙———

Cameron wasn't sure what had made her the most confused: the odd and totally unexpected from-out-of-nowhere job offer—a dream job, if the truth be told—or seeing Ethan across the dining room with a lovely woman.

Paul Drake had actually carried a contract with him. "Our lawyers have made me promise them that if I talk jobs with a candidate, I will have papers in hand," he'd said and insisted, with great hopefulness, that she take them with her to review. "Something about writing the meal off as a legitimate business expense—or some such legal nonsense," he had added, smiling.

Now she tossed the folded pages on her desk and her bag in the corner. Shrugging off her coat, she let it lie where it fell. She kicked off her shoes as she lowered herself onto the window seat and faced west. When she pressed her face against the glass, she could see a sliver of Otter and West Park.

Ethan lived on Otter—several blocks due north and a block east.

She wondered if she would see his truck heading home.

He had still been in the restaurant when they left. She wondered who that woman was. She was pretty certain the woman wasn't local. She dressed too well, wore too edgy a style of glasses, and her hair in too young of a design for her face.

She had to be near forty—a very sophisticated forty.

Cameron stared at the cars as they passed below her window.

And her hair was colored. I would bet on that.

Ethan pumped the accelerator three times, then waited. It was the routine that most often resulted in his truck's engine starting in the winter. He twisted the key. The engine sluggishly turned once, twice, and then fired. He feathered the gas pedal a few times, waiting for the engine to fully engage. He rubbed his face with his hand. A puff of black smoke chugged out from the back of the truck.

He put the truck into gear and pulled out onto the street, heading down West Park … heading toward home.

He pulled into the driveway behind his house, got out, and carefully shut the door to his truck. He could no longer park in the garage; the space was filled with materials *not* used on the Carter restoration. He made sure the garage door was securely shut, twisting the handle one last time.

He stopped in the soft gray light of the moon. His breath came in little puffs in the quiet and cold, like tiny clouds of life exiting his body. He took in a very deep breath.

I didn't call her because it would be an insult to Lynne. That's the reason.

He stood still, hearing the traffic from town, a few cars rumbling through, a horn off toward the river.

I was stupid to get involved with her. She is way too young for me. And … I couldn't do that to Chase. It would be an insult to the memory of his mother. I have to honor that past—my past with her. The mother of my son.

Ethan resumed walking, wondering if he even came close to believing what he was trying to force himself to believe.

Cameron woke with a start. She had nodded off while sitting on the window seat. She blinked, swept her hair off her face, brought her wrist up close to her eyes, and squinted at the tiny numbers on the watch face.

"4:30."

She put her feet on the floor and tried to focus. She moaned as she tried to stretch her back. Sleeping sitting up, leaning against a cold window, was not a way to get proper rest. She debated on going back to sleep in her bed. Still jangly over the night before, she knew that rest would elude her. Instead she took a blanket, sprawled out on her couch, and watched cable news on television.

She stirred again at 6:00. After a long, hot shower and four cups of coffee, Cameron felt almost ready to face the day. It was still only 7:15—hours before she was scheduled to appear at *The Derrick* offices. But she went early, more to get out of her silent apartment than any other reason. And she'd get a lot done with no one around.

When she entered the building, holding coffee number five from the convenience store down the street, she was surprised to see the light on in Paige's office.

Editorial operations at a morning paper seemed to come alive only in the later afternoon, when stories were due and when pages were laid out. *The Derrick* was no different. Paige always got there at 8:00 sharp but hardly ever before. Most often Paige and Clara would be the first to arrive at 8:00 and might be the only people in the office until 10:00, other than the advertising people. Cameron was friendly to all of them, but the two operations did not often overlap.

A stack of paper teetered on the edge of Paige's desk, and all Cameron could see was the older woman's back, bent over one of the files from her desk.

She tried to make as much noise as possible as she entered, so as not to startle anyone.

"Cleaning up? Moving? Quitting?" Cameron said as she tapped at the doorframe.

Paige rose slowly, twisting and grimacing. "Maybe all three. Last night I was looking for something—I don't even remember what it was now—and couldn't find it. I have all these files from decades ago that should have been tossed away years ago. At my age, you have to strike while the mood is right. So I'm purging. Simplifying. Getting the 'feng shui' in the correct alignment—isn't that what those people say on those clean-sweep programs on cable?"

"It is. And speaking of cable television …"

"You had dinner with Paul, didn't you?"

A little surprised, Cameron nodded. "I did. And he said you know about all this. You never mentioned it to me."

Paige pulled her already-full wastebasket closer. She grabbed a clutch of papers and wedged them in. "I didn't say anything because he has done this before. I don't mean talking to you, of course. But he has called me about one thing or another over the years. Not many of them come to anything. I knew he was in the area. I called his father last night. Apparently, he's on a family-sanctioned mission."

Cameron picked up a stack of bulging file folders from the chair and laid them on the floor, where the stack promptly tipped over, fanning out papers for a couple of feet.

"So it was a legitimate offer?"

"Apparently. They have read your stories. And they did call and talk to me. I didn't say anything earlier because … well, because I didn't want you to get excited only to be disappointed if they never showed up."

Cameron nodded as if this was most logical.

It was obvious that Paige was braced for a more emotional response toward the job offer. But Cameron's thoughts were anywhere but in Pittsburgh.

"I saw him at dinner."

"Saw who?" Paige looked puzzled. A second later, her expression changed. "He was there? Ethan Willis?"

"With some woman. I don't think she was from around here. She looked more … sophisticated."

"An older woman?"

"No. Well, yes. Older than me. Close to middle-aged. Maybe … late thirties. Or even forty."

Paige appeared to be considering her words carefully. "Was it a … date?"

"I don't think so. Maybe. I don't know. It was early." Cameron took a long, deliberate, slow sip of her coffee.

"And you're upset over this? Upset over him or excited about the job offer?"

Cameron slumped down into the chair. She moved some of the files on the floor with the toe of her shoe. "I don't know. Maybe both."

"It's been a long time, Cameron. If this were a soap opera, by this time the characters would have married, had children, and been divorced and remarried already."

"I know. I know it's been a long time." Cameron looked down at her coffee cup and twirled the cup in small circles. "I know."

Paige waited for a long moment, then arched her eyebrows and bent back down. Once again she began to riffle through the sea of yellowing papers in her bottom desk drawer.

⁓

As Ethan stepped up on the front porch of the Carter place, he heard laughter, feminine laughter. He glanced at his watch. It was 7:00—still early for most of the crew.

Then he remembered: the kitchen designer.

Emily and Joel looked up when Ethan entered the room.

"He hates where we put the Sub-Zeros," Emily said with a grin. "He said it impedes the traffic flow."

Joel appeared sheepish, as if he had been caught taking two cookies instead of one. "She asked my opinion, Ethan. I think it's too close to the doorway. It should be centered."

Ethan set his thermos and lunch on the plywood table.

"So, Ethan, time for honesty, even though it's early. What do you think?"

Emily stood, hands on hips. She wore some sort of tailored navy blue blazer and flippy skirt. Ethan always had trouble describing women's apparel, but her skirt was shorter than most skirts he had seen in Franklin this year. Her hair was pulled back with some sort of silk band, or scarf. Ethan thought her outfit was attractive—very attractive—but perhaps a bit inappropriate lengthwise for a work site, soon to be filled with a half dozen of his male work crew.

"I take no stand on kitchens. That's your territory, Joel. And yours, of course, Emily … I mean, Ms. Harrington."

"It's Emily. It was Emily at dinner last night. It's Emily this morning," she answered with a coy smile.

Ethan suddenly felt most uncomfortable. He knew Joel would not have given their dinner last night a second thought, but the way it was announced made it sound like there was more involved than just eating.

Joel glanced at Ethan, at Emily, then busied himself by staring at the kitchen blueprints.

"Well?"

Ethan grew perplexed and stuttered, "The Sub-Zeros. Well … I think they're fine where they are."

Emily beamed in triumph.

And on that morning, Ethan was never so heartened to hear the clump of the crews' boots on the wooden porch and the squeal of the front door.

The bell rang, and the clamor and confusion began in a rush as twenty-five eighth-graders jumped to their feet, charging out toward lockers and toward the lunchroom. Even though Elliot was more interested in lunch than most, he took his departure cues from Chase, who set a much more leisurely pace and walked, rather than jogged, toward the cafeteria.

They sat in the same place every day—the far left table by the rear doors, just one up from the trash cans. A few of their friends would sit with them sometimes; sometimes they ate by themselves.

Today was a by-themselves day.

"So, you going out for the Oilers this year again?" Elliot asked. "You never said."

Chase had been on the Oilers hockey team for two years. It was a club sport—not sponsored by the school—but paid for by parents and boosters. The Oilers were one of the better junior hockey teams in Venango County—in fact, one of the better teams in all of northwestern Pennsylvania.

Chase shrugged. "My dad didn't ask."

"Think he forgot?"

Chase shook his head. "I dunno."

"I bet he didn't," Elliot said, tearing open a second bag of Fritos. "Dads don't forget about stuff like that." He stuffed a handful of Fritos in his mouth. "At least your dad wouldn't. My dad … maybe."

And Chase hoped against hope that his dad had forgotten.

But he knew he hadn't.

A wise man will make haste to forgive,
because he knows the true value of time,
and will not suffer it
to pass away in unnecessary pain.

—SAMUEL JOHNSON

Many of us crucify ourselves
between two thieves—
Regret for the past
and fear of the future.

—FULTON OURSLER

CHAPTER FIFTEEN

For Ethan, for his crew, for CeCe, for just about everyone involved in the Carter Mansion project, work had gone on just about long enough, thank you very much, and everyone wanted it to be over. But the work would not be over for some time yet—weeks for sure, Ethan knew ... more likely a couple of months. At this same point in every major project, when the majority of the work was done, it was easy to feel overwhelmed and as if there was no light at the end of the tunnel—only another dark tunnel after the dark tunnel they were in now.

In recent days Ethan had not made his life easier ... nor his crew's, nor CeCe's.

"But I don't like that trim, Ethan," CeCe said as she strolled about the former ballroom on the third floor, staring at the walls. "I thought we had already discussed this."

Joel looked on from the side of the room, having finished stacking a few hundred board feet of authentically styled, historically accurate Victorian trim that had just arrived from a mill in southern Venango County, which milled authentic trim with authentic, historically accurate router bits. Ethan had been so excited when the source had been discovered and more excited when he'd discovered that their running costs were only a couple of dollars per board foot more than the trim the local lumberyard carried.

She picked up a stick of the trim and held it at arm's length. "This is just too—I don't know—but it's too something, for sure, for the feeling my interior designer and I are after up here."

Ethan really disliked her dismissive tone.

"I wanted everything to work off that more simple crown molding we picked. More like that feeling. Simpler. This is too ... too ... not right. Didn't I say that I was leaning toward a simple molding?"

Ethan had held his temper, held his words even, held any response at all, despite the fact that the pile of trim now stacked neatly on the floor had been paid for and was purchased on a nonrefundable basis. If he couldn't use it for trim, it might become costly firewood.

Even Joel had cautioned him against buying it without confirming with CeCe.

"Just buy a foot of it," Joel had said. "She might not like it."

But Ethan had bought it—and bought enough of it to trim the entire third floor of the Carter Mansion, because of the time constraints.

"But it's here, Mrs. Moretti. The trim was available so I jumped on it, thinking it would save some time. We won't have to wait for another run of material, and it's before the price increase goes into effect. This saves us both time and money."

By referring to her as Mrs. Moretti only, Ethan was hoping that his subtle refusal to use her first name would indicate how much turmoil he was in.

"This trim matches the original exactly. It may have been cut using the very same router bits that cut the original trim in the rest of this house. The owner of the mill was almost certain that his mill was the same one that ran the material for your great-grandfather. That is such an amazing coincidence—and we never knew they existed until Jack stumbled on this little lumberyard while riding his motorcycle in Venango County."

CeCe appeared unimpressed and unmoved. "That's terribly fascinating, Ethan, but I still don't like that trim for up here. It doesn't matter if one of your crew discovered it in a prehistoric cave somewhere. It's just too … fancy. I like what I like."

Ethan thought that if he tried just one more time, CeCe would recognize the validity of his argument and finally recognize the value of keeping the past alive—and all she would have to do is agree to use the authentic, historically accurate trim work. How hard could that be? She had to see the rationale behind his purchase.

She did not.

"Ethan," she said firmly, before he had a chance to continue the discussion, "I am not talking any more about this. I do not want this trim on this floor of my house."

She moved closer to him, as if she was concerned that their disagreement would be heard by more than just the two of them. She smelled of anise. She probably carried several biscotti in her purse, Ethan thought.

"Ethan, I appreciate your passion for the past. I really do. But I will not have that trim here. I don't like it here. And I don't want to fight about this anymore. Take it back. All of it. Get a refund. Or not. I don't care. Just finish this house according to the plans you have been given. It's my house. It's my life. If it's not right, then I have to live with it, not you."

She turned, then stopped and looked at Ethan. "I like you, Ethan. I really do. You do wonderful work. You are a great craftsman. But this is the last of it. This is the last of our disagreements over style. I do not want to have to deal with another situation about you making a decision that has not been approved by me. Are you okay with that?"

"But the trim is perfect, CeCe," he said, now emphasizing her first name. "This is the same trim as what was here originally—and what's still here in all the other rooms of this house. It would be so unified, and so much simpler."

"Why does it matter to you, Ethan?" CeCe asked, imploring. "It's my house. Are you willing to lose this job over your loyalty to what somebody did over a hundred years ago? I mean, really—are you?"

Ethan looked in her eyes, his eyes unwilling to give in, but after a long, long moment, he eventually nodded and replied with as much anguished resignation and defeat as he could muster. "If that's what you want."

CeCe sighed, loud and dramatic. She sighed often—at least while supervising Ethan and his crew. "You're taking all the joy out of this, Ethan. I love this house. But I don't want to fight over everything that goes into it. I don't want to fight with you, especially. I hate to say this, but I'm beginning to dislike coming here—because it's always a battle with you. You're too loyal to the past. The past is past. You have to let it go, Ethan. Get on with life. Or simply let me get on with mine. Okay?"

Ethan waited a long time to answer—time enough, he hoped, for CeCe to soften and to change her mind. None of that happened. It was only when he realized that she would not give in, that she would not use the authentic, historically accurate trim, the one that honored the past and her great-grandfather, that he finally nodded.

"Okay. We'll do it your way."

He knew it was obvious from his tone that he still considered her way wrong—dead wrong, absolutely wrong—but he had to complete this job or dire consequences awaited. She wasn't making the right decision, but she did hold all the power. Ethan did not like this feeling. He wanted to say that he would install the authentic, historically accurate, architecturally correct trim on his own dime, because that's what this house needed, called out for—but he said no such thing. He could not absorb that expense. And CeCe knew it.

"Good. That's all I wanted to hear," she stated.

It was nothing at all that Ethan wanted to hear.

Apparently, there would be no more discussion. Everything was now decided.

And it was nothing that Ethan liked.

***

Cameron woke early on Sunday. Arising early, in itself, was not unusual for her, but she was up, out of bed, showered, dressed, with minimal makeup, having consumed her typical breakfast of a bagel and cream cheese with coffee and juice, and was ready a full hour before the church service started. That was unusual. Totally atypical.

She had always been somewhat of a morning person and had been a rather early riser, but just barely qualified as a true morning person. For a starting time of 8:00 a.m., Cameron considered 7:15 to be a sufficient time to arise. It was true that Cameron was punctual, but always *just* punctual. On time, to Cameron, was just on time, never even more than a couple of minutes early.

Being awake on Sunday for church was different; being early for church was just that much more unusual for her. It was not that Cameron had ever positioned herself against attending church. Her family went sporadically and occasionally enthusiastically, but Cameron, while considering herself a Christian—whatever that really meant—did not consider herself a card-carrying churchgoer. Church was fine, she said, for those who needed it. She had seldom felt as if she needed it all that much.

Now ... well, now she was reconsidering her position on church.

Here it was, a cold winter Sunday, gray and overcast, and Cameron was looking forward to the act of going to church.

Odd, isn't it? she thought.

She sat on her window seat, sipping her coffee and leafing through a magazine, and checked her watch every few minutes until it was time for her to leave. It would take her no more than five minutes to walk there. Church started at 8:30. She left her house at 8:10.

Walking briskly up the wide brick steps of Franklin Community Church, she entered the building. She didn't expect to see anyone she knew—other than, hopefully, the kindly old man who greeted her during her last visit. Maybe this week, she told herself, maybe this week would be different. Last week, the pastor had asked everyone to stand and shake someone else's hand and introduce themselves. Cameron did that, of course, along with everyone else in the church, and immediately forgot the name of the middle-aged couple who first offered introductions. Cameron told herself that this week would be very, very different and that she would remember someone's name for more than a few seconds. Maybe she needed to meet some new people, and this was a good place to start.

"Miss Dane."

Cameron looked around for the source of her name.

"Charlie Ochs. We had coffee last Sunday. So nice to see you again." He took her hand as enthusiastically as before. "I know the coffee wasn't that good, so you must be back here because of me."

He smiled with his grandfather's smile—warm, inviting, and just a little mischievous.

"Of course," Cameron replied, hoping that Mr. Ochs shared her sense of humor. "Only because of you, Mr. Ochs. I don't remember anything about the sermon. Something about the Bible, I bet."

Charlie grinned. "Sometimes that is the case. But our new pastor is good, isn't he? Even *I* remember the sermons—most of the time, that is."

Others moved through the doors, removing coats, looking for hangers, rubbing hands together from the cold, calling out names, extending hands, or sharing hugs. Greetings and hellos spread out like the warmth from an unseen fireplace.

"I better find a place to sit down before the singing," Cameron said. "You don't want me to get on the bad side of the worship director, do you?"

Charlie waved his hand in dismissal. "Not to worry. He's a nice fellow— but that 'breaking the worship mood' stuff … pay me no mind. I'm just a fixture around here."

"More like a pillar, I would say."

He handed Cameron a bulletin and held open the interior door to the sanctuary. "The sermon today is all about forgiveness. Let me tell you, Miss Dane, that's the secret to a long life."

Charlie led her to a pew on the left side of the church, only a few rows back from the front, much closer than she would have picked herself if she had been doing the seating.

"The secret? What's the secret?" Cameron asked.

Charlie surprised her by sliding into the pew next to her and sitting down. He wore a most uncharacteristic serious expression. "Forgiving. Sometimes you're the one who gets forgiven. I mean, we all can be forgiven, you know what I mean—in the biblical sense, that is. Sometimes in life we have to accept forgiveness, but more often, and more importantly, we have to be the ones who forgive others—or even forgive ourselves. You don't forgive, the anger comes out as bitterness, or just turns inward and festers. Kills you early, I always say."

"Well, that's good advice. Living a long life is good."

Charlie nodded, as if he were agreeing with himself. "Someone once told me, Miss Dane, that one of the rewards for living a good life is a good life. That's part of it, for sure." He paused. "I have a feeling … I think you need to pay attention to the sermon today, somehow. Forgiving. Accepting forgiveness. I'm old, but sometimes I get a feeling about someone …"

He chuckled under his breath. "Or maybe you need to tell somebody else about forgiveness? I don't know. I just have this feeling."

At a loss for how to respond, Cameron simply said, "Thank you, Mr. Ochs. You're right. I will pay attention."

And with that, Charlie stood up, straightened his crisp sport coat, and headed back toward the narthex, smile on his face, hand flexing, ready to be extended, ready for the next person or persons to come through the doors.

Cameron watched him as he walked away. Her aunt—the aunt who had acquired a full dose of religion later in life—often had those sort of feelings, spiritual feelings, and she would tell everybody about them, whether they were interested or not. Even while she had dismissed them—and her aunt—as being sort of nutty, this one, coming from Mr. Ochs, felt anything but nutty. This one felt … very unnutty. She was absolutely certain that she should pay close attention to the sermon today.

———⸻———

Elliot stared at the bucket. Then he stared at the bag of cement, placing his finger on the chart of mix ratios printed midway down the bag. The printing was a little smudged, but Elliot could make out the numbers. Then he stared at Chase, who had taken a three-by-five index card and appeared to be focused on an intense math problem.

"I figure you need to do six variations," Chase said as he placed the carpenter's pencil behind his ear.

"Six? That sounds like a lot. Can we do like four instead?"

The boys were in the Willis basement. Since the house was well over a hundred years old, the foundation walls were made of stone. With the low ceiling, still air, and few windows, a tiny hint of mildew always seemed to be pooled in the chilled darkness.

Chase picked up a paint stirrer. "No. We can't do four. I mean … you can do five. But six will look better. And you need a good grade on this, right?"

Elliot pulled an old metal stool closer to the workbench and lifted himself up, pulling even closer, the metal legs squealing on the concrete.

"I guess. But a B would be fine. Would five varieties get me a B?"

Chase looked at his friend and shook his head. "Elwood … you are such a prize, you know that?"

Elliot grinned. He liked being called "Elwood." He'd told Chase he often wished his parents had named him Elwood instead of dumb old Elliot and that once he turned eighteen, he would legally change it. It was a boast both knew was just a boast, especially since Chase knew Elliot had no idea of how someone would go about legally changing his name.

"Well, no sense in overworking—especially if five would get me a B. My mom would think I could, like, make it into Harvard if I came home with too many As. And you don't want to disappoint her, do you?"

Chase lightly hit his friend over the head with a paint stirrer. "Just get busy gluing these together. We need six of them, okay?"

In a few minutes, several miniature troughs were glued and clamped. The boys added a strip of cardboard to each end. Once the glue set, they would begin to mix the concrete in small batches or varying consistencies and pour each concrete mixture into a small form. It was detailed work, work Chase enjoyed and Elliot merely tolerated.

"Are you sure I couldn't do a science project about blowing things up with firecrackers? I would like that."

Chase piped a thin line of glue into the last form. "Are fireworks legal in Pennsylvania?"

"No," Elliot replied. "But I know where we can get them. Arnie's older brother knows a guy who knows a guy."

Chase fastened a clamp over the form. "So we could use illegal fireworks in a school science fair?"

Elliot thought for a long moment. "Oh … yeah. I guess not. It would
be cool, though." He used a thin strip of duct tape to hold the cardboard
ends in place. "My mom asked me about hockey. She asked me if I wanted
to play."

"Really? Your mom asked? I didn't know you were interested in
hockey."

Elliot was less than a graceful skater, but his mother continually tried
to get him to expand his horizons.

"And I thought she said you couldn't afford it," Chase concluded.

"We can't. But somebody at the beauty shop or grocery store said that
somebody's kid had a full set of gear they wanted to give away. I think she
thought I could use it. Like it would fit me. Can you see me on the ice in
that?"

Chase looked at the bag of Sakrete again. He lined up six large plastic cups. "These will be for the concrete mix. We need another six for the
water. Did you ever tell your mom you wanted to play hockey?"

Snorting back a laugh, Elliot pretended to wobble off the chair. "No.
I hate skating. I'm afraid of thin ice. Speaking of hockey—did your dad
sign you up?"

"Nope."

"Come on. You said he was, like, some ace in hockey when he was
your age. Doesn't that automatically make you like some sort of legacy ace
or something?"

Chase ran his hand over the workbench. "I don't think so. I don't
think hockey is inherited like that. And, like I said, I'm not playing this
year. I don't care what he was when he was a kid or what he wants me to
do."

Elliot made a whistling noise. "You talk tough now. But you'll play.
You'll have to play if he spends all that money on registration."

"Nope, ain't going to happen, my friend. Now, get that measuring
cup. We need to measure out twelve cups of this mix."

Elliot took the cup and was about to rip at the bag.

"No. Not that way," Chase said. "You see that little white string?"

"Yeah."

"You pull that."

Elliot pulled it and it unraveled, and he kept pulling and pulling, and the top paper seam simply fell away. "Cool. That was cool. I would have just ripped it open."

"Easier when you know the secret," Chase said.

———◇———

Cameron walked into the office on Monday morning carrying three coffees and a bag of muffins. The office had its own coffeemaker, but Cameron imagined that it had had its last thorough cleaning during the Clinton administration. She drank that office coffee only in emergencies—when nothing else was available and she was fighting exhaustion. If anyone on staff wanted good coffee, that person brought his or her own.

On Mondays, the advertising department did not arrive until ten. The rest of the editorial staff arrived at varying times, and the office was not officially full until after lunch. On most days, Cameron shared the quiet mornings with Clara, and Paige, of course.

That's why three coffees would suffice for the entire crew.

But she also brought a dozen muffins. This way the three of them would get their pick and the rest of the muffins could be left for the later arrivals.

Paige waved hello. Cameron held up the bag and coffee carrier and received an enthusiastic smile in reply.

"Bring 'em in. You have a blueberry in there?"

She did. Cameron started in on her cranberry-orange muffin.

Paige tore the paper off the muffin and took a large bite off the bottom. Confused, Cameron lifted an eyebrow.

"I like the tops best," Paige explained. "They're crustier. Eat the bottom first and get that out of the way. Then you have something to look forward to."

They both chewed their muffins.

"Have a good weekend?" Paige asked.

"I did," Cameron answered, then waited a measured moment before adding with some emphasis, "I went to church."

"You did?" Paige said coolly. "Which church?"

"The community church down at the end of Otter."

"Really? Franklin Community Church? Really?"

"Really." Cameron took her coffee and sipped at it. "You sound surprised, Paige. Surprised that I went to church, or surprised that I went to *that* church?"

Paige offered up a shrug—her best noncommittal response. "I don't know. Maybe both."

"Well, it felt like it was time. And I can walk there."

"True. That's a great reason to find religion," Paige said, slightly rolling her eyes.

Cameron laughed and muffin crumbs spilled on her blouse. She brushed them away, then looked over at Paige. "Sorry."

"Like a few crumbs are going to make a difference in here. We have to talk to the cleaning crew. I've got a herd of dust bunnies under the desk."

"But didn't you say that the cleaning people aren't allowed in your office? You said they mess up your filing system."

"I said that? Really? Well, remind me to rescind that order. This place is a pigsty."

Cameron wadded up the muffin wrapper and tossed it into the trash.

"Did you like the service at the church? How's the new guy—Seth, isn't it? Seth Johnson? Is that right?"

"That's right. Pastor Johnson. I like him. And the music is really loud. You would hate it."

"I don't mind loud. But I do mind rock 'n' roll. If you ask me, that's what's driving everyone crazy these days—iPods and loud music. What's the matter with a good old-fashioned organ? Or even a piano? Do they have to have electric guitars and drums and amplifiers? Good heavens. So much noise. I go to church to be comforted."

Amused, Cameron cupped her hand to her ear. "What? What? I can't hear anything at all. It wasn't like this … it wasn't like this at all on Saturday."

Paige scowled, but with good humor. "Okay, so the music is loud—just like you like it—so it drives out all the old fogies like me. Satisfied?"

"Extremely. Don't trust anyone over thirty. That's their motto. They have that written over the sanctuary door."

"Very funny, Missy, but I don't need to tell you that I know how old you really are."

It was Cameron's turn to scowl with good humor. "Point taken. But their 'new guy' was really good. At least I thought he was."

"Was the church full? After Pastor Black left, that church was dying on the vine, or so I've heard. Down to a handful of people."

"It was pretty full. Over a few hundred people, I would guess. Lots of them younger. Some older. A few empty spots. Toward the front."

Paige stood and brushed the crumbs off herself, aiming, in a loose fashion, at the trash can. Very few of them actually made it in.

"No one sits in the front two rows of any church," Paige said. "Saved for all but the most righteous. So this young Johnson fellow was good?"

"He was. Very understandable. No thees and thous. And he was funny."

"Funny," Paige harrumphed. "Since when do preachers have to be funny?"

Cameron fussed with the brown cardboard sleeve around her coffee cup. "Paige, can I ask you a serious question? It's about … faith, I guess. And you're the only person I really know in town who claims to have that."

"Well, sure. Ask away. I don't have all the answers, but I'll try."

Cameron bit at her bottom lip as she often did when considering a hard question. "Pastor Johnson said yesterday that grace is free … and when we come to Christ for salvation, we are forgiven."

Paige appeared to be tussling with her answer. "Well, yes, but there's more to it than just that. To be saved by grace, to be given grace, one has to accept the gift of forgiveness—you know, God's gift of Jesus, His sacrifice for our sins. What he means when he says that grace is free is that there's nothing we can do to earn it. It's paid for by Christ's death. Forgiveness is a gift we don't deserve. That's what it means to be saved by grace. But you have to … you know … you have to accept it by faith. Take the gift. Believe."

Cameron was nodding as Paige spoke. "I know. I get that. But what I want to ask is that he said that the best way—he may have said the only way—to fully understand grace is to be fully forgiven."

Paige broke a piece off of her muffin top. "Well … yes. I guess. You can experience it and extend it to others when you've accepted forgiveness yourself."

"I want to know, Paige … can a person like me be fully forgiven?"

Paige appeared at the cusp of some emotion, perhaps tears, perhaps something else altogether. "Cameron … you can be. Of course you can be. Even the worst of sinners is not beyond God's healing love. Sinners like me. I once heard someone say you can never be too bad for Jesus, only too good."

"Are you sure that's what the Bible says?"

"I am sure, Cameron. I would stake my life on it. I *have* staked my life on it."

"Okay, then," Cameron said, rising from her chair and brushing more crumbs onto the floor. "Then I'm forgiven. That's what happened. I received the grace."

<hr />

Cameron did not tell Paige the whole story of Sunday. She wasn't sure why she didn't, but she didn't. But Paige had looked pleased anyway by what she had shared, and had given her a Bible—a "newer version" is how Paige described it.

The sermon had been about forgiveness, as Mr. Ochs had said. Cameron had nestled herself against the wooden end of the pew as she listened. The radiator on the other side of the aisle, under the pastoral scene on the Tiffany window, clanked softly, spreading a pool of warmth around her that made her feel peaceful, safe, and welcome.

In the rack on the pew back in front of her were two smallish Bibles, a stack of visitor cards, and two yellow pencils in individual holes on either end. The pastor had encouraged everyone to read the passages with him. Cameron was not a Bible student and would have had to flip to the table of contents every time, but the pastor had called out the actual page numbers, so she was able to find them easily. Two verses stood out to her—*I have swept away your sins like a cloud. I have scattered your offenses like the morning mist. Oh, return to me, for I have paid the price to set you free (Isaiah 44:22)* and *I am writing to you who are God's children because your sins have been forgiven through Jesus (1 John 2:12)*. The words were suddenly and amazingly clear to her—not convoluted as she remembered the Bible from her youth-group days, and made clearer by the explanation that followed.

And then, in no time, the message had been over.

The pastor had stepped down from the brass pulpit to the first step of the stone altar. As he walked closer, Cameron was surprised to note just how young he was.

He might even be younger than I am, she'd thought.

"Every week, at the end of the service, I invite anyone who might need prayer to come meet with me in front. I am making that same invitation today. If you want prayer, please come up. And the rest of you are dismissed. Go in God's grace."

Cameron had anticipated standing, gathering her things, and leaving. But she did not. She had sat and waited. The noise of several hundred people exiting and talking had soon diminished. A few people came up, shook the pastor's hand, exchanged a few words, then left.

In a few minutes, only Cameron had been left. The pastor had smiled at her and had walked to her pew. He'd extended his hand to her.

"I'm Seth Johnson," he'd said, and asked her name. "Would you like me to pray for you, Cameron?"

Cameron had no idea why she started to weep, but she did—weeping as she had that terrible morning so long ago when the ocean swallowed her little brother and never gave him back. Weeping for all the years of living with that nightmare. She could hardly talk—no, she couldn't talk at all through her tears—and had held her hands up and open, trying to communicate ... something.

The pastor, if he had been taken by surprise, was very good at keeping that concealed. He just sat next to her in the pew, took one of her hands in his, and began to pray quietly, saying words Cameron barely heard audibly but heard in her heart. She knew this prayer was for her and her alone. Then she felt a soft Light and an overwhelming Presence all about her, as if she were standing on a beach, arms outstretched, at daybreak in a warm summer wind that embraced her and carefully, gently made her pure as the dark clouds all around her were blown away.

"Father God, I know You love Cameron, and that You forgive her completely, because of Jesus' death and resurrection. Though she believes that she's failed, Lord—by Your Spirit, let her know the beauty of Your grace and allow her to accept Your forgiveness and forgive herself. Let those who have hurt her, who are not here among us, Father, offer their forgiveness to her. Let our sister pass this forgiveness on to others. Accept her as Your treasured child. Let Your perfect peace pour into her heart and into her soul and into her mind. Heal her and make her whole in You— Your forgiven daughter. Give her a joy that she cannot contain."

And Cameron could only weep and weep and nod.

That's why she didn't tell Paige what had happened that Sunday, when the Light filled her heart and, for the first time in her life—for the first time *ever*—Cameron felt free and without guilt.

Just how could she explain that to anyone?

He who cannot forgive breaks the bridge
over which he himself must pass
if he would ever reach heaven;
for every one has need to be forgiven.

—GEORGE HERBERT

We are all on a lifelong journey
and the core of its meaning,
the terrible demand of its centrality,
is forgiving and being forgiven.

—MARTHA KILPATRICK

CHAPTER SIXTEEN

THE BANNER OVER THE gymnasium, neatly written in blue and red poster paint, proudly declared, WELCOME TO THE FRANKLIN SCIENCE FAIR. The last two words crowded closer to each other, the *I* and *R* almost touching, so FAIR looked like FAR.

Cameron smiled as she pulled off the sticky backing to her official nametag—CAMERON DANE. *THE DERRICK.* JUDGE—and applied it just above the pocket on her blouse. She still wasn't exactly sure why she had been asked to be a judge for the event. She was not a scientist—far from it. In college, she had taken just a single science course. More than that one had not been on the list of requirements for a journalism degree. And in high school, she had barely gotten through biology and chemistry, and probably would not have made it had it not been for the generous assistance of two very smart—and very willing—boyfriends.

But the Franklin Middle School Science Fair always included several "celebrity" judges from the community. Cameron had laughed at being put in the local "celebrity" category. Her name appeared in print, often, and apparently that was more than enough to be on the "A" list—at least in Franklin, anyway.

"But what do I know about science?" she had complained to Paige after being asked to participate.

"You probably know nothing at all. But if you want to be a fair judge, just evaluate the projects on the basis of how effectively they communicate their ideas. You know about communication, right?"

Cameron hadn't thought of that aspect. And as a result, she walked through the doors of the crowded gymnasium with a sense of purpose, wanting to do a good job.

What she encountered when she entered dismayed her. Inside were rows and rows and rows of science exhibits—as if every eighth-grader had done one. Which, of course, they had.

How will I ever get through all of this?

Just as she despaired, a short woman with a nametag, clipboard, and a fierce, determined look appeared at her side. "Miss Dane? You can go directly to row one. All entries there have been preselected as finalists. Your clipboard and judge review notes are at the head table. You can just follow me."

The woman spoke fast. She had not stopped talking before she started walking, her low heels clacking on the wooden floor. Cameron wore soft, flat-heeled shoes for that very reason. When she attended high school, no one wearing heels was ever allowed on the golden hardwood of the gym.

Her official judging clipboard held a sheaf of papers, each one numbered to correspond to an exhibit, each paper with a short paragraph on the scope of the project and the hypothesis being explored, as well as the name of the student scientist. The bottom third of each page was reserved for "Judge's Comments."

Good grief … I have to write that much for each project?

Another judge, from the chamber of commerce, made his way past. Cameron recognized him and offered greetings.

"How much are you writing?" she asked as she drew in close to him, conspiratorially. "I'm not all that good with science."

Without smiling, he replied, "And I almost flunked out of Penn State because of freshman biology."

He held up his clipboard. In big bold letters, he had written *GOOD JOB!!!* on the first page. He turned to the second page. *Wonderful research!!!*

Relieved, she grinned and nodded. "Thanks."

She started at one end and slowly made her way down the line. The exhibits, for the most part, were well presented. The displays included experiments in cleaning-product effectiveness, plant-growth rates with and without fertilizer, the tensile strength of various formulas of concrete mixes, all sorts of curious attempts at finding and using scientific methods to prove or illustrate some manner of everyday life.

Impressed with several, Cameron made notes providing her insights of how well each student handled the communication process. Judging was to take place from noon to 1:30. Results would be tallied, and winners would be announced at 2:30. Judges were asked, if possible, to stay for the awards ceremony.

She made her way down the aisle of finalists, then back up the other side. In all, some thirty exhibits were judged as having outstanding merit, and out of those thirty, five top awards would be presented. Cameron was nearly done, one exhibit left, with five minutes to spare.

The last exhibit was complex—a model of a house, a couple of feet tall. It was a small-scale replica of a life-sized house, cut in half, showing all the construction techniques, exposing joists and rafters, all components neatly labeled and explained, with weight-to-span ratios detailed. It was a remarkably complete and intricate scale model—not proving a hypothesis so much as explaining hidden matters. She glanced at the nametag on the table: *Chase Willis.*

Cameron's heart took to a fast beat. Chase, of course. Ethan's son. Chase—the boy with something behind his eyes.

The poor kid's gonna be living that nightmare forever.

She looked up.

At the rear of the table, Chase stood, his hands at his side, his blond hair neatly combed, in a white shirt with the sleeves rolled up to his elbows, and khaki pants. He stood there, a small-scale replica of his father.

"Miss Dane," he said, his words soft, but clear and firm. "I didn't know you were going to be a judge. I would have taken more care with my written presentation."

She had to smile at him.

"Your presentation is wonderful, Chase. I have always been fascinated by models like this—that show what goes on inside of things. I helped my dad build me a big dollhouse once. We see houses all the time, but we never see what they hide."

"That's why I picked this topic. I like that too."

A voice over the speakers announced, "Judges! You have three minutes. Please turn your evaluations in."

Cameron clicked her pen and wrote on Chase's evaluation form, writing fast, but not carelessly, nearly filling in the entire bottom section reserved for judge's comments. Since she was standing right next to the head table, she simply handed her clipboard to the short woman who had initially greeted her.

"Well … my job is done. Good luck, Chase. You did a great job."

"Are you staying for the awards?" Chase asked. Cameron wasn't sure if he was simply being polite.

"I … I guess. I mean, I don't have anywhere else I need to be this afternoon. And I would like to see who wins."

"I understand that the winner gets their picture in the newspaper," Chase said.

"They do. The photographer is here. I've seen our Bart, snapping away."

"You're not doing the story?" Chase asked.

"No. I don't do education stories all that much. Lydia Fox usually covers school events."

Chase nodded.

"But I'll stay. To see the winner. Might be you, right?"

Chase smiled, a smile that let her know he knew he wouldn't win but would not be disappointed when he didn't. "The student council is selling Cokes and stuff over in the lobby. They're always selling something. Do you … do you want a Coke or something while we wait? I … I could treat."

Cameron wanted to cry, the invitation was so sweet and uncomplicated and generous. "I would love a Coke or something, Chase. That's very nice of you to ask."

Chase stepped from behind his house and pointed. "It's over this way. We can go around if we use this door."

Cameron set off behind Chase, knowing he wasn't sure if he should wait for her to draw even with him or if he should simply feel comfortable leading the way.

Ethan folded the bank check back against the perforations, and ran his finger along the edge. He tore it out and slipped it into the envelope.

Being the owner of a small construction business required more office time than most people realized. Besides all the actual construction work and ordering materials and supplies, Ethan had to verify statements; pay bills; calculate payroll, withholding taxes, and insurance; send invoices; deal with bids and contracts.… Everything that a large business did, Ethan had to do himself. It seemed more complicated—and would be too costly—to hire someone to help with office work than to handle it all himself.

With each check he wrote, Ethan entered the numbers in a small calculator and tapped the minus key. And with every deduction, his spirits, and his optimism, sank a little further. His checking balance grew smaller and smaller, and the pile of unpaid bills remained an inch or two thick.

He could simply delay paying a bill or two, depending on the supplier. The big outfits—the companies that provided lumber and other materials—would hound him if he skipped a payment, but once lumber was cut up and nailed in place, there wasn't much they could do. They would wait a month, then start with the late notices, then the phone calls asking for payment, negotiating payment installments and amounts.

Ethan hated this part of being a contractor. He hated when his finances were this skinny. He took slight comfort in the fact that most small contractors lived close to the edge financially. He did not want to be known as one of those contractors, but he didn't see a good way out of this current tangled thicket. He had several more bid requests to quote. Contractors, regardless of their current workload, always kept soliciting new projects. Otherwise, how would they keep their crews busy? Ethan had bids out on four or five jobs in addition to the ones on his desk. The Carter project would be over in a couple of months, and he would need another major project to begin.

What he didn't want to do, but began feeling he'd be pressured to do, was to use the deposit a new client paid to finish off the bills from this current job.

It's done all the time. Everybody does it in the contracting business. It's only a money float for a few weeks—that's all. That's not so bad, he told himself.

But Ethan did not want to go that direction—unless, he resolved, it was the one and only way to get through the next several weeks.

He paid one more bill, tapped in the numbers, and grimaced. Picking up the stack of invoices in his hand, he shuffled through them in order.

I can pay this one, this one can wait, this one I have to pay, this I can pay in small chunks….

He slipped one invoice onto the desk, and carefully stacked the remaining ones, placing a paperweight on top of them. The last invoice was from the Oilers' traveling team. Hockey was not an inexpensive sport. For the season, each skater was assessed a $250 fee—for ice time, the cost of regional meets, and liability insurance.

He mentally gulped as he wrote this last check. As he tapped at the calculator again, he saw, with a sinking feeling, that the amount was now getting close to his minimum balance.

Not much of a cushion left. But Lynne loved hockey and she loved watching Chase skate. He needs to know that. This is important. He needs to know how important it was to his mother. I can't just let this die.

He ripped the check from the checkbook, tucked it into the envelope, and sealed it.

Then he leaned back in his chair and wondered if there was something he was forgetting.

———⋙⋘———

"Over here," Chase said, holding the two Cokes, one in each hand. "There's an empty table over here."

Cameron followed him through the jumble of tables and chairs. He had insisted on paying for both drinks, and Cameron let him, watching him carefully extract two single dollar bills from his wallet. He refastened the Velcro on the red nylon fabric wallet after paying and shoved it back into his hip pocket.

"Your project was really well done, Chase. I learned a lot about building, and your presentation was very clear."

"Thanks."

Cameron looked around. The gym lobby was filled with parents and students, teachers, younger brothers and sisters. Female teenagers possessed the remarkable ability to squeal in such a unique fashion when meeting friends, punctuating the afternoon with their voices.

"You like working for the newspaper? I always thought it might be cool to do that. You get to write a lot, don't you?"

"It is cool. And I do write a lot. Sometimes it's fun, sometimes it's more like work. But I enjoy it."

What do young teen boys talk about? she wondered. *I guess … I could treat it as an interview.*

"Why did you pick the scale model house as a project?" she asked.

"I dunno. I guess 'cause my dad builds things."

Cameron saw nervousness in his eyes.

"Was it hard to put together?" she asked.

"Naw. I mean, I build models a lot. It's all balsa wood. That's really easy to cut. The only hard part was doing the captions and labels. I used the computer, but I had to cut them out and paste them on cardboard. Some of 'em I had to do five times."

"Are you going to be a builder when you grow up?"

Chase shook his head rapidly. "No. I mean, it's okay and all. But I don't want to do that. I think my dad worries a lot about everything all the time. A lot of things can go wrong."

Cameron took a sip of her Coke. Chase did likewise, but tilted his head back until the can was nearly upside down and vertical.

"My friend Elliot's science project is pretty cool too," he said.

"Which one is that?"

"It's the one about the concrete."

"Oh, yes … Elliot. I thought that one was really well done too," Cameron answered.

She could see his uncomfortable look again.

"It's kinda like people, you know?" Chase said after a moment. He looked right at her then.

"Like people?" she asked. "How's that?"

"Like, how they are on the outside isn't the same as they really are."

"You mean … they could look as though they've got it all together, but inside they're crumbling?" she asked.

"Yeah … something like that."

Cameron could feel an ache in her heart as she heard Chase's words. He looked down and tapped one foot on the rung of his chair.

Cameron quickly surveyed the busy lobby, giving him a minute to regroup before she asked, "School's good?"

Chase glanced up and nodded.

"Are you doing … basketball? Is it still basketball season? Or does track and field start now? I ran cross-country in high school, but the seasons here are different than in Philadelphia."

"No. No sports right now. Hockey starts soon. But … I don't think I'm going to play this year."

"No? I bet you're good at it. You're good at baseball."

He shrugged as only teenagers can shrug, accepting and deflecting a compliment at the same time.

"My dad wants me to play hockey. I think he does, anyhow. He was some sort of star when he played hockey in high school. Like he scored the most goals in one season. There's a big trophy somewhere in the attic with his name on it."

Cameron pushed the hair from her forehead and tucked it behind her ear. "You don't want to play? Why? I mean, if you're good at it and all."

He shrugged again. "I don't like it anymore. When my mom … my mom liked it a lot. It's hard. Hockey's real hard, I mean. And the practices are real early in the morning. I don't know. I mean, I don't hate it. But … maybe I do. I guess he's going to be real disappointed in me—but I just don't want to play it anymore. I was only doing it because … I didn't want him to be mad. He kept saying Mom would have loved to see me play."

The small ache in Cameron's heart grew bigger.

A bell rang, as if signaling a change in classes, and Cameron jumped in her chair, almost spilling her Coke. Chase remained unperturbed, but looked down at his hands, as if he thought he may have shared too much.

"I don't hear that sort of bell anymore. I forgot how loud they are," she explained.

"You get used to it, I guess."

"Well … I guess I should head back to the judges' area."

"Yeah. I need to get back to the exhibit."

"Thank you for the drink, Chase. That was very nice of you."

She touched his arm as she complimented him, and he might have blushed a bit.

"That's okay, Miss Dane. I was thirsty too."

———

Chase stood behind his table and watched the judges gather in a cluster. He expected his father to have come. His father had said he was going to be busy that day, but that he would make time for a brief stop. "I'll be there for the awards, okay, sport?" he'd said, again using the nickname Chase disliked.

But Chase hadn't seen him at all that day.

Maybe it's better that he's not here. I'm not going to win anything, anyhow. And if I don't win, why should he waste his time coming?

Chase was fairly certain that he would not take any of the top five awards. He imagined that the honorable mention might be as high as he would go.

The judges started at the bottom—number five was announced. The elated student walked self-consciously to the stage and received his award ribbon. Then fourth place was announced. When the third-place winner was named, Chase was excited and sort of stunned when they called out his friend's name.

"The third-place award, for outstanding achievement in an experiment explaining and demonstrating tensile strength of concrete goes to—Elliot Hewitt!"

Chase peered down the end of the row of chairs and saw Elliot's mom jumping up and down, and his father just standing, but with a smile Chase could see from where he stood.

Academics were not a playing field on which Elliot often excelled. He wasn't slow; he was actually quite bright. But he just wasn't an overachiever. And Chase knew that the combination of their work on the project made it look absolutely like a student had done all the work—which was true for Elliot. That must have been the deciding factor, Chase thought. The project was really good, but the fact that it was all done by a kid made it better somehow. The work that parents did was pretty obvious on most of the projects. Even Chase could tell a kid's project from a kid's-but-mostly-parents' project. Chase's was a kid's-only project, too, but he knew that it didn't really solve or prove anything. It was simply a pretty cool model. And it did make it into the finalist row for an honorable mention. That was something.

And now Elliot had won third place. He was happy for his friend, because Elliot did not win many awards.

This would be a really big deal in the Hewitt house for a long time.

He wondered if Elliot would get his picture in the paper as well. Maybe he could talk to Miss Dane about that. They were sort of friends now—and maybe as a friend, she could pull some strings. If Elliot had his picture in the paper—well, his mom would just about burst with pride.

Chase figured he should ask Miss Dane right away, while the photographer guy was still there and while Elliot's white shirt was still white and tucked into his pants.

Ethan stood and stretched. He bent backward, then at the waist, expecting to hear his back make some noise—but he heard nothing. A good stretch without a crack or two felt unsatisfying.

He shuffled all the invoices and matching statements into a neat stack. The unpaid bills that had been under the paperweight on his desk, he tucked in the upper-right-hand drawer. The bills with checks inside, he placed in the alcove by the phone. It was Saturday, after the mail carrier came by the house, so waiting until Monday would suffice. Maybe an unexpected check would arrive on Monday morning—but Ethan knew that would be almost an impossibility.

The house was quiet.

Chase must be at Elliot's.

He grabbed his work coat and headed outside. After paying bills, after feeling uncomfortable and anxious, he thought a walk would clear his thoughts and settle that uneasy, jangled feeling that filled in the spaces around his heart.

The day was drab and overcast, not really cold, but there was enough humidity in the air to give a man a chill—a biting, cold, damp chill that cut through his thick work coat without slowing down.

He began to walk faster, hoping that picking up the pace would keep him warmer. It did help, a little. After twenty minutes, Ethan found himself only a block from the Carter Mansion.

Ethan might have been working Saturday if it had not been for the paperwork.

He had the key to the front door on his keychain, so he slowly walked up the long flagstone walk, opened the door, and quietly shut it behind him.

A stack of new trim lay in the hall entry. Pails of mortar and five-gallon buckets of paint were lined up against the wall. The path of brown paper taped to the floor was torn and ragged. He told himself that it would be replaced on Monday. CeCe worried all the time about the walnut floors, which were original to the house, with an exotic inlaid border of ebony. Ethan imagined how they'd look when sanded, stained, and finished to a satin glow. He hoped that new, clean, smooth paper would help settle her nerves.

He took the stairs up to the third floor and began walking through each room, creating a mental checklist of sorts, as to what projects and work remained. As he did so, he kept a separate tally of a more unsettling number: the costs incurred when the owner of the house overrode his choices for trim or wall placement or any number of other frustrations.

As he passed the site of each battle and loss, he mentally figured the financial cost of each one of those lost battles. The authentically styled light fixtures that he thought would be perfect, she hated. They were returned, of course, for credit, minus a 20 percent restocking fee. The trim in the third floor ballroom-now-party-room was a complete loss. It sat in his garage now, balanced on three pallets. Perhaps he could use it on another job. If not, his choice cost him over two thousand dollars, plus time. The stairs, too narrow for CeCe, cost him another forty board feet of tread and riser material. The too-short stair tread and risers were stacked in Ethan's garage as well. Maybe he could find a use for them, but if not, that was another five hundred dollars. By the time he arrived back on the first floor, he had a long list of unfinished work and an account sheet that ran into the red.

If I had that money ... this job would be profitable. But as it is ... if I break even, I'll be doing well.

He sat on the first step of the wide staircase and stared blankly ahead, stared at the closed door with the frosted glass sidelight panels that he hated and CeCe had insisted on. He had forgotten that. Another lost restocking fee. And as he added that three-hundred-dollar loss, he felt a sweep of anxiety and fear pass over him, as if a cloud, dark and black, had just positioned itself between himself and everything that was good and hopeful in the world.

He lowered his head and cradled it in his hands, wishing and willing that what was, wasn't.

It was not an unfamiliar feeling to Ethan.

It was not unfamiliar at all.

———

Cameron felt again the unfamiliar feeling of peace that was becoming more and more familiar.

She looked up from her reading and out onto West Park. As daylight faded to a flinty gray, the streetlights were just coming on and began to glow faintly through the tall windows as she sat in her turret room.

The Bible, called *The Message,* which Paige had given her, lay open in

her lap to a section in Romans 3 titled "God Has Set Things Right." She
read the passage again.

> *Since we've compiled this long and sorry record as sinners … and
> proved that we are utterly incapable of living the glorious lives God wills
> for us, God did it for us. Out of sheer generosity He put us in right stand-
> ing with Himself. A pure gift. He got us out of the mess we're in and
> restored us to where He always wanted us to be. And He did it by means
> of Jesus Christ.*

Farther down the page, she read, out loud this time, there all alone in
her apartment: *"Having faith in Him sets us in the clear…. God set things
right. He also makes it possible for us to live in His rightness."*

As the sound of her reading filled the turret, all the words she had
heard in church as a girl, all the things Paige had said, all of Pastor
Johnson's sermons—all these were somehow coming together to form a
single truth for Cameron.

God sets things right. For me.

She had a sudden memory of early summer evenings with her grandparents and the one-thousand-piece puzzle of some sort that they'd
bought at the Ben Franklin. It was always out on a card table on their
screened porch, and their heads were bent together over a lighthouse or
farm scene, over zebras or a flower garden, as the twilight around them
faded with the chirping of crickets. Her grandpa always had them begin
with the simpler edge pieces. He said that once the borders were complete,
the rest of the more difficult pieces in the center could then be found
more easily—and perfectly, almost magically, form a pretty scene from
what was just a pile of random, irregular pieces.

That's how this is, she thought. *Knowing God is like that.*

And as she sat in the silence, she could feel a thousand pieces, the
pieces of her life, falling into place. She could feel the miracle, the beautiful picture emerging, the puzzle coming together, as the Light came and
illuminated the words in her heart.

Forgiving is not forgetting;
it is letting go of the hurt.

—MARY McLEOD BETHUNE

Forgiving turns off
the videotape of pained memory.
Forgiving sets you free.

—LEWIS B. SMEDES

CHAPTER SEVENTEEN

IN THE DARKNESS, a Roman candle poofed and sent a glowing red ball wobbling up into the cold night air. Chase and Elliot stood in the yard—five minutes to midnight, a box of matches at their feet and a bag of illegal Roman fireworks on the porch. Ethan had purchased them from a friend who traveled down south and bought them in Tennessee or Florida.

Ethan tried not to be the sort of parent who too closely monitored his son, nor the kind of parent who closed an eye to serious infractions, either. He remembered shooting off fireworks at midnight on New Year's Eve as a child, and using dangerous fireworks—the sort that might blow off a finger or two if handled improperly.

But Roman candles offered a more benign celebration. They were neither noisy nor explosive, and only moderately dangerous. With each glowing orb they sent skyward, Elliot and Chase would "ooh" and "aah" in unison, knowing that excitement over a Roman candle was sort of childish, but that they were sort of excited anyway.

Both boys, too young to be invited to a real New Year's Eve party, were spending the night with Ethan. He'd allowed them to rent a few scary movies (nothing too terrifying) and a few brainless comedies (nothing too graphic), and had stocked his refrigerator with nacho fixings, sweet snacks, and pop.

Ethan had been invited to two New Year's Eve celebrations, which he obviously had turned down. One was at Joel's house.

"A bunch of people will be there," Joel had explained. "I think Marcy is making her special chili. You want to come?"

The other was a tad more formal, with an engraved invitation to a *Ring in the New Year Fete* at the Phipps Conservatory in Pittsburgh. It was signed in gold: *Emily Harrington.* She added, also in gold pen,

> *I would love to have you be my guest, Ethan. Let me know and I'll make arrangements for you to spend the night.*

Ethan wondered if a coded message might be hidden in her few words. He read them through several times and didn't sense an underlying assumption. Nevertheless, he did not show the card to his son. Chase would not have understood. He did the right thing, however, and called Emily. He got her voicemail and left a message that he appreciated the invitation but could not make it.

What would I have worn to a conservatory? And just what is a conservatory, anyhow?

Now Chase and Elliot each carried lit Roman candles. They held them aloft like the Statue of Liberty holds her torch and ran up and down the deserted street. Glowing red and blue and green balls fuffed into the air as the boys called out "Happy New Year!"

Their calls to celebrate were almost drowned out by the louder fireworks that echoed up and down the river valley. Apparently, more than a few people had made stops in Tennessee or Florida or wherever south they had traveled this year.

Ethan stood on his porch with his work coat pulled around him tight, watching the two boys slide on the fresh dusting of snow on the street and welcome, officially, a new year to the town of Franklin.

He smiled, but it was more of a relieved smile than a smile that actually welcomed the New Year.

Ethan would wind up in Pittsburgh soon after New Year's, much sooner than he had ever anticipated.

———•◦•———

Snow fell gently over the streets of the neighborhood where Cameron grew up. It was just the right sort of snow—snow that made the scene pretty and picturesque but didn't seem to lie heavily on the street and make driving dangerous.

She did not like driving on snow, was not very adept at winter defensive-driving techniques, and winced every time the weatherman mentioned a possible snowstorm. She had returned home to Philadelphia for the Christmas and New Year's holidays. No snow had been forecast, and she had taken a week's worth of vacation, leaving Franklin early in the morning of Christmas Eve day, heading east and south, and had made it home in just over seven hours. Her father always quizzed her on the duration of any trip; when her parents visited her, they made it from their home to her apartment in just under six hours, despite her mother's pleas for more frequent stops.

"Seven and a half hours, Daddy, but I stopped twice for gas, once for lunch, and once for coffee," she'd reported when she arrived home.

Christmas included a whirl of relatives and family parties and friends stopping by and obligatory trips to grandparents and two visits to the huge King of Prussia Mall. On New Year's Eve, it had begun to snow. Cameron had been invited to a party by an old high school girlfriend. Her parents, knowing how she felt about winter driving, offered to give her a ride there on their way to a late dinner and midnight celebration with friends at their country club.

At the party, Cameron was introduced to a young man, Alan Bradley, whose name seemed so familiar. A recent graduate from the University of Pennsylvania Law School, he seemed eager to fill Cameron in on everything that had transpired in his life. She felt good seeing old friends—good, but odd in a way as well. Many of her friends had stayed in the area, within a few miles of West Chester, and had commenced starting their lives in earnest. Of course, many of them had married, and already had their first child.

When asked, Cameron told people she was from Philadelphia, even though she really wasn't. She actually had grown up in West Chester, a suburb of Philadelphia, but if she said West Chester, people wouldn't know where it was, and then she would have to say Philadelphia anyhow.

And in fact, her parents' home was closer to Goshenville than anywhere else, but Cameron was positive that no one ever heard of Goshenville, which was a few miles north of the larger town of West Chester.

The party was in Goshenville at a pretty, upper-middle-class colonial that her older brother would refer to as the *Leave It to Beaver* house. It was white with dark green shutters, a sunroom, and a finished basement, complete with a bar, a foosball and a pool table. Drinks had been set out on the bar, bowls of chips and vegetables with dips were scattered about, and plates of warm appetizers made their way around the room. The noise level wasn't quite as high as a high school party, but it was loud—lots of people talking, lots of women and men Cameron's age laughing loudly, the sort of loudness one hears after a few drinks, with some of the laughter on the shrill side.

Cameron learned that Alan Bradley had just joined the firm of Brooks, Bradley, and Kenney, specializing in injury law. "I'm not a partner yet, but my father says that if I apply myself, in a couple of years, well, the sky's the limit."

Alan told her a lot about his law school experience, which, Cameron later reflected, seemed to revolve around spring breaks spent partying in Cancun and on ski trips to Aspen.

The party began to break up at 2:00 a.m., much earlier than college parties, she noted, and much to the displeasure of Alan and his single friends. When Alan offered her a ride home, she checked first to make sure he was sober enough. Since it was still snowing, she was relieved that she didn't have to drive.

He implored her to come with him to another party in "downtown Philadelphia. One of the junior partners has this way cool loft with an incredible view. We could really chill out there."

Cameron wondered why she begged off, saying that she was tired and would be leaving town the following day and had to pack. It was a weak excuse, but it was the only excuse she had. It felt odd. She was intrigued by the idea of doing the "downtown thing" again, but at the same time, she was repelled by it. She realized that living in Franklin, she didn't miss the excitement of big-city life as much as she thought.

During the ride home in his new silver BMW SUV, Alan asked—repeatedly—when she would be back in town "so we could get together, you know, and maybe pick things back up where we left off."

Whatever that means, she thought as she got out of the car. "Maybe at Easter," she had answered.

He walked her to the door, grabbed her waist, and began kissing her, even though she had done nothing to encourage him. She succeeded in keeping it very short, clearly shorter than he wanted and enough for him to try a second time.

She was prepared and gently ducked under his clumsy embrace. "Good night, Alan. Thanks for the ride."

"I'll call you in …"

"Franklin."

"Yeah. *The Derrick,* right? I have your card, right?"

"You do."

"And you have my card, right? You can call at the office anytime. Okay? We'll call each other then?"

And Cameron agreed with him. She thought it might be the only way she would be able to shut the door and stop more snow from blowing in on what had been her grandmother's Oriental rug in the foyer.

———

The following morning, New Year's Day, Cameron mentioned the young man from the party to her mother.

"Alan Bradley?"

"Yes."

"From Goshenville?"

"Yes."

Her mother furrowed her brow. "Is he younger than you?"

"I think so. Maybe. He just graduated from law school."

"His father is a lawyer?"

"Yes," Cameron answered, bewildered a bit by her mother's questions. "Some multiple-name law firm. He said he'll be a junior partner there soon."

Cameron's mother nodded, folded her hands in front of her, and looked down at the table. "That's Betty and Robert's son. The Goshenville Bradleys."

Cameron shrugged. "I guess."

Her mother was quiet. Cameron had the feeling that she was disturbed and wondered why. She didn't have to wonder long.

"Alan was one of your younger brother's best friends … back in first grade. They went to preschool and kindergarten together."

That was why.

And as soon as she said it, Cameron realized that it was the first time in years that her mother had mentioned her younger son, even in passing. She looked at her mother's face and tried to read the emotions there. For the first time, she could see the lines, the shadows, the toll that the years of grief and loss had taken on it. Cameron was sorry then that she'd said something to bring her little brother to her mother's thoughts today, on the first day of the New Year, when all things should be bright and positive and hopeful. But she knew thoughts of him were still never far from her mother's mind.

Cameron wanted to tell her everything—about the guilt, about being forgiven, being free from the past, and all that was taking place in her heart.…

She tried to mouth the words … and simply could not get them out. Not now, at least—not this day.

But she was sure that she would … someday. Someday very soon.

On January 2, Ethan's cell phone rang, surprisingly a few minutes after seven. Joel never called this early. CeCe rarely called. Chase was upstairs. He scrambled to flip the phone open.

"Willis here."

"Ethan. I am so sorry to call you this early. No one gets up this early, do they? I know I don't. At least not often. Unless I have to. And today is one of those days."

The voice was several sentences into the conversation before Ethan recognized it.

"Hello, Emily. How was your New Year's Eve party?" He attempted to be polite and gentlemanly.

"Perfectly … wonderfully … dreadful. It would have been fun if you had been here. But since you weren't, it wasn't," she answered with a bit of a pout in her voice.

Ethan had no idea how to take that, so he did his best to ignore it.

"But that's not why I'm calling," she continued brightly. "The fact that you turned me down for New Year's means you must say yes this time."

Ethan measured his words with care. "You first have to tell me what it is."

"Well, you simply must be here this Saturday. Remember the big old house I'm restoring? I told you all about it at dinner. I have a bid—two bids—for the work and I don't think I trust either of them. I am afraid they might simply see me as a meal ticket and bump up their numbers to cover the cost of their children's orthodontist or college education. So I simply must have you come down for a single day. I'm going to the house Saturday, and I want you to walk through it with me and look at the bids and help me determine what really needs to be done and what doesn't."

Ethan started to sweat—not really sweat—but he could see this might be trouble.

Almost as if she had read his thoughts, she quickly added, "Ethan, I won't hold you to anything. You can be assured of that. I simply need a professional person who is well versed in restoration to tell me if some of the things they say I need are really and truly things I need, or not. You can do that, can't you? It's not like I'm asking you to take the job, though that would be nice—very nice. Be a sweetheart and come down on Saturday. Please. You'll be rescuing me, Ethan."

Ethan wondered if she might be using him to play one contractor off another. It didn't sound like it, but it had happened often enough to make him nervous.

"I'll pay you for the entire day—your hourly rate, travel time, meals, and any other expenses, Ethan. I really do need you. I have lots of friends in the business, but none of them know anything about old houses like you do. I really need you."

Her words, at least now, sounded most sincere.

"Okay. I can do it. Give me the address and when you want me."

Leaving Franklin at six in the morning was not the way Ethan wanted to spend the first Saturday in January, but at the end of the day, he would be several hundred dollars richer, he reasoned, and at this point in the Carter project, a few hundred dollars would prove to be a substantial sum in the Willis bank account.

Not a huge city, or even a major metropolitan area, Pittsburgh still intimidated Ethan. The freeways confused him. The heavy rush of traffic always going ten miles an hour faster than Ethan thought prudent intimidated him. The geographical layout of the city intimidated him. Someone said the only way to know your way around Pittsburgh was to be born there. Ethan knew his way to the zoo, since he and Lynne had taken Chase, and the stadium, because he and Chase went to a Pirates game a few times. They'd gone to the Carnegie Museum once last year as well to see the dinosaurs.

But Emily's house was near none of those landmarks. It was south of the city, across the Monongahela River. He took the 79 South Freeway, which led him smack into downtown. Even with pages of MapQuest directions, finding the Smithfield Street Bridge was horrendous, having to navigate a thicket of one-way streets and construction closures. He hated not knowing where he was and the best way to get to his destination

Eventually, he found his way to Mount Washington, looming over downtown, and to Emily's house. He parked his truck and got out and stretched, trying to relieve some of his nervousness, and looked around.

The house was a magnificent example of an Italianate Victorian, with angled bay windows and large eave brackets under the flat roofline. It had a square cupola and a Corinthian-columned porch. It was a disaster, at least from the outside, but still magnificent. It stood three stories high, on the south side of the street, an open lot between the house and Pittsburgh. The city and the stadiums and the three rivers lay several hundred feet below. He could see why Emily had bought it. The view alone was worth hundreds of thousands of dollars.

But the house—well, the house was another story. Ethan could easily see that it had once been a prize. White aluminum siding had been added poorly, and all the exquisite trim work had been painted a cold, flat white, so its details were all but lost. The house should not have combination storm and screen windows, Ethan knew, but it did. It didn't want a rickety staircase leading down from what Ethan surmised was its second-floor apartment, but it had that as well. The place needed a vintage fence and new landscaping. A new walk and two new entrance pillars, which were cracked and crumbling, were also needed. All these things quickly became crystal clear to Ethan, even as he stood fifty feet away.

He imagined the worst for the inside.

"Ethan! You came! You are such a dear."

Emily nearly bounced down the sidewalk, having exited her red Jaguar. She embraced him on the street, tighter than he imagined was appropriate between a client and a consultant. Ethan wanted to pull back, thinking that she shouldn't be hugging him where everyone could see, but then remembered that he knew not a single person in Pittsburgh, other than Emily, so he relaxed.

"Let me show you inside my money pit. I bet you already think it's horrible and I am a fool for thinking of restoring it, right? Am I right? Just light a match, right?"

That wasn't far from the truth, but Ethan shook his head. "Let's take a look first. And show me your quotes. Did you bring the preliminary drawings like I asked?"

"Bids and drawings are inside. As well as coffee, I hope. My assistant was supposed to bring coffee and donuts or rolls or whatever … she's a vegetarian. Do vegetarians eat donuts?"

The front door opened onto a truly impressive space. A double-wide helical, or spiral, staircase, flowed up and around from the foyer. The floor plan of an Italianate Victorian was typically asymmetrical, Ethan knew, and this one was no exception, with a large light-filled drawing room to the right, and a cozy library/study to the left. The rooms, with their high ceilings and tall windows, felt spacious and grand. They had wonderful architectural details. Despite what had been done to the exterior, most of the interior was fairly "virgin," including the fireplaces, which were dark-veined marble with burnished cast-iron inserts. With the exception of some temporary walls constructed of cheap sheets of dark paneling that could be easily removed and a lot of plaster repair work to be done, Ethan was excited by what he saw.

"This way to the kitchen, but let me warn you: It's straight out of the 1930s. Hasn't been touched in eons. Just like the bathrooms," Emily said.

For the next three hours, Emily and Ethan went from room to room, Ethan commenting on the quotes, Emily holding the drawings in her hand, sweeping around each space, rhapsodizing about how wonderful it would all be when restored.

Ethan noted only a few instances of excesses in the plan, or too costly an item, given the work required. Most of the quotes included in the bids were well within the range of acceptability, Ethan told her, adding a few percentage points because it was, after all, a bigger city than Franklin. And Ethan was certain some materials would be more expensive. He knew the labor was higher, much higher, than what he paid his crew. But he could see the potential in the place if someone like Emily wanted to invest the money it would take to bring it back to its original grandeur. And the location certainly warranted it.

"Ethan, you have been such a comfort," she said, taking his arm and squeezing it, holding him tight. "I feel so much better now. Let me take you to lunch. There is a wonderful Italian place just down the road with the same view as this house. Please say yes."

Ethan said yes.

The Venango County Airport had few departures to Pittsburgh. Really, there was only one on Saturday, and two a day during the week. The lack of options made Cameron's choice that much simpler.

At ten o'clock, she boarded a jet plane parked on the nearly empty runway at the airport. The plane was small enough that she could shake the hands of all her fellow passengers if she wanted, without unbuckling her seat belt. She took a deep breath, and the plane took off for Pittsburgh. The pilot was about the age that her younger brother would have been, and while it didn't cause her great worry, neither did it inspire great confidence.

The short plane ride took less than twenty-five minutes and saved her the two-plus hours of driving time. For that she was most grateful. During the flight, rather than looking out the oval window, which would have only served to make her more nervous, she studied the script and episode outline that Paul Drake had mailed to her before the Christmas holidays.

She hadn't told her parents of this new opportunity—not because she was nervous about it, which she was, but because she didn't want to raise any expectations if it proved to be a fluke. She had imagined the worst at times—forgetting lines, freezing up on camera, stumbling with words and generally making a fool of herself. Resulting, she was sure, in being replaced by some other more accomplished host. Better that Mom and Dad not know, she told herself, than to know and expect too much of their daughter.

Paul Drake met her at the airport and whisked her off in his fabulous car toward her first assignment—an old house on the south side of Pittsburgh that would be the initial project documented in the first episode of the show, now officially titled *Three Rivers Restorations*.

He chattered as he drove along, Cameron trying to appear nonplussed, hoping that she was keeping her anxiety under control. In less than forty-five minutes, they pulled up to a massive house overlooking Pittsburgh from a high ridge along the south bank of the Monongahela River.

"This is it," Paul said with satisfaction. "The owner is an old friend of mine. She did my kitchen in my row house in Shadyside. Personally, I think she's going to lose her shirt on the project, and if she does, it will make perfectly fascinating television. You have memorized the script, right, Miss Dane?"

The creased and folded papers lay in her lap.

"Sure. I think I did. I mean, if I miss a word or two, that's okay, right?"

Paul buttoned his cashmere overcoat and carefully adjusted his Burberry scarf. "A word or two would not be an egregious error. I imagine even Shakespeare missed a word or two at times." He paused and took a long look at the house. "This was once a spectacular home, but it is in desperate need of restoration."

She peered up at the house. "It is sort of ugly, isn't it?" Cameron ventured. "Don't these fix-it shows pick prettier houses?"

Paul flicked some lint from his sleeve. "Some do. Our plan is that this little show will feature ugly ducklings turned into showcases. Or ugly ducklings crashing and burning. Both ways, we win. That's the secret of television, Miss Dane: keeping the audience engaged and guessing. Will it turn out fine? Or will it bankrupt the owner? It's a great hook. And western Pennsylvania has more than its share of ugly ducklings to choose from."

He took a purposeful step forward. "The crew is on their way. You should take a tour of the house. Get acquainted with the owner. We'll do the first setup in front of the place."

He stopped and surveyed Cameron with a critical stare. "Your outfit will do just fine. You have a marvelous fashion sense. Classic is good. You could stand more color, though. Your makeup is a bit on the pallid side— needs some definition. We'll add a little something to your cheeks."

She followed him up the wide front steps and across the porch that creaked with every step. He knocked so vigorously on the front door that she could hear the echoes inside the empty house.

⸻

"Where's your dad, Chase?"

Elliot and Chase had sprawled on the couch, watching the last remnants of yet another college football bowl game. Neither of them was sure what this bowl was called, and while they knew the colleges that were playing, they had no personal favorite among either team.

"He said he had to help some designer look at an old house in Pittsburgh."

"He's going to work in Pittsburgh? That's like a long drive to get to work in the morning. My dad complains that he has to drive to Oil City—and that only takes ten minutes."

Chase grabbed a handful of potato chips. Ethan would not have let them have chips for breakfast and lunch, but somehow, a bowl of salty snacks was just the thing for an overcast winter day.

"No. It's sort of a one-day thing. That's what he said. Just sort of consulting or something."

"Consulting?"

"Yeah. He said consulting is telling somebody what they already know and charging them for it."

"You can do that?" Elliot asked, amazed. "And get paid for it?'

"I guess."

"Sweet. I can't wait until I grow up. I want to be a consultant."

Chase laughed as he munched another handful of the discount-store chips. "It does sound like a sweet deal. Maybe we can go into business together."

As Paul's knocking echoed in the old house, three large white panel trucks pulled to the curb behind his black Lexus and a red Jaguar, and in front of a pickup that Cameron thought looked vaguely familiar. Then the door was opened.

"Paul! You're here. Perfect timing. We just returned from lunch. And we're ready to get started."

Paul gently embraced the woman. "Emily, once again, I am so grateful for you allowing us this privilege to document your project. Emily Harrington, I would like you to meet the new host of *Three Rivers Restorations,* Miss Cameron Dane."

"Nice to meet you, Cameron," Emily said.

As Cameron extended her hand to the woman she had immediately recognized, she saw over Emily's shoulder a face that shouldn't be there. But it was there, and it caught the breath in her chest.

"And you have to meet my construction consultant," Emily said, "Mr. Ethan Willis."

An unforgiven injury binds you
to a time and place
someone else has chosen;
it holds you trapped in a past moment
and in old feelings.

—CAROL LUEBERING

⸺✧⸺

To forgive,
one must remember the past,
put it into perspective,
and move beyond it.

—BEVERLY FLANIGAN

CHAPTER EIGHTEEN

CAMERON GAVE ETHAN CREDIT. When they were introduced, he smiled politely and said, "Miss Dane. It's so nice to see you again."

And then again, she was angry at him for pretending they didn't know one another better than that. But she also realized that if he had acknowledged they indeed knew each other well, then further explanations would have been required, and that could have allowed the moment to get too personal—and messy.

Cameron didn't want messy. So she responded in kind. "Mr. Willis, it's nice to see you again as well. Are you going to be doing some of the work on Ms. Harrington's project?"

Emily interrupted loudly. "I wish he was. But he keeps turning me down. Fancy steak dinners, Italian lunches with lots of wine—nothing will get him to change his mind. I may have to resort to more drastic tactics."

The tone of Emily's words left nothing to Cameron's imagination, but she refused to look or act upset. *If that's where Ethan is at the moment, then so be it,* she told herself.

"No, I couldn't work down here. Too much traffic," Ethan added.

And with that, Emily took Cameron by the arm and ushered her farther into the house, pointing out details with the rolled-up architectural drawings.

That left Paul alone in the entry with Ethan....

"Paul Drake," he said, offering his manicured hand. "Television guy."

Ethan expected a limp handshake but got a very, very firm grip instead. "Ethan Willis, construction guy."

Paul pulled out the monogrammed cuffs of his starched white shirt a bit, leaving an elegant quarter-inch showing. He moved a step closer to Ethan and whispered, "Is our Ms. Harrington a lunatic, or do you think she can make something of this monstrosity?"

If Ethan had been taken aback by Mr. Drake, he did another good job of hiding his feelings.

He whispered back. "It's horrible, isn't it? But it has great bones, as we say in the business. A diamond in the rough. If she does things right, this will be a jewel."

Paul pursed his lips together and nodded, then offered a sardonic, twisty smile. "But it might crash and burn, mightn't it?"

Ethan shrugged. "That could happen as well. That's always a possibility in the construction business—especially when restoring an old place like this."

"Delightful," Paul replied. "Makes for such fabulous television, don't you think?"

And as if on cue, the first television crew member barged through the front door, carrying a clipboard under one arm and a rather expensive-looking and cumbersome video camera under the other.

He stomped his feet, tilted his head back to see from under his sunglasses, then asked, "Is the talent here, Mr. Drake?"

"Besides me?" Paul asked, smiling.

It must have been a familiar joke because the crew person could only offer a weak smile in return.

"Yes," Paul added, with a tiny hint of petulance. "Miss Dane is being given the grand tour by the owner. She says she knows her lines. But we need Ava here immediately. Someone needs to do something with the poor girl's cheeks."

"She's getting her kit now. We'll start with all the interior shots. It's starting to snow, and that just pooches any good exterior shots for today."

———◦◦◦———

Ethan had attempted to make his escape right after the first small segment had been taped. Emily would not hear of it.

"I am paying you for the entire day, Mr. Willis, and if I spent that sort of money, you must stay with me for the entire day. I need moral support. I need technical support. Please, please, Ethan. You must stay."

He relented. "But I have to leave by five."

"We'll be done long before five."

Actually, Ethan didn't mind staying. He felt he was somewhat in the way, but he had never watched the filming of a television show. Paul Drake's crew had brought two cameras with them—a big one mounted on a tripod, and a smaller mobile one, like the cameramen on the sidelines of football games used. That cameraman went from room to room, taking shots of everything inside the house.

"We'll add sound to these shots later," the cameraman said to Ethan when he asked. "This is all footage to show what the house is like—and the talent will do a voiceover once we edit it down. No sense in doing sound setups in every room."

Ethan followed them around, leaned against walls with his arms crossed, watching as they took multiple views of each space, seeing what detail they focused on, watching as they keyed the camera's attention on the Victorian moldings and old fixtures, scraps of original wallpaper, little details that echoed from the past. They even filmed in the attic, festooned with cobwebs and old boxes stacked in corners.

Ethan noted with surprise that the house had been constructed with care—better framing than he usually found, thicker joists than necessary, overall quality work done by the original builders.

Maybe Emily will be one of those people who really respects the past and the beauty of the original design.

Ethan watched Cameron, with cheeks more sculpted-looking and lips redder than they had been in the morning, stand with Emily in the ancient kitchen and ask interview-type questions.

"What attracted you to this house?"

"Do you know any of the history of the house?"

"You're a well-known designer of kitchens. What will you do to this kitchen?"

"How long do you think the project will take?"

"Do you plan to do any of the work yourself?"

As Cameron spoke, a boom microphone dangled over her head, and large illumination spots filled the room with bright light. A whole crew of people stood behind the camera, observing, taking notes, adjusting things, holding cables—a hive of activity. Ethan marveled that she was able to hold her composure and actually sound like the interview was spontaneous and unrehearsed. Every few questions, the director, a stout man with a matted black beard, stopped the proceedings and barked out, "We need that again. That word was garbled. I don't like garbled. Please be careful and speak clearly."

Then the question that had been asked would be asked again and the answer repeated.

Cameron never once looked like she was perturbed by any of the interruptions. Ethan was impressed. If someone interrupted him while he was measuring or doing any precise sawing, he'd become flustered and usually would have to start the task all over again.

Not so with Cameron. She would simply nod at the instructions, smile sweetly, blink once or twice, lick her lips, and start over again, ever nicer and sweeter and more inquisitive the second or third or fourth time than she was the first.

Ethan looked at his L.L. Bean watch. It was close to five. Paul Drake stood beside him and looked at his own watch—a large, expensive one, gold and stainless steel with an array of buttons on one side and a series of tiny dials on the face.

"Are we overtime at five?"

The entire crew, almost in unison, shouted out, "Double time."

Not ruffled, but firm, Paul then called out, "Then this will be the last setup. The entire script has been filmed, right?"

The director replied, "Right. More than enough in the can."

"Interiors all filmed?"

"Right."

"We have everything we need in the can?"

"We'll need voiceovers after editing."

"Right."

"Then, this—gentlemen, ladies—is a wrap."

And in that moment, Cameron chose to look up directly at Ethan.

He couldn't decipher her expression. It could have been relief or anger or satisfaction. Ethan just didn't have the language to translate it.

Ethan, Paul, Emily, and Cameron all exited the house at the same time. All stood on the porch, staring out to where Pittsburgh should have been, and none of them could see anything at all. Snow had fallen earlier in the day. While it wasn't a heavy snowfall, combined with warmer air swirling up the river valley, it brought a layer of dense fog to the city along with a blanket of white.

"Well, that's a real pretty sight," Paul said just as his cell phone rang. He unsnapped it from his holster and listened for a moment. "Miss Dane, your flight has been cancelled. Apparently, the Venango Municipal Airway and Screen Door Company has some safety standards after all."

Cameron's heart sank. "But how will I get home? I didn't bring anything with me."

"You could rent a car," Paul suggested.

"I could take you to a hotel for the night," Emily offered. "The manager of the William Penn downtown is a personal friend of mine."

"Well, dear Miss Dane, this is a predicament," Paul said. "A woman alone. Normally, I would offer to drive you home. It is only a few hours, after all. But tonight, of all nights, is simply booked solid. There is this charity ball sort of thing at the Carnegie Museum. I would simply slough it off if I were only attending the boring event, but unfortunately, I am one of the sponsors of the gala. It would not do if I were absent. I am so, so sorry."

Cameron's lips pursed in thought. *If he's not going to offer to hire a limo for me, I could spend the night, I guess. I could buy a toothbrush. I could ...*

"I could take you back."

Everyone looked at Ethan.

"Well, of course, my good man. You are heading back that way, are you not?" Paul said, now back to being chipper and happy.

If he had been observant of anyone other than himself, Cameron thought, *he would have noticed the scowl that slipped on and off Emily's face.*

"Are you sure, Eth— I mean, Mr. Willis? I would hate to impose," Cameron asked.

"We are going to the same place, Cam— Miss Dane. Of course I can take you."

Cameron's only discordant thought was, *Then why didn't you volunteer right away?*

"It might be a bit slower driving with the fog and all. But I'm sure it will be fine."

―――――

Everyone said good-bye and gave firm handshakes as Paul announced loudly to all that Cameron had done a marvelous, fabulous job and that the camera just adored her ... a rare talent indeed.

"You'll come back to the studio in two weeks for the voiceovers, Miss Dane. Hopefully there will be no fog then. And no wardrobe and makeup worries, either."

Emily walked Ethan over toward his truck. "I want you back in a few weeks too. The same as today—I'll pay you for time and travel. On a Saturday. Supervise what's going on here. I need your help, Ethan. Maybe you could stay through till Sunday," she said and slipped her arm through his.

"I'll ... I'll try to do it. If I can."

"That's my dear man," Emily said with enthusiasm. And before he could move, and just after Cameron began walking toward the truck, Emily grabbed Ethan and gave him an enthusiastic, firm hug that lasted much longer than he thought appropriate. And as she released him, she made sure she looked intently in Cameron's direction, just to be sure she noticed.

Clearly, Cameron had noticed. But once more, she remained sweet, professional, and—mostly, one would have thought—unaffected.

How does one know if she has forgiven?
You tend to feel sorrow
over the circumstance instead of rage,
you tend to feel sorry for the person
rather than angry with him.
You tend to have nothing left to say about it all.

—CLARISSA PINKOLA ESTÉS

CHAPTER NINETEEN

CAMERON REMAINED SILENT AS Ethan navigated his way down Mount Washington, across the bridge over the Monongahela River, and met up with Interstate 79.

The roads were wet, though not snow-packed, and the fog was thick, but not that thick. Ethan drove slowly—a safe, sane fifty-five miles an hour. The headlights of the truck illuminated two long ovals of white light in the road ahead. The wipers clicked back and forth, intermittently, a few passes every half minute, slapping with finality, a sound of comfort, of safety.

Nearly twenty miles had passed, and then thirty minutes slipped by, until either of them spoke.

Cameron broke the ice. She pointed to the sign for the next exit: EXIT 12—MARS—11 MILES. "Mars? I thought Mars was farther away than that."

Ethan jumped right in. "No. The government moved it here last year. Said it would save money for NASA. Instead of a rocket, the astronauts can just take a Greyhound Bus."

Cameron laughed, in spite of the fact that she didn't want to laugh or appear to enjoy this man's company. But she did and it felt so good.

Since the door had been opened, Cameron asked the question that had been hovering in her thoughts all day, distracting her, and keeping her slightly off balance. "Ethan … why were you in Pittsburgh today? How did you wind up in the same place I did? I was trying to calculate the odds of that happening, and had I not nearly flunked out of the only math course I took in college, I may have come up with an answer. But, obviously, I didn't."

Ethan appeared to be expecting the question. "I was about to ask you the same thing."

"I asked first."

Ethan laid out how he had met Emily—that she was working on the Carter Mansion, that she had purchased a house in desperate need of renovation, that she wanted an unbiased observer to look things over, and that she had begged him to come down this one particular Saturday.

Cameron had turned to him as he related the story. She had loosened her seat belt a little so she could take in his profile, illuminated by the orange lights of the dashboard. She watched his mouth move as he spoke, observed his strong hands as he gripped the steering wheel, and drank in the scent of his truck—the earthiness of wood and coffee.

"And you? Of all the people in the world I might think of seeing in Pittsburgh, you might not be at the top of the list. Well, I take that back. Odds of seeing you there weren't astronomical, but seeing you as a television star—that made the odds a bit higher. So, how did all this come about?"

And Cameron, still sideways in the seat, told Ethan of Paul Drake and his surprising visit and more surprising part-time job offer and how she resisted the idea at first but then figured that it wouldn't hurt to try it and that's what brought her to Pittsburgh that day.

"All that and a very small aircraft. I am so glad that the fog arrived and I'm not on it now. I'm pretty sure that the pilot was too young to drive a car, much less fly a plane, and that he was following the roads on his way down. Being on earth, being in a car—it's a much better way to travel."

Both stories, once released, were followed with another few minutes of silence. But this silence was less tense than before. Words had been exchanged. There had been no apologies or explanations, but there was dialogue and any dialogue was good—a good place to start, at least.

Cameron was the first to speak this time as well. "I saw your son at school a few weeks ago."

"Chase? For what? Why?"

Cameron heard in Ethan's words a certain edge, a particular tone, and she knew that Chase had never mentioned a word of their meeting to his father. She wondered, in that moment, how much of their story she should tell.

And as that thought jumped into her thoughts, another image jumped in as well—just as clear, just as sharp, just as critical.

She saw, in her mind, Pastor Johnson speaking ... walking the platform, pointing, smiling, holding his arms open as if in supplication. But this time he wasn't asking God for His attention; he was asking the church for their attention and telling them to pay attention to those moments when God and faith and human interaction coincide.

"Hear with your hearts, friends. God brings people in need to you. Listen to them. Help them. Share God's love with them. That's what we do. That's what true Christ followers do. That's what you must seek to do each day. Don't let another opportunity go by," he'd said, and Cameron had imagined him staring directly at her and her alone.

Cameron still wasn't certain if she could be considered a card-carrying Christian—or "Christ follower" as the pastor called it. She didn't really know if she qualified yet as a true believer, but she knew she was experiencing God's love in many ways. She knew a lot more about Christ's teachings than she did even as recently as last summer. Just about every day, she'd been reading the Bible that Paige had given her just about every day, finding herself oddly drawn to it. She looked forward to curling up with it in her turret, seeking and receiving comfort and guidance.

Some of the verses in Paige's Bible had been highlighted. One she read many times was 1 John 1:9:

If we admit our sins—make a clean breast of them—he won't let us down; he'll be true to himself. He'll forgive our sins and purge us of all wrongdoing.

While she still had a lot of questions, she was getting a lot of answers at church. Deep inside, she knew more about forgiveness than she had ever known because she herself had been forgiven. She felt hopeful that it could be true for Ethan and Chase as well. She wondered, in this sliver of a moment, if this was one of those God-and-me-and-a-needy-heart sort of moments she had been told to look for—and not let go by.

Maybe it was, because she felt the hurt and anger with Ethan that she had harbored for so long begin to slip away.

"I was a judge at the science fair. Apparently, I fulfilled the requirement for celebrity judge. I guess that's in the bylaws."

Ethan hardly smiled. That's when she knew she had been right. Chase had not said a word about meeting Cameron at the science fair.

"I missed the whole event," he said after a long pause. "He told me about it and how he was a finalist. I had made a note of it and just wound up at the Carter place doing some figuring. And by the time I realized it, the fair was over and Chase was home."

"Oh. I wondered why you weren't there."

"I wish I had been."

"His project was so well done. It should have won something. I gave it good marks."

Ethan took one hand off the wheel to rub his cheek, as if rubbing dirt away. "I saw it. He did a really good job. But I guess it wasn't scientific enough. That's what he told me."

"I suppose. That's what he mentioned to me as well. No hypothesis, apparently. His friend won third—Elliot ... Elliot something. Chase said he helped him a little. He seemed really pleased about that for his friend."

Ethan finally smiled. His eyes softened, and Cameron watched his lips expose a bit of teeth as he did. She remembered how much she liked his smile.

"Elliot is not the premier Franklin student, I guess, so it was a big win for him. Chase said Elliot's mother was just beside herself. He said it made everything worth it to see how proud she was of her son that day. I guess Elliot was just beaming. And to get his picture in the paper? It was a good day," Ethan said.

"I enjoyed it more than I thought—especially seeing how happy Chase was for Elliot."

"They're good boys," Ethan answered rather softly.

It was at that moment that Cameron wanted to forgive this man. He was sensitive and caring and insightful. But he had not asked for forgiveness, she thought, and if someone doesn't ask, then how does that work?

In her old way of thinking, it had seemed that any form of forgiveness that happens that way is cheap, perhaps unwanted, and most likely undeserved. But she didn't believe that anymore. She knew her being forgiven by God was completely undeserved, an act of grace, and that made all the difference. The need to reach out to Ethan—and to Chase—with a kind of love that she never knew she could have was almost overwhelming. She wanted them to take the gift too....

A moment passed, then another mile. She longed to reach across the space between herself and Ethan.

"I imagine that you'll be wanting to finish as well."

Ethan spoke, but the words did not make sense to Cameron.

"Finish?" she asked.

"The article. On the Carter place. We're almost done."

She took a breath. "Sure. Yes. I do want to finish. Yes. When? I mean ... what would be a good day for you?"

She reached into her purse for her PDA. She clicked the pen that was wedged into the pocket of the cover and brought up her calendar.

"Maybe in two weeks?" Ethan answered. "You could begin the story now. There are only a few things left to be done."

She wrote a line. "I could call you when I get back to the office on Monday and we can put it on our calendars. Would that be okay?"

"Sure. Monday is fine. Just so it doesn't interfere with any of Chase's hockey practices. That starts in a week."

"Hockey? Chase is going to play hockey? Really?"

"Sure. The Oilers. Original name, huh? You sound surprised."

Cameron was silent.

Should I be listening—or talking? What do I do, God? she prayed.

"Ethan … Chase and I had a Coke together at the science fair. He was such a little gentleman. I asked him about sports. I knew about baseball …"

The word seemed to cause Ethan to stiffen, just a bit. At least that's what Cameron imagined.

"… and he said that you wanted him to play hockey, that you were a real good hockey player when you were a boy his age."

"I guess I was. I loved hockey. And Chase's mother—she loved watching him play hockey. You could hear her cheer even outside the rink."

Cameron waited … for inspiration, for guidance, for a nudge in one direction or another—but she felt as if she were on her own here. She decided to trust her heart.

"Ethan," she said softly, "Chase told me that he wasn't going to play hockey this year … that he didn't like it and was only doing it to please you."

Ethan didn't speak for several minutes. A month ago, Cameron might have prattled on, expanding the discussion, trying to make it more understandable. But this evening she simply sat, silent and still, feeling a certain peace, watching Ethan process the information.

"He never mentioned that to me."

"There was a lot I never told my parents, either. Things I wish I would have said. Things that would have saved all of us a lot of grief and hurt and guilt," Cameron said. *About my little brother. About daring him. About holding his hand. About never having the chance to say good-bye.*

She wanted to reach over and take Ethan's hand, offer some reassurance, but she thought it unsafe because he was driving.

"He's such a great kid. I don't want to get him in trouble with you about this, Ethan. I know raising your son is your job—a hard job, alone—but I felt … I felt like I should say something about this."

"No." Ethan waited a long, uncomfortable moment before continuing. "No … I mean, you did the right thing. I won't say anything to Chase about this … that you told me you talked to him. That wouldn't be right, I know. But I should ask him about it—I mean, about playing hockey— if he really wants to do it or not. I don't think I ever asked him what he wants. I should talk to him. We need to talk more."

Silence returned.

"My car's at the airport," she said. "We just passed the first sign for the exit. You can just drop me off, if that's okay with you."

She sat alone in her car and watched as he drove away, wishing for something else, wondering if she had said too little or not enough. Yet she was satisfied—slightly satisfied—that she had taken a small step and said something that showed she cared.

*To understand
is to forgive,
even oneself.*

—ALEXANDER CHASE

———◦◦◦———

*To forgive is
to set a prisoner free
and discover
that the prisoner was you.*

—PHILIP YANCEY

CHAPTER TWENTY

ON SUNDAY EVENING, Cameron reached for her PDA calendar. She knew she had made an appointment for early Monday with someone at some restaurant for a breakfast meeting but recalled nothing more specific than those cryptic details. Her purse yielded no calendar, nor did her briefcase, or second purse, or desk, or junk drawer in the kitchen. She then checked the front seat of her car, and the backseat, and her very cluttered trunk, which she seldom, if ever, opened.

She stood outside in the growing dark, in the biting wind, frustrated and angry. She really, really needed that calendar.

It's in his truck! It's in Ethan's truck.

She remembered taking it out of her purse there and thought she remembered putting it back in her purse, but it could have slipped out.

I've looked everywhere else. It has to be there.

And then she realized that she would have to go to Ethan's house and retrieve it. She could call him but thought it would be simpler and easier just to go in person.

I don't think a phone call is what I want with him right now.

She ran back up to her apartment and threw a gray sweatshirt over her

head, then ran back down and jumped into her car. She first drove by the
Carter house, thinking he might be there doing work. But the house was
dark, and there was not a single vehicle in the driveway.

He must be at home.

She hurried over toward Otter. As she slowed, she noted lights on in
the Willis house. She didn't see Ethan's truck on the street.

Maybe he parked it in the garage, though it's usually outside.

She took a deep breath before she opened the door of her car. She
offered up a quick prayer as well. It wasn't something she had been in the
practice of doing before, but since starting up with this "church thing"
again, prayer felt like the right thing to do—even if she didn't think she
was always doing it the right way.

*Maybe I should get a book on this or ask Paige or Pastor Johnson. Maybe
there's a better way to do this … like an approved version or something that I
don't get yet.*

She could only shut her eyes. Bowing her head would have made her
feel too obvious or too pretend pious.

*Dear God. I think I'm supposed to be here tonight. Help me with the right
words to say. And help me find my calendar.*

She blinked her eyes twice, then shut them again.

Amen. I forgot to say amen.

She debated whether she should knock or try the bell. Sometimes
doorbells didn't work and then you had to stand there for several minutes
trying to decide if the bell didn't work or if the people really weren't home
in the first place. Knocking took one variable out of the equation.

She knocked three times—as politely as she could. She didn't want it
to sound like someone pounding.

Of course she stepped back, back into the pool of light from the overhead porch light. You always wanted the person inside to be able to
quickly see the person outside and not think that it was a robber or door-
to-door salesman or anything invading their space, she remembered.

Are there still door-to-door salesmen? Girl Scouts, maybe.

She quickly adjusted the hem of her sweatshirt with a green *Clarion
College* logo on it, and pushed her hair back from around her face.

I should get a haircut or something.

The clumping of footsteps grew louder ... not the sound of an adult, but the horselike trample of a young man deliberately descending wooden steps. She saw Chase's face pushed up against the glass of the sidelight. She could see his smile turn into a confused smile. He disappeared behind the door.

"Miss Dane," he said as he opened it. "I thought you were Elliot. He's the only one who comes here at night."

"I'm sorry, Chase, but is your father at home? I think I might have left something in his truck. My calendar—and I sort of need it before tomorrow."

He pulled the door open as an invitation for her to come in. She did.

"No. He's not home right now. He said something about the Carter place."

"I checked there. It was dark."

Chase shrugged. "I dunno where he would be, then. But ... you could ... come in and wait. He's never gone late or anything. It would be okay if you waited."

Cameron would have never come in before, never have imposed, most likely explaining that she would call in the morning. But tonight she felt a small, strange nudge to say yes.

"Okay. If you don't mind. I really do need my calendar."

"Sure. It's okay with me. I mean, my dad always says to never let anyone come in—except Elliot. I think he's worried about burglars. I don't think you're going to steal anything, are you?"

Cameron laughed. "Not tonight. I'd probably wait until you're both out of the house to do that."

Chase smiled broadly. Cameron imagined that he was smiling because he was now being sort of a grown-up, acting like an adult might act— sophisticated almost.

"I could get you a drink while you wait. Like a pop, I mean. Not a drink drink. Or coffee. I think my dad has some instant out in the kitchen. I don't drink it. He might have some stuff to make real coffee with."

"No, I'm fine, Chase."

"Tea?" Chase said brightly. "I can do tea. That's boiling water and a teabag, right?"

Chase was so disarming that she had to agree.

"Tea, then. But let me help." She followed him out into the kitchen. "My goodness. This is so nice. And tidy."

Chase ran some water into an electric kettle. "Yeah, we're both pretty neat, I guess. I mean, you should see Elliot's room. He's my friend—the one who placed at the science fair. He lives down the street. There's like stuff up to your knees in there. I couldn't do that."

He poured hot water into a mug and handed her a teabag. "There's sugar in that bowl on the table."

They both sat at a sturdy round table. Its top was made of beautiful old barn wood worn and finished to a soft patina, handcrafted by Ethan, Cameron imagined.

She let the tea in her cup steep for a moment, then took an experimental sip. "This is good. Thank you."

Chase smiled even wider, nodding.

"This is a very nice house, Chase. I've always admired the way it looked—from the outside—when I would drive by."

"Yeah, it's real old. My dad fixed a lot of it up. Some of it is still real old. My mom wanted to, like, tear some of this stuff out, but my dad said he didn't want to. He always says that he likes things the way they were, like in the olden days."

"Well, it's still very nice."

Chase looked around the kitchen as if he were seeing it for the first time. "Like this kitchen. It's neat and all, but she wanted an island or something and that wall over here taken down so we could have a bigger table and stuff. My dad said he liked it the way it was. And since … you know, since my mom died, my dad hasn't done any more work on the inside."

Cameron sipped again. She could sense Ethan in this house, keeping the lines and proportions just the way they were when the house was first built. The kitchen felt cozy—useful and cozy.

"You want a tour of the rest of the house? You know a lot about architecture, right?"

"Well, a little. But I would like a tour. If you think it's okay."

"Sure. It's just a house. You can see it."

Chase took Cameron through the first floor, pointing out some things that his mom had insisted on being changed, and some things she had wished to change, and the things that had remained the same. The house was inviting and thoroughly charming.

"You want to see my room?"

Cameron shrugged. "Sure, why not?"

It was the room of every teenage boy, Cameron thought—just like the rooms her brothers had occupied, filled with posters of sports teams and banners, trophies, photos taped to mirrors and newspaper clippings tacked to a bulletin board, and a large worn and weathered sign for Kennywood Park.

"It's the most awesome amusement park in the world," Chase explained.

Cameron saw an old unfinished pine bed with a windowpane check comforter and pillow shams, a nightstand, two matching chests, a student-sized desk and a couple of lamps. An overstuffed chair filled a corner.

"This is so nice, Chase. It fits you so well. Did your mother pick out the furniture?"

"Yeah. She was good at that. She was going to paint it, I guess, but never … she bought me that old Kennywood sign. She found it at a garage sale or something. It's really cool."

The poor kid's gonna be living that nightmare forever.

Now … there was a nudge in Cameron's heart … *now.*

"Chase, I wanted to tell you how sorry I was when I first heard about your mother … how it happened."

She could see in his eyes that while the words hurt, he really wanted to hear them.

"I was so sorry … especially when I heard that you were there … in the car and all that."

For a moment, Chase looked surprised. Then something akin to relief showed in his face. "You knew that?"

"I spoke to a reporter on the Erie newspaper. The reporter wasn't there when it happened, but he had heard that … that you were in the car that day."

Chase sort of nodded, acknowledging the truth. "Yeah. I was. Hardly anyone knows that I was. I mean, it wasn't in the papers or anything. No one ever asks me about it."

"The newspaper never mentioned it. They thought it would be best that way."

Chase shrugged. "Maybe it was."

Cameron could almost see his thoughts whirling about in his mind.

"Hey, would you like to see my secret room? Only me and Elliot know it's there."

Cameron didn't hesitate. "Sure."

Chase led the way again, switching on the closet light, removing the secret panel, cautioning Cameron to duck, "'cause it's real low in here."

She scanned the narrow room, dimly illuminated with a low-watt bulb in an open socket. The room held the faint smell of old comic books and dust, of carpet and insulation. She touched the elegantly installed plasterboard mosaic walls with a fingertip.

"You can sit in that chair."

She slid the lawn chair out an inch or two from the wall and sat down carefully, the webbing and metal frame creaking gently in the quiet.

"We found that in an alley in town. Somebody was throwing away a perfectly good chair."

Chase sat on the floor.

Cameron noticed a small, handcrafted wooden box in the darkness of the eave.

Now.

"What's that, Chase?"

Chase slowly pulled it closer and angled it toward Cameron. His hand lingered on the clasp. "Some stuff … from my mom."

Now.

"Would you show it to me? I'd like to see it." Her words were kind and soft, like a parent speaking to a damaged child. Cameron was not a parent, but she had heard her parents speak that way to her when she was small and wounded.

He hesitated only another instant, then carefully lifted the lid. He handed her a program. "This was our hockey schedule. The Oilers. I'm in the back row. You sort of need a magnifying glass to see me."

Cameron held it close to her face. "You're right there," she said, pointing. "I can tell by your smile."

He smiled up at her.

Now.

"What else is in there?"

He put his hand on some fabric, a shirt maybe. Cameron could not tell what it was.

"Just this, really. It's a ... it's a hockey jersey." He pulled it up and out—a small white jersey with a penguin in the center and a stain on one corner. "It's an old Pittsburgh Penguins jersey."

Now.

"Chase ..."

"That's why we went to Erie. That's why we were there that day. I wanted this jersey, and no one in Franklin had one just like this. I bugged her for weeks to get me one. I think I even cried about it, so she gave in and we went to Erie to get it. I was so happy when we found it. I mean ... that was just the best thing in the world. Then we were driving home and that mean guy came over to the car and started yelling. I saw the gun and heard it go off. Then the glass broke and the car hit the curb and stopped."

Cameron reached over and placed her hand on Chase's left shoulder.

"She didn't say anything to me. She just looked surprised and hurt. There was all this blood, like everywhere. She was trying to say something to me, but I couldn't hear it. I was in the backseat and was trying to get closer to her, but I must have been buckled up in the seat belt 'cause I couldn't get any closer to her. I dunno ... she sort of reached over somehow, with her hand ... reached out to me and touched my leg." Chase paused and swallowed hard. "And then she died, I guess."

Cameron squeezed his shoulder. She could barely see from the tears that brimmed.

"That was the last time she touched me." Chase was crying now, crying without shame, crying freely. "That was the last time …"

Cameron leaned forward.

"It was because of this stupid jersey. That's why we were there. To get this jersey for me. That I wanted so bad. It was my fault that we were there. I know that's what my dad thinks."

Now.

"Chase," Cameron said, "none of that was your fault."

"It was. Because of this stupid jersey. It was."

"Chase," Cameron said, her words edged with conviction, "none of it was your fault. It was a horrible thing, a horrible tragedy, but it was not your fault. It wasn't, Chase. Sometimes terrible things like that just happen."

He simply cried without responding.

Cameron waited, hoping for the right words to say, praying for some deep spiritual insight, some theological explanation that would make things right for this boy. No words came.

Instead she slipped off the chair and got down on her knees beside him and gently took him in her arms and held him tight. She held him there as he sobbed.

"Chase, when I was a little girl—a little younger than you are—my younger brother drowned in the ocean. And I was with him. I almost saved him. But I didn't. And he was in the water because I dared him. Every day since that day, I blamed myself for his death … that it was all my fault. But I couldn't carry that weight anymore. It was crushing me."

"What did you do?"

"I asked God to forgive me."

Chase sniffed. "That's all?"

"Yes, Chase … you just have to ask. And He will forgive you, too. He will, Chase."

Chase closed his eyes and, after a long moment, Cameron saw his lips move. She knew what he was asking, and she knew what the answer would be.

When he stopped, she said softly, "He has forgiven you, Chase. And I forgive you. You are forgiven."

He cried even harder, but she knew these tears would help wash the pain away, cleanse him. They were the tears he should have cried so many years ago.

So she simply held him close, stroked his hair, and whispered, "It's all right," over and over into his ear.

Eventually, his crying stopped. She let go of him and he looked up into her face.

"Is it really okay? Really? I'm forgiven?"

"Chase, I know that God forgives you, and that He loves you. No matter what. I know that, even if I don't know much else."

He looked down, then wiped his eyes with his palms. "Thanks, Miss Dane. Thanks a lot."

That urgent whispering had been what it took for Cameron to get off her chair and offer forgiveness—forgiveness for a lost young boy who did not know how to find forgiveness on his own … and for a father who did not know he needed it.

That boy just needed someone to offer him the gift.

Moments later, Cameron reached over into the footlocker and extracted a beige envelope—the size of a greeting card. Chase watched as she opened the flap. It was a Mother's Day card.

Inside, under the printed sentiment, were the carefully written words of a five-year-old:

I miss you Mommy. I hope heaven is nice. I hope you are not angry with me.
I love you,
Chase

Cameron tried her best not to weep but could not help herself. Her tears flowed as she asked Chase, "Have you ever talked to your father about this?"

He shook his head. "He never asked."

"He needs to know, Chase. You need to tell him what happened and how you feel."

Chase shook his head again. "He doesn't want to talk about it. He's mad at me and thinks it's my fault. I know he does. That's why he never wanted to talk about it."

Cameron couldn't stop from hugging the boy again. "Oh, Chase ..."

After a few more minutes, Cameron helped Chase fold the hockey jersey again and laid it, with great care, back in the footlocker. She placed the card and the program on top and lowered the lid gently.

She waited for Chase to reinsert the secret door back in place.

"Miss Dane, I'm really tired. Would it be okay if I just went to bed?"

"Of course that's okay, Chase." Cameron was well aware that such a torrent of tears could be exhausting.

"Could you wait up for him, Miss Dane?"

"I could, if you want me to."

"And maybe, could you tell him that it wasn't my fault?"

Cameron hesitated. She knew that Chase had to talk to his father—but maybe she was here this night for this one specific reason.

"Sure, Chase. I'll tell him. You sleep well, okay?"

And she kissed him ever so lightly on the forehead, as her mother did to her so many years earlier.

Forgiveness is the key
that unlocks the door
of resentment and the handcuffs of hate.
It is a power that breaks
the chains of bitterness
and the shackles of selfishness.

—CORRIE TEN BOOM

CHAPTER
TWENTY-ONE

CAMERON STOOD IN THE entryway of Ethan's home, debating what to do next. She wanted to jump in her car and start looking for Chase's father. There were not that many places to hide in Franklin. She could drive past the few restaurants that were open, back past the Carter house, maybe over to Fountain Park or to Joel's house.

That would mean leaving Chase alone upstairs.

But he was alone when I got here, she told herself.

She went as far as retrieving her car keys from her pocket, then stopped.

If I start driving around, I may not find him. Then I'll have to come back here ... and what if he's still not home? I would have to make sure the door is locked if I left, and I wouldn't be able to get back in. And if Ethan was home then, I'd have to explain that I was here earlier—and that might not be all that simple.

In the end, Cameron decided to stay where she was. When he drove up to the house, she would go outside and meet him.

That puts us in neutral territory, she told herself, as if being in the house he had shared with his wife might complicate what Cameron had to say.

This isn't easy. God, please give me the words.

She paced back and forth, walking softly from the kitchen to the front door. She repeatedly stopped at the door to look through the sidelights, scanning Otter Street in both directions. There were so few cars on the street after dark; it would be impossible to miss Ethan's truck.

Two framed pictures hung on the wall between the alcove with the phone and the doorway into the kitchen. The first time Cameron passed them she only glanced at them, knowing what they were without having to stare. She did not want to stop and examine them more closely. But as she paced, her eyes kept being drawn to them, again and again.

She finally stopped and faced them.

One was a wedding picture.

Ethan stood on church steps, very handsome in a tuxedo. Next to him was his wife, Lynne. Ethan was a little thinner, his hair a little fuller and longer. He wore a wide, happy smile, as if everything that day was exactly the most perfect it could be. His wife had her arm through his, her bouquet in her hand against the white of her dress. She was gorgeous, Cameron thought, with hair the color of summer, of wheat, of the sun, and hauntingly piercing eyes. Chase's eyes were like hers. He had inherited her hair as well. His mother looked as if she would be equally lovely and at home in a wedding dress as she would be in torn jeans and a work shirt.

Cameron felt an ache in her heart and scolded herself for feeling it.

The other picture, the same size and framed to match, featured all three of them, at a park, during a bright summer day. Chase, no more than three at the time, sat on his father's lap as his mother stood behind them, proud, happy, content. Again Cameron felt that ache, but this time it was for Chase, and for Ethan as well—an ache for what they both had lived and had lost.

She was hardly conscious of the movement, but she brought her hand up to that picture and placed it ever so gently on the image of Chase and his father and mother.

She turned and walked to the front door again, echoes of ghosts in her thoughts, faint images of what this house once held and would hold no more.

Perhaps on the twentieth circuit, or maybe the fiftieth, Cameron stopped and stared hard down Otter Street. A set of cone-shaped head-lights angled at the corner; a vehicle slowed. From the illumination of the streetlight midway down the block, Cameron knew it was a truck—a dark-colored truck … Ethan's truck. It came gradually to the curb. Perhaps the driver saw Cameron's car and slowed down sooner, confused or concerned.

Cameron took a huge breath, opened the door, and hurried off the porch, making sure the driver could see her. Half-waving her hand in the cold darkness, she smiled so he would know everything was all right.

"Ethan," she called out, not loud—not too loud, anyhow.

"Cameron, what are you doing here?"

He was at the sidewalk now, holding a grocery bag in his arms.

The grocery store. I never would have thought to go past the grocery store.

"I came over looking for my calendar, Ethan … my PDA. I think I left it in your truck. I knocked on the door and Chase saw that it was just me. I told him what I needed, and he invited me in to wait for you."

She could see a flicker of something in Ethan's eyes.

"He said that he knows the rules, but I promised that I wasn't a bur-glar. He said you would be right back."

Ethan appeared to be about to say something, but it also appeared that whatever it was did not fit that moment … did not fit it at all.

"Ethan, I don't want to interfere. I really don't. It's not really my busi-ness … but Chase had offered me a cup of tea and then he showed me around the house. He knew I was interested in architecture. And, Ethan, he showed me his secret room."

"Secret room?" Ethan asked, shifting the grocery bag from one arm to the other. Cameron could see a loaf of bread in the bag, and maybe a half-gallon of milk.

"Just through his closet. It must run under the eaves on that side." She pointed.

Ethan nodded. "I … knew that was there. I guess. He never men-tioned …"

Cameron took a step closer to him. She had told herself she wouldn't, but she did, and placed her hand on Ethan's arm. "He showed me what he's been hiding all these years, Ethan."

Ethan waited.

"It was the hockey jersey that his mother bought him that day in Erie. The day that she was ... when it happened."

Ethan didn't speak. He didn't move, really, but she could tell he was staring at the ground. After a long moment, he looked at her and said, "I never knew what happened to it. The police gave it to me. I guess Chase found it. I thought it was gone. I thought I threw it away. I wanted to throw it away."

Now.

Cameron moved her hand slowly on his arm. "Ethan, he thinks that you blame him for her murder. He thinks you hold him responsible for his mother's death."

A moment passed.

"He said that?"

"Ethan, he did. I know you don't. But he said you two never talked about what happened that day. He says you're angry and that's how he knows you believe he was the cause of it all."

Ethan's lips were pressed tight together. "I never talked about it ... because ... I thought it would hurt too much. I thought ... it would be better for Chase that way."

Now.

Cameron stood beside him and put her arm around him. "Ethan, you have to talk about this with him. You have to tell him it's not his fault."

She could see a tear course down his cheek.

"All this time? He really thought I held him responsible?"

She nodded.

Now.

"You need to talk to him. He's asleep—but you need to wake him up and tell him."

"It's too late, Cameron."

Now.

"Ethan, you had a right to your anger. Anger over what happened and anger over the fact that she died that way. But you have to give up that anger. Give it up, Ethan. For you and for Chase. It insulates you too well. Let go of the past. It's not too late. It's never too late."

Ethan shifted the bag in his arms again. "Okay. Come inside with me."

Cameron looked at her feet. She wanted so much to go back inside with Ethan ... but she also feared it ... what it could mean for their relationship.

"Please?" She took in the pain and sadness on Ethan's face.

Then she slipped her hand in his, and the two of them walked up the stairs together.

———◦❊◦———

Cameron sat in the kitchen and made another cup of tea. She added three teaspoons of real sugar to the cup—a forbidden, but wonderful, pleasure.

She sat and sipped at the sweet tea, not moving, save to look about the kitchen and imagine Ethan's wife here ... to see what she had so wanted him to change in the room. She imagined the scent of macaroni and cheese in the evening, of toast in the morning, of brownies baking in the afternoon. She saw Lynne play-chasing a wispy-haired toddler around the kitchen, making airplane motions to feed him in a high chair at this table.

The creaking of steps brought her back to the present.

Ethan walked in, his eyes red. But he was smiling.

"He's asleep again. He showed me what was in the wooden footlocker."

Cameron reached out and took his hand. "I'm sorry. I know that it must be hard."

"Thanks. But what was hard is that he was alone with it all these years. He carried that pain all alone. I never knew. I never understood. I was so wrapped up in my own pain...."

She squeezed his hand.

"I told him I forgive him. I told him how much I love him."

More tears fell.

"And he told me how he talked to God tonight."

Ethan wiped his eyes. "Cameron, thank you."

"It's okay."

"Cam?"

She looked up into his eyes.

"Will you ... can you ... forgive me? For being so stupid. For being ... so ... angry. So selfish and foolish and stubborn. Can you?" Ethan asked, his words, tender, soft, heartfelt.

She waited less than a heartbeat, then rushed to open her arms and embrace him and hold him in the fiercest, most earnest, most crushing embrace she had ever given anyone, ever before.

*Compassion is ... the knowledge
that there can never really be
any peace and joy for me
until there is peace and joy finally for you too.*

—FREDERICK BUECHNER

———❦———

*Forgiveness is
giving up the possibility
of a better past.*

—UNKNOWN

CHAPTER
TWENTY-TWO

CeCe Carter Moretti had promised to put on the biggest, grandest, most amazing open house Franklin had ever seen.

And she did.

Ethan and his crew finished the last bits and pieces of the project just after Easter—and Easter was exceptionally late that year.

"No matter," CeCe had insisted. "The work went on way too long, but now that it's done, I'm so happy with it. It was worth it all. Everything turned out terrific."

The third-floor ballroom glistened, decorated by Tessa Winberry with elaborate arrangements of spring flowers and scores of candles. It was filled with Franklin's finest and the best and most beautiful. There was even a scattering of tuxedos—something the town of Franklin seldom saw outside of weddings.

The mayor was on hand to offer a speech of dedication—or "rededication" as he remarked, and a toast: "The Carter name and Franklin go hand in hand. We are so proud to have a Carter back in the Carter Mansion. Here's to Mrs. CeCe Carter Moretti and her remarkable vision in restoring this gem of a house. May it stand proudly for another hundred years."

The crowd broke out into applause at that, and if the mayor had further remarks to make, he thought it best to go out on a positive note and simply bowed to the homeowner.

CeCe beamed the entire evening. She had vindicated her grandfather's name and reputation. The house was beautiful and she said she could see his pride showing through.

Even if she had changed some of the original lines, Ethan thought.

He wore a new tie that evening, as did Joel, Jack, and several members of the crew. Doug wore a new sport coat over a black T-shirt and slacks—and for him that was excessively well dressed, almost to the formal level.

Seldom had any of the crew been invited to an event like this, where they were made to feel almost like celebrities. Ethan's crew had all been asked to sign a plaque, which was going to be hung in the entry, giving credit to each man who had worked on the long project.

Ethan saw that as a touch of real class.

CeCe brought in a disc jockey for the evening. She would have used a real band, but few bands in Venango County could play Italian love songs and standards from the '40s—the music she loved—along with polkas and old Broadway theme songs.

The music started thumping as Ethan made his way down to the first floor. CeCe hurried around, encouraging her guests to eat more.

"*Mangia, mangia!*" she said as she herded them toward the food. She had spread every surface in the kitchen, which *did* look like one in a Tuscan villa, with platter after platter of Italian dishes—from linguini with clams to homemade mushroom ravioli with bits of green stuff, which Cameron informed Ethan was arugula, tossed in with its cream sauce.

Ethan headed to the lavish dessert table in the dining room and passed up the tiramisu and cannoli for the biscotti platter. He took two, slipped out the front door, and stood on the porch, now brought back to its original resplendence, taking in deep breaths of the cold, spring air. After every invoice had been presented and every bill had been paid, Ethan had wound up with a grand profit of a few thousand dollars. It wasn't much—much less than he had planned, and much less than it could have been, had he not been so headstrong. But with all the publicity, well—he imagined he'd do pretty well in the long run.

Even though he disagreed with some of the final design, it was CeCe's house after all. And on this project, he'd learned a lot about himself—and restoration—in the process.

Everyone did seem to love it.

With a few dollars' profit, and all the recognition this job had given Ethan, he knew it was okay to hope for a better summer than he had seen in years.

Cameron followed Ethan out onto the porch. She didn't say a word but simply slipped her arm around him and held him close, the two of them, alone, side by side. He put his arm around her shoulder in response. Dozens of votives that lined the railings flickered in the crisp breeze.

"Where's Chase?"

"Where else? At Elliot's. He didn't think this would be his sort of party."

The music's bass line vibrated inside and upstairs. Laughter and loud conversations echoed over the beat.

Ethan didn't speak for a long time. At last he said, "I wanted to thank you, Cam. I don't think I did—at least not for this."

She squeezed him harder. "For what?"

"For being a roadmap."

She dropped her arm and turned to face him, her face a puzzle. "A roadmap? I've been called a lot of things, but never a map before."

He took her hands. She could see the seriousness in his eyes.

"You showed me the way to make it right. No one else could have done that. You showed me something in my son that I never saw, or even suspected. You were the one who really knew what he needed. And you showed me how to get there too."

He dropped her hands and stepped to the railing. He looked out over the river, over the lights of Franklin.

"I held on to the past too tightly, Cam. I held on to what wasn't there anymore. And I was angry—angry at everyone who didn't suffer like me."

She came up behind him and encircled his waist with her arms. "It's okay, Ethan. I understand." She rested her head against him. "We both needed forgiveness."

He turned and embraced her firmly. "Thanks for showing me the way back to God."

Under her breath, she whispered, "You're welcome."

Anger makes you smaller,
while forgiveness forces you
to grow beyond what you were.

—CHERIE CARTER-SCOTT

Forgiveness does not change the past,
but it does enlarge the future.

—PAUL BOESE

CHAPTER
TWENTY-THREE

CHASE, LIKE EVERY OTHER student in school, waited with great anticipation for summer to begin. To a fourteen-year-old, those three months stretched out before him like an endless, golden paradise.

He stood in his front yard and waited. He held his new baseball glove, a first-baseman's mitt, personally autographed—a real signature with a Sharpie pen—by the Philadelphia Phillies' current first baseman, Greg Dobbs.

Miss Dane had gotten the glove for him from her older brother, William, as she'd promised.

"I know some people put these kinds of things on a shelf and hope they'll become more valuable over time," she said when he had unwrapped the gift. "But I want you to use this. Greg Dobbs wants you to use it. It'll be more valuable if you use it—otherwise, it's just a piece of leather with writing on it."

Chase did not have to be asked again. It was a cool glove and a cool autograph—even if he really didn't like the Phillies all that much. This season he planned on watching some of their games, though. After all, he had that glove. And Cameron was from Philadelphia. So was his mom.

Cameron pulled up to the curb in her car. She waved as she walked up to the house. She wore jean shorts, a T-shirt, and sneakers, and her hair was gathered in a ponytail of loose curls. Best of all, she carried her own glove.

"But it's a softball glove," Chase had said the first time he saw it.

Cameron had shrugged. "It still works. Don't worry about it."

He tossed her the baseball as she jogged across the sidewalk. She flipped it back to him, a little harder than he had thrown to her.

No sense in being pampered, she thought.

"Hey, not so hard," Chase said, joking, but not really joking.

"Can't take a pitch from a girl?" she called back.

And in the afternoon sunshine, the two of them tossed the baseball back and forth, without really talking, but with great contentment.

Ethan's truck rumbled up the street and he jumped out, calling, "Hey, Danish, let me borrow your mitt."

She laughed, tossed it to him, and retreated to the shade of the porch. She pulled up the wicker rocker and sat, rocking slowly, as the two of them, father and son, threw the ball between them. She could see where Chase got his pacing and rhythm—everything he did was echoed in Ethan's movements ... the long arm, the graceful pitch, the quick reflexes. The two had a balance, a harmony between them.

Every few pitches, one or the other would turn with a smile toward the shadows of the porch, looking for Cameron's face, as if asking for something. Was it validation? Approval? Each time Cameron would smile back. A comfortable smile ... a welcoming, accepting smile.

After awhile, after both were sweaty and thirsty, Ethan called it quits. His son walked toward him, and the father placed his arm over his son's shoulders as they walked to the porch.

"Let's get something to drink."

Ethan stood by the rocking chair and Cameron stood too. He embraced her tenderly and gave her a quick, happy kiss.

If anyone had watched Chase's face at that moment, they would have seen a look that combined a good measure of emotional disgust at their public display of affection with an equal amount of pure joy and absolute, complete satisfaction.

Though no one can go back
and make a brand new start,
anyone can start from now
and make a brand new ending.

—CARL BARD

Forgiveness is the
highest, most beautiful
form of love.

—ROBERT MULLER

EPILOGUE

CAMERON RAN UP THE brick walk of the Willis home. She yanked the screen door open and ran into the kitchen.

Ethan and Chase both looked up from the table, their eyes and faces welcoming her, smiling—one as wife, one as mother—all three tanned from their week at the beach on the Delaware coast.

Cameron waved the paper in front of her. They followed it, trying to see what it contained.

"You know that grandson who didn't want to sell? Well. He's changed his mind. Paige told me about it. Her realtor friend in Titusville has the exclusive on it."

"Grandson? Whose grandson?"

"Who changed his mind?"

Cameron took a step forward, holding the paper out, holding it with both hands.

And on the paper was a picture of a large house, a Victorian house, with three stories and an enormous turret, its paint weathered to a milky yellow, in need of some tender loving care and a restoration expert. It was almost hidden by trees, with a stream running next to the house, and in the foreground, a field of flowers filled the nearly perfect little valley, its one side draped with a weeping willow....

And in a moment, that paper was crushed between Cameron and Ethan as he picked her up and swung her about the kitchen in a wild, happy, joyful dance, accompanied by the laughter of their son.

ABOUT THE AUTHOR

 After eleven coauthored books with her husband, Jim, Terri Kraus has added her award-winning interior designer's eye to her world of fiction. She comes to the Project Restoration series naturally, having survived the remodel, renovation, and restoration of three separate personal residences, along with those of her clients. She makes her home in Wheaton, Illinois, with her husband; son, Elliot; miniature schnauzer, Rufus; and Siberian cat, Petey.

Visit Terri Kraus at her Web site: www.terrikraus.com.

Other Books by Jim and Terri Kraus

... a little more ...

When a delightful concert comes to an end,

the orchestra might offer an encore.

When a fine meal comes to an end,

it's always nice to savor a bit of dessert.

When a great story comes to an end,

we think you may want to linger.

And so, we offer ...

AfterWords—just a little something more after you

have finished a David C. Cook novel.

We invite you to stay awhile in the story.

Thanks for reading!

Turn the page for ...

- **A Note from the Author**
- **Discussion Questions**

A N o t e f r o m t h e
A u t h o r

Writing a novel set in the world of the restoration of old buildings has
always been a dream of mine. The idea of renovation is in my family's
blood. I'm an interior design professional. My brothers are rehabbers. My
husband, Jim, and I have survived the renovation of three houses.

I know the upheaval well, the despair of having no control, the agonizing over style decisions, the budget constraints, the disagreements
between contractor and owner, and the emotional roller coaster of unexpected problems and unanticipated gifts along the way. Together my
clients and I have accepted big disappointments, celebrated tiny successes,
and experienced the inexpressible elation at seeing what was once in
ruins—old, broken, useless—become, with all its quirks, a beautiful, completely renewed, and usable place for people to share life again. Looking
back on all those projects, I can echo the sentiment in the opening line of
Dickens' *Tale of Two Cities*: "It was the best of times, it was the worst of
times."

Many of you are probably, like me, HGTV fans who watch the many
shows about fixing up old houses. You find yourself glued to the glimpses
of contractors and owners engaged in the process. You live vicariously
through the rehabbing, renovating, and restoring.

I can relate. I've always been captivated by old buildings. Poring over
books about art, architectural styles, and decoration from all over the
world has always been one of my favorite pastimes. As I've traveled inter-
nationally and visited many of the places I've studied independently and
in the course of my education in design, I've become even more passionate about restoration. (I'm the woman you might see sitting on a bench
along the wall of the Sistine Chapel, silently weeping as I take in
Michelangelo's magnificent masterpiece in the simplicity of that sacred
space.) I can talk forever about the importance of preserving buildings
that are testaments to the creative impulse, the hours of painstaking effort,
the motivation and dedication of artists, designers, craftsmen, and artisans

from previous eras. All were, no doubt, imperfect people—but people used as instruments in God's hands to create perfectly rendered works of art that endure and can stir our hearts so many, many years later.

For me, there's something quite magical about walking into an old place, with all its history, where so much life has been lived, where so many events and significant moments have taken place—the happy ones, the sad ones, and all the everyday moments and hours in between. Imagining who might have inhabited a house, how the family came together, the love they shared, their conversations, the tears and laughter, is irresistible to me. I find inspiration as I imagine how they celebrated and grieved, how they overcame adversity, how they survived tragedy, then moved on to enjoy life within the old walls once again.

One of the joys of my life was visiting the little northern Italian village, nestled among olive groves high up in the Apennine Mountains, where my maternal grandparents were born, grew up, and married before emigrating to America in 1920. A short lane connects their two families' farmhouses. In between them stands a small, now empty house of ancient, mellowed stone where my grandparents lived as newlyweds. How full my heart felt as I walked over that threshold! I pictured them as a young couple in the first blush of matrimony, with all their hopes and dreams … before their brave journey (separately) across a wide ocean to a strange land where all was unknown. Within those aged walls, did they speak of their fears as they prepared to leave their homeland, certain they'd never see their parents and siblings again? What kind of courage did that require? What words did they use to comfort and reassure one another? I wondered. I could see, in my mind's eye, my grandmother stirring a pot of pasta as my grandfather stoked the fire. I could even hear the crackling of the firewood, smell the slight aroma of wood smoke....

A few artifacts remained of their time there, and I was delighted to be able to take them back to America with me. Now I treasure and display them in my own home because they connect me with that place and time and remind me of my rich heritage—all stemming from that small structure, still standing, solidly built so long ago.

I love the metaphor of restoration, which is why I came up with the idea for the Project Restoration series—stories that would follow both the physical restoration of a building and the emotional/spiritual restoration of a character. Ethan, Cameron, and Chase, whom you just met in this book, are just the beginning. Perhaps in *The Renovation* and the following books, you'll find a character who mirrors your own life and points you toward the kind of restoration you long for.

After all, God is in the business of restoring lives—reclaiming, repairing, renewing what was broken and bringing beauty from ashes. I know, because I've seen His renovation firsthand. For many years, I've worked in women's ministries. I've seen many women—as well as the men and children they love—deal with scars from their pasts that shape their todays and tomorrows. They all long for restoration—to live joyfully and productively once again—but that also requires forgiveness. Forgiveness of others (whether they deserve it or not) and, perhaps most importantly, forgiveness of oneself in order to be healthy and available to God. Clinging to past hurts or "unfairness," hostility, anger, grudges, resentment, bitterness, or allowing abuse to alter your self-worth renders your life virtually useless. Unforgiveness shapes your perception of yourself, your outlook on life, the kind of relationships you have, and keeps you in "stuck" mode. It leaves you in a dark, emotionally paralyzing, spiritually debilitating, physically draining state and causes so much unnecessary pain … even addiction.

Yet God Himself stands and waits, extending the gift of restoration. The light of His love shines on all those dark places deep within us, exposing what needs His healing touch. This is the type of restoration I've become passionate about too. For when our souls are gloriously freed through God's renovation, we become whole, useful, and able to extend the forgiveness we have experienced to others. Then individuals, families, churches, and entire communities can be transformed!

What event in your past do you need to let go of? It is my hope and prayer that you, too, will experience the renovation that awaits you through saying yes to God's invitation of heart restoration … and the life-transforming joy that will follow.

D i s c u s s i o n   Q u e s t i o n s

1. What hints do you see, early on in the book, that there is an underlying issue creating tension in the relationship between Ethan and Chase? Have you ever been in a situation where there was tension in a relationship, but neither you nor the other person involved were talking about the real issue? Explain.

2. Why do you think Chase felt responsible for his mother's death? Are there any ways in which Ethan could have behaved differently? If so, describe. If you were in Ethan's shoes, how would you have handled the situation?

3. Do you think Ethan carries his passion for respecting the past too far when he engages CeCe in battles over how "original" to keep her house? Why or why not? If you were a rehabber, how would you handle a client like CeCe?

4. Does Ethan's respect for the past carry over to any other areas of his life other than rehabbing the Carter Mansion? If so, what areas, and how?

5. When have you felt yourself clinging to the past? How did it influence your life at that time? What about now? Explain.

6. Why is Chase's secret room so important to him? If you had a secret place growing up, where was it? Why was that place so important to you? Who did you risk sharing it with (if anyone)?

7. Do you agree with the advice Paige gives Cameron about her interest in Ethan? Why or why not? How did Paige's sharing the past events in her life influence Cameron's spiritual journey?

8. How did Cameron deal with the guilt she felt about her little brother's

drowning? Have you found yourself in a similar position—where you've felt guilty about a past event? If so, what happened?

9. How did the tragic event that happened in Cameron's childhood color her adult life? How did it impact her attraction to Ethan, and to Chase? How has tragedy influenced the way you respond to others? The way you think of yourself?

10. How did Lynne's death affect Ethan's life? His work? His faith? Have you ever felt "stuck"? If you've become "unstuck" since then, compare your journey with Ethan's. In what ways are your journeys the same? How do they differ?

11. Who do you think was more aware of how the past tragedy affected Ethan's life: Ethan, or his son, Chase? Explain, using clues from the story.

12. How did Cameron's parents deal with the tragedy in their family? In what ways did this affect their daughter's life? If you were Cameron's parents, and you could go back and relive life after the tragedy, would you do anything differently? Explain.

13. What made Chase and Elliot's friendship special? Do you think Chase identified Cameron as a kindred spirit? Why or why not? Who was your kindred spirit when you were growing up, if you had one? Why do you think you were particularly drawn to this person?

14. Why did Ethan turn away from the church? Do you think this was inevitable, given the circumstances? Why or why not? What, if anything, could have prevented his spiral into doubt, unbelief, and anger toward God? Have you (or a loved one) found yourself in a similar situation due to life circumstances? If so, when?

15. In chapter 5, Ethan wrestles with blaming God for his wife's murder. How would you respond to the questions he asks as he contemplates why bad things happen in this world?

16. What risks did the following characters take in choosing to change the course of their lives:
      Ethan?
      Cameron?
      Chase?

17. Have you ever taken a big risk in changing the course of your life? When? What happened? Tell the story.

18. What science project did Chase help Elliot with? In what way(s) is it symbolic of what was happening in Chase's life?

19. What did you think of the appearance and timing in the book regarding the arrival of
      Emily Harrington?
      Paul Drake?
Have you ever had to choose between two people to love or be attracted to? How did you make the choice? Looking back, did you make the right choice? Why or why not?

20. In what way(s) did God orchestrate the lives of
      Ethan?
      Cameron?
      Chase?
Take a step back into your own past. In what specific events can you see God orchestrating your life to get you to where you are right now? Tell the story. Better yet, why not write it down for the generations to come?

Get Lost in Life-Changing Fiction!

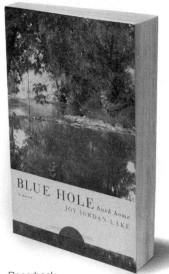
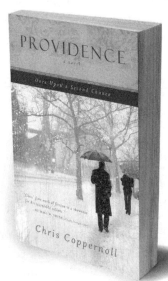

A medical researcher comes face-to-face with the unfathomable love required to sacrifice an only son.

"Taut with emotional suspense, author Sandra Glahn catapults readers into the world of medical ethics, exploring the desperate lengths folks will go to find a cure." —Mary DeMuth, author, Watching the Tree Limbs

Paperback
ISBN: 978-1-58919-109-9
$13.99

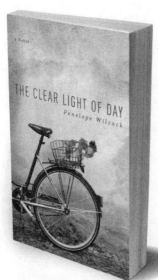

Lonely, divorced, and newly assigned to a rural parish full of quirky characters, Esme Browne rediscovers the beauty of friendship in a most unlikely place.

"... reveals a remarkable depth of spiritual wisdom. Highly recommended." —Davis Bunn, best-selling author, Heartland

Paperback
ISBN: 978-0-7814-4553-4
$13.99